MW01120468

# Once A
# SAMURAI...

## By
## D.C. Rhind

*This book is a work of fiction. Any resemblance to actual events or persons, living or dead, is entirely coincidental.*

"Once A Samurai...," by D.C. Rhind. ISBN 978-1-60264-409-0.

Published 2009 by Virtualbookworm.com Publishing Inc., P.O. Box 9949, College Station, TX 77842, US. ©2009, D.C. Rhind.. All rights reserved. No part of this publication may be reproduced, stored in a retrieval system, or transmitted in any form or by any means, electronic, mechanical, recording or otherwise, without the prior written permission of D.C. Rhind.

Manufactured in the United States of America.

For Carol
and for Sean,
who believed in me
when I wasn't sure
if I believed in myself.

# Prologue

Halifax, Nova Scotia, 2008

Mike threw himself backward, his back slamming against the hard stone of the outer wall. In a blur, the vampire was suddenly in front of him. Eyes glowing with anticipation, cat-like fangs exposed in a malicious grin, he thrust with his katana. Mike ground his teeth and grunted. He barely dodged the heart-thrust. The blade felt white-hot as it entered his shoulder, just below the right clavicle.

How in hell did he ever get caught up in this mess? The answer to that was complicated and almost as old as he was.

# 1: Kung Fu Samurai

Halifax, Nova Scotia, January 26, 2008

The clang of steel blades rang loud in his ears. Mike kept his eyes just a little out of focus, never quite looking at his opponent attacking with a blunted *katana* or samurai long sword. His adversary wore traditional Japanese gi top with hakama, the loose, skirt-like pants of the samurai, still worn in kendo. Mike wore the sleeveless jing-mo of southern style kung fu, bright red silk, yellow trim, with black silk pants.

Mike was careful to control his speed. He'd been born with unusual reflexes, something in the brain wiring, he supposed. His reactions were fast. Too fast a reaction could hurt this guy. And this guy was a piece of work—all flash and drama. He was a fourth dan black belt, a grade above Mike, but his movements were all power, no finesse.

Mike moved with speed and surgical precision. He knocked the blade to the side with a power move, then became the attacker. He twisted the sword in his hand, back of the blade coming down on a wrist. A powerful flick caught the round guard and sent the opponent's sword across the room.

He whirled in a circular blur, his leg slashing a backward arc. The heel slammed into the cheek of his opponent. Dazed, the man dropped to his knees, clearly trying to retain enough balance not to fall on his face.

Mike stepped. His katana became a high-speed blur that stopped abruptly, just touching his opponent's throat.

A ripple of applause sounded in his ears. The audience was limited—three judges, the dozen competitors, and a few companions or students of the competitors, some potential students and curious members of the public.

Mike walked to a bench where a stocky eighteen-year-old, whose build mirrored Mike's, handed him a towel.

"Nice job, Dad," the boy said. "I doubt if he saw half of what you did, but I know he felt it." The boy grinned in pride. Mike just gave a half smile.

"I'm tired, Sean. Let's get a bite to eat, then we can catch the last ferry."

"Sifu Cameron is once again the victor," a soft, accented voice commented as they were about to leave.

Mike nodded to an elderly Japanese man. "Takimura-Sensei." He took the old man's hand in his.

The old man then turned to Mike's son. "And you, Sean-san, I compliment you on your demonstration. Your father is clearly a good teacher.

"Michael, I analyze your style each time and I now see your secret. You act as if the katana is just an extension of your arm and apply subtle kung-fu moves. It is very unorthodox, yet very effective. I hear you spent a few years in both China and Japan. Who taught you this?"

Mike shrugged. "It just comes naturally to me, I guess. The Japanese masters frowned upon it, but they respect the results. The Masters in Hunan who honoured me with their teaching approved but had little interest in the sword. It amused my teachers in Tibet, but they were more interested in skills of the mind." He shrugged again.

Takimura smiled. "If you would honour me with a month or so of your time, an hour or two a day, I believe I could award you your chi-dan—your fourth degree. Perhaps along that path, I could gain a better sense of this amazing style of yours."

"You honour me, Takimura-san. May I consider this? I've been through much. Teaching is an outlet for me, but more study might not be good right now. I'm still not at peace with some of the events in my life."

Takimura nodded. "You have grieved long, Michael-san. Speak to me if you feel ready."

Mike nodded, then gestured for Sean to head for the door.

---

Mike and Sean were almost the only passengers on the last ferry back to Dartmouth. It was an unusually mild night for January and they rode up top in the open air, enjoying the view of Halifax Harbour.

"Nice change," Mike commented. "I was wondering if we were ever going to get the January lull. We've been inundated with snow."

"Global warming, my ass," his son replied.

Mike gave Sean that "watch your language" glare.

His phone made a musical sound, alerting him to missed calls and three voice mails. He'd had the phone's ringer turned off during the evening's competition.

"Tony?" he mused. "Tony rarely calls—maybe once a year. Now I have four missed calls and three voice mails."

He 'okayed' the phone to contact his voice mail, punched in his password, and listened. A voice with a cultured British accent urged him to call, sounding more anxious with each message."

Mike glanced at his watch—nearing midnight. "Surely this can wait 'til morning," he mused. "It's too late to call anybody tonight."

*Tony?* Mike thought. *Calling my cell phone now? He writes, he almost never calls. I didn't even know he had my cell number.*

It was a strange relationship lasting most of his life—the man who'd worked with his father all those years ago, yet kept in touch with Mike through the years. He smiled, remembering how they met. Even that was strange. How could he forget.

# 2: The Haunted House

Sydney, Nova Scotia, 1973

Mike Cameron stared at the dark old house and swallowed hard.

"Go on, Mikey" his brother Billy taunted, "I dare you!"

"You go first, if you're so brave," Mike challenged.

Billy hesitated. The lanky sixteen-year-old ran at the ancient stone wall, scrambled over the top, and landed hard with a painful grunt.

Mike shook his head. He ran, leapt, caught the wall, pulled higher, then rolled over the top. He landed lightly in the grass, dropping into a crouch.

Even in the dark, he could see the annoyed look of envy on his older brother's face.

"Make enough noise coming over the top?" Billy taunted.

"Not as much as you when you belly-flopped onto the ground," Mike shot back.

Billy raised a fist. "Quiet, or I'll give you a pounding."

Mike ignored him. In the yard, hoary old oaks, looking like dead, skeletal forms in their autumn nakedness, cast shadows like terrible claws clutching at him. Icy shivers raced up and down his spine.

He glanced around but could no longer see his brother.

"Billy!" he hissed.

"Over here, ya big sissy," came a taunting reply.

Peering into the darkness, he finally made out Billy's form crouched near the steps at the back of the house.

"What are you doing?" he demanded, creeping closer.

Billy was only three and a half years older, but he towered seven inches over Mike's compact, more solid build. And he flaunted his superior age and height like a trophy.

"I'm trying to listen, and it would be a lot easier if you'd be quiet."

Mike was shocked. Was there a hint of fear in Billy's voice? He wasn't going to mention it. He was too busy taking meager comfort from the fact that he wasn't alone in his terror.

The old Cowell house had been empty for years and had a reputation for being haunted—a place of great evil. Some parents smiled at these stories, but every kid within six blocks of Bentinck Street knew stories of ghost sightings, chains rattling at night, and muffled sounds of screams. The ancient stone edifice was one of the oldest residences in Sydney—some said as old as almost anything in Halifax.

Rumour had it that some stranger had bought the place and, sure enough, lights had been seen on late at night—but only late at night. There was never a sign of life in the day time.

More imaginative kids in the neighborhood had decided that a vampire or a an evil warlock had come to live there. Who else would never be about in the daytime, only at night?

Several dares had been passed around. Of course, Billy had been the loudest of the challengers. So now, Billy had taken up the gauntlet. He would enter the house, take some pictures of the inside, then be able to show everyone that he'd done it. Their mother's Polaroid would even show the date on the pictures.

"I hear something moving, Billy! Let's get out of here!"

Mike clutched at his brother's jacket sleeve, hoping to encourage him away from the place. But Billy shrugged his arm free.

"No way!" He whispered. "There's no lights. It could just be rats. Besides, if he's really a vampire, do you think he spends the night at home watching TV? 'Course not. He'd be out sucking out someone's blood until before sunrise." He used a Bela Lugosi accent, bared his teeth, and flexed imaginary claws at Mike, hoping to scare him. "Come on."

Sneaking up the steps, Billy flicked open the blade of his Gerber buck knife. It had a deadly-looking serrated edge and a locking blade. The lethal item had been a gift for his last birthday, from their indulgent uncle who seemed to specialize in gifts that made their parents frown. With a deft technique that made Mike's eyes widen, he slid the blade into the door jam, levered against the tongue of the lock, then eased it back, pulling the door open.

"Where did you learn to do that?" Mike demanded.

Billy rolled his eyes.

"About fifty movies and several episodes of *Columbo*," he replied in an acidic tone. "Don't you pay attention to anything."

"I saw it," Mike insisted, "but I didn't know it really worked."

Billy gave him a withering look, then slipped inside.

Mike followed so close that he had to work hard to keep from bumping into his brother.

They seemed to be in what his grandmother called a mud room. Next came the kitchen. The air had the awful stillness of a place that had been closed up for years. There was a tangy, moldy smell that made Mike want to gag.

He would have loved to have said something to his brother in hopes of making him take a picture of the kitchen so they could get out of there, but he was afraid to speak. He had the eerie feeling that there was someone in the house. He couldn't have explained it—it wasn't anything rational, just a terrible sense of presence. There was something there.

Billy snapped a picture in the kitchen. The small built-in flash fired off a burst of light that illuminated the room like a flash of lightning. One second the room was lit up, then it was a memory, and he was blinded, his night vision gone.

Mike thought his heart would stop. He so desperately wanted to get his brother's attention—tap him on the shoulder or something—and convince him to get out of there. But terror of the presence he was sure he could feel kept him silent. What if Billy told him off and the vampire heard? Surely the creature could already hear his heart pounding. Couldn't vampires do that? Could they smell fear? *No, that's dogs*, he told himself.

A rustling sound told him that his brother was nonchalantly placing the polaroid picture in his jacket pocket.

They were now in a large hall. Mike breathed carefully. There was a hint of a musty smell, but nothing more. Still, vampire lairs were always dusty and full of cobwebs. He was afraid the dust and dirt would make him sneeze. Anyone in the place would hear that.

Billy paused at the bottom of a huge stairway. The faint glow of the street lamps coming through the curtained windows in the foyer exaggerated haunted house look. Archways to the right and left yawned like huge, dark mouths waiting to swallow them. Terrible things, servants of the dark, lurked beyond those openings, he just knew it—*servants of a dark master*, he thought.

As he turned to look toward one of the archways, he bumped a table to one side of the stairs. A porcelain vase toppled.

Mike's shot a hand out, catching it before it could rattle down onto the table or possibly hit the floor and shatter.

Billy aimed the camera at the stair, then flashed another picture. This time Mike's heart did stop. The light of the flash had illuminated a man at the top of the stairs. He was sure of it.

"*Billy!*" he screamed.

Grabbing his brother by the back of his jacket, he pulled hard, then ran for the kitchen and the door they'd left unlocked.

Both boys raced for the back door.

"What do you boys think you're doing?"

The voice was right in front of them! It was impossible!

*No*, Mike thought, *vampires can do that. They can materialize right in front of you, too fast for the eye to follow*.

They dashed to the right. There was a door in the shadows. Maybe they could get to the front door and escape.

But the door seemed stuck.

Billy turned the knob hard, throwing himself against the door at the same time.

"No!" the voice commanded, "that's the—"

Billy let out a frightened cry. There was a banging, thumpity-thump sound of him falling down stairs.

Instantly, Mike was seized from behind by the most powerful hands he could imagine. Their father, who'd been a boxer in the navy and liked to race sailboats, had strong hands. But the strength of these hands was as far beyond their father's as their father's strength beyond theirs.

The hands wheeled him about. Eyes that seemed to glow in the dark stared into his.

"Stay put," the voice ordered. There was no disobeying this voice.

A hand seemed to lash out in the dark with amazing speed and accuracy, flicking a light switch. Ancient wooden stairs leading to a cellar were illuminated. The man disappeared, then reappeared almost instantly with Billy in his arms.

"Get the switch to the left of the door," he ordered. His voice was calm, cool, yet there was a sternness to it. It was the voice of someone who would take charge when others panicked.

Mike found the switch which lit the kitchen. It was astonishingly clean, though very old-fashioned, except for a few modern appliances.

"Wet that cloth and follow me to the parlour."

Mike did as he was told. It was weird. Somewhere in the back of his mind he was terrified. Somewhere, part of him was screaming silently, "Escape!" But it was as if that part of him was a prisoner in a dungeon. What remained would obey. Even his heart seemed to have stopped pounding.

"In here," the man said, turning left into one of the dark archways. "The light switch is to the right of the doorway."

The room came alive with the light of two antique lamps sitting on heavy mahogany tables on each side of a nineteenth century sofa. He watched the man set his brother down. For the first time, as the man carefully set a pillow under Billy's head, Mike took in details.

He wasn't as tall as he'd thought—maybe five-foot-ten. His hair was light brown, not quite blonde, and he had a thin mustache. Something about his hair style and manner made him seem like a character from an old movie. His clothes weren't old at all. He wore expensive trousers and a vest—part of a 3-piece suit—shiny black shoes, and a white shirt with a starched collar. There was no tie and the shirt was open at the neck.

With a blurred motion, he seemed to open the buttons of his vest. He opened four buttons faster than most men might open one.

Mike could see why the vest might have annoyed him. The man had a muscular, athletic chest and a lean waist. How could he even breathe in that vest? But, as the thought came to him, he stared. He couldn't see any evidence that the man breathed at all!

The man turned a handsome face to him, took a breath and said, "Now, let's have that cloth." He smiled and extended his hand toward Mike. He seemed to be staring at Mike's throat.

Mechanically, Mike placed the cloth in the well-manicured hand, and watched in amazement as the man gently wiped Billy's face, then began patting a nasty bump at the corner of Billy's forehead.

"You'll find ice in the icebox in the kitchen," he said, giving Mike a stern nod.

Mike started for the kitchen. Once out of the room, he seemed to come to himself. His heart started pounding. He ran for the back door.

He was almost in the mud room, the door to freedom before him, when the voice seemed to be right behind him.

"The icebox is in the corner."

He wheeled about. It felt like his heart had pounded its way up into his throat so high that he might choke on it.

There was no one there! The man was still in the living room—he called it a parlour. He also called the fridge an icebox. That wasn't so weird, though. His grandmother called it an icebox.

He opened the top, pulled out a tray, and got six cubes. Forcing himself to return to the man in the parlour took all his courage, yet, with every step, it seemed to get easier. The closer he got, the calmer his heart became, the more the frightened part of him seemed to go back to being that prisoner locked away in a dungeon.

His eyes widened as he approached the man. The latter just smiled and held out his hand for the ice.

"Thanks," he said, giving him another smile. For the first time, Mike noticed just the hint of a British accent—a bit like that Ashley Wilkes character in that dry old "Gone With the Wind" movie his grandmother always watched whenever it came on TV. He also noticed that he was very pale—not the grey look they liked to give vampires in movies, just the pale look most blonde kids had by the end of winter. The lips looked kind of red against the paleness of the face, but his mouth seemed normal. No sign of fangs.

The man smiled so that his teeth showed. The canines actually seemed thinner than normal. Heck, he knew kids in school with bigger fangs. Again the man's eyes fell to Mike's throat.

"That ice will melt if you keep holding onto it." The smile seemed harmless and gentle.

Mike felt stupid. He gave the man the ice, and watched as he wrapped it in the cloth and placed it gently against his brother's head.

"Time to wake up, Billy," the man said.

"How did you–?"

"How did I know his name? Simple, Michael—I heard you both talking."

"We didn't talk inside," Mike insisted.

The man smiled and nodded. "No, you didn't. But you did rather a lot of loud whispering outside." He pronounced 'rather' sound almost like 'rother.' "And there's the fact that I know your father. You're William Cameron's boys. You live just down the street."

Billy let out a groan, his eyelids fluttering.

"That's it," the man said, "almost there. You gave yourself a concussion in that fall. Now you need to wake up and stay awake for a bit. That's it. Now, look at me. Look carefully."

Billy's eyes opened, looking deep into the stranger's.

"Jolly-good. Now, what's your full name?"

"William James Cameron," Billy said in a dull, hypnotic tone.

"Very good, William. Now tell me, where are you?"

"I'm in your house—the old Cowell house."

"Very good." The man nodded. "You've been shaken up a bit, but everything works. Do you like tea?"

Billy made a half shrug. "It's okay. My gran' likes it."

While he spoke, he wrapped the cool cloth about Billy's right forearm, covering an area that was beginning to show purple bruising, and was a bit swollen.

Turning to Mike, he smiled a winning smile. "And you, Mr. Michael Cameron? Will you drink some tea? William needs to settle his system a bit and tea is good for the nerves. It will also help him stay awake a bit until we're sure there's no vascular damage in his brain. It's well past midnight. Since you've obviously snuck out while your parents were asleep, they aren't likely to miss you for a few hours.

"My name's Tony, by the way. Now, you two sit still while I put the kettle on."

The boys seemed calm as Tony left the room but, as soon as he was gone, both became uneasy.

"We need to get out of here," Billy hissed.

Mike shook his head. "We'd never make it. You saw how he got to the back door ahead of us. And he can read our minds. I'm sure of it."

"So you want to just stay here and be eaten— sucked dry like spider bait? It's your throat he keeps staring at."

Mike shook his head again.

"He could have done that to you and left you in the basement. Instead, he carried you in here and made me get ice for your head. Then he put a compress on your arm. And I think it's my scar he's staring at."

Billy removed the cloth, his eyes widening at the bruise. He wiggled his fingers.

"Is it broken?" Mike asked.

"No," an ethereal voice said out of the air.

Startled, the boys looked about. They were still alone. Yet, Tony's voice had sounded as if it were in the room with them.

"How did he do that?" Billy hissed.

"You two have a tendency to whisper in a loud hissing manner," Tony replied. As before, though he was still in the kitchen, his voice seemed to be in the room with them.

"You're arm's not broken, William," he continued, "but you did bruise it rather badly—bit of a sight, actually. Still, so long as you don't do anything too strenuous with it for a few days, you'll be right as rain.

By the way, tea's almost ready. And I just found a tin of biscuits I didn't even know I had."

"*Biscuits*," Billy spat out derisively. "I won't even eat them when Gran' makes them at Christmas."

Mike rolled his eyes. "He means cookies," he explained. "He's English."

"Jolly-good, Michael," Billy taunted, imitating Tony's accent. "I say, old boy, did you read that somewhere?"

"At least one of us can read," Mike quipped. "You Neanderthals barely reached the level of speech." He stuck his tongue out at his brother. "Until you were born, the scientific community thought Neanderthals were incapable of speech."

"Careful, *squirt*, Neanderthals can crush book *worms*."

They were interrupted by a chuckle from the doorway.

"I say, are you two always like this? I shouldn't wonder that your mother doesn't keep a whip and a chair handy."

"Aw, we just rag each other a lot," Billy blurted, "It don't mean nothing."

"It doesn't mean anything?" Tony offered.

Mike grinned. Billy started to scowl, then relaxed.

Tony entered, setting a silver tray on the table. On it were a silver tea pot, three ancient cups and saucers, a matching creamer and sugar bowl, and some antique tea spoons. There was also a new-looking rectangular box of assorted cookies.

Mike examined a spoon.

"Hey, is this Georgian?" he asked.

Billy groaned. "Here comes another lesson," he muttered.

Tony smiled. "Actually the spoons are French, given to me by a lady I met during a mi... well, during a visit to France. They're from the same time period—about 1780's, I should think. The pattern is similar to some English work at the time, which would be Georgian, of course.."

"Our Aunt Olive has some Georgian silver, and it looks a bit like this," Mike said simply.

Tony just nodded. He poured tea and passed a cup and saucer to each of the boys.

"Help yourself to milk and sugar. The milk is powdered—I hope that's all right. I don't use enough milk for it to keep. Probably silly to put it in that old creamer but, well, old habits die hard, as they say."

"Kind of weird getting all this stuff out for us," Billy announced. He was eying Tony with suspicion. "We're not exactly the Bishop of London or the Duke of Edinburgh. Don't you have some old mugs?"

Tony's smile broadened.

"You are my first official—or should I say *unofficial* visitors since I rented this old relic. I don't get to use this set much, though there was a time–" His face took on a far away look and seemed to sadden at some thought. "I don't get a lot of visitors. In fact, if it weren't for Welcome Wagon or whoever they are, I wouldn't even have the biscuits. My work keeps me from eating at home, though I do like a bit of tea now and then, even if I can only manage a sip." The last part of the sentence trailed off, as if he were thinking out loud.

"Are you going to kill us?" Billy asked suddenly.

"*Billy!*" Mike hissed.

Tony chuckled. "Why on earth would I want to do that? Besides, I think your father would disapprove."

"Because you're a vampire. Isn't that what vampires do?" Billy asked. There was a defiant air to his tone, somewhere between trying to be brave and trying to force the inevitable.

" And just why do you think I'm a vampire? Your father would gather more evidence before leaping to such an unscientific conclusion."

"What do you know about my father?" Mike demanded.

"He's Detective William Cameron of the local constabulary. Our paths have crossed due to my work. I'm here to assist him with a case, actually."

"Yeah, right," Billy sneered, but Mike cut him off.

"What work?"

"I'm sort a what the Yanks call a profiler. I help the police find certain serial killers by trying to anticipate their behaviour, their reactions to certain things. Seems you have a nasty fellow killing people hereabouts, and I've been asked to lend a hand. I worked a similar case with your father about seven years ago, 'round about the time you got that scar on your neck, Michael. How is that, by the way? It seems to have healed well—your voice seems normal."

"Yeah," Billy taunted, "he has the voice of an angel. Had to dress up with a tie and sing in solo festivals all over the province 'til he got out of it this year. *There once was a shepherd who lived on his own...*" Billy did a warbling, girlish parody of singing.

Mike felt the blush come to his face.

"I take it that your voice was undamaged by the accident," Tony offered.

Mike shrugged. "I came third once and second twice. The judges' report said I would have come first last time but I forgot the second verse and sang the third twice." He made a grimace. "I got nervous."

Tony nodded. "It takes some experience to grow out of that. Well, your folks wouldn't like you being out at such an hour. I trust you can sneak back in as easily as you snuck out."

Mike unconsciously touched the scar on his neck. All he remembered about it was coming off his two-wheeler the first night he'd ridden without training wheels. He'd fallen against a jagged piece of pipe someone had driven into the ground as part of a wire barrier to keep people off their lawn that spring.

Billy took the Polaroids from his pocket, selected the shot looking up the stairs, and handed it to Tony.

"You don't photograph very well. I didn't notice any mirrors in the house but, if you had one, which I doubt, I bet you don't cast a reflection."

"Actually, I wasn't there when you took the picture." There was an amused glint in Tony's eyes. He seemed to be enjoying the banter. "May I?" He gestured to the camera showing from the pocket of Billy's windbreaker.

Billy handed it to him with reluctance.

"Hmm, you're lucky. I was sure the fall down the stairs would have broken it." He held it out before his face, closed his eyes, and snapped. With a whir, the picture came out of the front, dropping into his hand. He watched as it developed. "Not bad," he commented. "Better than my driver's license usually turns out."

He handed the blurry shot to Mike.

"As for mirrors," he added, "there's a large one in the dining room, one in each bedroom, and one in both the upstairs bath and the downstairs power room."

"You heard my voice and thought I was at the top of the stairs," he explained. "I came down the back stair to the kitchen. That's how I cut you off at the back door. Any other evidence?"

"You're only about during the dark hours, never in daylight."

"Actually, I'm up and about at various times, but I do most of my work at night. I have an aversion to sunlight and ultraviolet rays."

"Like a vampire," Billy insisted.

"Or an albino," Tony offered.

"Your hair's too dark for an albino," Mike countered. "And your eyes are blue-grey. They aren't pink like an albino."

"Oh, not you, too," Tony complained, giving Mike a disappointed look.

Coming around to Tony's side of the table, Mike spooned some sugar into his tea, then suddenly picked up the shiny silver pot. He struggled with the weight of the full pot, trying to hold it closer to Tony.

"I can see myself in the silver," he said, then sighed. "I can see you, too."

Tony showed a hint of a smile. "Does this mean the local constabulary won't be here at 9:00 am, armed with garlic, holy water, crucifixes, sharp holly stakes, and the parish priest? Don't you think they'd laugh at you for such an absurd accusation?"

Mike felt chagrinned. "I feel stupid. It's obvious you're not dangerous."

"Not dangerous!" Billy argued. "He's a vampire! Do you think he's Casper the Friendly Ghost? He kills people to stay alive."

Mike turned on his brother. "If you read more instead of just watching movies and God forbid, *thought* about what you read—Vlad Dracul was a monster even as a human. He impaled people on stakes. He had spikes driven into some guys' heads because they wouldn't take their hats off in his castle. An evil man became an evil vampire. So, if a good man got turned, couldn't he become a good vampire? Vampires don't have to be like monsters in the movies."

Tony sat back, watching the boys' faces. Holding the saucer in his left hand, he slowly raised the cup to his lips. He watched the boys argue the point for a couple of minutes, then set his cup and saucer down.

"If I had to pick one of you as my solicitor, I think I'd pick Michael," he offered in a low tone. "But, since we're theorizing, let's try this: What if vampires *were* like people? What if most of them peacefully coexisted with humans, but there were a few, rather like sociopathic humans, who chose to kill—not because they think they need to, but because they like it?"

"Vampires are vampires," Billy insisted.

"Ah," Tony replied. "And dogs are dogs. We should kill them all, in case one decides to bite you."

Billy's eyes narrowed in anger.

"Mikey may read a lot, but I see details just fine, and not just in movies," he declared. "For example, let's see you take a big gulp of that tea. You only poured yourself half a cup. You did it so naturally and picked it up so fast you probably thought we'd assume you had a whole cup, just like us. While we were arguing, you made a lot of motion and display of sipping your tea, then set your cup down. You're hoping that we'll think you started with a full cup and drank half of it. But you started with half a cup and, in spite of all your pretense, you still have half a cup."

Very deliberately, Tony picked up his cup and drank a noisy slurp, then set it down again.

"Better," Billy admitted. "It was almost a teaspoon that time. And you didn't even gag. How long have you been working at drinking tea like a normal human?"

"What about the polaroid?" Mike countered, looking back at Tony. "He also makes a reflection in the tea pot."

Tony nodded. "You've a sharp, keen mind, Michael. You have remarkable reflexes as well. Quick, accurate movements. I once knew a chap from Hong

Kong like that—amazing fellow. Perhaps you should study the martial arts. With your mind and reflexes, I think you'd be good. More important, I think it would be good for you—channel your abilities into something exciting."

He looked at Mike for a reaction.

"I've talked to my dad about it," he admitted. "He's thinking about it, but Billy's not interested."

Tony nodded. "Perhaps I'll mention it to him," Tony suggested. "He needn't assume that William here must take the classes with you.

"But, coming back to this absurdity. If I were a vampire, couldn't I just fix my hypnotic eyes on you, like Bela Lugosi, and make you forget ever seeing me?"

Billy and Mike both nodded, but it was Mike who spoke. "Just like you made me relax when we were in the same room. But, when I left for the kitchen, I was afraid again. The further I was from you, the more my feelings and thoughts were my own."

Tony sighed.

"I can't win," he said. Then, "How's the head, William?"

"Okay."

"No headache? Blurred vision? Ringing in the ears?"

Billy shook his head, then sat up. He shook his head more vigorously. "My head's fine."

"Good," Tony said. "Perhaps there's no concussion after all. In that case, if you two promise to go right home, and you can get back in the way you got out..." He looked closely at Billy as both boys nodded.

"Very good, then. Off you go. And, should you decide to visit again, please, just ring the doorbell."

Next evening, just as the sun was disappearing behind the houses across the street, there was a knock at the door.

"I got it," Mike shouted. As he pulled it open, he stood and stared.

"Hello, Michael," Tony greeted. Turning, he glanced back through dark sunglasses at the disappearing sun, then stepped into the entry hall. "Hmm," he whispered. "That's two cardinal rules for a vampire that I've broken. I'm out of my coffin well before dark and I neglected to be invited across the threshold."

He removed his shades, pocketed them, then looked in the mirror, giving his mustache a slight brush with a finger.

"Nice mirror," he teased, giving Mike a wink. "Is your father in? We have a meeting at the station tonight and he kindly offered to drive me. I thought, if I came over early, I could broach the suggestion to him about your martial arts lessons."

# 3: Attack

Mike's reverie was interrupted by the bumping of the ferry against the rubber fenders of the terminal dock. As they exited the terminal, he handed Sean the car keys and his sword in its silk sleeve, then walked down along the landing toward the little city marina.

"Dad, you just bought a new boat," Sean called. "Aren't you done lookin' yet?"

Mike grinned. "One can always look," he said. "I'm just curious to see how many tried to stay in the water. They've got a bubbler system here."

"Okay, I'm comin.' Hold up."

Mike heard the slamming of the back hatch of his Cherokee, followed by the sound of his son jogging after him.

An odd smell assailed his nostrils. He couldn't place it—stale, dirty—a faint but unpleasant odor.

Something nagged at his peripheral awareness— something off to one side moving very fast toward him.

All senses were alert.

"Sean, get back to the car. Get in and lock the door."

Sean ignored the command. "Dad, what is it? Whatever it is, I'm a brown belt, for cryin' out loud. I don't need to hide in the car like a kid."

He never got to argue. It came out of the shadows of a tent-like pavilion at the corner of the boardwalk. A shadowy figure loomed at him, a huge hand lunging at his throat. It looked about six feet tall.

He tried to parry the hand away but it was like slapping at a tree trunk. He drove a front kick into his attacker's groin, then pivoted, driving the same foot into the solar plexus. There were two grunts. Then he was airborne. Leaping, he spun, whipping a reverse roundhouse into the attacker's head.

The attacker staggered, but kept on coming. Charging in, he latched onto Mike's throat, lifting him off the ground with one hand.

Mike was astounded. He was five-foot-eight and solid. He might look like one hundred seventy pounds but he was every bit of one ninety. And this thing lifted him with one hand.

The grip was powerful. His head started to spin.

He thrust his foot into the solar plexus again, then drove a toe kick into the throat.

His attacker made a painful gurgling sound, clutching at his throat with one hand. The force of Mike's kick broke the grip on his throat and propelled him back. He fell to the pavement, rolled backward onto his feet.

What he saw by the light of the pole lamp froze his blood.

"Sean, get away! You can't help!"

The face was ugly, with sharp fangs for canines. The features were brutal, masked by the pain of Mike's defensive attacks.

And it was fast. He'd never encountered an adversary so fast. It took all his speed to dodge attempts to hit or grab at him. And the strength of the thing was terrifying.

Suddenly the attacker drew a weird, wicked-looking knife and slashed.

Mike parried with his right palm, drove his left into the inside of the attacker's elbow, attacking nerves, then tore the knife from the attacker's grasp.

Wheeling, he slashed the blade across the thing's throat. He felt the heavy blade tear through muscle and cartilage, the tip grating against cervical vertebrae. The head remained attached, but the trachea and esophagus were severed.

The thing clutched at its ruined throat as if to keep in the fast-escaping blood. It glared at him, then fell to its knees. The look in its eyes was feral. Then it began to struggle to its feet.

Mike felt a rare surge of panic. Stepping in, he drove the blade into the thing's throat so that it severed the spine. Finally the life left the thing's eyes and it sank to the pavement.

Sean hugged his father and Mike returned it one-handed, keeping his bloody right arm away from his son.

"You okay, Dad?" Sean asked in a subdued voice.

Mike nodded. "Shaken, I guess. That thing isn't supposed to exist outside of movies. I told you to go to the car."

Sean ignored the reprimand. "Is it really a vampire, Dad?"

Mike didn't answer right away. "I don't know," he said finally. "It was impossibly strong and has the teeth."

He flipped open his phone and called 911. "How do I report this," he asked himself.

A police car pulled up and two officers got out, hands on their sidearms. One cop was older. They assessed the scene and put handcuffs on both Mike and Sean.

Squatting next to the body, the older cop called out, "Go easy on those two. Look at this." He pulled back the corpse's lips to expose long sharp teeth, like those of a large cat.

They were getting Mike and his son into the back seat of the patrol car when an unmarked car pulled up.

"Jeeze," the younger officer hissed, "I was expecting CID but it's the inspector himself, even before Forensics could get here!"

The inspector was tall, balding, stern of expression. As his eyes caught Mike's, a ghost of a smile appeared. Another detective got out of the car, pulled on latex gloves, and went over to the body of Mike's attacker.

"Lose the cuffs, officer," the inspector said.

The senior patrol officer looked puzzled, but complied.

As soon as Mike's hands were free, the inspector shook his hand. "Been a long time, Mike. How's your dad doing?"

"Inspector MacDonald," Mike acknowledged. "Dad's doing as well as can be expected. SeaView's a good place. I wanted to take him in with me, especially after I got my new place finished, but the doctor wanted him under more steady supervision."

"Lung cancer is no picnic. And Mike, you used to call me 'Pete' before you went away all those years ago," the inspector reminded him. "Christ, Mike, I'm your godfather. I went with your dad to see you in a couple of tournaments. God, you were fast. By the looks of things, you're still one fast, dangerous son of a bitch."

He turned to a young uniformed officer and said, "Officer, why don't you duck over to Tim Horton's and get us all some coffee. Take young Mr. Cameron with you. Here." He handed the younger cop a twenty.

"I'm not under arrest?" Mike asked.

The inspector blew out a heavy sigh. "This is a mess Mike—no, not you, though your experience tonight is part of a bigger mess. We've been dealing with these kind of attacks for almost three weeks. At first the guy seemed to get around—rather a broad hunting ground. A week ago, we had two attacks, about the same time, similar MO, happening far enough apart to require two assailants. Three nights ago, there were three at about the same time, too far apart not to be three perps. Each one looked like some whacko pretending to be a vampire.

"We brought in a specialist as a consultant—an actual English Lord, if you can believe that. Works with Interpol and police departments have used him in the past. He worked with your father and I, back when you were a kid. He talked to me about wanting to have you help him."

He looked cautiously at Mike.

Mike gave brief, ironic chuckle. "So Tony really is Lord Anthony Dewhurst. I guess I know why he's been trying to call me. We've kind of kept in touch." He shook his head. "I can't imagine what help I can be."

"Take a look, Mike." MacDonald gestured toward the body. "You've already been a help." He shook his head as if he couldn't believe what he was seeing—or didn't want to believe. "Back then, early seventies, your father and I were partners. When Lord Dewhurst came on the scene, he and your father did a lot of work without me. It was like they were trying to shut me and other detectives out. I could see maybe the other cops, but I was his partner. I guess I resented it." He sighed. "Now I know why he kept me from learning all the facts—facts that were kept from the public, even kept out of the files. I wish I could have remained shut out. Mike, just how strong and fast was this guy?"

Mike felt a shiver run down his spine. All the talk had put up an insulating wall from the events of less than an hour ago. Just having the two cops arrive had been a comfort. The question yanked him right back into the reality of what he'd just experienced.

"Too fast and too strong," Mike said.

MacDonald seemed to repress a shudder. "When you were nineteen, Mike, you were like a freak of nature. I remember a tournament at the Forum. You were too fast to follow. You still that fast?"

Mike thought about it. "Arthritis makes my hands feel stiff some mornings, and I don't feel so fast. I'm forty-seven, Pete, forty-eight in August,—but yes. I must have slowed some but most times in combat practice it feels like I'm still that fast."

"Yet you think this guy was too fast."

Mike nodded. "I can still bench press three hundred pounds. This guy had a grip like a vice and impossible arm strength. He's big but he's sloppy big. He's no Arnold Schwarzenegger. Yet he picked me up with one hand."

"Inspector," the other detective called.

"That's detective constable Legendre. He's good—science major, like you."

As MacDonald walked over to the body, Mike followed.

"No wallet," the detective said, "but I've got a note in Russian. The printing is crude and uneducated. I can't read Russian, but I know Cyrillic when I see it." He pulled out a zipper baggie and slipped the note into it, flat, then handed it to the inspector.

The inspector glanced at the note.

"André, this is Mike Cameron, Inspector Will Cameron's son." Then, to Mike he added, "Detective

Legendre doesn't like to wait for Forensic Identification and carries half a dozen baggies of various sizes."

At that moment, a compact Cadillac pulled up. The man who got out was tall, maybe sixty years of age. He was well groomed and his clothes were expensive and of European tailoring.

"Sorry I'm late," he said in an Oxford accent. "They've excavated part of Ochterloney Street."

Mike wheeled about and stared.

"Hello, Michael. It's been almost thirty years—perhaps if I'd sent photos with my letters..."

"Tony? It's not possible. You look about ten years older and it's been about thirty."

"Be that as it may, Michael, 't is I, none the less."

"Well, I'll be damned!" Mike blurted. He stepped forward and gave the other a resounding hug. " Still working with the police, I see. I gather you're still with Interpol. Man you must be seventy, eighty, even! How do you do it?"

"Careful attention to my diet," Tony quipped with a smile.

"What's going on, Tony? This guy attacked me out of nowhere, as if he was laying in ambush. He was fast—way too fast, and strong like he was on steroids. He's got fangs like a vampire and smells funny. Don't tell me it's a psycho with roid rage."

"We need your help, Mike. There's no way to ease into this—have to just dive in off the deep end."

"Was that thing that attacked me really a ..."

MacDonald cleared his throat in a loud manner. "We've got one or more psychotic serial killers with a bizarre fetish, going around killing people, trying to act like vampires. The last thing we need is a lot of panic and people buying crosses and garlic.

"You're an amazing man, Mike: BSc in Biology and Math from Acadia, BEd from Dalhousie, level two instructor in Wing Chun and Bak Sil Lum Kung Fu, third degree black belt in Shotokan Karate, and a master's ranking in swordsmanship." The inspector paused, flipping through a leather-bound notebook. "Let's see. You also have a 25-ton captain's license from Bermuda and did twelve ocean crossings. What happened with that? You suddenly moved back ashore."

"She died," Mike snapped. "Her name was Susan. It was melanoma—nothing they could do. We used what time she had to do something we'd loved doing together. We hit a derelict shipping container, got picked up by a freighter. She took a turn for the worst."

"Now you've come home, returned to teaching, after a fashion, and bought a smaller boat."

Michael shrugged. "Life goes on."

"You came home," MacDonald repeated. "After she died, you taught martial arts in the Bahamas for a bit. You moved to the States, tried to write, got published, had a disastrous relationship, then came home, bought a house and another boat, and started a new Kung Fu school. And you have a new publisher."

Mike shifted his glance to Tony. "What's going on? I got attacked by a vampire, and the inspector of Criminal Operations doesn't seem surprised. I was forced to kill my attacker and everyone's just taking it in stride. Now I'm listening to my personal history like I'm under a microscope."

"Keep your voice down," MacDonald insisted, looking about as if to see if anyone heard.

"He's not the first one I've dealt with, Michael," Tony said. "Perhaps you recall the case in Sydney that your father and I were working on all those years ago."

"At first we thought there was just one," the inspector said. "Then it looked like two, then three. Lord Dewhurst believes there may be more."

"Lord Dewhurst?" Mike queried, staring at Tony.

Tony nodded. "I don't use the title much, except when it helps grease certain bureaucratic wheels. We can talk about it later."

Mike raised an eyebrow but held his tongue.

"Anything useful on the body?" Tony inquired.

"Can you read Russian?" MacDonald asked. He handed Tony the bagged note.

"Cheap notebook paper, written in pencil, crude penmanship."

"Right-handed, used a number two pencil, and not well-educated by the penmanship," Legendre added He left the body and joined them.

Tony nodded. "The latter is confirmed by several misspellings, "Cherokee," for one."

"Cherokee?," Mike interrupted, "I drive a Jeep Cherokee."

A look of alarm appeared in Tony's eyes. "Red? A Grand Cherokee Limited?"

Mike nodded.

"You read Russian," MacDonald cut in. "Damn it, man, what does the damn thing say? Read it!"

"Sorry, old chap. It says, and I quote, "five-foot-eight, muscular build, greying dark hair, blue-grey eyes. Drives a 1999 red Jeep Cherokee Limited, license plate DYC 635.""

Mike felt an even colder chill shoot through him. "Why me?" he demanded.

Tony sighed. "My fault, Michael. I think someone knows why I'm here and that I was trying to get in touch with you. My guess is that either my cell phone or home phone has been compromised or else someone has found a way to intercept my e-mails."

"With the right spy-ware, the latter is the easiest," Mike said.

"I've discussed you with the inspector, here, and I'm in constant touch with a colleague in London. Nigel will be coming over in a few days. We've discussed your talents and how you might be of help to us. I guess I painted a rather dramatic picture, enough for someone to try to remove you from the playing field before I could even ask you to join the team."

"Team?"

The inspector cleared his throat. With a glance at Legendre, he led Mike away, lowering his voice.

"Mike," he began awkwardly, "this can't get out. We can't even let the rest of the department know. My God, man, can you imagine the panic? I'm trying to keep the police as much out of this as possible. If even a tenth of the legends are true, the police are helpless. We can't shoot them; they just heal. Lord Dewhurst has an uncanny talent for finding these monsters, but we need someone who can destroy them. They're strong and they're fast. We need someone of your ability, someone we can trust."

"Let's face it, Michael," Tony chimed in, "it's not as if we can arrest these chaps and give them their day in court."

Mike nodded slowly. "I can just hear the judge: You are here by sentenced to a stake through the heart, decapitation, and having your mouth stuffed with garlic."

"Actually," Tony said, "a stake through the heart only incapacitates. Severing the ventral root, as you did, is the best method. Removing the heart is also good, but more time-consuming. If the vampire can remove the stake from his heart, it will heal and he's back in business in a few days, all-be-it weakened. Fortunately I'm acquainted with the night ME and he knows to separate the head from the body. If the knife is removed, the spinal nerve tissue could regenerate enough to reattach."

"That's not possible," Mike objected. "Trust me, my degree was medical biology. Major nerve tissue like the spinal cord does not regenerate."

"Not in humans, no," Tony replied, "but the regenerative capabilities of vampires are more amazing than those of a lizard. Cut off a lizard's tail and he grows a new one, fully functional, sensory and motor nerves included."

"So the coroner is in on this, too?"

Tony nodded. "The night ME is well acquainted with the situation." He turned to MacDonald and added, "Perhaps this would be a good place to leave the official part of this, Inspector," Tony suggested. "And, the more I think of it, the more I fear bad luck between here and the ME's office. Excuse me."

Tony went over to where Legendre was standing by the body, and seemed to stare into his face.

Mike watched in amazement as the detective took an extra pair of latex gloves out of his pocket, handed them to Tony, then turned and stared at the harbour. Tony donned the gloves, took hold of the huge knife in the throat of the corpse, and levered down—first to the right, then he removed the blade, reinserted it, and levered down the other way until the head was severed. He laid the knife on the chest and pulled the head several inches away from the body.

As Tony returned, the inspector let out a sigh. "Now I have to figure out how to explain that to the Forensics boys. A knife in the throat is self-defense. Cutting the head off is hard to explain."

"I'll have a chat with them," Tony said. "Here they come now, behind that patrol vehicle."

"At least that means the coffee's here, too."
MacDonald turned to Mike and said, "I've got your
statement. There'll be a copy at the Dartmouth Station,
in the Spicer Building, behind the hospital. It'll be at
the front desk tomorrow. Just drop in and sign it.
Forensic Identification will want photos of your hands
and arms. You have a few bruises that are clearly
defensive wounds, and you've got bruising about the
throat. It makes it easier to rubber stamp this as self-
defense, though Lord Tony may have just complicated
that."

The patrol car pulled up, followed by a van labeled
"Forensic Identification Unit."

Sean brought coffee to his dad, eying Tony with
curiosity.

"Sean, this is Lord Anthony Dewhurst," Mike said.
"Tony, this is my son, Sean."

Tony smiled and shook Sean's hand. "A pleasure
to meet you, Sean. Your father's mentioned you a lot
in his letters over the years. And your grandfather
speaks very highly of you."

"You the guy who sends Dad books all the time?
They're great. I've read some of them myself."

Tony smiled. "Excuse me a moment."

He walked over to the forensic team just getting
out of the van, and seemed to get their attention so
completely that the conversation was one-sided. "Make
sure you bag the head separately," Mike heard Tony
say to the lead CSI.

"Bring that camera over here before you
photograph the body," the inspector called out. "Mike,
we can probably get into Alderney Gate out of the cold
for a torso shot. You'll have to take your shirt off."

Mike handed his coffee to Sean, removed his Helly
Hansen sailing jacket, then pealed off his turtleneck.

The photographer gave a whistle, apparently due to the many scars on Mikes arms and upper torso.

"Been in a lot of knife fights?" he asked.

"Sword training," Mike said. "Usually the blades are dulled. Sometimes they're not."

Mike was just pulling on his sweater and jacket when MacDonald said, "That's all I need. Peters, get rid of that photographer or at least move him far enough away that he can't get anything too detailed." The constable nodded and moved toward the press photographer just outside the cordoned area, snapping away with a digital Nikon.

"Damned police scanners," the inspector muttered.

Mike ground his teeth. "I don't need this."

Tony said, "If you can drop Sean at home, I'll follow, then take you for a drink somewhere. We need to talk—aside from catching up."

Mike sighed and nodded slowly.

"He's got his license. He could drive himself home, but I'd rather he didn't. I expect he's a bit more shaken by this than he knows. Okay, Tony. I could do with some scotch right about now."

# 4: A Strange Offer

Mike sat on the edge of his son's bed. Sean was on his back under the covers, hands behind his head.

"Dad, will Tony get in trouble for hacking that guy's head off? I mean, that's like tampering with evidence. He had to, you know. If the severed nerves ever touched together again, the guy could regenerate."

Mike smiled. "Relax, Sean, it's over. It's not like the movies. Some of the cops think he was just a psycho with tooth caps."

"No way, Dad, I saw him. He picked you up with one hand."

"And he went down from a few well-placed kicks. Here, take this." Mike held out two tablets and a glass of water.

"What is it?"

"Herbal Nerve. It'll just relax you and help you doze off. It'll probably keep you from dreaming about tonight."

"That'd be a relief. I thought I was about to lose you, too, Dad."

"No chance," Mike said, smiling.

"Still, I guess it's there in the back of my mind—one of those stupid things like a phobia."

"Get some sleep. I'm just going for a drink with Tony. We need to talk a bit. Haven't seen each other in a long time."

He shut the door, leaned against the wall, closed his eyes, and drew in a long, slow breath. It was like fighting vertigo. Images of the horrific encounter flashed through his mind. He squeezed his eyelids tighter, willing them to go away.

"I say, old man, if anyone ever looked like he could use a drink, it's you." Tony was there next to him. Mike had left him seated in the living room, admiring his antique piano and the guitars hanging on the wall.

———————

Mike knew of a pub not far from where he lived that stayed open past the usual 1:00 am. They took a quiet booth in a corner. Except for country music coming through the speakers, there was little life in the place.

"Those sword scars look like they'd have been quite painful when inflicted," Tony commented. "Bit dangerous, don't you think?"

"So's living in the sun in Bermuda, exposing your skin to all that UV. So's crossing Portland Street at 5:00. What's your point?"

"That you don't mind danger, but you may be a bit reckless."

Mike sipped his Glenlivet and thought about Tony's comment.

"I suppose I do. When you're in your teens and twenties, you think you're immortal. Your prospective changes a bit after thirty. After forty, your views *really* change, especially when your wife dies in her thirties. My mother thought I was being reckless when I dragged Sean to Japan, China, and Tibet for almost two years after I left—well, you know. My folks *loved* that. But, it was good for him, and it was very good for me. Actually, I think some part of my father understood or at least tried to."

"You and Sean seem very close. He has some of your gifts. He also has your build, your dark hair—and working on being taller than his father."

Mike chuckled. "He'd stretch himself on the rack if it would help. He competes with me but, yeah, we're close—at least I have that. And he has his mother's eyes, some of her features."

While he was talking, Tony had his eyes fixed on Mike. He suddenly felt a vague buzzing in his head. *Relax, don't fight it.* The thought pushed at him, a thought not his own. *There are things you're going to have to accept. Your definition of what's real and possible in this world has been altered. Trust me. You're upset and angry about tonight. That's why you respond with sarcasm. That, too, will pass.*

Mike stared back into Tony's eyes. He took a deep breath, relaxed, then pushed. *STOP THAT!*

"That was remarkable, Michael—a very forceful push. Did they teach you that in Tibet?"

Mike blinked and shook his head to clear his mind. "Been to Tibet yourself? I never had to push any of the Tulku out of my mind like that. They felt gentle, easy to push out. With you it was more like having to slam a door against an intruder."

"That's a good analogy, Michael. Of course, the Tulku are gentle, non-aggressive in their outlook, like most lamas. If a vampire pushes into your mind, he'll be as gentle as your attacker tonight. Mind you, a vampire's mental talents depend both on how long he's been a vampire and how strong his mind was as a human. I rather expect your attacker tonight was weak-minded. Have you ever used your talents in combat against an opponent?"

Mike shook his head. "Sometimes I can get a glimpse of what a guy's going to do before he does it. It helps.

"So, what brings you back to Canada, Tony? Is it these Ripper killings? Dad talks about it so much that I think he wishes he weren't retired."

Tony nodded. "I've talked your father into accepting a small consultant's fee. He was always very good at this."

"Thanks. It'll help pay the bills at SeaView, and make him feel like he's still in the loop. He insisted on staying in the house after Mom died but, when the lung cancer hit, well, it was just too much for him. He never said you'd be in town.

"And thanks for all those books, by the way," he added. "I know I wrote to thank you each time, but this is in person. You never missed a Christmas or a birthday, and I always loved them. I especially loved Rice and Elrod. The Lustbader books were a surprise. I thought for a while you really had a vampire thing going, but his ninja series and the Sunset Warrior series were an interesting change of direction."

Mike stopped and stared. "All those vampire novels—you were preparing me for something like this. When you suggested my Kung Fu training all those years ago, were you prepping me for a career as a hitman against the undead, the *nos feratu*?"

Tony shook his head. "No, well, perhaps on some unconscious level. Actually, I was hoping to prepare you for something else, but we'll get to that. How's your own writing coming?"

Mike shrugged. "Five books, no huge success. Still, I enjoyed the writing. And you're very good at evading the issue."

"I read the one you paid to have published in the America," Tony said. "I thought it was quite good. Fantasy is a tough genre. I notice your best heroes are warriors—even some of the wizards."

"Write about what you know," Mike quoted with a smile.

"Michael," Tony began after a long pause, "do you ever feel like a warrior who lives in the wrong world? A warrior who longs to wage war with his sword against evil? Lost in a modern world where swords are no longer allowed and a swordsman just has no place?"

Mike became pensive and introspective.

"What if..." Tony hesitated. "What if I could provide you with that—not walking around in daylight with a sword, dueling with bad guys—but going after real evil. You might even get to use a sword on occasion."

"Evil," Mike almost jeered. "Right. Do I get a cape and a mask? No that would be too overt. One must be covert when killing vampires."

Tony pulled a folded section of a newspaper out of the pocket of his long topcoat and tossed it on the table. He then unfolded two stapled sheets of photocopy paper and placed them next to it. "You've been through a shock tonight. If I could have reached you by phone sooner, I might have averted that. I'm sorry."

Mike glanced at the papers. The lurid headline was of the Ripper Killer. He nodded. "Like Jack the Ripper, he slices up his victims." His brow furrowed. "Very little blood at the scene."

Then he glanced at the photocopy. "Victims died of exsanguination. He completely drains them of blood until the heart stops. Cut open with surgical precision, throats cut, sometimes gutted." He looked up. "Rather a devious modern day vampire. My attacker had a knife that looked a bit like an Indian kukri."

He turned the page, read, then looked up. "Forensics found no cast-off blood stains or splatter stains—so the slashing is post-mortem—but there was enough trace at the scene to make them believe they weren't killed elsewhere.

"So why you, Tony? What made you a vampire hunter? And why do you really need me?"

Tony sipped his tea, barely a spoonful. "How much do you recall of our conversation the night we met?"

"Enough."

"What if there were as many different kinds of vampires as there are people. Some want to play a useful role in the world, some don't give a damn just so long as they can go unnoticed, and some are predators, serial killers. Today, even in smaller cities like Halifax, it's actually easy to kill as a vampire and go unnoticed. In Victorian times, it was hard. People believed. Drain a body of blood, leave it lying about, and people yelled 'vampire.' Today you can do it and they think it's a serial killer or some kind of gothic Satanic cult. Kids dress in black and call themselves vampires. I saw a chap once who'd had fangs installed by a dentist. No one would notice a real one if he walked in right now.

"Think hard, Mike—remember the night you met me."

"Okay," Mike chuckled, "I'll play along. You're very pale. You have some sort of allergy to ultraviolet light—photophobia. But you came to my house before sunset."

"Anne Rice's Lestat could rise before sunset and stay up until just after sunrise. Patricia Elrod's Jack Fleming wanted to live a normal life and not kill. She was wrong about the cows' blood—vampires need a regular transfusion of human blood. We're immune to reactions to most differences in blood type, but it must be human. We just don't need much."

Mike felt Tony's mind pushing into his.

*Like you said, Michael, a vampire could have pushed inside your mind, forced you to forget. Instead, I influenced you to calm you. I sensed in you the beginnings of a person that I would want to know—as a friend, not as a convenient tool when I needed it. I didn't want you to forget meeting me. And, no, I didn't learn this from a Tibetan tulku.*

Mike pushed him out, but what Tony was saying was falling into place.

Tony sighed. "I can see by the look on your face this isn't going to be easy. Very well."

Mike felt his stomach tighten and could feel the blood draining from his face.

Tony pulled out a small pocket knife. "It must be sharp—our skin is more resilient than yours—especially at my age." He glanced about to be sure no one was looking, then drove the blade into his arm.

"Jesus!" Mike blurted.

"Not to worry, old man," Tony comforted, "it'll close quickly enough."

Taking a napkin, he blotted most of the blood that was welling out of the wound.

"See? It's already stopped bleeding."

Mike sat very still as shock and incredulity faded into frightened belief. The wound closed, and slowly healed, leaving a red scar. Mike stared at the scar.

"After a good day's sleep, even the scar will be gone," Tony promised.

"But you cast a reflection."

"That's a myth—the assumption that we can't be seen in mirrors. Religious superstition led to the notion that we are of the devil, and not of this world. Simple physics of lightwaves, Michael. If you can see me, I have to cast a reflection."

"Have you killed people?" Mike gasped. It was barely a whisper.

Tony nodded. "Yes, but never as a vampire. A long time ago, during a chaotic time in history, I was forced to kill some rather persistent Frenchmen, but that was survival, and the cause was noble. As for taking blood, it's rather like giving blood, really—a pint here, a pint there—two people a night is fine unless I need major healing. I can use hospital blood if it's warmed. I once brought my own wine to a party. Of course it was 80% O+ and 20% claret. I had a devil of a time keeping this cute little minx from pouring out of my bottle. I finally had to hypnotize her, after a fashion."

"So you hypnotize your victims?"

"Michael, will you relax? You've backed your chair up half a meter in the last four minutes, and it's still creeping backwards. Look, if I were a danger to you, you'd have been dead the first night you entered my house. Besides, with very little training, you could as easily hypnotize people, assuming you can't already. You required very little effort to push me out of your mind tonight."

"So how would you profile your victims?" Mike challenged. "Young, healthy boys like Lestat? Women? Or do you seek out evildoers, like Lestat in the beginning?"

"Oh, my, no." Tony demurred. "The latter wouldn't do at all. First, I select for health. They're less likely to miss half a pint or so. I prefer happy, optimistic people. You'd be surprised how much mood and psyche is tasted in the blood. I have a theory that feeding on villains may be part of what turns vampires into monsters. You see, we do gain some of the knowledge and psyche of our victims when we feed—not through the blood but from their minds. Constant feeding on criminals would foster increasing criminal thoughts in a vampire—at least that's a theory. Of course, it has a lot to do with the kind of person one is before one crosses over, so to speak.

"One thing is for sure—killing becomes addictive. I've interviewed many vampires over the years, and a pattern emerges. We feel what the victim feels. If we feed like a monster, inciting horror in our victims, that horror becomes exhilarating, addictive. The vampire looks for more and more of it. He's more likely to kill and his attacks become more violent, more horrific. Apparently, taking the victim into death in this manner is very addictive. Before you know it, what you have is more the profile of a serial killer than that of a vampire. He kills for the psychic thrill.

"Most of us use hypnosis to lull the victim into a sense of peace. What we get psychically from them is calming and soothing. In return, they find the experience rather sensual. Both Rice and Elrod were quite accurate in that."

"So you mesmerize your victims, like Dracula." Mike seemed to have traded disbelief for some sort of cynical disapproval.

Tony thought a moment, then called, "I say, miss?"

As the waiter approached, Tony fixed his eyes on her. She came to the table and stood, her eyes locked on Tony's. As Tony continued to hold her gaze, she opened a button near the top of her blouse, pulled the collar to one side, and leaned in toward him, her throat exposed to one side.

"I'm sorry," Tony said, "but we seem to be out of napkins. Could you bring more?"

"Certainly," she said in a dreamy tone. Picking up the obviously full napkin dispenser, she gave them one from the adjacent table, and took theirs away.

"I'm not exactly unattractive," he commented, "but I'm no Cary Grant. It does work. Like I said, with the right training, you could be good at it. Don't look so shocked. The Great Ravine wasn't a vampire, nor was the Amazing Kreskin. You picked up a lot of mental talent in Tibet. It just needs focusing."

Mike pushed his chair back away from the table. In a flash he drew a Gerber knife clipped to his belt and flipped the blade open with his thumb. Just as quickly, he reversed the grip, holding it more for stabbing than slashing, the spine of the blade parallel with his forearm. Gripping for slashing was what most people would have thought of, but the grip would be weaker. With something like a boxer's right cross, he could slash the blade across a throat with maximum force, slicing with the full length of the blade rather than just the tip. He watched Tony carefully, his heart thumping in his chest.

"That was very fast, Michael. I barely saw you move. But, please, listen to me a moment." Tony's voice was low, calm. There was no sense of an attempt at mesmerizing, just a desire to reason. "Think, Michael. I know this is a lot after what you've been through tonight, but think. What kind of man are you? You're a trained warrior, potentially a killer. Tonight you became a killer. But is that who you are? You're a caring man. You're an idealist. You always want to do the right thing. It's like an obsession with you. So, if I infected you with my blood, what kind of vampire would you become. Would the changes in your physiology created by whatever this virus is turn you into a predator, a heartless taker of human life? Or would you try to exist in your new form while still retaining the same ideals you've always had? Oh, yes, you'd try to exist on animal blood at first, but in a few weeks, when you weakened, even sickened just like a human trying to live on potato chips, you'd realize that you can't exist on infusions of animal blood any more than a human can tolerate a transfusion from a pig or a

cow. So what would you do then? You'd look for ways
to take from humans without hurting them. You'd
gravitate to young, healthy people, people strong
enough to easily spare half a pint. Being a male, you'd
prefer women. But you'd realize that an athletic man
was a better donor. Your first donor would teach you
that your mind absorbs the emotions of your victim.
You'd want to soothe them, keep them calm. You'd
prefer happy, optimistic people. Anything else would
be too unsettling. When you didn't age, your friends
would find it odd at first, then a bit unnerving. You'd
avoid your friends, live a solitary life. After a few
generations, you'd long to meet someone you could be
friends with. If you could meet them young and nurture
them carefully to the idea of accepting who and what
you are, perhaps you might dare reveal your true nature
to them. Imagine the prospect: for one lifetime, you
could have a true friend. They might even feel a bit
like a son or a nephew."

Mike realized he'd been holding his breath. He
exhaled slowly, closed the blade, and clipped the knife
back on his belt. He began to nod slowly.

"Now," Tony continued, "imagine a different man,
one who has always moved through life as a taker, a
user. He thinks society owes him something. He
discovers the joy of his strength and his ability to prey
on these weak, pathetic mortals. He finds joy in killing,
joy in tasting their fear, their terror of what he is the
moment he attacks. That's what attacked you tonight.
But there's a worse kind. That's probably the one thing
Stoker captured accurately in his novel. Imagine a man
who, all his life, felt superior. Perhaps he's a sociopath.
Perhaps he's a spoiled, predatory member of European
nobility who sees the members of the so-called lower
classes as having been put on Earth to serve his needs.
He's educated, intelligent, and he doesn't care a whit

for the suffering of these peasants he chooses to feed upon. That kind is much more dangerous than the creature that was set upon you tonight."

"This is a lot for me to swallow at once," Mike declared. He gulped the rest of his scotch and signaled the waiter for another. "You say my perceptions of the world have been altered? That's a damned understatement if there ever was one! This afternoon I was an aging martial arts instructor trying to prove to a stadium full of kids that I still have it. I was a divorced widower trying to be mother, father, and big brother to a teenage son, trying to teach him that the world needs hard work, not shortcuts. Trying to convince a publisher that my work deserves a bit more attention than they're giving it. My monsters were yearly taxes and threats to the western world by extremist radical Islamic fundamentalists. Tonight I live in a world of real monsters, one of whom was set on me to kill me because I might be asked to help hunt him down. Someone I've thought of as a dear friend for most of my life is also one of these monsters, except that he's not really a monster. Oh, yes, and I'm now expected to become some sort of modern day samurai hit man, whacking these monsters' heads off with a katana or something. That kind of thing went out the window over two hundred years ago with the Meiji Restoration."

"I'm sorry, Michael. My intention was to ease you into this. I'd planned to reveal what I am under calmer conditions, though I'd assumed some dramatic demonstration like I did here would be required. I had no idea that you'd be attacked, forced to kill, forced to learn about this under such terrifying circumstances."

"Look, I need to get home," Mike said suddenly.

"Can we continue this another time? Perhaps tomorrow evening?" The look on Tony's face seemed almost to beg.

Mike nodded slowly.

Tony took out a card and wrote on the back before handing it to Mike. "I'm renting an old house on Hawthorne. Anytime after 6:00."

Mike gave him a half smile. "Probably about 7:00."

After Tony dropped him off, Mike sat in his room at his computer desk for a half hour, sipping on another scotch. He wasn't a regular drinker, though his tolerance was high. He was hoping to numb himself into falling asleep. It didn't work. His dreams were restless.

He found himself reliving an episode from his late teens.

*He's walking along the Halifax waterfront at night, heading toward the ferry terminal after a movie. Someone steps out of the shadows and slashes at him with a knife. There's a sharp pain and the warm flow of blood from a shallow wound in his abdomen. As the blade returns in a backhand pass, he goes into reflex mode. His hand catches the wrist, twists. His foot drives into ribs as he yanks on the wrist, twisting and wrenching. Releasing the wrist, he launches a high roundhouse kick at the man's head. The man falls to the pavement, bleeding from mouth, nose, and ears. Mike has broken his jaw, cracked his skull, broken his wrist and elbow, dislocated his shoulder, and broken two ribs, driving one into his spleen.*

*Mike stares at the fallen mugger. The mugger fades from view. In his place is another man in seventeenth century samurai armour. He's been beheaded, one arm severed, one leg almost severed.*

*Mike's own hand, partially obscured by samurai armour of the period, holds a katana. Blood drips from the blade.*

Mike sat up in bed, beads of sweat on his forehead and cheeks. He wiped his face, then lay back, staring at the ceiling.

"I haven't had that dream in almost twenty years," he said to himself. "Well, if that nightmare's going to come back to haunt me, tonight's definitely the night."

# 5: Pressure

Next morning Mike's computer woke him up far earlier than he would have liked.

"It's Sunday, for crying out loud," he muttered. "What appointment can I have on a Sunday?"

His memory reminded him just as his *iCal* program displayed the memo. He had to sing with his church choir for two services, and he was playing the bagpipes as the minister recessed down the aisle after the service. And he had to be there to rehearse at 8:30. He groaned. It was 7:30. After a trip to the bathroom, he went to the kitchen and put the coffee on, then banged on Sean's door.

"I'm up," Sean called. "We have to be in choir. Did you remember?"

Mike shook his head. He could remember Thursday night's rehearsal but that now seemed ages ago, part of someone else's life.

"I sing bass in the choir, I teach kung fu and swords, I sail, and I kill vampires on the side," he muttered.

He just couldn't get past the unreality of last night. He looked at his arms. There were traces of bruises and a faint hint of blood spatter up his arm from having driven that oriental knife into the monster's throat. He went to his sink, soaped a cloth, then scrubbed at his arm, trying to get what he'd missed last night. He glanced in the mirror. The bruises around his throat were more purple this morning.

*Great*, he thought. *Maybe my collar and tie will hide it. Shit! The Ghillie shirt I wear with my kilt won't. And I have to duck out of the choir loft and change before the end of service, then change back for next service and start all over! How do I get myself into these things!*

He had trouble swallowing toast and mostly just drank coffee.

"Late night?" Sean asked, grinning. "Guess you and Tony had a lot to catch up on. I got your choir book here. Are we walking or driving?"

"Driving," Mike said, loading his Dunbar pipes and a wardrobe bag into the back of his jeep. There was fresh snow on the ground. He drove the short distance with the window down, hoping the crispness would help wake him up.

During the service he studied Sean when his son wasn't looking. The boy seemed nonchalant, as if nothing had happened last night. He often wondered if it was a good or bad trait. Everything just seemed to roll off his back: his mother's death, his grandmother's, Mike getting mad at him. After a certain interval, he just seemed to pick up and go on. Mike worried that he might be in denial or worse, bottling it all up inside.

"That went better than expected," Mike commented to Sean after church. Sean, on a whim, had recently joined the tenor section of the choir.

"Yeah, you looked like you were struggling to stay awake during the sermon," Sean teased. "I loved watching you sneak out to become the Highlander.

Why didn't you just pull your pants on under the kilt and let the gown hide the pirate shirt?"

Mike let his chagrin show. "I didn't think of it. Too much on my mind, I guess."

Sean grinned. "That's my dad, brain so far into overdrive you missed the speed bump. We going downstairs for coffee?"

Mike thought about it. "No, I think I'd rather get a quick lunch, then go down to the boat. I want to check on the tarp, then we need to go see your grandfather."

Sean snickered. "You don't need any more coffee. You must have had three cups between the first and second service. And, yeah, we do need to visit Grampy. I haven't seen him in a week. I wish you'd let me bike there—the snow's not a problem, Dad, I put snow tires on my Suzuki. I could take the back way and stay off the *Circ*."

"Not today."

"And here's the duo with the dulcet tones," the minister greeted in a put-on Irish brogue.

"I thought you were Scottish, Sandy," Mike said.

"Ah, but me sainted mother was Irish. We're a confused lot, as if being from Cape Breton isn't enough."

"Careful," Mike warned. "Half your congregation are Capers—the better half, if you ask me."

"Aye, Cape Breton *is a good place to be **from**.*" Mike and the reverend finished the adage in unison, making both laugh.

"Can we have a talk downstairs after I'm through here?" Sandy asked.

Mike made a face. "I'm coffeed out and was hoping to get down to the boat before going to see Dad."

"I think it's important, Michael. I had a visit with your dad yesterday."

Mike was about to press him further but the reverend found the best way to forestall him. Beaming, he simply reached past Mike and Sean, grabbing an elderly lady's hand. "Ah, Mrs. Ferguson, I'm so glad to see you out today. How's the heart."

"See you downstairs," he added to Mike out of the corner of his mouth, giving him a wink.

When the reverend finally made it downstairs, he headed straight for Mike, making short work along the way of saying 'hello' parishioners attempting to waylay him. He took Mike by the arm and led him well away from any listening ears.

"You look great in a kilt but aren't you a bit heavily armed for church?"

"Ah, but the *sgian dubh* is a traditional part of the outfit."

"Aye, laddie, I know it," Sandy mimicked, lapsing into a Scot's brogue. "But isn't it just one *black knife* in the right sock? Michael, you've got one in each sock and an even heavier one in your belt. Maybe you're feelin' a bit unsafe. Maybe you've a right to feel unsafe.

"We've known each other a long time, Michael," he went. "I remember the day you came to my door. The Youth Council had dumped in your lap the idea of a teen coffee house at this end of town. I thought it was a good idea, went toe-to-toe with the more anal members of session, and kept a discrete watch as you ran things in a mature fashion. You kept kids well-behaved and created a good time. And, I might add, showed amazing promise as a musician."

Mike eyed the reverend closely. "Why the trip down memory lane?"

"Ah, yes," Sandy mused. "Well, Michael, I had a talk with your father yesterday. Have you ever been with someone who desperately needs to talk about something but feels he can't? He did his best to dance around the edge of something without shining a light on it. He's worried about you. There's something he wants you to do because you're the best man for the job. But he fears for you at the same time. There's someone else that he trusts completely, but something about this man scares him. Then there's today's paper. Have you seen it?"

Mike's memory flashed on the photographer from the night before. His heart sank. "No," he admitted. "It's probably still on the unshoveled doorstep, under the snow."

"Ah." Sandy pulled a large clipping out of his pocket and handed it to Mike. Most of it was a dark photo, the article was short, but it was clearly from the front page. In the distance were the forensic crew going over a body. In the foreground was Mike, in profile, talking to Inspector MacDonald. The bold headline read "LOCAL HERO DISPATCHES VAMPIRE KILLER?" The article was full of speculation as to who Mike might be, whether or not he'd been attacked by a vampire, and how, since there'd been another vampire killing over in Halifax, there might be more than one. They connected it to the Ripper Killer, making it clear that they'd henceforth be calling him the Vampire Killer.

Sandy pocketed the clipping as soon as Mike was through with it.

"I've been following this, Michael. I've had an uncomfortable feeling since it started—not the troubled feeling I get when I see terrible things reported in the paper. This is something like a sense of real evil. We Celts are a superstitious lot, but I've never had a feeling like this before. The United Church—well, Mike, we're not like some of our Roman colleagues or the southern evangelists. We don't see the devil in everything that's bad in the world. For us the devil is more of a metaphor for man's innate capacity to do evil. But, Michael, when I saw this, it was as if everything fell into place—your father's fears—all of it."

Mike felt very weary. Two church services back to back, being in the choir, playing "Go Now In Peace" on the bagpipes—it had created kind of a buffer between the reality of today and the impossibility of last night. Now that buffer was ripped away. What had happened was real once more. What Tony had revealed about himself was real once more. It was like finding the evidence of blood on his arm again. He sighed, then looked Sandy in the eye. "And?"

"I remember more of you from the years before you left than you may know," the reverend continued. "I saw many of your tournaments. You probably thought I didn't even know about that part of your life. I once made a quick hundred and fifty dollars betting on you with another spectator. I've seen you do displays with a samurai sword. You move faster than seems humanly possible. In the best way possible, Michael, you really are a warrior at heart. You believe in good and right. I also think God brought you home for a reason. Maybe he has a lot of reasons. Maybe this is just one of them. Maybe you are meant to rid us of an evil in a way that only you can."

"Where are you getting all of this?" Mike demanded.

Sandy glanced about, as if making sure no one was listening, but kept his voice down all the same. "Well, Mike, as I said, your father put a lot of effort into not saying things, but it wasn't hard. He worked with a man named Tony who specializes in profiling a certain type of psychotic killer. I suddenly got the image of

Lord Tony as a vampire hunter. Your father's fears led me to suspect that Lord Tony is an expert because he himself is a vampire. I'm a man of God, Michael, but I live in a world of science. If vampires are real, then I suppose, like humans, some must be good while others are predators. I doubt if the world is ready to acknowledge the existence of vampires, much less sentence one to life imprisonment for being one. Secretly weeding out the bad ones may be the best way. It saves us from having to handle the reality of such frightening creatures."

Mike couldn't believe what he was hearing.

Sandy smiled. "As I suspect, it's a huge shock to you. Mike, I'm having this talk with you for two reasons. I think this may be something that you are meant to do. Some people have to take on terrible tasks because they can and no one else can. And if I can be of help..."

"Free crosses and holy water?" Mike quipped.

The minister made a wry smile, then said, "What I was thinking is that, if it ever seems so huge, so beyond your ability to grasp, and you need somewhere to turn, well, I'm here for you, Michael."

Mike sighed. He was beginning to feel trapped, like there was no escape from this. "I may need to take you up on that," he admitted. "And, between you and me, crosses and holy water are a waste of time."

"I had a hunch," Sandy said.

He found Sean at the doughnut table and steered him toward the side door. If possible, Mike was more confused than before. The idea of seeing his father, hearing him add his voice to those trying to sway him, seemed too much, too soon.

"Sean, I think I'm going to work more on the boat today and see Grampy tonight or tomorrow."

Sean looked puzzled but just nodded. "Shelly did want to go to a movie," he mused.

"There you go," Mike said, giving Sam, his thirty-five-pound corgi a boost over the stern from the top of the ladder. The short-legged dog scooted across a cockpit seat, breaking into a grin. Sam loved boats. Mike smiled and gave him a pat, then went back down and adjusted the tarp lines. Where a grommet had torn loose on each side he punched in replacements, two grommets replacing one, dividing the load.

Sam watched with a cocked head as Mike crawled about under the tarp, pushing up to heave snow off. He then had to climb back down and tighten the lines again. That done, he took notes and did some sketches of improvements he hoped to make to the instrumentation layout, changes in the galley, and measured for a new propeller. It took all his concentration. He loved sailing and took boats seriously but, as hard as he tried to keep his mind away from thoughts of vampires, it just didn't work.

Sean was at the movies with a new girlfriend. He seemed to just carry on as if it had all been a bad dream.

Finally, between the cold and the distraction, Mike called it quits. He needed some hot coffee and had to get home and make supper. The whole world seemed in danger of crashing in on him, as if it were all part of a conspiracy. Instead of making him feel part of some destiny, it made it all seem too far-fetched. And then there was the promise to meet Tony. He suddenly wished he hadn't made that promise.

# 6: Tony's Story

**M**ike swallowed hard as he approached the front door of the old house. The large Victorian brought back a flood of childhood memories—he and Billy climbing the wall and sneaking into the old Cowell house the night he first met Tony. He hesitated, then knocked with the big door knocker.

"Punctual as ever," Tony's crisp Oxford accent greeted him as the door opened. "Come in, Michael."

"I was half expecting something like 'Enter of your own free will and leave behind some of the cheer you bring.'" He was aiming for humour but his anxiety made it sound sarcastic.

Tony just chuckled. "Stoker did much to help keep us safe. He was a superstitious man and fond of his whiskey. Still, it's a good read. Curiously enough, just as Rice portrays in some of her works, there used to be a lot of superstitious vampires who did recoil at crosses and thought they could never enter a House of God without bursting into flames. Some even called themselves The Damned."

"Do you go to church?" Mike found himself asking.

"Not as much as I once did. I try to get to the late night Christmas service every year, but I can't take communion." He made a wry smile. "And, while I can move about in daytime, sunlight really hurts my eyes

and will burn my skin. But I have attended on the odd
cloudy Sunday."

"So the legends are right about daylight?"

Tony nodded. "Right down to smouldering and
bursting into flame from excessive exposure."

"Maybe vampires retain magnesium in the skin,"
Mike suggested. Somehow, treating it like an academic
problem kept it at a distance.

"You may have something there. I'll ask Jonathan
to run a tissue analysis on your attacker."

"Your night man in the morgue?" Mike asked.
"Did you hypnotize him?"

"Oh, heavens, no. Actually, he's a vampire, older
than I am. He's also a source for blood. Contrary to
what I implied last night, I rarely feed on live blood."

Tony gestured through an arched doorway. "Take a
seat in the living room. I made coffee for you."

Mike found the living room furnished in Victorian
style, rather like his grandparents' house in Sydney
from almost thirty years before. The furniture was
reproduction. He stood admiring paintings, one an
original Turner.

"Are you as old as I think?" Mike called out.

"How old do you think I am?"

Mike started. Tony was right behind him, handing
him a large mug.

"How do you do that?" he blurted.

"To paraphrase Brad Pitt in *Interview With the
Vampire*, I move pretty much the same way as you do,
only faster. I caught you off guard that time, but you
could follow my movements by eye when you were
young. I'm sure you could do the same now. With
practice, you'll get better. You'll need to."

Mike shook his head. It felt like he wanted to
dislodge cobwebs. He stared at the large wine glass in
Tony's hand. It held close to a pint of dark red liquid.

"That's not merlot, is it?" It was more statement than question.

"No," Tony said in a quiet tone, taking a seat.

Mike fought the mounting anxiety. "This is going to take some getting used to. So, how old are you."

"My name should give you a hint," Tony replied.

"Tony Dewhurst," Mike said slowly. "Tony Dewhurst. Lord Anthony Dewhurst." He began nodding to himself "You had to kill a few persistent Frenchmen—a chaotic time in history. So, I'm guessing that you're *the* Lord Anthony Dewhurst, of the League of the Scarlet Pimpernel."

"The very same," Tony drolled, making a poking gesture with his finger. "Sorry, that was one of Percy's expressions. I found it funny just then."

"But I thought that was just literature, fiction."

"Oh, no, I assure you," Tony argued. "The Baroness Orczy was rather colourful in her writings, but she was fairly close to history most of the time. She was researching in London libraries, after escaping the peasant revolts in Hungary, and there was a researcher there, doing some work of his own for the foreign office. I was what the French liked to call an *agent provocateur*. In those days, *spy* didn't have the romantic ring that it has today. I found it ironic that she wanted to write about Percy, Andrew, Edward, and myself. So, I told her a few stories. Of course I couldn't possibly tell her the one I'm going to tell you now.

"It all started with the revolution and what came to be known as 'the terror' in France. The country had gone mad. A few of us who had been school chums were outraged at what was happening and got it into our heads to see if we couldn't find a way to rescue some of the French aristocracy from the guillotine. We were all titled snobs, rubbing shoulders with young

George, the Prince of Wales. George was such a fop that he gave us a kind of cover without even knowing it. His father King George III was in and out of mental care so much that young George was running the country. But he was such an effeminate dandy—you'd probably call him a sissy—that no one took us terribly seriously, since we were part of his circle of friends.

"Actually, it was Percy who was his closest friend—that would be Sir Percival Blakeney. Percy was only a knight-baronet and didn't even have proper standing in the House of Lords, but he was the richest man in England, and absolutely brilliant. George befriended him because he wanted to keep the Blakeney fortune within his sphere of influence. And, having the ear of the throne, Percy knew what was happening as fast as the crown did. That proved very useful as time went on.

"Anyway, by 1789, Percy was mucking about in France, helping William Pitt and secretly getting on Chauvelin's nerves. In June of 1792, his wife's brother, Armand St. Just, had gotten himself into trouble in Paris, and Percy, along with Andrew—Sir Andrew Ffoulkes—set about to rescue him. They succeeded. It was mostly a lot of cunning and disguises, and very cleverly handled. They'd also rescued the Duc de Bonnefin from the guillotine, just before saving Armand. So, in August, there we were in Percy's study, listening to Percy and Andrew bragging about what they'd accomplished. Percy had been cheeky and left Chauvelin a note, using his father's ring seal as a signature. The seal was an imprint of a pimpernel flower, done with red wax.

"Of course we were all jealous and wanted to be a part of it. Percy would be in charge, with Andrew as his second. I was third in command. Laughably, that was based on the fact that I could beat Andrew in tennis and polo, and had beaten Percy a few times. That seemed to give me a reputation for being clever. I was also something of a swordsman, though most of us were.

"There were also Lord Edward Hastings, Lord John Bathurst, Lord Stowmarries, Sir Edward MacKenzie, Sir Philip Glynde, Lord Saint Denys, and Sir Richard Galveston. By January, ten more joined, including Armand, Marguerite's brother. The League of the Scarlet Pimpernel was now twenty in number.

"For three years we had the most hair-raising adventures. I'd run off and married my wife, Yvonne, and was less active in the League than I'd been. Yvonne de Kernogen and I had eloped, since approval of our marriage wasn't abundant on either side of the family, especially mine. But, there was the dauphin, the young crown-prince of France to rescue and smuggle into Austria, and a few more rescues to make, so, with my wife's blessings, I made a few more trips to France.

"What no one ever knew is that there was a certain French Baroness who had been the best source of information Sir Percy could have imagined. He never spoke of her. When he finally did, it was because she'd become a recluse in her chateau in northern France and Sir Percy had lost all contact with her. He never knew how she was able to learn so much about the plottings of the Chauvelin and his Committee. Now she'd become silent and there were rumours that she was in trouble.

"Percy's little brigantine, the *Daydream*, took me across the Channel one cold day in early December of 1794. I insisted on landing near Dunkerque instead of the usual Calais. Things had cooled off but, so close to the end, I was taking no chances. Lady Dewhurst wanted to have children and I figured she'd rather have me there to contribute than hear of me languishing in the Temple Prison." He grinned. "Still, with old Robespierre's date with Madame la Guillotine the previous July, much had changed.

"Of course, Chauvelin was still about. On the other hand, with Percy, Andrew, and Hastings in France to rescue two more, I imagined Monsieur Chauvelin would be searching for them, instead of me. So, while they were liberating Maurice Reversac and Josette Gravier, I was hoping to rescue a countess 'all by me one-sies.' If Chauvelin caught wind of Percy's presence in France, he'd be watching Calais for his escape. And he'd be watching for the *Daydream*. So I opted for the surf at Dunkerque, with a planned escape on a fishing boat out of Berck-Plage."

Tony's face took on a sentimental look, a wistful smile forming.

"I recall my last moments in Percy's cabin, looking at a miniature of my wife and promising, as if in a prayer, 'When this one's over, Yvonne, there'll be no more adventures for the league—no more adventures for me.'

"I remember looking at a second miniature, one of the countess. It was a beautiful face—perfect. I was suspicious of perfect faces. I decided she was probably somewhat less beautiful that the portrait allowed. Painters were known for their flattery. Still, there was something in the eyes that was startling. Then I thought, 'I don't know how you've done all the things you've done, Madame, but you've earned sufficient gratitude for us to see to your safety.'

"The captain landed me in the dark. The wind had lulled and there was little surf. Once ashore, I made my way up the beach, over the dune, and began searching for a path to the road. My clothes, like the spare set in my bag, were plain and comfortable, of French style, yet gave an impression of some affluence. No one would accuse me of being an *aristo*, but I'd get the respect due a successful *bourgeois*.

"Fearing that the village of Dunkerque might be watched by Chauvelin, I passed through silently, making my way on foot. I had no intention of presenting myself in a coastal town, looking damp from the sea, and asking to hire or buy a horse. I might as well present myself to the local prefect for arrest. So I walked. By the time the sun was peaking over the horizon, I was many miles along the road to Lille and had my part worked out in my head. From behind me came the sound of an approaching wagon. I spun a story about my horse dying on me, and begged a ride to Lille.

"Two days later, I was nearing the countess's chateau. I'd purchased a horse in Lille—I had no intention of walking the whole way—and was coming up the road to the chateau late in the afternoon, maybe an hour or two before sunset. I remember how the late afternoon sun hit the windows of the chateau, seeming to set them on fire."

He let out a sigh and took a slow sip from his glass.

"Excuse me a moment."

In a blur of motion he was gone, back into the kitchen. Mike heard the sound of the microwave for about thirty seconds. Tony seemed to just reappear in the room, but this time Mike had been able to follow his motion as he entered.

"I forget when I'm talking how fast this can cool off. Microwaving breaks down the cellular structure, so I heat a marble and put it in the glass."

"I suppose it needs to be warm," Mike agreed.

*"Body temperature, Renfield, body temperature."*

It was an excellent Bela Lugosi parody. Mike surprised himself by chuckling. "*Love At First Bite*— not very accurate, I'm learning, but amusing. So, what about the countess?"

Tony nodded, his expression troubled.

"There was a gang of ruffians at her door, dragging what seemed to be a long chest out of the house—it seems strange to call it a house—the place was huge. Anyway, they were peasants—filthy, coarse in their actions and manners. They seemed to be stealing from the chateau. My first thought was that they'd done harm to the countess and were looting the place. They dropped the chest on the portico and began attacking it with axes. Two servants who fought to stop them were hacked to death.

"I remember feeling incensed. I drew a pistol from my belt—I'd loaded and primed the pan before taking to the road—and spurred forward. At first, they blurted a barrage of nonsense at me in illiterate French— something about the devil's daughter and cleansing the world of evil—but, when I showed no sign of slowing and took aim as I came on, they scattered like cockroaches when a light comes on.

"By the time I slid down from the saddle I was alone with the chest. Upon examination, it turned out to be an elaborate coffin, now so badly broken through in the top that I could see a beautiful face inside. It was the countess. I was too late—she was already dead, dead for a many hours, considering how white she was.

"Then, much to my horror, as the evening sun hit her face, it began to smoke. I was aghast. I'd never heard of such a thing. I didn't know what to do. Then, the impossible. Her eyes snapped open and she began screaming!

"I panicked. I tore at the lid, then found the latches and released them. I pulled her from the coffin and dragged her into the chateau. Her face and arms were starting to blacken. Once we were away from the door, away from the sunlight, the burning of her skin stopped, but I was completely unprepared for the next horror.

"Without warning, she turned on me. One moment she was screaming in a panic, the next she was on me like a ravenous wolf, sinking her teeth into my neck. There were horror and panic, then a feeling of peace and tranquility. A voice in my mind seemed to be calming me and apologizing at the same time. I felt my heart slow. Then everything started to go black.

"I heard someone saying, 'No, No,' and 'What have I done?' Then there was a flood of warmth into my mouth. It was like nothing I'd ever experienced. It was like swallowing the strongest brandy possible, yet it wasn't. Heat, knowledge, a sense of power—all these things seemed to pour into me.

"My senses cleared a while later. I opened my eyes to find myself in a well-furnished parlour. As my vision cleared, I saw the countess bend over a servant. The man was seated in an expensive chair and the countess seemed to be embracing him. I was startled and began to think I was hallucinating. When she straightened, there was blood on her lips. I then noticed a small wound in the young man's neck and a vacant, seemingly intoxicated stare in his eyes.

" 'I offer my deepest of apologies, monsieur,' she insisted. Her tone was so sincere it was almost pleading. 'Caught as I was in the sunlight, all was madness and the need to survive. I've hidden in the cellars for days with no food, monsieur. I was not truly awake when you rescued me and, with the sun, well, it was the madness of panic, monsieur. In my panic, I took you too close to death. I had to chose—let you die or make you what I am.'

"Turning to another servant, seated on the divan, she said, 'You must assist now, Marie. We must feed our rescuer before the maddening thirst sets in. It shall be I who draws it, since his teeth will not form for several days.'

"I thought I'd gone mad, Michael. There I was in a chateau in the north of France, servants seated as comfortable as you please on the best seats in the parlour, a dead countess drawing blood from them, and all the while implying that, if she didn't feed me on the blood of her servants, I should go mad and attack out of 'the maddening thirst.'

"I watched in horror as she bit into the neck of the maid, Marie, then held a large goblet to the wound, filling it. She bit one of her own fingers and held it to the wound. It seemed to staunch the bleeding almost immediately. Bringing the goblet to me, she held it out. 'Quick, monsieur,' she said, 'you must drink before it cools.'

"I expected to gag as she brought the cup to my lips but the moment I inhaled the smell of the blood something inside me made me take the goblet and drink it down.

"She dismissed Marie and told her to send Cecile in. She then told Claude, the man, to saddle two horses. When Cecile came, she repeated what she had done with Marie. 'That should be sufficient,' she assured me. 'It will take days for the change, but we have no time, monsieur. We must make haste and ride from here. The peasants will return in greater numbers. They now know what I am and will be determined to burn this place to the ground. My servants must flee, as well. They can make their way into the village, tell whatever tales they like of escaping horrors—whatever guarantees their safety and their futures. I will give them money to tide them over. Some day I shall return and rebuild.'"

Tony stared at the floor a moment before looking up once more.

"And there you have it," he concluded with a weak smile. "The rest is a dreary tale of traveling day and night. Claude and Marie accompanied us, posing as a poor couple transporting his dead parents to the place of their birth for burial. By day, we were in the meanest of coffins.

"Once at the coast, I was in a panic. I didn't know how to explain to Percy what had happened. The countess, however, was very clever. She'd lived in this form for more than a hundred and fifty years. She knew something of rare diseases, and knew of a tropical malady that makes one weakened by sunlight.

"It took nearly two weeks for me to change fully. The countess must have given me almost half of her blood. There were moments of great agony. My old cells were being taken over by this new virus. My senses sharpened, my strength grew, my canine teeth changed. At rest, they are little longer than those of most mortals. But when the hunger comes, they elongate perhaps an extra seven or eight millimeters. They seem to extend and retract from the upper jaw bone. Unlike what is seen in some movies, my lower teeth remained normal.

"The ability to climb is really just a matter of strength, just as in talented and experienced mountain climbers.

"But, coming back to my tale, we made it to the coast, where a certain fisherman awaited our arrival. He took us halfway across the the Channel, rendezvousing with The Daydream late one night. Our caskets were shipped aboard as part of the countess's belongings.

"Percy was aboard, much to my concern. The countess told a wild tale of me being injured and contracting a fever from one of her servants—a fever that left me overly sensitive to sunlight. The old boy never showed an ounce of suspicion. To the contrary, he was most solicitous of my well-being.

"Once back home with Yvonne, however, it was another matter. She was never truly happy with my changed hours. Things became strained, but we were British—stiff upper lip and all that."

"What did you do after that?" Mike asked. "I guess you couldn't have children."

"Actually, we adopted two rather quietly," Tony said. "Yvonne, in her pride, insisted on pretending they were hers. I went along.

"Over time I learned to hide my lack of aging. After all, I'd been part of the League of the Scarlet Pimpernel. If Percy could make people in the Place de Gréve and the Gates of Paris think he was an old hag, I could make my self age little by little. Even now I choose to look older than I need to. It adds credibility to what I do."

"I was about to ask you," Mike commented. "I'm guessing you were in your thirties when it happened, but you looked about fifty when we met, and look about sixty now."

"A matter of diet," Tony explained. "Without blood I would age until I looked ancient, rather like in the beginning of Stoker's *Dracula*. If I routinely drank my fill, I'd look the age I was when I died, perhaps a bit younger. I drink just enough to look this age. Preserved blood, while keeping me healthy, doesn't rejuvenate as well as fresh blood.

"But back to my story—I eventually tired of the pretense and felt a need to move on. Yvonne was tiring of waiting on her invalid husband. So, one day, I died.

The countess, posing as her own daughter, came to visit me in my room—something never allowed, normally—and 'found me dead.' There was much wailing a moaning. Yvonne was quite distraught. I felt very guilty, but I'd grown weary of the subterfuge. I was buried in the family vault. The night of my burial, the countess liberated me.

"I embarked on a career as a criminologist. I even found and destroyed the real Jack the Ripper. Of course it never could be known. It was clear to me that he was a vampire, and a twisted one at that. He left devious clues that pointed in many wrong directions, including befriending a talented and somewhat deranged painter, allowing him to paint portraits of some of his victims. There was a book not long ago about that painter being Jack.

"The real Jack was a late riser, as vampires go— never up and about until the final failure of twilight. I, on the other hand, was an unusually early riser. That started about the middle of the eighteen hundreds. I think it's a mix of how strong the countess was (and her blood in me) and how long I'd been a vampire. Anyway, he woke up one night, and there I was, sharp axe in hand.

"He's the only vampire I've ever killed myself. I simply swung and struck off his head. Unfortunately for me, it wasn't so simple. As he died, there was a massive release of psychic energy—a bit like in the Highlander series and movies, but without all the special effects. It was like I could feel everything he'd ever felt and experienced. It gave me nightmares for days—daymares, I could say," he made a wry face. "Anyway, I vowed I'd never kill another vampire myself. I often wondered if the creator of the Highlander stories had ever killed a vampire."

"But what about the body? Jack the Ripper, as far as official knowledge, ceased to kill and faded from the news."

Tony shook his head. "A certain detective from the Yard knew—Frederick Abberline. He knew all about Jack—helped me drag him, box and all, into an empty hovel in a slum area that was about to be redeveloped. We burned it to the ground."

"So how much of the legends are true?" Mike asked. "The cross thing, of course, is absurd. I'm sure there have been Jewish, Buddhist, Hindu, or Islamic vampires who weren't disturbed by Christian symbols. What about garlic, roses, hawthorn, wooden stakes, etc.?"

Tony shook his head. "Garlic is pretty much a myth. It has always been known for curative properties, so primitives thought it warded off evil— much the same with other plants you mentioned and some you neglected. Wooden stakes have a limited basis in fact. We heal quite rapidly, as you saw. We can encyst a bullet and heal around it. Wood, on the other hand, we can't seem to heal around. A primitively cut stake of softwood, like pine, if it passes completely through the chest and pins us to the ground, is rather hard to pull out. It's also rather incapacitating. It creates great pain and limits our abilities rather noticeably until pulled out. Of course, in this modern age, the movies like beautifully-made hardwood stakes, and love to show some vampire hunter turning them out on a lathe. Hard and smooth as they are, they're much easier to pull out. No, a softwood stake, crudely hacked with a hatchet, will hold a vampire in place long enough to cut his head off. The stupid irony missed by the scriptwriters is that it takes much longer and much more effort to pound a stake in than it does to slice off a head with a machete."

"So cutting off a head works?"

Tony nodded. "Your Hollywood chaps have the notion that vampires can regrow severed hands, severed arms, and that cut hair grows back in an instant." He chuckled. "Healing and growing hair are actually related. In both, your body is sending protein to a location and making it part of the tissue there. But, of course, you taught all that, didn't you. Some people heal fast and grow hair faster than others. Cut a long-haired vampire's hair short and he or she would grow it faster than you could, but not all that fast. I think our assimilation of protein is less random than yours. While you're healing a cut, your hair still grows. Vampires seem to devote protein to maintaining our bodies. Our blood cells don't last very long and we can't make them as easily as humans. That's why we need a blood supply. That bit about us remaining the same as we were when we were made is nonsense. I had long hair when I was made. I get a trim about every two or three weeks now. However, just as you can't grow a new arm, neither can I. But, if it was cut off and held in properly in place, the connections would regenerate. That's why I had to cut your attacker's head off."

Mike pondered this. "So, if I'm ever facing off against a vampire and have a sword, whacking off a hand or an arm narrows the odds."

"Considerably," Tony agreed.

"Ancient vampires wouldn't turn to dust, either," Mike mused. "More Hollywood. No matter the age of the vampire, the tissue is still protein. Killing them doesn't turn them into mortals and return them to the state their bodies would have been in had they died a mortal death when they were made."

Tony nodded. "More superstition, I'm afraid."

"Can you rise up into the air?"

The vampire shook his head. "I climb well—a regular spider-man, actually. It's all about finger strength, really. But I can't crawl across a ceiling."

Mike nodded. "All very scientific—like a virus that changes the flesh, making it more resilient, faster-healing, non-aging. The major flaw is fatal damage from ultraviolet light. Otherwise, decapitation is the only way to kill you. And I assume fire, since you burn in sunlight. The virus doesn't let you make your own blood. You need a regular intake, part for blood components, part for protein and glucose needed for food. I replace all my blood cells in about two months, if I remember my histology lessons from Acadia. You, obviously, need to replace them faster. Foreign blood doesn't last in your system very long."

The idea came rapidly. "Ever feed on someone and find you needed less blood for a couple of days? Or feed and find it sustained you a little less than expected."

Tony seemed to go deep into memory. He nodded slowly. "Yes, I'd have to say 'yes' to both. I can see it in your eyes. You have a theory."

Mike nodded. "Your system is powerful. It doesn't wimp out like a mortal's at blood incompatibility, it modifies or destroys blood that would create an immune reaction. The closer the blood is to your own type, the more it sustains you. The more antagonistic it is, the less good it is to you."

"I say," Tony responded. "All I need do is check for a donor card before I indulge! Or do some covert research and develop a sort of short list of regular donors, so to speak."

The thought made Mike uncomfortable. He wanted to change the subject. "What was it like working with my dad? How did that come about?"

Tony sighed. "That's something of a long story. Suffice it to say that my friendship with Percy and my association with the League of the Scarlet Pimpernel gave me a taste for adventure of a noble purpose. In various guises, I've worked for the Home Office, consulted with Interpol, even worked with MI5 and MI6. I met your father when Interpol sort of loaned me to your RCMP as a profiler. I was hunting killer-vampires in the guise of specializing in certain types of serial killers. It was the RCMP who recommended me to your Sydney constabulary when you were young. Once CSIS learned of vampires, they took over, especially after 9/11 and the panic about terrorism."

Mike stared at the floor for a long time, thinking it all through. Finally he looked back at Tony.

"How much does my dad know?" he asked.

Tony pursed his lips. "Tough one, that. Deep down, I think he knows it all. That serial killer when you were a kid stopped killing the same day as a bizarre case of spontaneous combustion. Some poor chap just burst into flames, in the middle of the day, for no apparent reason. We found him in a basement, in a darkened room. I helped your father drag him out into the rising sun, then had to escape—both the sun and exposure to the psychic energy."

"And you think he knows?"

Tony pondered this again. "He's familiar with some of my other cases. He knows enough to put it all together—he's a very smart man, like both his sons. He must know about vampires and I think he has guessed about me. I think, somewhere along the line, he decided that he didn't want to know, if you follow me."

Mike nodded. "What of my involvement? Does he know you're trying to recruit me?"

Tony nodded. "It was his idea. I think that he understands you better than you know. I think he saw long ago the part of you that doesn't quite fit into this modern world, which has no place for a romantic warrior like you. He sees how this side of you became tragically, I dare say dangerously, unhappy after the loss of your wife. Sean's need for you held you together for a while. Now Sean needs you less, and you need something like this."

Mike pondered this, uncomfortable with the truth of it. "You brought up my studying the martial arts, you talked my father into my first lessons, you found my first instructor. Were you working toward this?" He looked Tony in the eyes, watching for a reaction. "It was you who wrote that I should go to Japan after my marriage broke up. I'd lost some in the market crash, but was okay, yet you sent me plane tickets and a cheque. You even told me what sensei I should visit. Did you tell him to send me to that sifu in the reopened Shaolin temple in Hunan? Did you tell Master Ying to send me to that particular Tulku in the temple high in the mountains of Tibet?"

Tony shook his head. "I recommended the Ito school," he said. "You chose the Yagyu School instead."

Mike felt his anger fade. He wanted to let Tony find a way to make an excuse.

Tony took a deep breath. "I didn't secretly recruit you at the age of thirteen. I saw potential and did what I could to foster it. I knew that, the more you could become, the happier you'd be with yourself. Michael, I think you may be a great warrior from another time— the reincarnation of a knight or a samurai or a Shaolin priest. It might explain why part of you doesn't fit in today's world, yet found it so easy to learn your arts, as if you'd done it all before. I didn't set out to turn you into a potential vampire killer. But, deep down, part of me hoped you had it in you to become one, ever since that first night. You are the only mortal who can actually track me with your eyes when I move fast."

Tony looked awkward for a moment, then went on.

"There's an aspect to this existence that most movies never portray. We have no real friends. Oh, they often show us having vampire friends, and sometimes we do. But some of us long for human friends. It's hard to be friends with someone for more than a few years. They soon become suspicious. I saw something in you—something imaginative and clever, something that might be able to accept what I am. It was my friendship for you, more than anything else, that wanted you to be the best you could be in areas where you were talented. But then affection for you also made me send you lots of vampire books, books about good vampires, like Elrod's Jack Fleming."

"So no one else knows what you really are?"

Tony shook his head. "I have a colleague from London. He knows what we're dealing with, but I think I've managed to keep Nigel in the dark about me. He'll be here in a few days."

# 7: From Out of the Darkness

**B**arbara Fenwick wanted a promotion and grabbed at the chance to go into the office on a Sunday afternoon to clear up extra paperwork for her boss. She liked to think of herself as a paralegal. She was the assistant, *personal assistant*, she reminded herself, to a hotshot lawyer in a posh office on Barrington Street. Working late had its perks. First, overtime pay was nothing to sneeze at on her salary. Besides, she was hoping the office would approve her request to study law part-time at Dalhousie. It would dip into her hours, so she needed their blessing. She was hoping they would actually help pay her tuition, and she needed the references they could write directly to the Dean of Admissions. No, working 'til 10:00 and getting it all caught up was no problem under these circumstances.

She decided to cut straight down to Water Street before continuing on toward the ferry terminal. She usually walked along Barrington, then down the hill at George. Tonight she wanted a change. The sea-smell coming off the harbour was invigorating, though the breeze off the water had carried a bone-cutting chill.

She'd just crossed the street and was passing a dark alley when she heard a moan—no, not a moan—a groan of pain—agony. She paused to listen. She could barely hear it—something–

"Help." It was a long, drawn-out cry—feeble, helpless in its tone—the cry of someone severely injured.

Curiosity overcame caution. What she'd thought was an alley turned out to be a walled courtyard with steps up to another courtyard off a restaurant. Odd— both the street light and the pole lamp in the courtyard were out. She strained her eyes to see something. Nothing. Then—a hint of movement on the ground— something crawling?

"Hel-l-lp me." It was so weak she could barely hear it.

She steeled her nerve and approached with caution. Rummaging in her purse, she found a can of pepper spray and a small flashlight. She hoisted her purse straps high onto her shoulder, leaving her hands more free—light in one, spray in the other. There was a man lying on the at the top of the steps, struggling to crawl toward her. Then she saw the blood coming from a wound in his neck.

"Oh, my God!" she cried, and rushed toward the man.

She thought to find her cell phone in her purse and call 911. She thought, *Maybe if I go back to the street and yell for the police, someone will hear.* But there was time for nothing past thought.

Something loomed out of the darkness and seized her by the throat. It was a hard, impossibly cold hand. Fear invaded and logic fled. She couldn't scream— hell, she couldn't even breathe.

It lifted her completely off the ground, as effortlessly as if she were weightless. Red eyes blazed out of a pale, almost white face.

"Must be my lucky day," a voice chuckled. "I barely finish dinner and here is dessert. I love this town."

*European accent. Why waste time on such foolish thoughts? Do something! You're about to die! The pepper spray!*

She forced the hand to move fast. But the monster's hand was faster—so fast it wasn't possible. It tore the can from her hand, crushed it flat. There was a bursting sound, a hiss that fizzled rapidly.

She could only stare in helpless fascination. His teeth—upper canines, thin and sharp like a cobra's.

"Oh, you like my teeth?" he asked. "Hah!" He lunged his face toward her.

She felt warmth down her leg as she peed herself.

He laughed.

"Arr!" He repeated the attacking gesture with his face, stopping just short, as before. He laughed, delighted with it. "My teeth will like you, too, pretty one. Oh, yes!"

He slammed her against him, his teeth going into her throat. She had a flash of having seen a cobra strike in a movie. She had no control now, the thoughts came as they pleased. Underlying it all was fear and the knowledge of her impending death—*a slow, terrible, agonizing death*, something in her mind said. No—not her mind, *his* mind. His mind wanted her to feel terror.

"That was just a taste, pretty," he said. He let her see the blood—her blood—dripping off his fangs.

She was starting to black out. Her head was swimming from lack of oxygen.

As soon as she was conscious of this, his grip loosened.

Red eyes stared into hers, piercing into her mind.

"Quiet, now," he ordered in a soothing tone. "Very quiet. We want no interruptions."

"Hahh!" It was like a taunting snarl as he launched his teeth at her again, biting into her face.

"That's just for fun," he said. "I can't feed much from there. The breasts, though—oh, yes, a couple of good blood vessels there. Let me show you."

He glared at her. Raising his free hand, he showed her his fingernails—thick, long, cut sharp like claws. For a moment they lingered in her view, then they raked down the front of her jacket, tearing through nylon, lining, and the blouse underneath. Strong hands ripped it all wide open, tearing her bra away in the same motion. Then he held her higher as he attacked again.

"Oh, you're so tasty," he taunted.

*Boom-boom. Boom-boom. Boom-boom. Boom-boom. Boom-boom.*

Was some insane person beating a drum? Then she knew. It was the pounding of her heart.

"Time to drain you," he hissed. "Sorry, pretty, but it's over now. You're like that chocolate milk commercial, and I just can't drink it slow. This is where you die. Are you ready?"

Again he fastened on her throat.

*Boom-boom... Boom--boom..... Boom---boom........ Boom----boom............. Boom------boom.*

She could feel it slowing down. It got harder to hear. She felt it stop. Then feeling, hearing, and thought faded into nothing.

------

*Is this foolhardy or good practice?* The dark figure thought as he looked up at the imposing blue-grey edifice. It wasn't well-lit here at the back. He'd climbed a fence, walked across the flat roof of an adjacent one-story building that framed a courtyard with the taller building, and dropped silently into the courtyard. Part of him thought what he was about to do was risky and stupid—childish even. But part of him loved the joke and the daringness of it. It was a prank, like a child's prank, but he hadn't been a child for a very long time.

He flexed his fingers, adjusting his claws. He took a deep, cleansing breath, then started to climb. He forced the claws into mortar between the large concrete blocks. Higher and higher he went, always keeping his eye on a particular window. Many of the windows were in darkness. This was one of the ones that showed light through the drawn curtains.

Three floors up he stopped. He glanced back at the moonlit view of the harbour. The moon was just peaking through a break in the cloud cover. No wonder they'd named the place as they had. It was the best seniors' facility in the area, as big as some small town hospitals.

He paused outside the window. It was open a crack. After all, the night was unseasonably mild. No screen. Perhaps maintenance wasn't keeping up. He eased the window open further, little by little, then silently slipped inside.

A man in his mid-seventies lay on the bed, head elevated so he could read. As the shadowy form dressed all in black approached, the man seemed to sense something. Lowering a crime magazine, he looked up. Shock registered on his face. His eyes widened, his mouth opened as if to gasp.

"Shh," hissed the intruder.

"Shush yourself, Mikey" the man retorted. "If nurse Barkhouse sees you, she'll call the police." He punctuated it with several bursts of coughing.

Mike made a wry face, unbuckled the ninja climbing claws from his hands and pocketed them. "Bark-face, that old bedpan-licker? I'll just say that nurse Carrie buzzed me in."

"Now you sound like your brother used to. And this stunt reminds me more of him than you. Why didn't you just let Carrie buzz you in?"

"Because, Dad, it's been a long, unbelievable couple of days and, with my luck, it would have been Barkhouse who answered the bell. She'd have given me the third degree and tried to send me away. Besides, I wanted the practice."

The older man shook his head. "She can't do that, and you know it."

"She thinks she can," Mike argued. "She thinks she makes the rules when she's on duty. Besides, after the conversation I just had, I wanted to see if I still had some unpracticed skills. As for Louie over there, we could hold World War III in here and he'd sleep through it."

William Cameron glanced at his snoring roommate.

"You're right there." His face took on a worried look. "Tony been in touch?" Again the hacking cough.

Mike nodded. "Has he been to see you?"

His father nodded back, still coughing. "Pete was here today, too. He's in a panic."

Mike grabbed a bottle of Benylin off the bedside table, handing it to his father. The older man twisted off the cap and took a swig as if it were a flask of whiskey. "I wish I could chase it with some Glenlivet."

Mike pulled a pint out of his back pocket and handed it over. "Hide it well."

Cameron took a small sip, then a longer swig, letting it ease down his throat in small swallows. Finally he eased out a slow breath, breathing in with caution.

"Better," he announced.

"So what did Pete want?" Mike's gut went tight. He feared the answer.

"He's between a rock and a hard place, Mike. He needs your help and it goes against everything he believes in. He's got a situation and the only way to deal with it is to farm it out to a civilian and ask him to work outside the law. Can you imagine how that makes him feel? He can't even face the reality of what he's dealing with."

Too much too soon. Mike wasn't ready for this.

"Heard from Bill?" He asked. He was surprised when his father picked a letter out of the bedside drawer and passed it over.

"Woah, a whole page, I'm impressed."

His father glared. "He's your brother, Mikey, be nice. You're the writer. You write letters to everyone, you write stories, you write letters to the editor. Billy doesn't communicate well. It doesn't mean he doesn't care."

Mike felt guilty and wished he'd kept his mouth shut. He'd tried for years to keep in touch with his brother but, like his father said, *he* was the writer, not Bill. He decided to get on with what he was avoiding.

"I saw Tony last night," he said. "I just came from seeing him again tonight."

"And?"

"He hasn't changed any."

Mike watched his father's reaction closely. There it was—the light of knowledge in his eyes, the inability to deny what he so badly wanted to deny.

"Dad, I need you to tell me about the end of that case—the serial killer in Sydney, when I was a kid."

"Which one: the first or the second?"

"There were two?" His mind suddenly flashed back to the night he met Tony. Tony had mentioned being in town seven years before.

"I guess you were too young to remember the first. Nasty. Tony got him cornered in some old hovel near the steel plant. The perp knocked over a kerosene lamp and set the place ablaze. Tony got out but the perp didn't. By the time I got there the place was raging. Next day we found the guy's bones.

"It was a couple of days after your accident. Remember? You pestered me until I took the training wheels off your bike. Off you went, 'round and 'round the block. Tony and I just happened to be coming back to the house—it was after dark and you should have been home—anyway, there you were on the sidewalk in front of the Snell house. Old Mrs. Snell had Sid drive some steel pipe into the ground and run wire around it to keep people off the front lawn. What a joke. The houses were crammed in at that end of the street. Her lawn was two patches about six by eight on each side of the front walk. Anyway, there you were in a huddle, holding your throat and crying. The pool of blood around you was frightening. I guess you hit the edge of a sidewalk slab where the frost had lifted it, came off the bike, and hit one of the pipes. Tony was out of the car—I never saw anybody move so fast. I don't know what he did, but he got the bleeding stopped—the doctor at the hospital said it was a miracle. You could see the carotid artery through the tear. But you healed fast. Of course, you were always a fast healer."

Mike flashed back to a childhood memory of Tony staring at his throat—at the scar, asking if it had healed properly, if his voice was undamaged. "I heard Tony was around then but I never knew he was there when you found me. You never mentioned him. Come to think of it. I'm not sure I knew that it was you who found me. I thought I went to the hospital in an ambulance."

"Of course I found you, Mikey, but you were six. I didn't talk about work at the dinner table. But the guy you asked about would be the monster who was roaming loose the night you and Billy climbed down the ivy trellis to sneak out. That was the night you really met Tony, wasn't it? You snuck over to see the new guy in the old Cowell place. It was the night before Halloween."

Mike stared, not knowing what to say.

"Mikey, I'm—I was—a cop, and a damned good one. Two sets of sneaker prints in the soft ground at the bottom of the trellis, ivy partially torn away in a couple of spots—you were damned lucky it didn't tear loose and drop you. You'd have broken a leg, or worse, your neck."

"It was Billy who tore the ivy loose," Mike defended. "I was holding onto nothing but lattice, and only close to where it was screwed onto the house."

Will chuckled. "And the next evening, on the way to the station, Tony tells me of meeting you—what talents you seem to have and how lessons would foster them, give you something to carry with you throughout life."

Mike nodded. "Now skip ahead two weeks to the night you found the guy."

"I never found a damned thing," Cameron growled. "Months of legwork going nowhere, and Tony Dewhurst comes along and cracks it like a fresh egg. He had the guy profiled down to the kind of house he'd live in—houses, actually—he had two. He knew they'd be in rundown neighbourhoods, knew basement windows would be boarded over, inside and out. He stalked the guy, prediction his haunts, brought us to a body that was still warm. Tony seemed more upset than we were. Pete MacDonald and I were partners. Pete was unnerved, as I was, but Dewhurst seemed shaken to the core. Kept going on about how this guy had bitten her in different places, prolonging it, feeding on her fear, her terror.

"Only two houses fitting his description had been sold in the six months prior—one on Union Street, near Center, and one on the Esplanade. Both were way too close to Bentinck Street for my peace of mind. Tony left us in a coffee shop for about thirty minutes. When he came back, he announced that we should wait 'til just before dawn. Pete should call for backup and take the Esplanade, while Tony and I would go to Union Street. We had warrants for both places.

"Mikey, that clever limey knew exactly what he was doing."

Will started to cough again. Mike poured some scotch in a glass and passed it to him. A slow sip made the cough subside.

"Don't ever smoke, Mikey," he gasped. "And keep warning Sean. I should go on TV and warn these stupid kids. I swear to God, Mikey, I haven't had a cigarette since that day your mother caught Billy and you smoking out back. You were twelve. Not even that morning—I had several stiff drinks back at the station, but not one cigarette. And I needed one so bad.

"Yeah, Tony Dewhurst knew what he was doing. He sent Pete off to the other place, knowing what we'd find on Center Street. Never batted an eye. He went to the back of the house to the bulkhead doors—remember how some basement doors were in those days? The doors were padlocked from the outside, but he just grabbed that lock and hasp and tore it off like he was tearing staples out of cardboard. Mike, the hasp was through-bolted and he just tore it off. Then he led the way down into the dark cellar.

"There was an inner room, locked from the inside with a big dead bolt lock. I was going to shoot out the lock but, before I could, Tony got this angry look in his eyes—scary eyes they were at that moment—kind of red. He just hauled off and slammed both palms into the door, near the lock. The jam splintered and the damned door almost got tore off the hinges.

"Inside was just a metal frame bed, like an army cot, and a light hanging from the ceiling. Not a window, not a table, nothing. On the bed was our guy. He had blood on his hands, under his nails, trace spatter on his clothes—hell, the bastard even had blood on his lips.

"Tony said we didn't have much time. I had no idea what that meant, but he grabbed the guy off the bed and headed for the bulkhead doors. It was the damnedest thing. I still had my gun drawn, waiting for the guy to wake up. I was all set to blow him away, if it came to it. But you'd think he was in a coma. He was dead weight. Tony's a skinny guy—I mean, he's got good build across the chest, but he looks like a swimmer. Yet he lugged that guy like the best weightlifter I ever watched in the Olympics.

"Just once I saw lips twitch on our guy and thought I saw sharp fangs. Tony said there were freaks out there who paid orthodontists to alter their teeth like that.

" 'If you want blood samples from his clothes or fingernails, you'd better get them now,' Tony said. 'I have to be somewhere else in about fifteen minutes.'

"Well, Mikey, I got scrapings and cut a patch from his shirt. While I was bagging it, Tony dragged the guy into the yard and was gone.

"I kid you not, Mikey, he was gone. No sign of him leaving, no footsteps running off—he was just gone, nowhere to be seen. I couldn't believe it. I cuffed the perp and called for backup. I wanted a paddy wagon, as we called them in those days, to haul his ass down to the station. I didn't want to dirty the car with him, and figured there'd be a stink if I locked him in the trunk.

"Then the sun came up. As soon as the sun hit the body, it started to smoke. Then it just up and burst into flames. The guy's eyes flashed open. I thought I'd never seen eyes like that, but I had. The guy writhed about like a crazy thing, but he was burnt to the bones in minutes. It was the damnedest thing!

"But I'd seen eyes like that before, Mikey. I told myself I was wrong—nerves shook up, tired—for years I denied what I knew."

"If he burned but the bones were left, he must not have been very old," Mike mused.

"That's what Tony said when I saw him again that night," his father murmured.

"And the paper wrote it off to spontaneous combustion," Mike said.

"We'd never seen it before in Sydney, probably not in all Nova Scotia," the old detective added. "But everything from *Ripley's Believe It Or Not* to *In Search Of* had done an episode on spontaneous combustion. Now we had a case in Sydney. The press loved it. They wanted it to be spontaneous combustion."

"But you didn't buy that theory?"

His father shook his head. "I wanted to, but the teeth, the thick sharpened nails, and those eyes—then there was the way he was like someone in a coma with the sun coming up—but it was those eyes. Mikey, I gotta tell you who has eyes like that—you gotta know..."

But Mike was already nodding his head. "Yeah, yeah, I know—Tony Dewhurst. I've seen his eyes, Dad. His irises are larger and dilate 'til they almost disappear in dim light, making his eyes look black—or red, depending on how the light hits them." He immediately regretted the dismissive tone in his voice. "I'm sorry, Dad, I just have so much on my mind."

His father nodded, then placed a hand on his son's shoulder. Before he knew what was happening, his father was hugging him.

"You've been through a lot, son—Sue dying, your mother's sudden heart attack—we knew she had angina and that weird rhythm thing, but she'd only ever had little turns, nothing big like that one." He sighed. "I guess it only takes one. And now me. I quit before they ever put those surgeon general warnings on the packs, but the cigarettes got me anyway."

"Dad ..." He picked up the paper, riffled through it, found the front page. Then, folding it so that the two paragraph story was in the center, handed it to his father.

Will nodded. "Yeah, I saw it earlier. Some psycho, whacked out on PCP attacked an unknown victim with a knife. The victim got the knife away from the guy. Then, in a fit of panic, practically severed the guy's neck. He ran off. The police are still looking for the poor guy... at least that's what the papers say."

"It's a whitewash," Mike declared. "The perp had fangs and inhuman strength. I succeeded in fending him off and got in a few good blows. Then he pulled the knife. I didn't decapitate him, I just drove the knife into his throat, severing the spinal cord. It was Tony who later cut off his head and instructed the forensic guys to bag it separately. I think he hypnotized them. Pete was the detective on the scene. The guy was Russian and had my description, a description of my Jeep and license number on a piece of paper in his pocket. He was lying in wait for me."

His father stared, his face drained of colour.

"Jesus, Mike! Are you okay? What about Sean, is he all right? Pete told me most of what you just said, but he held back enough to make it seem—I don't know—like you were in less danger?"

Mike nodded. "Sean's fine. Today he seemed in denial. He went to the movies with Shelly. Tonight he's parked in front of his TV. But, Dad, the nightmares have started again—at least I had another last night."

"Headaches?"

Mike shook his head. "Not yet."

"Mikey, you have nothing to feel guilty about—not now, not then. You were just defending yourself. And I'm glad you were so successful. That night on Water Street all those years ago—the guy had a rap sheet almost an inch thick. He was out on parole."

Mike nodded. "I remember. Dad, I had a long talk with Tony tonight."

The old cop looked worried. "Don't take what I said about his eyes the wrong way, Mikey. I've seen so many come and go—good cops, dirty cops, crooked politicians, guys who got busted after one stupid mistake, and some of the meanest, coldest, nastiest bastards God ever put on this earth. I've learned to read people, Mikey. I've always had the gift, but I've learned to refine it and use it over the years. Tony's one of the good guys."

"I guess it's like cows and sheep," Mike said. "Picture us from their perspective. We're terrible demons, feeding on their kind. Most of us are humane and just take what food we need. But some of us are predators who like to kill, who feed on the fear we can create."

"Tony's no animal rights activist," his father joked, "but he endangered himself to rid the world of a monster that day. I figure he had to beat it home before the sunrise. It amazes me he could stay up as long as he did. It was one of the things that made me doubt for so long."

"Then you saw him again. To what pieces you already had you added the fact that he'd aged maybe ten years in almost thirty."

Mike's father nodded. "I feared for you, then I remembered how he'd kept in touch all those years— books for you and a bottle of scotch for me every Christmas. He say's you're special, Mikey. Of course, I always thought you were. I thought both my boys were special, but you were different."

He paused, looking guilty. "I'm sorry, Mikey. Sometimes I was a lot harder on you than Billy. I think I had trouble understanding how different you were. So many things seemed to come to easy to you—school, your Kung Fu. You see things other people don't see and you have a gift for what you do. I've read what you write, Mikey. The fantasy stuff seems weird to me, but you make me believe it while I'm reading. And you read people well. You have a good mind—I wanted you to go into forensics, not teaching, but you were a good teacher. Your students respected you.

"Tony says you're fast. I've seen you. You're forty-seven but you hardly look forty, and you're faster than these young studs in the action movies. I've never seen a human so fast. But are you fast enough, Mikey? And are your talents enough? Not many cops can look a killer in the eyes and shoot him. Can you look a monster in the eye and not give in to a moment of panic?"

"I don't know, Dad," Mike admitted. "Last night— it was a form of panic, but there was no hesitation. I was fast enough. If I watch for it, I can track Tony's movement. I don't know if I want this. Part of me does. Part of me wants something that this world can't give me."

His father held both Mike's hands in his.

"I watched you start to slowly die. The life had gone out of you. You were hanging in for Sean, but it was like you were waiting for your turn to die. Then the letters from way off there in the Orient started to sound better, more positive. Then you came home. I think something about being there made it possible for you to come home. Being home, teaching your Kung Fu and your samurai sword stuff—it gave you something back. Now I see something new in your eyes, Mikey. I see caution and uncertainty, but I see a sense of drive I haven't seen in the fourteen years since Sue died. If you do this—I think you should and I'm afraid at the same time—be careful. Learn from Tony."

They were interrupted by the entrance of a nurse.

"Well," she said, beaming a smile, "I didn't know you had company, William. Hello, Michael."

"Hello, Carrie," Mike answered. "Ahh, actually, no one knows I'm here."

Her brows furrowed. "Really? How did you manage—never mind. And Nel didn't buzz you in."

"Nell? Barkhouse's name is Nell? Sure it isn't Nettle?" Mike quipped, making a wry face.

Carrie chuckled, dimples showing. "You're bad," she said. But her eyes denied what she said. She looked to be about his age. His father once told him she had a grown son, in the navy, off on a ship, but there wasn't even the trace of a ring line on her finger.

*Divorced,* he thought. *Stupid bastard. She's cute, a sweetheart.* He couldn't bring himself to assume anything but that her ex had been the villain in any failure of the marriage. *Maybe she was never married,* he thought, then, *No, she's too cute to have stayed uncaught for so long. Even now they'd be chasing her.*

He abruptly chased such thoughts out of his mind. His life was just too complicated at the moment. He wasn't ready to let anyone in right now.

"Don't worry, I'll say I buzzed you in. How did you get in, anyway—no, never mind, I'm not so sure I want to know.

"Now, William," she said to his father, "I see you had your bath before I came on this afternoon. Emily must have cleared your supper tray. Would you like some tea or anything else before I go off shift?"

She eyed the bottle of scotch still on the table. She pursed her lips a moment, then smiled.

"Oh, I see you've already had some additional refreshment this evening."

Picking up the bottle, she opened the drawer, slipped it in, then closed the drawer.

"Don't let Nel see that. She can't really deny it to you, but she'll try to take it, complain to your doctor and the floor supervisor, and be a pain in the butt until someone makes her give it back."

Mike walked her to the door.

"Thanks," he whispered.

Carrie nodded. "He doesn't have much to look forward to besides your visits. A little scotch isn't going to shorten his life any. Nothing is going to change the lung cancer and how fast it's working."

She shook her head, a trace of a tear showing.

"His old partner came to see him today," she commented. "I think he's hoping your father can help him solve a problem. And there was a new visitor a couple of evenings ago. He'd never been before. Nel didn't want to let him visit, but I argued with her. He was English—he reminded me of the last actor who played James Bond—Pierce Brosnan—except his hair was lighter, and he was very pale. At first I thought he might be someone your father had put in prison who just got out, but your dad said they'd worked together."

Mike nodded, smiling. He'd have to tell Tony that someone thought he looked like Pierce Brosnan.

"Lord Anthony Dewhurst," he said. "He's a profiler of sorts—works with Interpol and gets loaned out to law enforcement agencies all over the world."

"Shall I put him on the list of close family and friends?"

Mike nodded. "I've known him since I was thirteen. I may be about to become a colleague of his."

"I hope that won't take you away from the area," she said, then quickly added, "I mean, your father would be lost without your visits and your son's."

Mike smiled, taking in the details of her appearance again. She was short, about five-three, five-four, with a mop of shoulder-length blonde hair framing a pretty face, green eyes shining with an impish sparkle. When she smiled, her whole face seemed to glow.

"I don't know," he admitted. "I'm home and don't want to go anywhere. After all, Sean's still in school, and I just finished renovating a house."

"And bought a sailboat, so your father says."

"Why, do you like to sail?" He couldn't believe he'd asked her that. He usually avoided chatting women up.

"I've never done it," she replied. Then, flashing a smile, she added, "But I love to be around water and I wouldn't mind giving it a try sometime."

The ring of his cell phone interrupted.

He glanced at the screen. The caller was unidentified, the number looked like another cell phone.

He flipped it open. "Yes?"

"Michael, this is Tony. Can you meet me in Halifax, Lower Water Street, just south of Prince?"

"What is it?" he asked. He felt a knot forming in his gut.

"There's definitely more than one. It's changing, Michael—escalating. It's rarely seen in his kind. There are two bodies—an elderly shop clerk and a young woman."

Michael sighed. "I'll be right there." He smiled at Carrie. "Sorry, duty calls."

When he reached his car, he opened his phone again and pressed a button on the side. "Home," he told the phone.

"Hey, Dad," Sean's voice greeted.

"I'm just leaving from seeing Grampy," Mike explained.

"How is he?" Sean interrupted.

"Fine. He'd love to see you."

"I can go tomorrow after school," Sean suggested. "I don't usually have homework on Mondays. I can take my bike and, before you say no, Dad, remember I've got snow tires and I know to stick to good roads and drive sensibly."

"Fine. Listen, son, I have to meet Tony in Halifax—business. I might be late."

"So, does this mean you're taking whatever this job is he's offering?" Sean asked.

Mike heaved a sigh. "Yeah, I suppose it does."

# 8: The Case

It took thirty-five minutes to get from Eastern Passage to the MacDonald Bridge, across the bridge, and over to Lower Water Street. Finding the exact location was easy. You could see the flashing patrol car lights reflecting off the snow from a block away. Mike pulled his Grand Cherokee against the curb in front of a meter and got out.

He noted the mixture of curiosity and suspicion on the faces of police officers as he approached the barricade. Finally one held a palm up towards Mike's chest.

"Whoa, there, mister. See the police barricade? This is a crime scene. You'll have to detour across the street."

Mike laughed inwardly at how pathetic and rooky-like the gesture seemed. He could have broken the cops arm at the wrist and elbow in less than a second with a simple two-handed crane maneuver. He knew a few cops—three attended his adult sessions regularly. Most were polite. This guy was rude and annoying. Instead of backing off, Mike stood still, folding his arms.

"Tell Lord Dewhurst I'm here," he said, his voice low and calm.

"Ah, Michael, there you are," came Tony's Oxford drawl. "He's with me, officer. Michael, you need to see this before they move the bodies. I delayed them as best I could, but these forensic chaps are getting impatient."

The cop gave a grunt of annoyance but let Mike pass. Mike noted the name *Jenkins* on the name tag.

"Mike," a cop in a suit called his name. It was Inspector MacDonald. Mike suddenly remembered the statement he was supposed to have signed today.

He shook the inspector's hand. "I'm sorry, Pete. I completely forgot about that statement. I guess I spent most of today trying to get things into prospective."

MacDonald nodded. "You and me both." He handed Mike a clipboard, the statement on top. It was a slightly more detailed version of the whitewash he'd read in the paper. Mike looked at MacDonald with a raised eyebrow. He scribbled a signature and handed it back.

"Were you expecting the detailed confession of a vampire-killer? Look, Mike, Lord Dewhurst wants your help and, well, damn it all, Mike, I need you."

Mike raised an eyebrow.

The inspector smiled. "I saw how Jenkins was with you. For a second I thought you were going to do a Kwai Chang Caine on him. Jenkins is young and has a chip on his shoulder—wants to flaunt the uniform to the public. His sergeant is just looking for a chance to take him down a peg."

Mike shrugged it off. "Three of my students are street cops," he admitted. "They're good—motivated, attentive, and learn quickly. Jenkins is just an asshole."

MacDonald hesitated, then spoke in a low tone. "I need you, Mike. Some of this case—if it goes through official channels and the media get hold of the real facts… Mike we're not talking about a town in a panic. It would either shake the world to the core or convince the rest of the country and the world that folks in Halifax are nuts. I understand now why the CIA has special task forces for handling things that the world would be happier not knowing about, and why our

English Lord over there is working through CSIS on behalf of Interpol." He held out two laminated ID cards.

Mike nodded slowly, one ID identified him as a special liaison with Interpol, the other was a permit to carry weapons, both concealed and non-concealed. He slipped them into his wallet and nodded. "I'm in Pete. And, Pete, I'm sorry I was a bit distant last night. It's hard to explain. Your my godfather but we haven't seen much of each other since I was a kid. I don't know—I've got relatives who breeze into town every five or six years, act like it's only been a week, and expect free room and board at night but disappear and play tourist all day. I guess you kind of got dumped into that department. It's been years and you just came on too familiar, too soon, if that makes any sense."

Pete looked somewhat abashed and nodded. "Sorry, Mike. I know it's been a long time, but your dad keeps telling me stuff about where you are and what your doing—he's so proud of you and was so worried after your wife died. I guess it just felt like we were never out of touch."

Mike smiled. "I'm home, Pete. It'll all fall into place." *I hope*, he added to himself.

Pete looked so relieved that Mike placed a hand on the inspector's shoulder. "Dad said you were between a rock and a hard place. I'll do what I can. Too bad I can't just carry a sword around in public. That might be a comfort."

"Actually," the inspector said, "with that weapons permit you can. It's not just for firearms."

"Time's pressing, Michael," Tony interrupted. "They want to move the bodies."

The courtyard was lit up like a hollywood movie set. Mike glanced at the walls.

"Minimal cast-off from the wounds. So the slices to the throat were postmortem. Minimal blood pooling on the ground."

"That's pretty good," a tech commented. He wore a navy nylon jacket with *Forensics* on the back. There were two others, but he seemed to be senior. "You train in forensics?"

Mike shook his head. "CSI, CSI: NY, and CSI: Miami, all programmed into the DVR. Oh, yeah—pre-med at Acadia and ten years of teaching human biology in the British school system."

"Sam MacGilvery. Call me Mac." He took Mike's hand in a sincere, firm grip. "I like the Vegas show and New York, but Miami's got too much grandstanding and too little forensics," the CSI said with a grin. "So, what do you make of the slashing of the throat?"

Mike squatted down to look. "He's torn the throat open with a very jagged blade."

"Close, but no. It'll surprise you. But first, look at this. I didn't catch it until I got to the first victim. He was careless. He was so tickled by her arrival on the scene that he finished with number one almost as an afterthought. He was sloppier. It's right up here."

He went up the few steps to the elderly victim and used his fingertips to close the gashing of the throat. In the middle of the closed gash were hints of the edges to two round punctures.

"Our villain seems to think he's a vampire, Michael," Tony suggested, giving Mike a wink. "He bites them, then tries to hide the punctures."

"But the slashing isn't linear like a blade would be," the CSI put in. "It's almost like he tears across with a cluster of small curved blades. Look at the pattern. There's a slight curve. That's hand motion. Drawing a blade across, even a serrated one, would leave a straight cut. It's torn, yes, but even a hacksaw blade would tear in a straight line."

Mike found himself looking at Tony's unusually thick, shiny fingernails. He glanced at Tony. He felt Tony in his mind. *Yes, Michael. Tell him.*

"Claws," he murmured.

"What?" the tech asked.

"Claws, fingernails."

"Good theory—great theory. It fits the image of a guy who had some ortho give him fangs, but human nails just aren't that strong."

"They aren't human nails," Mike said.

Tony gave Mike a look of warning. *For God's sake, Mike, were profiling a serial killer. Don't suggest he's a vampire. We can't afford humans to even consider that as a possibility. He has to remain a deranged serial killer.*

Mike just shook his head. The tech was staring.

"What do you mean, they aren't human nails. If they aren't human, then what are they?"

"Synthetic." Mike could feel Tony heaving a sigh of relief next to him. "If he can get a dentist to give him fangs, why not fake claws, epoxied on. And I don't mean nail epoxy; this nut might even go for something incredibly strong like West System. The nails might be acrylic, they might be polycarbonate—hell, they might even be made of real keratin protein. He files them very sharp and slices with a strong arm motion, almost like a shuto." He made a classic karate-chop gesture with his hand.

The CSI nodded. "I'll mention it to the ME. Maybe he'll find traces of something in the wounds that'll give us a clue. However, there's something else interesting you should see. We've identified this fellow as the first victim because of how thickened blood trace around him is. His blood was exposed to air longer, so he bled first. Now, she comes along, interrupts him, and becomes number two, right? Wrong. Look here."

He drew their attention to the ground, but Tony was already squatting, looking at the stains. "Gads, this chap crawled for more than two meters, bleeding the whole time!"

"If he'd already lost as much blood as I'm guessing," Mike surmised, "he wasn't crawling very fast. It took what little energy he had left and he probably died in the effort."

"Exactly," the CSI agreed. "He crawled pathetically slow. Look at the pooling—here—here— here—This guy crept a bit, then stopped, crept some more, then stopped, and so on."

A look of concern came over Tony's face. "He's not just escalating, Michael," he said, "he's broadening his pattern, his MO, so to speak."

"Exactly," the CSI agreed. "Our would-be Count Dracula just stood back and let him crawl, watching him die."

"No," Mike mused. "He wasn't watching him die, he was letting him cry for help. The bastard was using him for bait to lure another victim."

"It's possible that he wasn't even meant to die just yet," Tony added. "What if the blackguard meant for him to watch the death of the second victim, increasing his horror for when it was finally his turn to die?

"Are you all right, Michael?" Tony suddenly asked. "You look as if you could use a drink."

Mike nodded. "You're probably right. This guy really is a monster, isn't he? It's hard to imagine the type of mind that could do this."

"Why don't we let these scientific chaps continue what they're good at and wait for their report, shall we?"

Tony turned back to the CSI. "You will have someone call me and leave a message if anything else is learned? We'll want to know anything at all that adds to a picture of this blackguard.

"Now, Michael, the Glenlivet is on me."

---

It was late when Mike finally got home. He had a lot on his mind. The scene of the latest attack had shaken him. It was one thing to read about it in the papers but, to be at the actual scene—to see the blood, the bodies, to sense the lingering aura of evil—that was the worst part. His depth of sense, the result of his considerable *chi*, had felt the cold, soulless sense of malice that had lingered at the sight. Last time he'd been the victim, but he'd survived. Now he'd had a firsthand look at two who hadn't.

After being let out to take care of business, Sam followed him about, wagging his tailless butt back and forth, constantly bumping into Mike's legs. Mike chuckled. "Easy, Sam, you're going to trip me up one of these days."

He glanced in on Sean. As expected, he was asleep. Mike started to pick up some clothes and deposit them in the laundry bin the the corner, then sighed and gave up. His son's desk was a clutter of DVD cases, video game cases, and library books, with a computer CPU and an LCD screen rising out of the apparent rubble. He noted with some relief that there were also a few school books sitting on the desk chair. Mike wasn't exactly a neat freak but teaching his son a sense of organization was a daunting task. He wondered if it was something only a mother had the patience to teach. Perhaps if Sean hadn't been so young when Susan had died things might have been different. *No*, he thought with a smile, while neither was quite the extreme of Neil Simon's characters, he had been the Felix Unger to Susan's Oscar Madison.

Crossing the hall to his own room, he sat on the bed and collapsed backward. He'd just take a minute or two to collect his thoughts before getting ready for bed. The minute or two was all he needed to fall asleep.

The dream came again, a painful repetition of the previous night's nightmare. This time the body of the thug became the body of his vampire attacker, then became the dismembered body of the young samurai. Once again he saw the samurai long sword—the katana—in his hand, blood dripping from the blade. He awoke, went to the bathroom and splashed his face, then returned to bed.

He awoke with a start. There was a change in the vibes of the house. He'd heard the front door close. He bolted upright, then gathered his thoughts. Look at the clock—8:10 am. Of course—Sean had just left for school.

He could smell brewed coffee in the kitchen. He smiled, knowing what he'd find. Sean wasn't supposed to use the stove without asking but, in his loving and calculating manner, he seemed to think that doing something nice made up for ignoring this rule. Sure enough, he'd fried eggs, then made coffee as a bribe. Mike shook his head. Sean was a walking contradiction. The boy had a tendency to make his own rules, but he had a huge heart, and he and Mike were extremely close. This bond, partially a product of their natures, partially from how inseparable they'd been after Susan's death, was the main reason Mike tended to just sigh and not deal with certain of Sean's faux-pas. Mike was not exactly a liberal parent.

Next to the coffee machine was a note.

"Dad—Won't be home for lunch. Trying out for play (drama). Made you coffee. Have a good day. PS: We need more eggs. Love, Sean."

Mike smiled. "I'll bet we need more eggs. You eat four at a time."

He checked the green bucket under the sink. Sure enough, four egg shells and the end crusts from four pieces of toast.

Mike poured a mug of coffee, went back to his room, and sat at his desk. He fired up his Intel Mac, typed in his password, then sat back sipping coffee while his e-mail downloaded—some junk, some forwarded humour from friends, then an unexpected address—pimpernel@hotmail.com. He found himself staring at it before copying it to his address book.

The text was simple. "Hoping for preliminary forensics report later today. Have set up meeting at HRM PD HQ for 4:00 pm with Inspector MacDonald."

*Great*, Mike thought, *Sean will get home from school just as I'm heading out the door.* At least he could plan for them to eat together after the meeting and before Kung Fu classes at 7:30, assuming the meeting let him get back in time.

He noted the time of the e-mail—7:55 am, well after sunrise. He knew Tony wouldn't get the reply until he awakened, whenever that was—he was surprised that Tony planned to make a meeting before sunset. *No,* he mentally corrected himself, *the day after I met him, he was at the door before sunset.*

After dealing with e-mail, he wrote a bit, struggling with a chapter in a new book, then made a grocery list and headed for the store. He managed to get a host of other chores done in time to be home when Sean got out of school, before rushing across to Halifax in a light snow flurry. Fortunately, most of the rush hour traffic was going the other way, and getting across the bridge to the main police station posed little difficulty.

In the parking lot across the street from the station, he spotted Tony's small Cadillac just pulling into one of two empty spaces. He quickly pulled in next to his friend, got out, hit the 'lock' button on his remote, bringing a confirming *beep* from the Grand Cherokee's horn, then looked across at Tony just getting out of his car.

The vampire wore a heavy wool top coat and a large-brimmed felt hat pulled low over his face. A bright red scarf showed at his neck.

*"Who knows what evil lurks in the hearts of men? The Shadow knows!"* Mike quoted, finishing up with the chilling laugh.

"Thank you Orson Wells," Tony commented dryly. "At least it allows me some protection from old Sol when I venture forth this early." He adjusted his scarf and pulled his collar closer, timed the traffic, then became a blur, reappearing across the street.

Mike shook his head, wide-eyed, then darted after him.

Inside HRM Police Headquarters Tony gave his coat a shake, sending water droplets flying. "Good thing I'm rather immune to temperatures. Sink me! I've never seen so much snow."

Mike chuckled. "I thought Sir Percy's 'sink me' was something some scriptwriter made up, or maybe the Baroness Orczy. I guess you guys really talked like that."

Tony smiled. "Percy certainly did," he admitted. "He used every fashionable bit of slang, hamming it up to the hilt. He played the effete fop to extremes, portraying himself as the absolute antithesis of the Pimpernel. Some of us imitated it a bit, but that was possibly my only regular bit of slang. Probably rubbed off from Percy. Mind you, young George, our Prince of Wales and defacto king when George III was in and out of the loony bin, had a downright flair for it." He grinned and added, "We had our doubts about his preferences in certain areas." He gave a conspiratorial wink, then chuckled.

Mike grinned, shaking his head.

"I'd lose the hat and scarf PDQ, Tony," he teased. "There was a passable movie of *The Shadow* a few years back. A few of the cops we're about to meet with are bound to have seen it. They'll razz you into the middle of next January."

Tony pretended to shiver. "The middle of January in London is spring compared to this. I swear it'll be a blizzard by dinner time."

"This is dinner time or supper time," Mike pointed out.

"Tsk, tsk," Tony clucked. "You poor colonials. It's barely 4:30, a tad late for high tea. Dinner's not until 8:00, late supper around 11:00 or 12:00, should one wish to indulge.

"On to more serious things, we have a name for our foe. That brings us a step closer. Unfortunately, according to the fax from my friend Mason in MI6 waiting for me when I awoke, he may have five friends. I'm assuming one of them is your friend in the morgue." They were nearing the entrance to the Office of Criminal Investigations. "I guess you'll hear the rest inside."

"Ah, here's Mulder and Scully, now," a voice called jokingly as they entered the room.

Mike sensed tension in the room, as if they were unwelcome outsiders. "X-Files," he whispered to Tony. "A TV show. Two FBI special agents who investigated paranormal cases."

Tony nodded, then quickly donned his hat and scarf, wrapping the scarf about his face. "I prefer *The Shadow*, if you don't mind."

Mike thought the resulting good-natured laughter helped eased some tension. Tony had Interpol and diplomatic credentials, but Mike was a drafted civilian, even if he did carry Interpol ID. He hoped his martial artist reputation and being Former-Inspector Will Cameron's son might ease the way with a few.

Inspector MacDonald took the floor and brought things to order. He reviewed the details of the incidents to date before revealing anything new.

There was a minor interruption from the back as a plain clothes detective arrived late and took a seat.

"Kamensky, nice of you to join us," MacDonald quipped. "Now, for what the lab boys have turned up. Both of the latest victims were definitely bitten in the throat and blood sucked from the (he referred to notes) right exterior carotid artery. The woman was also bitten in the left breast."

"He's right-handed," Mike mused, not realizing he was loud enough to be heard.

MacDonald gave him a curious look, then nodded.

"That seems confirmed by the way he crushed her can of pepper spray. The lab lifted two clear finger prints from it. According to Immigration, they're from the right index and second finger of one (again he referred to the notes) Vladimir Ivanovitch Chernov, originally from Moscow."

Mike shrugged, explaining, "I'm ambidextrous, but I'm right-dominant. If I picture biting someone's neck, it seems more natural for me to tilt my head left than right."

He fought a smile as most of the cops in the room performed a subtle pantomime of trying to tilt right to bite, then tilted left, nodding at their discovery.

"Funny thing about Comrade Chernov that our ever-vigilant Immigration Department failed to notice," MacDonald continued, "It seems he was low level KGB for a bit, then Russian mafia before emigrating to Montreal last May."

There were murmurs about the room.

"A fax from British Intelligence confirms this," Tony interjected. "He also has five colleagues who disappeared from Moscow on the same day. MI6 found all five on the same flight manifest of KLM, a Dutch airline, destination Montreal. That was last June."

"It gets better," MacDonald said. "In August, he and his five friends were gunned down in some kind of hit. Automatic weapons. All six were taken to the morgue. Chernov and four of the other five must have still been alive. They disappeared from the morgue."

"And now they hunt by night," a cop quipped in a Transylvanian accent. "They can only live by night."

MacDonald wasn't smiling.

"Hey, wait a minute," a young cop called out, "what about that case last month where the big, long crate got stolen from the bonded warehouse in the middle of the night? Evidence pointed to the doors being opened from the inside. The chain-locked gate was broken out from the inside."

"Right," another cop droned in dry sarcasm. "Comrade Dracula awoke, broke out of his crate-coffin, nabbed a truck, and crashed the gate. I was on-scene. The gate had a SOBO high-security padlock—uncuttable and unpickable. We think the crate was an arms shipment. Yeah, the crate was long like a coffin, but so are crates for some rifles and ARs if they pack an ammo shipment in the same box."

"So," Tony interjected, "you think the perpetrator in this case climbed the fence to get in, picked the other locks, but the outer padlock forced him to commandeer a vehicle and crash through the gate."

The cop nodded.

Another muttered, "So what about four Ruskies walking out of a morgue after being hosed with machine guns. Now one of them is feeding from the throats of folks here in Halifax. And we're not supposed to believe in vampires?"

"Actually, if I may interject on that note," Tony put in, his eyes on the inspector, "bulletproof vests would have prevented death, but the impact of said bullets would most certainly knocked them down and rendered them unconscious. Perhaps whoever sent them to the morgue assumed they were dead. But, whatever one's belief in the occult and folklore, there are two obvious facts we can believe in. This fellow is very strong and very dangerous."

"If the subject is located," MacDonald added, "you're to contain the area and wait for Lord Dewhurst. That order comes from the chief, himself. According to Interpol and our own RCMP, Lord Dewhurst is the leading expert on this type of perp. Mr. Cameron is working with Lord Dewhurst. HRM PD will officiate over any arrests. Some of you know Michael Cameron's father, former Inspector William Cameron. Mike's reputation is such that, given a choice, I'll let him go one-on-one with this guy before I volunteer. And this guy may still have three colleagues."

"Don't you mean four?" a detective constable asked.

MacDonald shook his head. "One of those four was identified by fingerprints today—one Pavel Petrenko. While high on PCP, he attacked the wrong man last night and got his throat cut with his own knife by his intended victim.

"For the record, I don't believe in vampires—I think this guy is a nut case, albeit a very dangerous nut case. So I won't be signing any requisition orders for crosses or garlic."

The ranks dismissed to general amusement from the last remark, but the air of uncertainty and superstition seemed to linger.

"God, all I need now is talk of vampires," the inspector sighed. They were alone with him in the squad room. "Cahill will be bringing in sharpened stakes tomorrow, offering to sell them for five bucks apiece."

Tony shook his head. "Stakes might slow him down, but they're overrated. Hollywood hype, I'm afraid."

"Jesus, Lord Dewhurst, I wished you wouldn't say things like that. This is hard to take. I sometimes wish I could retire, crawl into a hole, and just hide—forget everything I've learned in the past few days.

"I'm running this Chernov and his friends' names through every database we can access. We're checking for credit cards, mortgages, documented leases, tax records—anything that will help locate Chernov. And I'm working on locating any or all of the others, just in case they're still in touch."

"It may be stretching coincidence to the limit," Tony suggested, "but check across Canada, maybe even over the border into the States for similar attacks, similar *modus operandi*. I don't mean to imply that the others are committing the same attacks, but it is a sort of starting point."

MacDonald nodded slowly, then gave Tony another deep stare. "Vampires. I wish I was going mad and this wasn't real."

Tony pursed his lips. "I've been doing this kind of profiling for a long time, old man. Don't let my boyish good looks fool you. I'm a lot older than I look. I've done this in about eight or nine countries, and I've seen some very strange things."

As Tony said, 'very strange things,' he caught the lieutenant's eyes in a direct stare. Mike held his breath and remained still. Tony's eyes took on a red tint and became quite bright, their intensity seeming to pierce into the lieutenant's mind.

"I think it's crucial that you and I meet alone from now on. Any new developments must come to me first. You and I will discuss what the detectives and patrol officers need to know. That nonsense about Chernov and his associates being gun down and then walking out of the morgue served no purpose but to create superstitious fear amongst the men. We can't have your men believing there are vampires out there. Nor can we have them thinking they can tackle one of these subjects like a rugby player in a scrum. Chernov would gut them like lake trout. And any thoughts you've had about me being unusual, any conversations you think we may have had on the subject—they're nonsense. Balderdash, man, absolute poppycock! Don't you agree?" The red faded from Tony's eyes and his intense glare became calm appraisal.

"Yes," MacDonald agreed. He nodded his head, seeming to slowly slip out of a trance. His face took on a sober look as he continued to nod. "You're right, Lord Dewhurst. I should have thought of that. If one of my men ever confronts the bastard, he might be hesitant to shoot. He could get killed because he had a moment's doubt about whether his bullets would work on the perp."

"Just so," Tony agreed, "however, we don't want them confronting these particular suspects. That must be left to Michael and myself."

"May I see those notes?" Mike cut in.

He ignored Tony's questioning glance and proceeded to leaf through the papers. Just as expected, the report about the incidents in Montreal came via police fax.

"Put him under again," he whispered to Tony.

The moment Tony had the inspector's attention, Mike slipped into an adjacent office. As luck would have it, there was a photocopier.

"Inspector MacDonald wants a copy of this," he said, handing the fax to the officer.

The officer looked at the paper, an uncertain look crossing his face, then glanced out at where he could see the inspector talking with the British profiler from Interpol. He shrugged.

"He should be copying this himself, not using a visiting civilian as an office boy. Standard copy?"

"Can you clean it up a bit?" Mike asked. "More contrast?"

The sergeant nodded and pushed a couple of extra buttons on the machine. "You want the cover page, too?"

Mike nodded. "Lord Dewhurst might want it, just in case."

"Here you go," he said, handing Mike the copy and the original.

"Thanks," Mike said, then headed back to Tony.

"I have a copy of the fax and an idea of how to fix part of this," he said. "There's an officer who knows about the copy, though. He made it."

"Inspector, you've instructed an officer to copy the Montreal report for me. You should probably thank him later."

Once more he released the detective from hypnosis. The inspector looked a bit dazed, then shook his head. "Oh, yes. I thought you might want a copy of that. Should have made one myself."

"Well," Tony concluded, "you have a lot to do, and I have a lot to think about and discuss with Michael." He shook the inspector's hand.

"Why did you want a copy?" Tony asked once they were back on the street. "I remember everything he said, and he read from the fax."

"I wanted the fax number and the letterhead logo, as well as the cover page. Ever do much with computers, Tony?"

"Not much," the vampire replied. "Mrs. Rice was right in an observation by Lestat. We tend to cling a little to the times in which we were changed. Our fashion tastes contain hints of our times. I'd look a bit eccentric in some of the togs I used to wear, but I still prefer suits with waist coats. We're slow to adapt to modern technology. I purchased a computer a few years back—what you chaps this side of the ocean call a laptop. I use it for e-mail and the odd fax, but nothing elabourate. Why?"

"I can send the inspector a follow-up fax from Montreal Police, explaining away the morgue incident. All I need is the cover page and a copy of their logo."

This time Tony crossed the street at Mike's pace, slipping into Mike's car once it was unlocked.

Tony smiled. "I like your forged fax idea. You're resourceful, just like your father."

Mike warmed at the comparison. He'd always been proud of his father. He'd been closer to his mother— her 'baby.' Now that she was gone, it drew him closer to his father as the surviving parent.

"I'm beginning to feel like the warrior in your hand-picked D&D team."

Tony smiled. "I'm actually quite familiar with Dungeons and Dragons," he confessed, "even played a few times. You may feel even more that way when you meet Nigel tomorrow. He's sort of a reformed thief

who helps me with research. He can hack into almost
any computer system, as you computer chaps like to
put it, and could have picked that SOBO padlock that
got crashed through."

Mike gave him a deadpan look. "You've got a
hobbit thief, too? Now I know I'm the fighter on a
D&D team."

Tony shook his head. "I'm glad to have you,
Michael, but you are so much more than that. There's
tremendous relief and comfort in having a true friend
that you know you can trust—someone you know who
accepts who you are—not having to worry that your
friend will learn the truth and be horrified, no longer
your friend."

Mike found himself smiling and placing a hand on
his friend's shoulder. "All those letters, all the books—
not just Christmas and birthdays, but the months in
between..."

"Yes, Michael. There was some irony in sending
you books about vampires. I knew you liked them. I
read them to see if the authors knew anything of the
truth or were just spinning yarns, but I knew you liked
them. At other times, after I read something well-
written and interesting, if I thought you might like it, I
sent it to you. And I kept in touch with your father
partially because I liked him and partially to aid in
keeping in touch with you. We can't have children,
Michael. We can bring others over, but even that
doesn't always work–" He hesitated, seeming
distracted a moment, then went on.

"Belle—Isobelle, the countess, was very old. She
insisted that, to survive, we must make close ties to
someone mortal. It gives us the illusion of living out
their lifetime, watching them grow, grow old. It keeps
something human in us, keeps us from living on the
outside and becoming predators like Chernov. I was

attracted to something in you when I met you. And I like your father very much. I have since the first day I met him. I suppose I could say that, if I must pick a human to adopt, so to speak, I prefer to find one for whom I can truly develop an attachment."

Without thinking, Mike found himself hugging his friend. Tony seemed to cling to it a moment, then pulled away, almost awkwardly.

"We don't hug very often," he confessed. "We Brits are famous for our reserve, and vampires come to associate such embraces with feeding, some as the prelude to a kill. You're a dear friend Michael. I don't think I cultivated you for this role, but I saw the possibility in you. As you matured and your skills sharpened, especially when you traveled to the Orient, honing your craft and learning new mental disciplines and abilities—especially your mental studies in Tibet—I began to hope that I might at last be able to work with a true friend, someone I knew I could trust."

Mike felt a bit embarrassed. "There's something else on your mind," he changed the subject. "Something came into your head a minute ago, breaking your chain of thought. It has to do with making other vampires, about it not always working."

"Chernov had five associates. All six were gunned down. Only five left the morgue. If they were made very recently and the change was not complete, perhaps the sixth was simply the one who couldn't change. It's no coincidence that literature favours eastern Europeans as vampires. If vampirism is the result of a virus, then the bug seems to work on less than one in ten."

"That would explain why we're not inundated with them," Mike agreed, "but it doesn't account for five out of six making the transition, if indeed they have."

"Ah, but they are Russian—eastern European. There seems to be a higher viability rate with Russians, Chechs, Rumanians, and Hungarians. MacDonald is looking for the remaining three and I have my own request in to the RCMP and CSIS for any available information about their whereabouts. They, in turn, will no doubt contact the FBI south of the border.

"Now, about your plan, how could you make the police think a fax was from Montreal Police?"

"Simple," Mike explained. "Computers can't think. When you send a fax using a computer, it places your fax number at the top of each page. But it only knows the number you tell it. You just go into the system setup and give it a new phone number and sender name, then change it back when you're done."

Tony shook his head. "It's so easy, it's a wonder this type of fraud isn't common."

"It is," Mike replied. "But anyone replying to the fax will soon expose the fraud."

"Well," Tony concluded, "at least now we have some names to go on. The police will be looking for possible addresses. And the inspector will be dealing with me before broadcasting to the rank and file. For our part, I have a long distance call to make, and you have supper with Sean and a class to teach. I'll try not to intrude on you tonight, but learning to sleep 'til noon might be a good habit to get into."

"We could meet later, if you like," Mike suggested. "Further out Main Street there's a bar that has karaoke Monday and Friday nights. It's a good time. Some are really bad, but some are really good."

"Assuming our friend takes a night off, I'll be there. What time?"

"They start around 9:00 or 9:30, but I probably won't get there 'til 10:00 or a little after. By the way, what made you decide to change MacDonald's routine?"

Tony became pensive. "Compassion, I suppose. I think it's becoming too much for him. After the cases in Sydney I felt I had to be straight with him. I regretted it immediately and almost hypnotized him then. Unfortunately he has to know that these are vampires. He can't be sending officers after them, thinking they can shoot useless bullets into them with impunity."

"Care to hypnotize me into not believing?"

"Sorry, Michael," Tony said with a smirk. "I need you too much."

The car door opened, there was a blur, and it closed immediately.

# 9: Carrie

**M**ike entered the karaoke bar a little after 11:00. Tony was standing at the bar, hoisting a drink in Mike's direction.

"I'd almost given up on you, old boy," he said, handing Mike a glass. "Scotch and water—Glenlivet. No ice. It took some effort to keep the girl from putting ice in it. Why anyone would want ice in this weather is beyond me. Is it snowing yet?"

Mike nodded. "It's just a light flurry at the moment, but it's supposed leave ten centimeters before dawn. Sorry I'm late. Class ended on time but I got the urge to do that fax before coming, and it took longer than I thought. I ran the logo through image software to clean it up a bit."

"Hey," a voice interrupted, "you sang here last week, didn't you?" She was a pretty brunette, about thirty. "You did that Elton John song. Man, you can sing. I couldn't believe it. So, what do you do?"

She was all wide-eyed and hungry looking. *Just broke up and on the rebound,* Mike thought, reading her signals, using instincts he'd honed through training. She was eying him up and down, as if gauging the cost of his clothes.

Mike hesitated, then made his face take on an embarrassed look. "I'm unemployed and I live in my mother's basement." He aimed for sincerity in his tone and abashed look.

"Oh." Her tone was suddenly uncertain and it only took a moment for her to wander off.

Tony was chuckling. "That was better-done than I've ever seen. You're quick. I hope you don't brush them all off that way, though. Keep things in perspective, Michael. You had a very happy marriage, then you made one colossal mistake. You were heart-broken and alone in the world, trying to father a very young son. You were starving for company and you felt desperate. You probably married her so quickly just to keep her from getting away. I think you're in a different place now, a much better frame of mind."

Mike shrugged. "There were enough warning signs—hell, the alarms were deafening. I just didn't want to hear them. I kept trying to convince myself she really loved me. But, as more time passed, it just got harder. The sad part is, I think that she really thought she loved me. She just had too much armour—too many walls, and too many defenses. And a fear of being vulnerable."

"So, now that all that is clear, just remember, there are caring women out there who do know how to love. Probably someone who's been through something like you've experienced and is also looking for someone who can love deeply."

Mike smiled at his friend. "You should have Dr. Phil's job. You'd be good at it."

Tony's brow furrowed, making Mike smile all the more.

"Never mind," he chuckled. "Here, give this a gander. It's a copy of what I faxed Pete."

Tony took the pages and compared Mike's creation to the photocopy of the Montreal PD fax.

"Nice job," he approved. "Looks authentic to me. And I like the touch—five of the six were wearing Russian-made kevlar. They were removed for evidence. Five went to the hospital, one to the morgue, but someone told the morgue to expect all six. Bollox in the paperwork. So the five didn't walk out, they never arrived.

"I like it, Michael. It's imaginative, believable, and doesn't make the Montreal Police look stupid. In my experience, rivalry between departments, especially with the French-English nonsense, might have made it acceptable, but cops would still rather blame it on someone else's paperwork. Very good, Michael."

Mike sipped his scotch.

"I sent it to MacDonald just before coming."

His voice trailed off as someone leaving the dance floor caught his eye. He found himself staring, smiling back at a pair of sparkling green eyes and a dazzling smile framed by dimples. The well-rounded figure was quite attractive. But it was the face, accented by a tasteful makeup job that he found stunning. He couldn't take his eyes off the smile.

"Steady on, Old Man," Tony whispered. "The pounding of your heart is fairly deafening! Sink me! Isn't that the nurse who looks after your father?"

"Carrie," Mike replied. "Yeah, she's an LPN. Excuse me."

Mike found himself abruptly leaving Tony, crossing the floor toward Carrie, who was walking toward him.

"Hello," she greeted, her tone musical. "Nice to see a friendly face."

"I could say the same," Mike replied. He felt like he was smiling from ear to ear and fought to tone it down. "I usually come Friday nights when I can and sing occasionally. Can't say as I've noticed you here before."

"I have tomorrow off," she explained. "This place is on my way home. My youngest brother was in the last contest here. Now and then I drop in for a drink, if I have the energy. And I love to dance. Do you dance?"

He took it as a hint and led her to the small dance floor. He couldn't take his eyes off her. She moved well. Indeed, she did love to dance. Mike, on the other hand, felt like an indifferent dancer.

"Actually," he found himself saying, "there was a time when I went to about six dances a year but never got to dance. I was lead guitar and lead singer in a local act. We played yacht club functions where I lived in the States."

"Well, Michael, you're not a bad dancer at all."

Mike chuckled. "Didn't you know? Guitar players learn to play so we won't have to dance." He hesitated. "My dad say's you're divorced."

Her expression clouded. "I'm doing my best to forget Mister Asshole and that twenty-five cent tramp he ran off with."

He nodded, wracking his brain for a way to put the smile back on her face. The way she smiled, any man with half a brain would make it his life's mission to keep the smile there. She was radiant when she smiled.

Before he could think of anything she said, "You're dad is very proud of you. He tells me you write books, and are being courted by a local publisher. He also raves about your Kung Fu school and how you teach some unusual system of samurai sword. And he told me about your music, sailing across oceans, scuba diving, and how you were a biology teacher. How did you squeeze all that in?"

Mike laughed. "I started young. There were a lot of things I wanted to try, things I just wanted to do."

"He also says you're a good father. He thinks Sean is just the best grandson ever."

Mike got a warm feeling. "He's pretty good as a son, too. He can't grow up fast enough. He'd love to

come here and sing. So how did you end up at
Seaview? Why not a hospital?"

"I was an RN in Emergency," she said with a trace
of pride. "I stopped working after my son was born.
When I decided to go back, I found I wanted to work
somewhere like Seaview. They needed LPNs more
than RNs. I had to re-certify after being away for so
many years and it was way easier to re-certify as an
LPN. And I like what I do. I find myself doing a lot of
PCW work, which makes the PCWs happy that I'm
helping out. At the end of the day I come home tired
but satisfied with who I am and what I'm doing."

"That's better than most people can claim and
wiser than what most strive for," Mike commented.

He suddenly realized that they'd danced through at
least four songs without him noticing the change in
singers. The next song was a slow one—'Amazed' by
Lonestar. He took up the classic ballroom waltz
position for a friendly slow dance. Before the first
verse was over, they'd both moved closer so that she
pressed against him. He felt mesmerized by the feel of
her against his chest, the way her arm came up over his
shoulder, the way the top of her head seemed to nestle
against his cheek, the fragrance of her hair. The song
seemed too short, over too soon. Holding her had been
a magical feeling, so soothing, so peaceful.

"I saw your friend, the English lord, at the bar with
you," she commented. "So, are you working with him
on these terrible murders? What kind of work are you
doing? Your dad thinks you'd make a great detective."

"Not too long ago I told a girl at the bar that I was
unemployed and lived in my mother's basement," he
laughed. "Now I'm ready to tell you anything you want
to know. Are you a witch?"

Her eyes sparkled. "I left my broom at the door so
the snow could melt off it," she joked. "The residents

say I'm easy to talk to. So are you. I guess, after all your father told me, I just feel like I know you."

"I guess my job will be to physically catch this monster," he said, "–whatever it takes."

She pressed her hand to his back.

"Ooh, you're almost soaked. I think we could both use a drink."

Mike grinned. "I don't dance much, but I guess you inspired me to put my heart into it."

Keeping an arm around her as they walked to the bar seemed natural. She also seemed to accept it as such.

Tony handed him his scotch. "And something for the lady?" he offered.

"I've got this one," Mike insisted.

"Just water," Carrie said. "I left a vodka cooler at a table with a coworker, but she'll have polished that off by now." The smile beamed at him. "Besides, I still have to drive home."

"How long have you been here?" Mike asked.

She glanced at the clock. "Is it midnight already?" She gave Mike a devilish look. "And you accused *me* of being a witch. You're the one who's making time race by."

She sipped her water, then took a napkin and mopped her brow and neck. Taking another, she handed it to Mike.

"You need a towel," she teased. "I got off at 10:45 and got here about ten after, just a little before you. I saw you come in, but you and–"

"Tony," Tony reminded her.

She nodded. "You and Lord Tony seemed preoccupied. I was about to come over and say 'hello' when you finally noticed me."

"Well," Tony interjected. "You two seem to have a lot to talk about, and I see a table to the side that just emptied. It seems just big enough for two."

"We can grab another chair," Carrie and Mike said at the same time. They looked at each other, then laughed.

"I need a trip to the ladies' room," she confided to Mike. "You grab the table and I'll hurry back. And Lord Tony needn't rush off."

As soon as she'd left, Tony commented, "You do realize that there are other people here, an entire room full, to be precise. She has certainly caught your attention. And you seem to have hers. I sense much from the auras people give off, part of being what I am. You two are definitely in harmony—quite rare and amazing."

Mike blew out a massive breath.

"It's a bit scary," he confessed. "I'm sensing massive waves of stuff from her. I can't explain it. I've never felt so comfortable, so natural around anyone— never this fast."

"Don't throw up too many walls," Tony warned.

"I'm not sure I could if I wanted to. I never thought I'd say this but, around her, being as natural and honest as I can seems the only way I can be."

"Good," Tony approved.

Mike furrowed his brow. "You say that now. Just remember, we're involved in something that has to be kept secret. And what are we to do next? Even if we locate Chernov's daytime lair, it's not like we can go in, treat the coffins with holy water and wafers, or plunge a crucifix into the coffin pillow. This guy probably sleeps in a bed in a blacked-out basement. None of the Hollywood ploys work."

Tony nodded, his manner grim. "That'll be where you come to the test. If you can find him by day, dragging him into the sun will be enough. If that's inconvenient, cut his head off. There's also burning the building he's in, but that's rarely a good idea. This chap is as likely to live in an apartment complex as a single dwelling."

Mike took a deep breath and blew it out. "So it really comes down to me having the balls to cut someone's head off." He winced, putting a hand to his temple. "Walking around in broad daylight with a thirty-eight-inch katana might be a bit conspicuous."

"What is it?" Tony asked, looking closely at Mike.

Mike could read concern in his face. He shook his head. "Nothing, just a bit of a headache."

It hit like a wave—sparks in his eyes, vision blurring, a bright cloud obscuring his sight. He squeezed his eyes shut, then looked down. On the ground before him was a decapitated and dismembered body, the head off to one side.

*Great,* he thought, *just what I need—visions of killing my first vampire.*

But this was no modern vampire. The corpse was wearing seventeenth century Japanese armour. He could see the armour on his own arms, katana in his hands, blood dripping from it. "Oh, God, no!"

Something smooth and cool touched his neck. "Are you okay?" The voice was soothing. The sensation was repeated at his cheek, then at his forehead. He closed his eyes, then raised his hand to his head, encountering a small female hand.

Heaving a huge sigh, he opened his eyes, relieved when his vision cleared, the pain receded. He nodded slowly.

"It hit like a migraine," he said, "but it left just as suddenly. I haven't had regular migraines since I quit teaching. Lately, they've been coming back at odd times. They come on fast, but they never leave that abruptly."

"Here," Carrie said, "I have some ibuprofen in my purse."

He shook his head, pulled a small pill container, decorated with an ornate Celtic design from his pocket, and popped two Excedrin Migraine, draining his scotch.

"Ibuprofen sends my blood pressure through the roof. I brought several bottles of Excedrin home from the States. Can't get it here. It's the only thing that works on headaches for me. Good for migraines, too."

"Have you seen a doctor about these?" Her voice was anxious, she gripped his right hand in both of hers.

Mike nodded. "Several, in four countries. I don't get them often enough for prescription drugs and they agree with the Excedrin. I'm okay."

He stared right at Tony. "It was weird. I saw something almost symbolic of what we were discussing. But it was more like a vision from the late 1700's."

Tony seemed perplexed. "Have you had advice on this?"

Michael gave a grimace of absurdity. "The suggestions range from drug flashback—rather difficult for someone who never took drugs—to past life memory, to a highly-developed imagination given to elabourate daydreaming. I used to have recurring nightmares. Now I seem able to have them when I'm awake."

"I've read about past life memory," Carrie said. "It's most likely to come through when events in this life are close to events in the past life, when the memory of that life can help us deal with events in this, or when we're trying to keep ourselves from making a mistake we made before."

"Mike, are you going to do a song?" The voice blared through the big speakers at the front of the room.

Mike could only chuckle.

"I say, great timing," Tony quipped in his dry tone.

Mike caught the DJ's eye and shook his head. "Not tonight, dear, I have a headache."

The audience response was a mixture of laughter and attempts to persuade.

"Maybe it'll take your mind of whatever's causing the headache," Carrie suggested. "Besides, I'd like to hear you sing." She still had a gentle grip on his hand, her green eyes sparkling at him.

Mike let a sigh escape. "Women," he breathed, smiling as he got up.

"Okay, Jim, what have you got there? I wasn't kidding about the headache."

"Anything you want, but I did pull U2, just in case."

"With Or Without You," Mike said. " 'Still Haven't Found' is too much for my head right now. I wasn't kidding about the headache."

As the song started, Mike fell in with the beat, one leg flexing in time, both hands resting on the mic in its stand, nodding his head in rhythm. He eased out the first few lines in a low baritone, deep but gentle, keeping his mouth close to the mic, letting the mic do the work. By the second chorus, he backed off the mic, fired his voice up an octave, driving the refrain in power-tenor, resisting the urge to scream the lyrics, keeping it melodic. There were a few cheers from the audience. He knew he closed his eyes a lot, but he couldn't help it. He tended to get lost in the music. It was just something he did. When he opened his eyes, he found the audience moving in time with the song, heads nodding, people smiling. As the instrumental ending faded, the applause and whistling retriggered his headache.

He nodded to the appreciative crowd, murmured a *thank you* over the mic, then made his way back to the table.

"Wow!" Carrie said, eyes shining. "Your father said you were good, but I thought that was just pride."

Tony commented. "I'd say your throat healed just fine." He was smiling broadly.

Mike shrugged. "I was born with my father's voice," he said simply. "I had some training as a young teen—solo festival stuff. You know, the kind of thing every kid is just dying to give up baseball and hockey for? Mostly I remember the smell of Brill Cream and the feel of the knot in my stomach."

He danced with Carrie through a long string of songs, especially enjoying the slow ones. Holding her close just felt good, but it was more than that. He felt a wave of feelings coming from her. Something told him that they were both sentimental types who loved expressively and deeply, who thrived on touch. Slow dancing, holding each other close, gave them something they'd been starving for without ever understanding it.

Next thing he knew, someone was calling, 'last call.' Moments later, the lights came on and the DJ was shutting down.

Mike walked Carrie out to her car, an arm about her shoulder. She started it with a remote. He stood alert next to her compact until she had the door unlocked.

"When are you coming to see your dad next," she asked. The hint of anxiousness in her voice sent an adolescent thrill through him. He felt like a nineteen-year-old, and he hadn't been nineteen for close to thirty years.

"You still on nights after tomorrow?"

She nodded. "All this week," she sighed. "I'm off this weekend, then back to days on Monday. I was supposed to have tomorrow off but I just remembered that I agreed to cover for a friend."

"So Saturday night is the best night to take you to dinner?" he suggested.

She seemed to ponder this. He could read the hesitation coming off her. *Somebody hurt her really bad,* he thought. *Even with the chemistry between us, she's still gun-shy and cautious.* He waited patiently. Trying to be convincing was not the way to go. Then, brushing her cheek with the back of his fingers, he said, "We can talk about it tomorrow afternoon when I come to see Dad. There's a nice restaurant that I like but don't go to very often."

When he told her the name, she nodded with enthusiasm. "Never been, but I've heard it's nice," she commented, then got into her car.

"Talk to you tomorrow," he promised.

"Tomorrow," she agreed. The dimpled smile and sparkle in her eyes brought back a churning of the butterflies in his stomach.

"She's very nice," Tony offered as Mike approached his own car. "Take a chance, Michael. She's special. You can date a bit and, if it doesn't work out, no harm done. I believe that she is the type who would remain a friend even if it didn't work."

"She scares me, Tony."

"This from a man who has taught policemen in several countries how to take guns and knives away from nasty fellows? This from a man who's last relationship, doomed as it was, was with a former model?"

Mike lowered his head, his smile tentative.

"She makes me feel like a teenager on prom night—all butterflies."

"And this is a bad thing? Michael, you're both over forty. People your age would sell their soul for that feeling again."

Mike took a deep breath and blew it out. He grinned at Tony. "I asked her to dinner Saturday night. She'll give me her answer tomorrow when I visit my father."

# 10: Nigel

His horse is foaming, lungs pumping like a bellows as he reins him to a halt in front of the line of warriors advancing to meet him. At their centre is the man he seeks, body protected by ceremonial gold-gilded armour, face bearing a haughty sneer. But it stops at the eyes. There is fear in the eyes. 'How Yoshihiro fights to hide that fear!' he thinks. Yet he can feel it.

"Let your men stand down, Yoshihiro," he shouts. "This is between you and me. It need not concern your retainers or mine, unless you fear to face me alone."

He makes an abrupt hand gesture and his own small company backs their horses away several paces.

Toda Yoshihiro's eyes blaze. "Why should I fear you, Yakura? When my great-grandfather was fighting Tokugawa Ieyasu, yours was probably mucking out some stable."

Yakura ignores the taunt. While his family have never amassed great wealth like the Toda, they have a long history of bravery in battle and loyalty to the Tokugawa. He draws his katana and dismounts, advancing on Yoshihiro, who does the same.

He breathes in deeply, as Master Chen has taught. 'Seek the inner calm,' he hears in his mind. 'All will flow from that. Your hands can move like the wings of the white crane. Let the sword be just another part of your arm.'

*With a roar, Yoshihiro attacks, battering at him with a barrage of heaving strokes.*

*'You attack like a butcher,' Yakura taunts. 'Did your ancestors cut meat for a living?'*

*Dealers in dead flesh are unclean, made to live apart from other people. There is no greater insult he could fling upon his enemy.*

*The rage it triggers makes Yoshihiro wild, out of control.*

*Yakura dodges and parries, waiting for the moment to feel right. He steps in, swings a mighty parrying stroke, carrying the other sword to the side, then cuts down. His blade slices through the connecting straps of* sode, *the upper arm guards, biting deep into the muscle.*

*As Yoshihiro gasps in shock, Yakura repeats the move on the other arm.*

*Yoshihiro's eyes widen in pain and rage. With a roar, Yoshihiro attacks wildly, his technique now limited by the pain and flowing blood.*

*Yakura parries again, his blade lunging in and cutting the straps of the upper leg armour. Left leg, then right. He feints toward the left leg again, then wheels a full circle. The blade comes down, almost completely severing the left arm, then flicks across Yoshihiro's throat, leaving behind a thin line of welling blood.*

*Yoshihiro is foundering, weak from the massive flow of blood at his shoulder. His eyes now show a mix of terror and desperation.*

*Yakura whirls again. His blade bites deep into the upper thigh, all but severing this limb. Tears of anger fill his eyes as he wrenches his katana free. Before Yoshihiro can collapse to the ground, Yakura spins and swings a backhand blow. There's a hush as Yoshihiro's head falls to the ground.*

*He stands over the body of his fallen foe, tears falling freely now. The anger has subsided, but the well of grief knows no bottom. She is gone. Killing Yoshihiro has not brought her back. Nothing will.*

Mike's eyes snapped open. His pillow was half on the floor, his body bathed in sweat. He leaned over and slapped the large button on his digital clock.

"It's 5:13 am," a computerized female voice announced.

He pulled his pillow back into place. The covers were a mess, clearly he'd been thrashing about. Details of the dream were fresh in his mind. He grabbed a book from his night table, unclipped the attached fountain pen, and began scribbling down the images and impressions before they could fade. An old sailing buddy who believed in the significance of dreams as both past life memories and a window on the future had given him the journal.

*So who is she and why do I feel such grief?* he wrote. He glanced back several pages and read about entering a garden and finding a young woman dying from a terrible sword wound to her abdomen. It was meant to look like sepuku, the ritual suicide of honour, but the depth and range of the cut was too much for a woman to make with a wakizashi or short sword. The blade had bitten into a rib. A man had done this with a katana.

*"Yoshihiro," she breathed, then died.*

"What is this and why does it haunt me?" he asked aloud. There was no answer.

He put the book down and collapsed back on his pillow. It took a while but he finally drifted back to sleep.

He bolted upright. The phone was ringing. The clock said 9:00 am.

His right hand lashed out, snatching the cordless phone out of its cradle.

"Hello?"

"'Allo, guv'nor. Sorry to ring you up in the wee earlies an' all, but I'm in a cab from the airport, crossing over to your 107, and I need better directions for the cabbie, 'ere."

"Ugh, who is this?"

"Cor blime! Don' tell me 'Is Lordship never told you I was comin'! Well, kick me down the Ol' Kent Road. Name's Nigel, Nigel Worthington." The cockney 'th' came out like a 'v.'

"Nigel," Mike reiterated, remembering Tony's comments.

" 'At's right. So 'Is Lordship *did* gimme a mention."

"You're his expert on locks and system hacks," Mike said. He sat up and rubbed his eyes.

"Well, let's just say ol' Nigel can get into just about anything. Did I wake you? Well, just gimme— better yet, I'll put the cell on speaker and you can give the cabbie the whatsits about finding your flat. Then put the coffee on, throw on the bangers an' mash, an' I'll be there in a jiff."

Mike found himself grinning. He'd worked with enough Brits in Bermuda that it only took a bit of waking up to wade through the crippled pronunciations and cockney slang. He gave directions, rang off, then got up, went to the bathroom, and splashed his face.

Plodding out to the kitchen, he ground the beans and put the coffee brewer on. He felt sluggish, almost irritable. He didn't like being awakened early. He often wrote late, if the muse was upon him. During the week, the sounds of Sean getting himself up for school often woke him, though he resisted. Then there'd be Sean's parting, "I'm outta here, Dad." He'd mutter back,

"Have a good day," before burying his face in the pillow again.

Last night had been a late night for better reasons than writing. The memory of it still lingered, giving him the same feeling of anticipation. He tried to visit his father at least twice a week, often more, but he never felt this kind of anticipation about going out there. It was almost enough to drown out how disturbing his nightmare had been—almost.

The nightmares had started during the summer before his first year of university. He'd been to a movie at the old Vogue Theatre in Halifax. He'd cut down along the waterfront toward the ferry—dodgy territory, he knew. A guy had stepped out of an alley and slashed with a knife, grazing Mike's stomach. What happened next was reflex. Based on the injuries, he could guess what he had probably done, but he had no memory. Next thing he knew he was standing over the guy, who was lying on the pavement bleeding from almost every opening. He thought the guy was dead and ran to the ferry in a panic, took the ferry across and caught the last bus home.

That night the first nightmare came. It was short. He was looking down at the bleeding thug. The thug went blurry and turned into the bloody dismembered body of a samurai. Mike's arms went from being the bare arms of an eighteen-year-old in a T-shirt to the armour-clad arms of a young samurai in red-lacquered armour.

His dad found the bloody T-shirt balled up in the trash can and confronted Mike, forcing an accurate account out of him. His father took a statement and settled things with the Halifax Police. This was long before the amalgamation into Halifax Regional Municipality. It turned out the guy's rap sheet was, in his father's words, thicker than the phonebook. He'd been out on parole but would be heading back to prison just as soon as he was out of the hospital.

"You really did a number on him, Mikey" his father had said. "Shattered ribs, ruptured spleen, right arm (his knife hand) broken at the wrist and elbow and dislocated at the shoulder. Fractured jaw and parietal skull fracture connected by one large bruise, presumably a kick to the head.

"He had it coming. He'd have gutted you like a fish, then looked for a wallet. He's done it before. Don't feel guilty, son. I'm just glad to know you can take care of yourself when you're out at night. Docks are a bad place after dark, though."

His memories were interrupted by a squeaky yawn and the feel of a heavy furry body against his legs.

"Morning, Sam," he said. "Ready to go find a bush?" The responding 'huff' could only be taken as a 'yes.'

Samwise Gamgee was a Pembroke Welsh Corgi—black and tan with a white chest. He gave his master a huge smile, his entire butt wagging from side to side, well making up for his lack of a tail. Mike fancied that he even looked like his hobbit namesake.

He opened the sliding door onto the deck just enough for Sam to squeeze out, shivering as a blast of arctic air forced its way in. Going to the cupboard above the coffee brewer, he got out a T-Bone snack and a Denta-Stix. The brewer was just starting to gurgle. He closed his eyes and sighed, smelling the aroma of the coffee as if he could absorb caffeine from the smell.

When he figured enough time had lapsed, he went to the door again. There was Samwise Gamgee, sitting patiently, smiling at him through the glass.

"Come on, it's cold," Mike admonished, opening the door and wishing Sam would waddle through a bit faster. "Is it cookie time?"

"*Huff!*" Mike had put a lot of effort into teaching Sam to contain his barking. He had a sharp bark and, like most herd dogs, was prone to being vocal. Unfortunately, when excited by anything, Sam usually forgot to whisper his 'huff.'

Mike held out the T-Bone at waist height. Sam struggled to rise on hind legs, then gave up and sat.

"You're getting old, Sam," Mike said. "You and me both." He dropped the cookie on the floor. Sam snatched it and ran under the baby grand piano in the living room. Moments later, he returned for the chew stick.

The doorbell rang just was Mike was pouring his first cup of coffee. Sam's reaction was immediate. He charged the front door, racing down the stairs of the split entry, barking all the way.

"Don't mind Sam," Mike said as he opened the door, "he's wired to the doorbell. He's our door-dog. If I don't hear the bell or a knock, I hear Sam."

At the door was a small black man, maybe five-one, smiling in a most cheerful manner. He thrust out a hand, grabbing Mike's in a firm grip.

"Nigel Worthington," he announced. (It sounded like *Worvington.*) "An' you must be Mike Cameron, our trusted paladin."

Mike wondered if the Dungeons and Dragons theme would become a running gag.

As Mike took Nigel's coat and hung it in the closet, Nigel went partway up the stair, glancing about at the kitchen and what could be seen of the living room.

"Cor, nice digs, gov'nor! Looks like the rest o' the neighbourhood from outside. You do all this?"

Mike nodded. "I had time on my hands, so I bought a place that had been neglected on the inside, gutted it, put down hardwood, moved a few walls, and designed a kitchen."

"Well, you done right proud for yourself." His eyes traveled over the 'granite' Coreon and mahogany cabinets in the kitchen, the stainless steel appliances, and the tiny work island with it's built in wine fridge. "Bet the ladies love this place. Sorry 'bout the knock-up an' all. 'Is Lordship might o' told you. Anyway, 'ere I am. You look a bit out of it. Rough night?"

"Kind of."

Glancing at the living room, Nigel dropped his bags and walked straight to the baby grand, sat down, and shocked Mike by launching into a Mozart sonata. He stopped in mid phrase, taking in the collection of guitars hanging on the walls.

Mike felt a bit off balance.

"Don't stop," he said suddenly. "I never get to hear anyone else play it. I'm just a hacker—a guitar player who taught himself to do a few things on the piano."

"She's a beaut, gov. How'd you come by 'er, then? An' I bet you're a bit more 'n an 'acker."

"Building a house with a library—the ex decided we needed a baby grand. I was indulgent, probably contributing to the problems, got a deal on it. It was made in 1920." He rattled it off in an emotionless rote.

As Nigel's eyes continued over the walls with their built-in bookcases, he added, "I see you also took the library when you split. Good on ya, gov. Are those Ovations?" His eyes were on the guitars, but the fingers were still pouring out Mozart.

Mike gazed fondly at his guitars and nodded. He had a 6-string and a 12-string, both dated limited editions, the former a present from Sean's mother. He was very attached to that one. Between them was a Les Paul, transparent blue, with Seymour Duncan pickups.

"You've done yourself up nice, 'ere, gov. No TV, though. How you manage wiffout TV?"

Mike smiled but said nothing. There'd be time later to show Nigel downstairs. Mike liked movies. His idea of TV was a nine-foot screen with a ceiling-mounted projector and 5.1 digital surround-sound.

Returning to the kitchen, he poured coffee. "How do you take your coffee?"

"Black, gov'nor."

Mike checked the fridge and freezer before taking Nigel his coffee. He set the mug on a coaster on the piano, then flopped into the sofa.

"You're in luck. There's no bangers, I rarely buy sausage, but my son hasn't totally eaten us out of house and home yet. I can manage bacon and hash browns, if that suits you."

Nigel gave a wink. "Down to the ground, mate!" he declared, hoisting his mug as if to toast. "I was kind o' joking wiff the 'bangers an' mash' bit—joking but 'opeful, you know? Anyffing you can manage is fine by me."

"Have you got a place to stay?"

Nigel shrugged. "I usually stay wiff 'Is Lordship, an' expect to this time. But, between you an' me, 'Is Lordship is *not* an early riser, *if* you know what I mean, nudge-nudge, wink-wink. I figure I can get started on a few things 'ere on the computer, if 'at's okay by you, gov, then catch a few hours' kip and taxi to Lord Tony's 'round about sunset—4:30, would you say? Did you check yer e-mail, then?"

Mike shook his head. "I had a late night."

"Oo, out wiff a bird, eh? Good lad."

Mike chuckled. Nigel looked at least fifty, yet seemed to be enjoying a prolonged adolescence. He took some getting used to first thing in the morning, but Mike couldn't help but like him.

"Let's just say it was a chance encounter with someone very interesting, that could turn into something."

"Sounds like every sane man's dream. Good luck wiff 'er, gov."

Mike nodded. "Thanks."

When Mike returned to the kitchen and started rattling through the pots and pans hanging above the island, Nigel abandoned the piano and followed, sitting on a stool.

"If you want to check your e-mail, I can put the apron on, gov. Breakfast for two?"

Mike grinned. "Just one. I'll just have coffee. You're lucky my son Sean is off to school. He eats enough for two."

"Teenager, then? Still growin'? I got two lads in the army, just 'ome from Afghanistan, finally. They'd been in southern Iraq, too. Cor! The way them buggers want to blow each other up, I say, 'let 'em 'av a go, then we start from scratch and deal wiff what buggers is left! My girl's the smart one—a solicitor like 'er mum, no less."

"It's tough raising kids in this day and age," Mike agreed. "When I was a kid, it was *Leave It to Beaver* reruns on TV. Beaver's biggest fear was staying after school or breaking something in the kitchen. He didn't have to pass through a metal detector at school to make sure none of the other kids were carrying guns or knives."

He made himself another cup of coffee, then headed back to the desk in his bedroom. He gave Mail his password, and watched as a steam of mail downloaded. Most was junk. One was from Tony. It contained the names Vladimir Ivanovitch Chernov,

Pavel Petrenko, Viktor Boris Chekinovich, Pietro Illich Vollinkoff, and Mikhail Bondarenko. Next to each name was from one to three others, under the heading of 'other known associates.' He flagged the text, ported it to Pages, enlarged the text and changed the font, then printed 2 copies.

"Breakfast is served, gov'nor. Can Sam 'av a nosh? 'E's dancin' 'round me worse 'n a Piccadilly pan 'andler."

Mike smiled but shook his head. The corgi was grinning hopefully. "Samwise Gamgee, you are a *dog*." Sam's ears went back and the smile faded. "You eat *dog* food—low calorie *dog* food for *older* dogs with fat bellies!" He gave Sam a loving rub on the head and whispered, "Your food is in your dish."

"I'll just e-mail Lord Tony, if that's all right," Nigel said. "After breakfast, if I can patch into your broadband. Whot kind o' computer 'ave you got, gov?"

"An Intel iMac," Mike told him.

Nigel nodded. "Nice. I've got software for doing searches for me. I wrote it for my Dell an' it won't run on your Mac—wiff the way Apple's going wiff their operating systems, it probably will by next year, but we don't 'av 'til then, do we?"

"Help yourself," Mike said.

A motorcycle growled into the driveway and went silent. Then, the front door opened, accompanied by the chiming *beep-beep-beep* of the alarm system.

"Hey, Dad. I smell food. Whatcha cooking?"

"What are you doing home?" Mike asked.

"It's Tuesday, Dad," Sean explained. "My off-block is just before lunch." Then, spotting Nigel, he switched gears without a blink. "Hi, I'm Sean."

"Nigel, Sean. Sean, Nigel," Mike said. "Nigel's a friend of Tony's, from London."

"Cool," Sean commented, then began to prowl the fridge.

"Back in a second," Mike said, then headed back to the bedroom. He retrieved his coffee from his desk, then rummaged through a file drawer, located a spare ethernet cable, plugged it into the router in the hutch cupboard above his heavy mahogany desk, and left the end dangling.

Back in the kitchen, he told Nigel, "There's an ethernet cable coming out of the cupboard from my router. Just set up on my desk."

"No need, gov," Nigel assured him. "Got a little gadget wiff me. I just plug it in to the wall, plug your e-net cable into it, an' boom, it transmits wireless to me. Made it meself."

"Wow," said Sean. "I'd love to see it. Sounds like Airport."

"Only a third the size," Nigel replied. Soon he and Sean were into an animated chat, ending up on the subject of movies. Mike shook his head. With Sean, sooner or later all conversations turned to movies.

"Dad's got a *huge* collection," Sean asserted. "You should see the theatre downstairs. The screen is *huge* and the speakers are *awesome*. He did it all himself, even made the speakers."

"Been holdin' out on me?" Nigel teased, looking at Mike.

Mike shrugged. "It's why there's no TV, just the little one there on the kitchen counter and one in Sean's room. Except for the news, I do my watching downstairs. If you like *CSI*, you certainly get to see all the details clearly."

"Good show, that. We get it in London. Tony said you were scientific—medical stuff, right?"

Mike nodded. "I taught anatomy, physio, and genetics in a secondary school in Bermuda."

"Good ol' Human Biology. I remember that. Failed me O-Level. Broke me muver's 'eart. Took up pickin' locks instead."

"You must have done okay in school to be a first rate computer hacker," Mike countered.

Nigel shook his head. "Weren't teaching 'at stuff when I was in it. Learned it in porridge when I was in me thirties.

"That's the joint—the slammer," he confessed to Sean, as an aside. "Keep yer nose clean. You don't ever want to go there—not a nice place. Anyway, 'ackin' is just another kind o' lock pickin,' i'n'it?"

Sean grinned. "You remind me of the guy in *Ocean's Eleven*."

Mike feigned a puzzled look. "Sammy Davis jr? I don't see the resemblance."

"*No, Dad,*" Sean groaned, rolling his eyes, "the *other Ocean's Eleven*—the one with George Clooney."

"*Oh, that one,*" Mike joked. "It was okay, but I still prefer the original Rat Pack version."

Sean rolled his eyes again. "Old people, jeeze!"

"Sorry, mate," Nigel said, "but I 'ave to stick wiff your dad on 'at one. Don Cheadle's a bit taller 'n me, but thanks for the comparison."

Once Sean was out the door, back to school, Nigel said, "Great kid! You 'n he always like 'at, then— jokin' n' banterin'?"

Mike nodded. "Pretty much. His mother died when he was young. We've always been tight. My last attempt at matrimony, a well-disguised disaster from the start—well, she didn't really want kids and had a problem with boys. The less said the better. Let's just say it made him a bit of a loaner. Mind you, I was a loaner most of my life, and I had a brother and great parents."

"Yeah, some of it is just the genes, i'n'it?"

"So how did you come to know Tony?"

"'Is Lordship? Well, now, that's got to be a bit of fate. Well, we were both in a bit of a pickle, weren't we. See, there was this bloke—real weird number, you know? Started showin' up at the local rub-a-dub-dub and givin' all the barmaids the willies. But, word 'ad it he was loaded. Never went to the bank, always 'ad the doh-ray-me on 'im. Well, the lads at the pub all reckoned he 'ad a huge swag stashed wherever 'e lived. So, I followed 'im 'ome one night in the wee earlies.

"Well, it seems this other bloke was followin' 'im, too. I could've missed 'im—'e was good, moved like a regular shadow—fast, silent, real smooth, you know? So, I tails 'em both. Well, second chap tails 'im inside an ol' stone building wiff a string o' flats inside. 'E waits outside the door to the bloke's flat 'til just as the sun's comin' up, calls someone on a two-way, then goes inside.

"Well, I figure 'e's up to the same game as me, so I goes in, ready to crack 'im on the 'ead and make off wiff the money. I barely gets inside—there's 'Is Lordship tryin' to open wot looks like a bedroom door, when, BAM! A hidden iron bar door slams shut blocking the bedroom door, and anovver one slams shut right behind me, lockin' me in.

"That's when 'Is Lordship sees me for the first time. 'E asks me wot I'm doin' 'ere. I tell him, probably the same as him. 'E says 'e doubts that, givin' me that smile 'e 'as. Well, I says, no matter wot we *were* up to, we gotta get out now, 'fore the coppers shows up, nicks the pair of us, an' it's off to porridge for the both of us, me for a longer stretch. Turns out there's a keypad by both doors. I figure there's one on each side of each door, since rich bugger don't want to be locked in, does 'e? Anyway, I pull the pad off the wall. Turns out it's pretty simple—just short out the right two wires an' *open sesame*.

"I'm about to take a powder when 'Is Lordship is suddenly between me an' the front door, shaking 'is 'ead. Says we need to get the ovver door open, too. I tells 'im the coppers might be coming, an' wot do you ffink 'e says? 'E says, 'course they are—'e called 'em on the radio. That's when I suggest 'e must be a nutter, from a long line o' nutters. 'E just smiles an' says, 'The police will not pose a problem.'

"Well, I shakes me 'ead, but quick as Bob's-your-uncle, I get the ovver door open. 'At's when this bobby shows up. 'Is Lordship tells 'im to pay me no mind—says I'm a colleague 'elpin' 'im out. Well, I been a colleague 'elpin' 'im out ever since, 'aven't I?

"Now, computer time. If I can connect to your router, I'll 'av a go at some o' them names 'n see if anyone lives in the neighbourhood, so to speak."

Nigel unzipped an ancient kit bag and rummaged for a moment. "'Ere's the gizmo." He pulled out a black metal casing the size of a deck of cards, with a telescoping antenna."

"Looks like the sender for my wireless in-ear monitors," Mike commented.

"Similar idea, actually," Nigel said. "Now, let's get 'er 'ooked up."

Back at his desk, Mike watched with interest as Nigel plugged the ethernet cable into the box, then plugged the box into a wall outlet. "Now we see what we got."

Returning to the dining room, Nigel opened a padded case and extracted a Del laptop. He booted it up, plugged what looked like a USB flash disk into a side port, then started tying.

"That's it?" Mike asked. "You didn't have to change any network commands?"

Nigel shook his head. "Naw, I use it all the time, don't I. Computer looks for the receiver, receiver looks for the sender, sender looks for ethernet info. Now we start nosin' into dark corners—tax records, leases, motor vehicles—wherever these blokes names might be."

"If you'll be okay on your own for a bit, I need to go out for a few hours."

"Sure thing, gov'nor. Long as 'ere's coffee in the pot. Don' mind if I make more, do ya?"

Mike smiled. "Help yourself. I'll get more while I'm out. Part of the trip is groceries."

"Oh, that. From the look in your eye, I fought it might be somefin' to do wiff 'at bird o' yours."

Mike fought back a smile. "I'll be visiting my dad. She's one of the nurses where he lives."

"Well, you 'ave a good one and don't worry 'bout me, gov. Wiff a bit o' luck, I may have some useful info by the time you get back. Stay outta barney."

Mike had to think a second. It had been a few years since he'd heard much rhyming slang. Barney was Barney Rubble, trouble.

"Can't get into much trouble at a seniors' home. Maybe we can hit a rub-a-dud-dub for a gold watch after meeting Tony tonight?"

"Ooh, I 'ope it's Glenlivet. I spotted a bottle on the buffet."

"Sure thing."

———

Mike felt almost nervous as he approached the third floor desk. Carrie was nowhere in sight and the dreaded nurse Barkhouse had just come on duty. He signed in, then headed for his father's room. Carrie almost caught him off guard. She appeared out of a doorway next to Mike's father's, taking a possessive grip on his arm.

"Nice timing," she said. "I just came on ten minutes ago and was starting to make rounds."

He eased his arm free and slipped it around her in a kind of one-armed hug.

"Hey there."

She flashed a smile. He felt like butterflies were holding a marathon in his stomach.

"Hi. Nice to see you," she said in her liquid, musical voice. "You look troubled. Anything wrong? Another headache?"

"No," he assured her, "just a rough dream—sort of an extension of the image that triggered last night's migraine. Then I had an unexpected guest. A friend of Tony's, showed up on the doorstep this morning when I would rather have slept in. He's a cockney from London. Interesting guy. I like him already. Anyway, he's playing detective on the computer, so I thought I'd steal away and see you—ah—Dad."

Carrie blushed just a little.

"I was hoping you'd come—to see your father, that is."

"We on for dinner Saturday night?"

"You don't need to do that."

"I want to," Mike insisted. "Aussie Steak House, just like I promised. They do great chicken, as well as steak. I don't go there much, but I do like it."

"Well, I've heard it's good—okay. What time shall I meet you?"

Mike shook his head. "I'll pick you up, just give me an address. How about 6:30?"

"It's all the way out in Fall River. You don't need to..."

He cut her off. "Not a problem. Besides, if we want to go somewhere else after dinner, we can talk while driving instead of playing car tag."

She seemed to think about it, then nodded. She pulled a pad from her pocket and wrote an address and phone number, using a pen that hung around her neck on a lanyard.

Mike carefully tucked the paper into his wallet.

"Good, now that that's settled, were you going in to see Dad?"

"As a matter of fact, I *was* about to look in on your father and Louie. Neither went down to the TV lounge today." She dropped her voice to a murmur. "Louie's been having bowel troubles and your father watches over him like they were old war buddies."

"That's my dad, 'Man down, officer needs assistance.'"

"Well, look at you two," Will commented as they entered.

"I found him in the hall," Carrie joked.

"Mmm hmm. I was a detective, Carrie. I was in and out with the lab boys enough to know chemistry when I see it."

"That will be enough out of you, Mr. Cameron," Carrie said. "Have you been to the bathroom today. Perhaps you need an enema. Shall I inform nurse Barkhouse?"

Will Cameron's colouring lost a shade, then he recovered. "You wouldn't dare. Besides, if I'm right, and I think I am, I can't imagine a better match up—the best gal I know with the best guy I can recommend."

"Woah, put the breaks on, Dad. That's two compliments in the same sentence. You been into the scotch early today?"

"Just you never mind, Mikey. I see a spark here. Give it a chance. Your head's in a much better place than it was last time."

Mike rolled his eyes, but Carrie leaned closer to where Will sat in his chair, *True Detective* in his lap, and whispered, "We're having dinner Saturday night."

Will beamed. "Good for you." He gave Mike a nod and a wink.

"And how are you feeling, Louie?" Carrie asked. Her tone was like a concerned mother with a sick child. While she tended to Will's roommate, Mike pulled a chair over next to his Dad's.

"You look like shit, Mike. Is it the case?"

Mike shook his head. "Just a rough night. Actually, it was a very nice night, but I got hit by one of those visions and a migraine flash, then had a detailed nightmare, then a friend of Tony's called on his way from the airport."

"Nigel?"

Mike nodded.

"Never met him," Will went on, "but I gather he's a genius on the computer. No system can stop him. Not too many locks, either, from what I gather from his record. He's on the up and up now, though. Tony says he's the best."

"Well, he's back at the house, prowling the net on his laptop, tracking lease and property records. Tony e-mailed a list of names. Anyway, I didn't sleep well, then he called early and showed up at the door soon after."

"About those nightmares—I know you've seen shrinks about them, Mikey, but I wish there was a way to get to the bottom of them."

Mike shrugged. "So do I. I've been on the couch, I've even been through hypnosis."

"Maybe Tony can hypnotize you and get somewhere. He's so good at it that it's scary. If the movies are right, it comes with the... uh ... his condition."

"Gee, I don't know... maybe. Anyway, no real news on the case. We're meeting with Tony tonight. Perhaps there'll be new developments. Maybe Nigel will unearth something."

"Just you think about it, Mike. Really. These dreams and visions have been going on for more than twenty-five years. They mean something. If they're more common now, it must be for a reason."

"And you don't think being asked to help kill monsters by hacking their heads off with a sword is enough reason to dream about chopping some guy up?" Mike whispered in a low hiss, so Carrie wouldn't hear.

His father paled, seemed to think about it, then shook his head. "I think it's making something come to a head, that's all. Please talk to Tony."

Mike stared at the ceiling, then nodded. "Okay. I will. I promise."

"Tonight?"

Mike hesitated, then nodded. "Tonight."

Will let out a sigh. He laid a hand on Mike's shoulder and smiled. "At least this vampire guy was quiet last night—nothing on the news."

"Maybe they're not giving anything out. Frankly, I'd be for keeping it quiet rather than creating hysteria. I don't think the public is ready to cope with that kind of knowledge. I'm still adjusting and I've known Tony, at least through letters and phone calls, for most of my life."

Will nodded. "So, what's with you and Carrie? How did that get started? And let me be the first to say I'm glad it started. She's a peach. I've been telling you that."

Mike shrugged. "I took Tony to Lakeside for a drink. It was karaoke night. She dropped in on the way home from work. We started dancing, talking,—I just found myself liking her company. There's something about her that just feels comfortable, like I've known her forever."

Will was nodding his head. "What did I tell you? Everybody in here loves her. She's an angel."

"I know when I'm being talked about," Carrie interjected, "so I think I'll just go look in on Annie and Rose, then come back to check on you, Will."

Mike smiled, trying to hide his embarrassment. "Now see what you've done? Anyway, I asked her to dinner Saturday night."

"Mario's?"

"No, the Aussie Steak House."

"Nice choice. After that, take her back to your place and play the piano for her. Sing to her. Serenade her off her feet. You're good at it and she deserves it."

"Jeeze, Dad, slow it down, will you?"

The old man smiled. "Should I be patient, Mike? Should I act like I have months, years to watch this unfold? Mike, I've been here for almost two years now, ever since I realized that it was just too hard for me to cope on my own at home. No, I'm not playing the sympathy card, and I know it's why you came home. My point, Mike, is that I've known this lady a while. She came in here one night and helped me up to the can when I'd been hacking so bad I almost passed out. She was late getting off shift that night, after one hell of a day with some of the more difficult ones in here. This might have been just weeks after that asshole left her to shack up with his mistress. She was all alone dealing with this disaster in her life. Her son was off at the Navy equivalent of boot camp. She was carrying a lot on her shoulders at the time. I'd catch her crying when she thought no one noticed. She could have come in complaining about wanting to get home. Hell, Mike, she could have called for a PCW to deal with me. But she didn't. She heard me coughing, saw me struggling to the can, and rushed in, telling me off for not buzzing her. She helped me to the can, waited, then helped me back to bed. She had this compassionate smile the whole time. Now what kind of woman would do that, Mike? I'll tell you: a deep, loving, caring, giving woman, that's who."

Mike just nodded. "No arguments, Dad. I can sense all of that from her. I sense a lot of things, mostly my own comfort around her. You've also called me 'Mike' about half a dozen times in the last two minutes. You only do that when you're really trying to get through to me. But, Dad, take a look at what I'm in the middle of. And now the nightmares again. My life is a bit chaotic at the moment."

"So make some space for yourself, even if it's just momentary islands of peace in a sea of chaos," Will rebutted.

Mike stared at his father. "Where did you pull *that* image from? Been reading Hemmingway instead of Hammett and Spillane?"

Will chuckled. "Actually, I think one of your characters said something along those lines in your first book."

Mike rolled his eyes. "Look, I've asked her out. I like her. I *really* like her. You're winning. Just don't use your condition to push me. It's not fair and the reminder is hard to take."

"Mikey, we all have to come to grips with things. One night, almost thirty years ago, you came to grips with the hardest decision a man may make, and you weren't even a man yet. You had to defend yourself knowing that it might require killing a man. And you did just that. You didn't kill him, but you thought you had. When you told me about it, I could see it all in your eyes. You'd made a choice to survive and your rigid Arthurian ethics were comfortable with it. Well, I've had to come to terms with my impending death. I'm not a rock star or a movie star being pulled out in the midst of a brilliant career. I've lived a life and done some good. I helped a wonderful woman raise two fine boys. And, God willing, when I'm through suffering through this hell of remissions and relapses, maybe I'll be with your mother again. I'd just like to have a sense that you're going to be okay before I go. Sean worries about you, too. Even he thinks you spend too much time writing, working on the boat, and teaching your Kung Fu and your swordsmanship. He thinks you should get out more. And now Tony's about to have you risking life and limb against monsters."

"And that's the life you want me to drag Carrie into?"

Will sighed. "Maybe you can keep it away from her. Maybe she can handle it and be supportive. Maybe you should give her enough of a chance to let her decide."

"Did I mention I'm taking her to dinner Saturday night?" Mike asked. "Dad, you're preaching to the choir again."

Will chuckled and gripped his son's hand.

"How often are you on oxygen?" Mike asked.

Will looked caught off guard. "Oxygen?"

"Yeah, Dad," Mike retaliated, "oxygen. You know, that big steel tank in the corner—the one with the cloth covering it? Care to guess how many times I've thrown a towel over a scuba tank to keep the sun off it? Don't you think I'd recognize an oxygen tank?"

"Oh, that." He tried to sound nonchalant. "I don't know—a little here and there, sometimes at night." He shrugged.

"Or whenever I'm not around?" Mike suggested.

"Get out of here, Mike. She's three doors down on the left. And you don't need to rush out here every day or even every second day. If your days get crazy, even a phone call helps."

Mike hugged him.

He found Carrie just as Will described.

"You two finished?" Her smile was just a step away from laughter. Mike couldn't help but grin, in spite of the tears he'd been fighting inside.

"When we were kids, he kept a dead horse in the backyard just so he could go out there and beat on it regularly," he quipped

That brought full, rich laughter out of her. Her eyes sparkled like emeralds. Mike felt the same weak feeling in this stomach that she'd caused the night before.

"I'll wait for you to finish, if you have time to walk me out."

Carrie looked at the resident she was tending, who replied, "I'm fine and he's too cute to let get away. Walk him out, then give me my meds. Ellen can help me get a bath after."

"Thanks, Annie," Carrie whispered.

The lady in the chair by the other bed grinned and gave Carrie a thumbs-up.

Carrie was chuckling when she joined Mike for the walk down the hall. "Your father means well. I probably told him too much about what was happening with me when Mr. Asshole left. I know I shouldn't have, but your dad is just so easy to talk to. Sometimes I'd open up about painful details before I even knew I was about to."

Mike nodded. "He's good. He was a hell of an interrogator. As a kid, I'd go through experiences that I didn't want to have to explain to my parents—you know how that is. Well, he'd catch a look on my face. I'd be determined to keep it all in but next thing I knew he'd open me up like a can of sardines."

Carrie nodded. She held onto his arm with both hands, then, becoming aware of watching eyes, let go.

Mike smiled. "Can't get away with much in here, can you? It must be a haven for gossip—all these poor people with limited mobility, waiting for someone to visit—too easy to find the life you're lacking in the lives of others."

"You put that well. I must read some of your work some time. I bet you're good."

Mike shrugged.

They'd reached the doors to the stairs. Mike gave her a quick kiss on the forehead.

"I'm looking forward to Saturday, but I'm hoping to see you before then. I need to see Dad as much as I can. I don't have much faith in remissions."

Carrie glanced to see if anyone was watching, then launched up on her toes and gave him a quick kiss on the lips.

"Bye," she whispered, then rushed off.

Sam met him at the door, butt wagging, huffing for attention.

"Hey, bear," Mike greeted, rubbing his head. "Nigel still here?"

"Right 'ere, gov," the cockney called from the dining room. "Still at it, but I got a bit o' news for you an' 'Is Lordship. Sean got 'ome a few minutes ago. Someffin' about quadrant equations or someffin.' Lot's of 'omework, I guess, but no worries. Says 'e'll be done PDQ."

Mike smiled. "Quadratic equations—he's in advanced algebra," Mike explained. "He can do math in his sleep."

"Ya," Nigel replied, "'e said someffin' like that—says 'e gets it from you."

"So what did you find out?" Mike asked, ignoring the secondhand compliment.

"Got one address—it's an 'ouse in 'Alifax, not far from the Angus L. MacDonald Bridge, 'bout a block up. It was just bought by a Gregor Chernov. I checked the Interpol Database. Seems our mate Vladimir 'ad a kid brother named Gregor. I say that's too much of a coincidence. From wot we know of Chernov, 'e's a nasty one, an' most likely yer Jack the Ripper wot did the ol' man and young woman at the same time. 'E's the leader. Might even 'ave made the others."

Mike nodded as he took it all in. "So we check out that address tonight?"

"More likely close to dawn, knowing 'ow 'Is Lordship works."

"Tell me something," Mike said, "Did Tony come right out and tell you he's a vampire? Did he tell you his story."

"Naw, 'e's too private for any o' that, isn't 'e? Gave me a yarn 'bout catchin' some rare tropical fever while stationed in 'Ong Kong wiff MI6. Says 'e got over it but was left wiff a painful sensitivity to sunlight an' 'as to keep to a strict diet. Well, 'e's a wiry one but 'e ain't no Arnold Schwarzenegger, is 'e, yet 'e can rip a door off its 'inges wiff his bare hands—I seen 'im do it. Sleeps all day, never seen 'im eat—you don't 'ave to be a bloody Einstein to put it together. I play along, but I figure, whatever changes 'em just makes 'em more o' wot they were before. 'E's a good guy and these others were nasty blokes from the start, 'at's 'ow I sees it."

Mike nodded. *So he never told Nigel the truth about himself, he only told me. Why do I find that comforting?*

"Well," he said, "I need to throw something together for supper—feed the boy before we head over to Tony's"

"Wot, no Kung Fu classes tonight?"

Mike shook his head. "Sean's in charge tonight. I teach Monday, Wednesday, and Friday, 6:00 'til 7:30. Sean, Johnny, and Frank his fellow brown belts, teach a ladies' self-defense class Tuesday and Thursday evenings for an hour."

"Great, that means I don't need to call a taxi and figure my way to 'Is Lordship's place."

"Do you always call him that? You never refer to him by name."

"Well, it's a Brit thing, isn't it? I mean, 'e's a real English Lord an' I'm a commoner—an bein' cockney is about as common as you can get back 'ome, less'n maybe yer Irish. Just comes naturally, don't it. Started as kind of a bit o' sarcasm from me at first, but now it's more out o' respect than anyffing else. Oh, that reminds me—got someffin' for you. Just a minute."

Attached to his duffle was an architect's tube, the kind designed to hold blueprints. He untied it and passed it to Mike.

"'Ad fun slippin' that through customs. Thought I'd need to use my Interpol Credentials and some sweet talk, but they never even checked me bags. 'Course, when I told Immigration I was 'ere on business as a special assistant to an Interpol agent, they probably gave me a free pass through customs. Never get through that fast at 'ome. 'Course some o' them know me well enough to check me twice, don't they?

"Anyway, 'Is Lordship 'ad some bloke named Paul Chen make the main bit, an' another bloke in London who specializes is this stuff did the rest. I talked wiff 'Is Lordship just before you came in. 'E said to give it to you before we came over, ravver than wait 'til we got there."

Mike just held the tube in his hands listening to all of this. As he turned his attention to opening it, he had an idea what to expect and was not surprised. Almost anyone involved with swordsmanship knew who Paul Chen was—one of the two most renowned makers of combat blades, made the way they had been made two hundred years ago. Sitting in a rack on his piano was a katana made by the other current master. In his bedroom was a Muramasa blade from the the early fifteen hundreds. He broke the seal, slipped the cap off the end, and pulled out a long object in a blue silk sleeve. He untied the tie that held the end of the sleeve folded over and slid the object out. It looked like an expensive walking stick, thirty-eight inches long, with a long handle—more like an elabourate hiking stick than a walking stick, he corrected himself. He tapped the shaft against his palm—no rattle—then pulled on the handle—no give. He gave the handle a quarter twist, then pulled, and a polished straight blade came free. It was straight like a ninjato or ninja blade, but the length of a katana.

"Well," he commented with a frown, "at least I don't have to figure out how to carry a katana without drawing attention—not that this will be inconspicuous. Hopefully I'll just look a bit eccentric. Still, drawing this will be a lot easier than freeing a katana from a sleeve and drawing it. No matter what kind of permit I have, I can't just go around carrying a katana in public. Still, I wish the blade was curved."

# 11: Revelation

Mike rang Tony's doorbell and waited, Nigel just behind him. "I brought you a house guest," he said to Tony when the door opened.

Tony smiled and extended his hand to Nigel. "Good to see you, old boy. Smooth flight?"

"Smooth enough, gov'nor," Nigel commented. "Still, bit o' gold watch'll take the edge off any grit, eh?"

Tony's smile became a grin. "You'll find a bottle of Glenlivet on the counter in the kitchen. Pour Michael a glass, as well. I've a feeling he might feel need of it before we're done."

Mike eyed Tony. "You have something new?"

Tony's face sobered. "Your father's deeply concerned, concerned enough to call me and, shall we say, make sure you keep a promise you made."

Mike let out a sigh. "I guess there's no escaping it. Do you think you can get to the bottom of these dreams?"

"Only time will tell, but I've had a few centuries to read, and psychology is a special interest, as you might imagine. And of course hypnotism is a trait that develops with my condition." He'd kept his voice down.

"You can speak normally," Mike said. "Nigel never bought the tropical fever story. He's had you figured out for quite some time."

Tony gave a slow nod. "I suspected as much. Well, I suppose it simplifies things a bit—one less pretense to maintain." He paused, looking Mike over. "Nice outfit. And I see you're carrying my little present."

Mike was wearing a stylish black trench coat with over flaps at the shoulder, a bit like the over-cape look of similar Victorian garments, and a heavy felt western drover's hat with a woven leather band.

"The designer's Australian," Mike said. "It's a trench coat styled after a drover's coat. I figured with my fancy new hiking stick I needed to go for a look that says, 'This guy's a bit eccentric.'"

Tony chuckled. "You tease me about looking like The Shadow. You look like Hugh Jackman in *Van Helsing*. Still, it works with the sword cane."

"I could probably conceal my *Muramasa* katana under the coat. I might be more at home with it than the cane. I'm not used to a straight blade."

Tony nodded and shrugged. "Whatever you're comfortable with, Michael. Driving your car with a katana under your coat might be awkward."

Nigel returned with two scotches, one neat, Mike's with water.

"I gather you know the truth of my condition." Tony watch for Nigel's reaction.

The cockney just nodded. "Well, it's just a case o' puttin' two an' two together, isn't it? Besides, we been workin' together for, whot—fifteen years now? Yer obviously one o' the good guys, ain't you? An' I been helpin' you weed out the bad ones." He shrugged.

Tony placed a hand on Nigel's shoulder. He said nothing but the look in his eyes spoke of trust and affection.

"I gather you have an address for us."

Nigel nodded. "I'm still working on others, but it's a start. Like I told you on the phone, it's an 'ouse in 'is brovver's name. Actually, it's like a set o' flats. I don't know 'bout these geezers over 'ere but, for a Londoner, it's walkin' distance from the last crime scene."

"You're shaking your head, Michael. What's the problem?"

"It's a decoy, maybe even a trap. The guy who attacked me last Saturday was a thug. He was strong, fast, and good with a knife, but that's all he was. As my American friends would say, he was just muscle, all his brains were in his biceps. But Chernov is different—he was KGB. Those guys were the FBI and CIA rolled into one. They didn't hire stupid people. He needs to hide his sanctuary. He's not going to use his own last name, even if he's convinced we know nothing about him. He'd have fake ID in a new name."

Tony nodded. "I agree. Interpol sent me what they have on him. He was low level, but he was no enforcer. He was an investigator on an organized crime task force. That's how he got connected with the Russian Mafia. He went dirty while he was still KGB—drugs."

"So we let the flatfoots checkout this place while we keep lookin' for the real deal, right?" Nigel suggested.

Tony shook his head. "No, Nigel, I don't think that's a good idea. If he's set a trap, I think we might be better prepared to find it, you better prepared to deal with any elabourate surprises he may have concocted. The police might get injured unnecessarily."

"Ya, but they get paid to get injured unnecessarily. Better them than me, I say."

"Sorry, Nigel. We're going. First, though, I have to help Michael with a personal matter. In the meantime, I'd appreciate it if you could check my computer. I told you about the attack on Michael Saturday evening. Michael suggested that my e-mails may have been compromised."

Nigel nodded. "Simple enough to check for. I'll start wiff a sweep for spyware. Where can I stow me stuff?"

"Oh, yes—upstairs, second door on the left."

With a nod, Nigel left.

Michael sat in a winged back chair and sipped his scotch. Tony pulled up a chair opposite him and smiled. "Relax, Michael. This is far easier than you might think. First, we'll just start with the event that your father believes triggered all of this—you were eighteen?"

Michael nodded.

Tony fixed his gaze on Michael. The eyes glowed red, as if engorged with blood. Michael felt like he was sinking in warm water. "Don't fight it, Michael. We'll practice fighting it later. For now, it will help you better if you just let go and float.

"Now, let's go back to that night. The cinema has ended. You're walking along Water Street. It's a warm summer night."

*He is headed for the ferry terminal. Lots of time before the last ferry to Dartmouth. A man steps out of an alley. There's a click—switchblade knife. No warning. The knife slashes at his gut. Instinct. Skip backward, lean the chest forward, suck the gut in away from the blade.*

*Good, but not enough. He feels heat and pain, wetness—blood welling from a cut. The knife hand returns, backhand. He blocks, crane-style, grips the wrist, twists, jerks hard. He pivots and drives a snap-sidekick into the ribs, pulling on the wrist at the same time, driving his left palm into the elbow. There's a scream—ribs shatter, wrist and elbow are broken.*

*The kicking foot comes back just enough to slam a high roundhouse into the side of the head. Another crack—jaw and skull. The shoulder dislocates just before the wrist is torn from Mike's grip by the impact of his foot. The attacker begins to collapse.*

*Two rapid thrust punches to the chest drive any remaining air from the lungs, and drive broken ribs inward. Mike spins. His heel impacts on the attacker's head as he goes down.*

*Mike stares down. Blood wells from the attacker's mouth, nose, and ears. The eyes stare at him. The chest seems still. Mike runs to the ferry terminal.*

"Very good, Michael. Take a deep breath. We're now back in my parlour. You're calm. Take a sip of scotch."

Mike looked at the glass in his hand, then set it on the little side table without drinking.

"I sort of knew from the injuries what I must have done—broken wrist and elbow, dislocated shoulder, broken jaw and fracturing of the parietal and mastoid bones, ruptured spleen, broken ribs, and a punctured lung from a rib shard. Once you know the damage, based your more instinctive moves, it's easy to picture what you must have done. But now I know for sure. Seeing him lying there, I thought I'd killed him. I panicked and ran. I was still a kid, really. I guess he must have started breathing again soon after I left. The guy had a rap sheet the size of the Sears catalogue. Dad fixed it so that I just had to sign a statement. The guy had two months in hospital, then back to Dorchester. I guess a few years later he got killed in a fight there.

"Anyway, that night the nightmares started. First I was looking down at the guy—reality—then I was in feudal samurai armour looking at a hacked up body, also a samurai. Actually, the correct term is *bushi*—warrior. Samurai was a term used by others jealous of the power of the warrior nobility. It roughly means 'servant.'"

Tony nodded. "Let us now take a look at these dreams and visions, shall we?"

Mike hesitated, then sighed and nodded. He took a sip of scotch. "Let's get this over with."

"Now, Michael, I want you to relax. We're going to go back in time. I want you to slowly take yourself backward, back through your youth, back to your birth, and now back before that. You have lived before. One of these lives involves a scene from your nightmares. We're going to go back to this life, this time in history, but only if it really happened. Can you find this life? Can you find this time?"

Mike slowly nodded.

"Now, Michael, lets find a time where you feel comfortable. There is a memory where you feel very safe in this life. You are happy. Let's find that. Any dates you use will be in the western calendar."

"It's 1683. I'm fifteen years old. My father is a daimyo under shogun Tokugawa Tsunayoshi. We're not rich, but we have a long and proud military tradition. Others have fought less but fattened on the spoils of war, fighting only where they could loot from powerful nobles who fell into disfavour. But we Tomomatsu turned any spoils we found over to the shoguns—Ieyasu, his son Hidetada, his grandson Iemitsu, great-grandson Ietsuna, and now his great-great-grandson Tsunayoshi." Mike's voice sounded like a young boy's in his ears, but that was okay. He was only fifteen.

"My name is Yakura."

"*Domo,*" said Tony. (Thank you.)

Mike nodded. "*Do itashimashité.*" (You're welcome.)

"*Wakarimasu ka, Yakura-san?*" asked Tony. (Do you understand?)

"*Hai, wakarimasu.*" (Yes, I understand.)

"What are you doing?"

*He is practicing the art of kenjutsu with his aging teacher, a master of the famed Yagyu school and a student of the teachings of the legendary Miyamoto Musashi. He'd been reading aloud to his master from The Wind Scroll, the fourth of five parts making up Musashi's "Book of Five Rings."*

*His speech falters and his master rebukes his lack of concentration*

*"But, Master, there's a girl in the tree behind you," he whispers.*

*"And she's been there for ten minutes, watching us, watching you, mostly. Now finish the passage."*

*Yakura focuses and finishes the remaining page.*

*Master Yagyu leaves and Master Chen enters, an elderly Chinese monk dressed in a sleeveless robe of saffron yellow, the badge of the southern Shaolin or Sil-Lum. He carries a bokken—a wooden sword. He takes a prepared stance and gestures for Yakura to draw his katana.*

*The monk advances with rapid chopping blows, but Yakura doesn't retreat. He responds with a series of parries and counters reminiscent of crane style Kung Fu, his katana merely an extension of his arm.*

*"Excellent! Now show me what venerable Yagyu has been teaching you with your katana today."*

*Yakura advances on him. The priest moves smoothly and easily, countering all of his moves quickly and effortlessly.*

*Yakura stops and ponders. "That was like the back of the hand crane wing block followed by the tiger palm thrust," he says.*

*The monk nods. "Let your mind flow and adapt. The sword is just an extension of your arm. All the techniques of the Sil-Lum can be adapted. There are many possibilities. You are already demonstrating adaptations that master Yagyu has yet to explore. With this broader base, few will be able to surprise you with their tricks, yet you will have natural responses that extend far outside the traditional boundaries they have set upon themselves."*

"But master Yagyu's ancestor knew the great Musashi Miyamoto!"

"Ah, the great innovator. Yes, he developed many new and unorthodox ideas. But there are still ideas that even he never explored. Just as there must be ideas that my masters never pondered in their far away temples. As you practice and meditate, you will come up with your own innovations. Already I have seen a few, just from how you adapt the Shaolin system to your own body and it's natural preferences."

There is a sudden crashing of branches and a young girl of ten or eleven drops to the ground. Yakura rushes over as she scrambles to her feet in embarrassment, eager to recover before he can assist.

"Are you hurt?" he asks, anxiety evident in his voice.

"No," she insists. Her pride tries to mask her embarrassment with bravado.

"You were in the tree watching my lessons with Master Yagyu, and now with Master Chen."

Her eyes drop in the shy modest fashion expected of her, but only for a moment. They snap back to face him. "Yes," she confirms. She braces herself as if expecting a lecture about the horror of a young lady, daughter of a daimyo, shaming her family, related to the shogun's, by being in a tree.

"That cherry tree is old," Yakura says, his eyebrows lifting, his expression imitating the wise and conspiratorial look his grandfather often used with him when advising him on something he knew Yakura's parents would not approve of. "You must avoid the *outer branches and stay closer to the stem. With an old tree whose limbs are becoming dry and more brittle, the outer lengths of the branches will not hold even your delicate weight."*

*She smiles at him warmly, giving a slight bow. "You fight well, better that any I've seen." Her eyes take on a teasing look. "Yet the old grandfather of China still bests you."*

*Yakura smiles. "Just as he would best any bushi. If Master Yagyu were to attack Master Chen with his katana, Master Chen, unarmed, would take the katana away from him." He drops his voice to a whisper. "And if his humour was greater than his respect, he might spank him with the side of the blade in doing so."*

*The girl went wide-eyed.*

*"Now, Akiko, you must return before your mother finds you missing."*

*"You know my name."*

*"Just as you know mine," he says with a smile.*

*Glancing anxiously at the limbs of the tree that lean over the wall well above her head, she looks worried. "But how?"*

*Gripping her hips from behind, he cautions, "Keep your back straight and reach up." He takes a slow, deep breath and blows it out through compressed lips as he lifts her off the ground until his arms are straight. As soon as she has a grip on a branch, he shifts his grip to her knees, lifting her higher as she pulls with her arms, until she is securely in the tree. Moments later she starts to climb down on her side of the wall.*

*"Tomorrow, Yakura," she says with a bold, sweet smile. "I'll be watching you."*

*"She is a bold girl to defy tradition," Master Chen says, finally approaching Yakura. "She has great courage. Who is she?"*

*"She is daughter to a second or third cousin of the shogun. And someday she is to be my wife. Our parents have arranged it."*

Mike paused in his narration. He just wanted to dwell there for a moment, lingering, enjoying the warm emotions inspired by what he'd just experienced.

"We'll stay in this time period, Yakura," Tony's voice said. "We'll pause, rest if you will, then move ahead to some important events. There is someone from this life who causes you trouble. Is he present in your life at this time?"

"Hai," Mike replies. (Yes.)

"What is he doing."

"He struts up and down the street, mostly before Akiko's home. He has a bokken in his sash, as do his companions. He is a show-off and a bully, but he never walks alone. Always his companions follow him. They are sons of warriors who serve his father. He likes to frighten younger children and the elderly. He brandishes his bokken but he has no style. He is like a herder waving a stick. Clearly he does not apply himself to his studies. He is too proud. He is a Toda."

"Toda, is that his family name?"

"Yes—Toda Yoshihiro. His home is on the next street. It is not his real home—none of these are our real homes. It is the shogun's law that every noble must maintain a home in Edo, where his wife and children live. We are informal hostages to the Tokugawa to insure the loyalty of our fathers."

Tony waited a few minutes, then said, "Now, Yakura, there is a terrible event in your life that is causing nightmare's in Michael's. I need you to tell me about this. Can you do that?"

Mike realized that his voice was older when he answered. Of course it was. *He* was older. He was twenty-one.

"What year is it, Yakura?"

"It's 1689. I am twenty-one."

"Is this event related to Akiko?"

"Yes." Mike spoke through clenched teeth, fighting the urge to sob. "He killed her. He murdered her and tried to make it look like *sepuku*."

"Who killed her?"

"Yoshihiro," he hissed.

"Tell me about it. Take your time."

"Akiko had told me how the haughty and vain Todo Yoshihiro had been trying to force his suit upon her, going so far as to threaten me, her betrothed. She continued to reject Yoshihiro's advances but he became more determined. He felt his honour was being insulted by her refusal. He couldn't distinguish honour from vanity and pride. Our families having betrothed us meant nothing to him. He thought his father should be shogun. There were rumours that he and his friends were plotting to assassinate Tsunayoshi to accomplish this very thing.

"On this particular day, I was to meet her in her garden."

*As he reins his horse before her Edo home, he knows something is wrong. He opens the doors and goes straight through to the garden. There she lies, her mother sobbing next to her, servants all about.*

*He tears off his* kabuto *helm and tosses it aside, rips at his* sode *upper arm shields until his arms are free, then collapses to his knees, taking the bleeding form into his arms. Weeping with great sobs, he tries to force her inner abdominal organs back inside her, but it's no use. She'd been cut with both a deep lateral slice and an upward stroke that bit into the bottom rib.*

*"Yoshihiro," she breathed finally as the light of life went out of her eyes.*

*Ignoring the pool of blood about him, drenching his* kobakama *and* shitagi *and staining the leather and iron armor that covered these, he continues to hold her, pouring out his grief and rage uncontrollably.*

*An older man runs up. He freezes, silent, then kneels next to Yakura.*

*"Why would she do this!" he wails. "She was happy! She spoke of nothing but your impending wedding, Yakura. Has she been dishonoured?" His grief was turning to anger.*

*"This is not sepuku," Yakura hisses. "Look!" Easing her body down, he points to the chip on the bottom surface of her rib where the blade had struck. "Few strong samurai can perform the upward cut with such force! This was done by another with a katana."*

*"But the* wakizashi *is here and it is bloodied. It is my fathers. I keep it here at the Edo residence."*

*"I could as easily dip a cryptomeria branch in her blood and lay it next to her. No. The rib says that the rest is a false story—a lie to hide a coward's act. She spoke his name with her last breath—Yoshihiro." He hisses the name as if it were an obscenity.*

*The older man's face falls. "It will mean war with the Toda."*

*"No," Yakura insists. "It will mean only death for Yoshihiro."*

*"But the shogun! It is not permitted."*

*He taps his katana, an expensive present from his father—an heirloom made by a master. "Yama Kaze will truly be a wind of justice. I shall speak to Tsunayoshi. He will either grant my boon or I shall be dishonoured. Either way, Yoshihiro dies."*

*Snatching up his* **kabuto** *and* sode, *he stalks out of the garden of the rear courtyard. When he reaches his horse, he tears the reins loose with his bloodied hands and, mounting, dashes off at a wild gallop.*

"*These are difficult times, young Tomomatsu-san. There is much to consider. There is dishonour in this, but there is the risk of war in denouncing the Toda for the vile act of one Toda son." Tsunayoshi's voice is calm, but his eyes show stress and fear.*

"*And what of his treason to you, my shogun? In the drinking places, the sake makes him bold late at night. He and his friends quietly boast of a new shogun—a Toda shogun."*

*Tokugawa's eyes flash. "My prefect of police has unearthed some of this," he snarls. "It will be dealt with discretely."*

"*And if I challenge Yoshihiro to combat?"*

"*Dueling is outlawed and I have ordered you not to. Your family has been a great ally to my ancestors and I have great affection for you, Yoshihiro."*

*Yoshihiro feels uncomfortable. It is no secret that Tokugawa Tsunayoshi feels great affection toward many young men, even to dressing as a woman for the occasion but, while custom accepts this, Yakura has always been repelled by the thought.*

"*I cannot stop you, Yakura. I tolerate from you that which I would not tolerate from any other. Against an edict from my great-great-grandsire you carry an illegal blade. The silk you drape over the tsuka does not deceive me, yet I overlook this. But know, Yakura, that if you insist upon this action, you will have to atone to save your honour. Muramasas have killed many a Tokugawa. Yours may have to end the life of a Tomomatsu. Think well on this."*

*So the price of killing his enemy, the murderer of his Akiko, is his own death by sepuku.*

*It requires more than a day of hard riding to reach the Toda estates, far from Edo. Yakura is accompanied by a small armed group. It is obvious that Yoshihiro has seen their approach, for he rides out to meet them on the field before the castle, surrounded by his own escort.*

*"There is no need for our warriors to shed each other's blood today, Yoshihiro. This fight is between you and I, if you are man enough to face me in combat."*

*"Over a woman? Over breeding stock?"*

*Yakura feels his blood run cold. He slides from his saddle and draws his katana.*

*"What would a meat cutter like you know of breeding?" Those who handled dead flesh are forced to live apart from the rest of Japanese society. Yakura has chosen the most provoking insult he could give a bushi.*

*With a roar, Yoshihiro attacks, battering at him with a barrage of heaving strokes.*

*Yakura dodges and parries, waiting for the moment to feel right. He steps in, swings a parrying stroke, carrying the other sword to the side, then cuts down. His blade slices through the connecting straps of sode, the upper arm guards, biting deep into the biceps.*

*As Yoshihiro gasps in shock, Yakura repeats the move on the other arm.*

*Yoshihiro's eyes widen in pain and rage. With a roar, Yoshihiro attacks wildly, his technique now limited by the pain and flowing blood.*

*Yakura parries again, his blade lunging in and cutting the straps of the upper leg armour. Left leg, then right. He feints toward the left leg again, then wheels a full circle. The blade comes down, almost completely severing the left arm, then flicks across Yoshihiro's throat, leaving behind a thin line of welling blood.*

*Yoshihiro is foundering, weak from the massive flow of blood at his shoulder. His eyes now show a mix of fear and desperation.*

*Yakura whirls again. His blade bites deep into the upper thigh, all but severing this limb. Tears of anger fill his eyes as he wrenches his katana free. Before Yoshihiro can collapse to the ground, he sweeps his blade in again with all his might. There's a hush as Yoshihiro's head falls to the ground.*

*He kneels in his father's garden, under the cherry tree that Akiko had fallen out of. Slowly he strips away his armour. He composes himself, drawing deep breaths. He feels oddly calm as he draws his wakizashi, the short sword.*

*Blood-red eyes pierce through the vision.* "That will be enough, Michael. It is Tuesday, January 29, 2008. You are in my parlour in Dartmouth, Nova Scotia. You are Michael Cameron. You are calm, but you remember everything that has happened."

Mike remained quiet, pondering all that he had seen. Much of it he had seen before in dreams and visions, but now it had context.

"I wonder if any of this can be confirmed," he murmured.

"Possibly," Tony replied. "Have you ever read anything by Laura Joh Rowland?"

Mike thought, then shook his head. "Never heard of her."

"A book called *Shinju?*"

Again Mike shook his head.

Tony nodded. "It's in a carton somewhere. I meant to send it to you and then packed it to give you in person. It takes place in feudal Japan during the year your Akiko was killed. Tokugawa Tsunayoshi appoints an out-of-favour samurai as police prefect for Edo. This samurai uncovers a plot to assassinate the shogun. When Tsunayoshi is attacked, he is parading through the streets, dressed as a woman. His warriors are prepared for the attack, and all the plotters are killed. Excuse me a moment."

He left, returning several minutes later with the book. Resuming his seat, he thumbed through the pages until he found something, then passed the book to Mike. There, staring up at Mike from the page, from a list of conspirators' names, was the name Toda Yoshihiro.

Mike looked at Tony. "Is there any way to contact the author and authenticate this? Is this documented or is it all fiction, including the names?"

Tony shrugged. "I can have some colleagues inquire. Perhaps they can contact her and ask. However, what we've learned explains a lot about you. You're an old soul, Michael. I've known it from the beginning. As a teenager you looked at me through something akin to an old man's eyes—eyes that had seen things before, eyes that carried the wisdom of past lives. Then there's your experiences with the martial arts. Whether Kung Fu or what you call Katana-Jutsu, whenever they taught you something new, you felt like you'd done it before, like some part of you already knew it. Then there's your sword style, very unique. You adapt your Kung Fu moves to the katana. You were taught to do that by a Shaolin monk, a Master Chen, in the late 1600s. You were taught your original swordsmanship by a renowned master of the Yagyu school.

"The traumatic attack of your late teens triggered initial memories of a violent episode in Yakura's life. The attack of Saturday night retriggered those memories. You are Yakura and Yakura is you. Of course, you are older, wiser, and more experienced than Yakura, but he does have unique experiences to offer. You mentioned in letters how some of these dreams showed up after your wife died. You saw Akiko in these dreams. The part of you that is Yakura wants to remind you that you have suffered great loss before. You wanted to die when Susan died, but Sean's needs kept you going. Yakura also wanted to keep going. He killed himself once and didn't want to do it again. Now that you must help in killing a great evil, he seeks to remind you that you have also done this before and can do so again."

Mike finished his scotch and stared at the floor, nodding his head slowly. "It all fits, makes sense in a Freudian sort of way," he conceded. "If the nightmares and visions stop repeating themselves, I'll know you're right. I mean, now that I'm aware of Yakura's story, no need to keep beating on that horse."

Tony smiled.

"All done 'ere, then?" Nigel appeared in the doorway. "Time for another gold watch, mate?"

Mike shook his head. "Thanks, but no—too much to think about."

"Yeah, I know wot that's like. Anyway, Your Lordship, your computer 'as a clean bill of 'ealth. No spyware, no hidden forwarding of e-mails, noffin.' Any leak of information lies elsewhere, as they say."

Tony nodded, then glanced at his watch. "Not even eight o'clock yet. I suggest we check out the address in Halifax. Ready, Nigel?"

Nigel nodded. "Yeah—I was gonna run a sweep o' the place, you know, checking for any kind o' electronic surveillance, but I guess I can do that later."

Tony glanced at Mike. Mike just nodded. Tony put a hand on his shoulder.

"It'll all fall into place. Give it time."

Mike tried to smile. "Some people have to deal with moving, settling into a new job, new house, new schools for the kids. Some get used to being divorced or widowed. In one week I'm adjusting to the existence of vampires, apparent proof of my own reincarnation, having killed a monster that's not supposed to exist, and finding that a life-long friend is a vampire. It strains the limits of credulity just a bit. I keep hoping I'm going to wake up, find I was dreaming, and have a good laugh."

Tony nodded. "Sorry, old man, but I'm afraid this is as real as it gets." He picked up Mike's sword stick and handed it to him.

The musical chiming of Mike's cell phone interrupted. He pulled it out. The caller and number were unidentified. He flipped it open and answered. A cold chill went through him. He closed the phone and put it away.

"That was SeaView. Dad's condition has deteriorated—he's coughing up blood. It's bad. I need to get over there."

Tony nodded. "Go take care of it. Nigel and I can do a reconnaissance of the address in Halifax. There's not likely to be anyone there now; we'll just look for evidence as to who resides there and wait until you can come with us before dealing with the place—perhaps around dawn."

# 12: Nasty Business

Mike felt numb. *Why now?* he thought. *Isn't there enough going on?* He took a deep breath and blew it out slowly. He knew this was coming, he'd just hoped there'd be more time.

Feeling under siege, he almost missed the turn onto Pleasant Street, the main artery to Eastern Passage. He spotted a police car at a Tim Horton's, checked his speed and eased up on the gas. Before long he was pulling into the SeaView parking lot.

He rushed out of the elevator, pushed past Nurse Barkhouse when she tried to intercept him, and hurried town the hall to his father's room. The door was open. He almost collided with Carrie coming out of the room.

"How is he?" Mike fought to keep the anxiety out of his tone, but it was hopeless.

Carrie looked puzzled. "Fine—I just brought him a cup of coffee." Dropping her voice to a whisper, she added, "It's decaf, but don't tell him that."

He moved into the room far enough to see William. His father was sitting in his bedside chair, sipping coffee and reading Mike's first book.

"Oh, hey, Mikey. I was just trying again to read this. I love the action, but these names—couldn't you have just name the wizards with handles like Charlie or Fred. I can't pronounce this guy here, and he's important."

Relief surged through Mike. "Alentius," he said, "A-lent'-yus. I'm thinking of shortening it by one syllable."

He noticed that the oxygen tank was no longer covered. The nose pieces rested on top, their long tube spilling down beside the tank. It looked like someone had just pulled the nose pieces out and set them on the tank.

His thoughts were interrupted as Nurse Barkhouse stormed in. Whatever tirade she might have launched was cut short. Mike moved closer, put a finger in her face, and snarled, "Don't start with me. I come and go as I please. Furthermore, I just had a call from a doctor here, telling me that my father had gone into severe bronchial spasms, coughing up blood, and that his condition had seriously deteriorated."

Barkhouse seemed in shock, staring at Mike's eyes. She took a step back and seemed about to gather nerve for a retaliation. Carrie cut her off.

"Doctor Taylor? She's not on this evening."

Mike shook his head. "This was a man's voice." He flipped his phone open and checked the last call. Name and number restricted.

"When Dad calls, SeaView Manor comes up on the screen. Caller ID isn't blocked."

Carrie nodded. "It's not blocked at the desk, either. It shows up at home. Sometimes they call to see if I'll take an extra shift. We can check the phone in Doctor Taylor's office. Your Dad's oncologist hasn't been in for two or three days. If the call wasn't from here, then it was a hoax—a cruel, nasty hoax."

"We can't just barge into..." Barkhouse began.

Carrie just smiled, her voice as sweet as always. "Well, Nell, this is important. I know Doctor Taylor would want to get to the bottom of it."

Mike flashed his new Interpol Liaison ID under Barkhouse's nose. "I can have a couple of detectives here in an hour, if you prefer that kind of interruption."

"No, no, that won't be necessary," Barkhouse stammered

"Need my cell number?" Mike asked Carrie.

Carrie just smiled and pulled his card from her pocket.

"Now, Mikey, why don't you come over here and sit a bit," Will said. "Did you talk to Tony like you promised?"

Mike sighed and sat with his father, phone in his hand.

"Yeah, Dad, he did his thing and, if you can believe what came of it, it answers a whole lot of questions, but it also opens a whole other can of worms."

He was about to go on when his phone rang. The screen said *SeaView Manor* and displayed the number. Mike closed the phone and wrestled with the implications.

"Someone wanted me here tonight..."

William was nodding. "… to keep you from being somewhere-else."

Mike nodded. "I need to catch up with Tony and Nigel."

William nodded. "Just give me the facts before you go."

Mike gave his father a condensed version of what he'd learned.

"Wow, Mikey, that's a lot to swallow. It explains everything, though—why it always seemed so easy to you—like you'd done it all before. Hell, Mikey, you did do it all before. It even explains your unorthodox sword style." He placed a hand on his son's, holding it there a moment. "It's a lot to take in. In just a week, your whole world has been rearranged and redefined. That takes getting used to. But you can't let it get in the way of staying sharp."

"Tell me about it!" Mike said.

His cell rang again. This time it said *home*. "Yeah, Sean," he said. "You got it turned off? You checked all the doors? Okay, call Dave across the street and have him come and help you check things out." Mike frowned and shook his head. "That's fine, just don't slip and burn the place down."

"What's up?" William asked.

Carrie came back in the room, a questioning look on her face.

"The plot thickens," Mike said. "Your call came up as *SeaView* and displayed the number," he told Carrie. "Sean just called. He got home from teaching a class and then the alarm went off at the house. He killed the alarm, then ADT called. None of the doors were opened. He's sitting guard now with a spare flare gun—there were two on the new boat, so I brought one home. Dave, across the street, used to be a cop. I told Sean to call him and have him help check things out, but I'd better check in there before going over to Halifax."

Carrie made a face. "You just got here and you're leaving."

"Yeah, life sucks sometimes."

At the elevator, she took his arm to turn him, checked to see no one was watching, then gave him a quick kiss. He returned it more slowly.

"I'm not watching," came a teasing comment from one of Carrie's co-workers, just arriving at the desk.

Mike felt troubled. He started his Cherokee and headed down Caldwell Road. The quickest way home was the winding trip down Caldwell, across Portland,

and down Dorothea. As he neared the light at the first intersection, a police car pulled out behind him. It maintained a fixed distance behind him for the next two miles until he reached a deserted stretch of winding road, then the flashers came on. Mike was puzzled. His speed was exactly to the limit and there was nothing wrong with his vehicle. He signaled, then pulled over onto the shoulder and killed the engine.

He watched the cop approaching in his wing mirror. The man's walk was a swagger. Mike lowered the side window as the cop approached. "What seems to be the problem, officer?" He asked.

"Both your rear lights are out."

The cop looked familiar.

"That's odd," Mike mused. "They were working fine a few minutes ago. I distinctly saw them light up the car behind me as I was backing out of the parking space."

The cop just grinned and walked to the rear of the car. He drew his short billy club and gave each rear light several backhand blows until the plastic lenses and bulbs shattered. "Well, they're broken now."

Mike got a cold feeling in his gut. This kind of nonsense only ever happened in movies. He wasn't sure what to do. He decided to play innocent and stay alert, ready to react. "Well, I promise to get them fixed first thing in the morning."

"License and registration." No 'please,' no courtesy, just chip-on-the-shoulder attitude.

"Sure." Mike reached into the glove compartment, pulled out the leather-sleeved book on the car, and extracted the registration and insurance slips, half expecting the cop to rip them up. The cop glanced at them, then passed them back.

"And the license."

Mike pulled his wallet from his back pocket and was starting to remove the license from its sleeve when the cop interrupted. His hand was out in a stopping gesture. "Leave it in place and pass me the wallet—slowly."

It was the hand gesture that let Mike place him—the cop who'd tried to stop him at the crime scene in Halifax a few nights ago—Jenkins. What was he doing driving patrol in Dartmouth? Asking for his wallet was a clear violation of procedure (as if breaking his tail lights wasn't.) They were trained to ask that the license be removed. Cops weren't allowed to handle a wallet.

Jenkins looked at the license in place, then began rifling through the other cards and ID. He removed the laminated card identifying Mike as a special liaison to Interpol and the local police. He glared at it before pocketing it, then pulled out the permit to carry concealed and unconcealed weapons. He tried to tear it but couldn't, so he dropped it on the pavement and ground it under his heel.

"Sir, I have reason to believe there are weapons in the car. Please step out of the vehicle." The cop had a sly grin. His right hand rested on his gun, the left pulled out a set of handcuffs.

Mike's mind raced. This could get dangerous. *Is it just harassment? Is he annoyed at a my involvement in police work? Was he put up to this by a resentful cop or detective involved in the case? Is this part of a set up to have me removed from the game the way I was set up that first night?* It felt like a cold hand gripping his gut. *Could this cop be working with one of the vampires? Could he be a vampire? Do I end this now or do I play it through? There can't be that many cops involved in this case. It can't be that hard to find out who this guy is helping out.* He decided not to let it go any further.

He eased the door open and stepped out.

"Turn and face the car."

Mike fixed his eyes on the cop's. "No."

"No?" Jenkins seemed torn between amusement and amazement. He placed a lot of confidence in the uniform and the Glock his hand was resting on.

"No," Mike repeated in a calm, level tone.

Jenkins pulled his gun and shoved it in Mike's face—just what he was waiting for.

Mike's right hand shot up, gripping the gun and fingers in a vice-like grip, wrenching to the right. His left palm drove into the cop's jaw. As the impact lifted Jenkins, Mike finished wrenching the gun out of the cop's hand. With Jenkins stunned by the blow, it was easy to spin about and slam the cop into the side of the car. Mike pocketed the Glock and cuffed Jenkins with his own handcuffs. He forcibly walked Jenkins back to his own car, retrieved his ID, then threw him onto the back seat. The car was still running. All he had to do was put it in gear and pull ahead fifty meters to where he could pull off the road, kill the engine, and kill the lights.

Returning to his own car, he opened his cell phone and called home. "Sean, is Dave there with you? Good. Put him on." The deep voice that came on the phone had a no-nonsense tone that put Mike at ease. "Dave, somebody is seriously trying to mess with me. I don't have all the details yet but it would really ease my worries if you could take Sean back to your place until I get home." Dave assured him it was no problem.

Mike thanked him, clicked off, then called Tony. The phone rang three times, then a recording kicked in. "The cell phone customer you have dialed is unavailable at this time."

The knot in Mike's gut tightened. What to do. This couldn't be just harassment. For a duty cop it was a career-ender if Mike reported this. Mike was too well-connected with the police for this to be brushed over. The fool wouldn't have done this unless he knew he was safe, that Mike would never report it.

He grabbed his sword and walked back to the police cruiser. Jenkins was glaring at him. Mike thought about it, then acted. He leaned his walking stick against the car. His hand shot out, slapping the cop. The shock in the cop's eyes said he never saw the blow coming.

"That's just to get your attention. Imagine what I'll do to get your cooperation. What was the next step—call someone?" No reply. Mike drew Jenkins Glock, pulled the magazine, all the time watching the cop's eyes. They bugged wide. Good. He thought Mike might shoot him. Mike ejected the chamber round, then tossed the gun and the mag on the floor of the front seat.

"You need toys like this, I don't. You need to remember who I am."

Mike's hand shot out again, two hard fingertips driving in under the cheekbone. The cop's eyes widened. Tears flowed. He opened his mouth to gasp but no sound came out.

"Hurts, doesn't it? It's hard to believe something can hurt that much. Of course, those nerves are protected by the cheekbone—usually. They don't get hit very often. Do you know there's a nerve plexus like that in almost every joint? Look."

He pressed in under the joint of the cop's jaw. This time there was a squeak, then more tears.

"Ready to answer? There must be over thirty spots like that all over the body, multiply by two—don't forget, you've got two cheekbones and two TM joints. We could be here all night." He drew his sword from the stick. "Or I could just get bored and start cutting things off. What's it going to be?"

Mike gave the cop's cheek a slap. He could see the relief in the man's face. The pain had eased. "I can put that pain right back—on both sides this time."

"There's a number I call on my cell phone."

Mike rummaged through the cop's pockets and found the phone. "What's the number?"

Jenkins sighed. "Press send and hold the phone to my mouth."

"Kamensky," the cop said into the phone.

"Dialing Kamensky," the phone replied. Mike heard a voice answer, then the cop said, "He's waiting for you, as planned." He then glanced up at Mike and nodded. Mike ended the call.

"He'll expect you to be cuffed and in the front seat of your car. I was to pull the battery connection so you couldn't use the horn to signal a passing car, not that there'd be many out here this time of night."

Mike nodded, then lashed out with a palm strike that walloped Jenkins's forehead between the eyes. The eyes crossed, then rolled shut, the head drooped to one side.

Mike hauled him out of the car and stuffed him in the trunk. He used the cop's shoelaces to tie his wrists and ankles, fastened the gun belt about his knees, then took the cop's trouser belt and pulled his elbows in together. Satisfied that he was secure, Mike cut the front of the uniform shirt and gagged him with it, then found the keys and removed the cuffs. He felt a certain righteous satisfaction as he slammed the trunk.

He walked back to his car, sat behind the wheel, and waited. *Who is Kamensky?* He'd heard the name recently. *Kamensky, nice of you to join us.* His mind flashed back on a scene at the police station, a detective arriving late at the briefing. Little about the man's appearance had registered on Mike. He'd been pale. *This is Nova Scotia and it's winter*, Mike thought. *Pale is the norm.*

It was cold. He wished he could run the car to keep warm, but it had to look like the battery was disconnected. Kamensky might arrive at any moment. He played with the handcuffs. He had to be wearing them, yet able to get out of them quickly. He was many things, but he was no Houdini. The spring-loaded latch where the ratcheted cuff arm passed through had a mild enough spring. He checked in the back of his car—yes, there was a roll of duct tape. He tore two thin strips and taped the latch back. A close inspection showed the tape but, at a glance, it wasn't very noticeable. He tried moving the ratcheted arm. It moved in and out easily. He could make it look like the cuffs were closed on his wrists, but a quick movement made them fall free.

One more touch—he opened the knife on his multi-tool and made a cut in the hairline above his left ear. He looked in the lighted makeup mirror over the visor. Good. There was enough of a trickle of blood for it to look like he'd been clubbed over the ear, possibly by a cop's handgun.

He was really beginning to feel cold when he saw lights in his rearview mirror. He adjusted the cuffs, positioned himself, and waited. The car drove past. *Shit! I don't need this. Come on, it's getting cold.*

New lights from ahead. The car slowed, made a U-turn, and pulled in behind him. The car was white, but unmarked. He recognized the pale detective from the briefing. As he neared the car, Mike shut his eyes down to relaxed slits. They looked shut, but he could see enough. His door opened. Kamensky pulled him out with a bit of a struggle—strong, but not the strength one expected of a vampire. He was breathing hard and, through his veiled eyelids Mike could see that the man was wild-eyed.

"Hey, wake up, buddy." Kamensky gave him a shake.

Mike let his head roll around, opening his eyes a bit more.

"Hey!" Kamensky was right in his face. The breath was foul, and there were the teeth—fangs but not fully developed.

*Shit, this guy really is a vampire!*

Mike jerked his hands free of the cuffs. His right hand came over the top, grabbing Kamensky's right wrist. His left palm drove into the elbow, forcing the arm up and around, slamming the vampire into the side of the car, the arm now behind his back. Mike made sure Kamensky's face hit the edge of the roof. He drove his left fist into Kamensky's lower spine, then walloped him in the base of the skull with a palm, slamming his face back into the roof. As the vampire dropped to the pavement, Mike snatched up the cuffs. He fumbled with them until he tore the duct tape free, then cuffed Kamensky's hands behind his back.

"Now, what to do with you?"

He popped the back and threw him in, covering him with a blanket. Starting the car, he took off, turned left at the next corner, and headed for Halifax.

On the way he called Sean's cell phone. "Everything okay there?"

"Yeah, Dad, everything's fine. Dave's here. We're almost done checking over the house. Want to talk to him?"

"No, that's okay. I'll talk to him later. Take Sam and go over to his house."

He could hear the teenage attitude in Sean's sigh. "Why?"

"Sean, just do it, please."

As he pulled up outside the address Nigel had come up with, his gut told him something was wrong. The house was in total darkness except for the garish light from North Street. He grabbed the sword from the seat beside him and glanced in the back. Kamensky had started thrashing about as they were crossing the MacDonald Bridge, but the cuffs held him. *Odd,* Mike thought, *I was sure a vampire could break handcuffs. Both the shaolin master in Hunan and the tulku in Tibet suggested that I could probably rally enough chi to break them. So why can't this guy?* His own logic told him. *The guy's new—he was changed recently. It takes time for all the changes to occur. It's not like the movies.* Kamensky was a lean man, lightly built. He hadn't been very imposing as a human. It might be years before vampire strength became very impressive in him. The thought made him relax a bit.

Now, what about Tony and Nigel?

Gripping the walking stick tightly, he approached the house and checked the front door. It was unlocked—Nigel had probably picked it. Inside, he found a corridor to two small apartments and a stair going up. Instinct drew him upward. He checked his phone—no signal. *Odd—is there a jamming device in the place?* He nodded to himself. *The place is a trap. So, now that you know that, don't get trapped.*

He drew his blade, reversing it so that the blade ran up the back of his arm, arm slightly out from his side. The cane/scabbard was in his left hand, angled in front of him in guard position as he slowly ascended the stairs. He stayed to one side, against the rail. He was in shadow and the stair treads wouldn't creak. At the top, the stairs turned onto a broad landing before a single door. The entire second floor was one apartment.

*So far, so good*, he thought, then examined the door. Nothing out of the ordinary. He tried the knob. It wasn't locked. Turning it gently, he eased the door open a bit at a time, then stepped inside, assuming a combat stance.

"Blimey! Fank God yer 'ere!"

Nigel's voice came from the living room, beyond an iron grate.

"No one else here?" Mike asked.

"No, just us, an' we're in a bad way 'ere. 'Is Lordship is in serious Barney, and there's a tickin' in the walls wot's got me nerves on a ragged edge. I fink the 'ole place is wired to blow, I jus' don't know when."

"What about Tony?"

"'E's bad and not gettin' any better while we're talkin.' We need to get this bloody cage open."

Mike nodded and examined the bars and the wall around them. There was an slot at the top and grooves in the side of the door frame. The bars had dropped from the top, presumably an attic above. There was no hint of a mechanism for raising them.

He sheathed his sword, set it by the door, grabbed the bars, and heaved. "Help me," he said to Nigel. He gripped the bars, focused, let himself relax completely, then power breathed, his legs, back, and arms slowly surging upward. Nigel grunted and groaned, heaving with him.

"It's no use, mate. When it fell, it latched into place somehow."

"What about that window?"

"No good, mate—heavy bars bolted on the outside."

"So what we need is a new door."

"A what?"

Mike unsheathed his blade and drove it through the wall a foot away from the door.

"Jeeze! Give a guy a warning!"

"Good," he said, ignoring Nigel. "It looks renovated. I was hoping this was drywall and not wooden laths with plaster." He pulled the blade, then cut downward through the outer layer, then across the top until he hit a two-by-four. Grabbing the drywall, he tore it away. He drew back, then brought his fist down with a sharp exhalation, smashing through a cross-stud, then tore the pieces free. He used his sword to cut across the top and down one side of the other layer of drywall. A rough wooden stake, over a foot long, was imbedded in the wallboard. "What's with this?" he asked.

"You'll see in a minute, an' it ain't a pretty sight," Nigel replied.

Mike struck repeatedly with his palm until he'd smashed the inner layer away, creating a narrow opening. Amid the rubble was a small magnesium flare, one end torn off and covered with tape. Hanging from the hole in the wall was a wire with a small detonating cap attached."

"It's a tight fit, but it's a door," he said. He squeezed through, then ran to where Tony lay on the floor. "Jesus, Tony!"

"It would appear that someone knew exactly how to incapacitate me." Tony's voice was a whisper. He lay on the floor in a pool of blood. Three wooden stakes were buried in his chest, one in his right leg, one in his left arm.

"There's a big pressure plate in 'e middle o' the floor," Nigel said. "I was lucky enough to be off to one side when 'Is Lordship stepped on it." He gestured to the wall Mike had made a hole in. There were almost a dozen stakes imbedded in the wall, most about chest-height. On the opposite wall was the launcher.

"We need to get him out of here," Mike urged. "You get the other arm."

He got one of Tony's arms about his neck and heaved him to his feet. Tony let out a weak groan.

"Sorry, old man," Mike imitated Tony's accent. "Got to be done. Stiff upper lip and all that. Nigel, once we're out, you can take his legs and we'll carry him that way. I hate to squeeze him through with the stakes in place, but he'll bleed to death if we take them out—at least a human would."

Nigel nodded. "I can't budge 'em. I tried. I fink he'd close up wiff 'em out, but 'e needs blood to 'eal."

Getting Tony through the aperture wasn't easy, but they managed. Once outside, they got him settled in the back seat. "Keep an eye on our guest in the back. If he gives you any trouble, cut his head off." He handed Nigel his sword.

"Guest? Wot guest? Hey, where ya goin'?"

But Mike was running back into the building. He pounded on the lower apartment doors. A European man in need of a shave appeared, looking like he'd been awakened. Mike told him there was a bomb upstairs, warning him to evacuate. He gave a similar warning next door, advising them to call 911 and report it, then did the same on the other side. Satisfied at the stir he'd created, he got in the car, started the motor, and set out for the bridge. He'd was barely a door away when he heard a dull *wumph* from the building they'd just left. He picked his bluetooth earpiece out of the cup holder, triggered it, and called MacDonald.

# 13: Cleanup

"Jesus, Mike!" MacDonald exclaimed. "Did you clear the area?"

"As best I could," Mike said. "It just went off but I haven't time to go back and check. Tony's hurt and I need to get him medical attention. And, Pete,–" He told him about Jenkins and Kamensky. Pete went silent, as if in shock. Mike stopped, lowered his window, and tossed three quarters into the fare basket on the Dartmouth side of the bridge. "You still there, Pete?" he said as the barrier rail lifted.

"Yeah, Mike. Sorry, that was a bit of a shock. Damn. Okay. I'll send a car to get Jenkins. I'll have his sorry ass up on charges first thing in the morning. Shit! What are we going to do with Kamensky?"

"Well, I have some questions I plan to ask him," Mike said. "Other than that, I have a very sharp sword and I'm not afraid to use it. This clown was all set to kill me tonight, and Jenkins set me up for it."

"Oh, trust me, Mike, Jenkins's charges will include conspiracy to commit murder. Any thoughts on how they knew what you guys were planning tonight?"

"It was all planned out in advance, Pete. There was a script and all our movements were directed."

"Yeah, Mike, I get that, but I think it all hinged on going to that house in Halifax tonight. How would they know you were going there? I didn't even know about the place."

Mike thought about it. "I'll get back to you."

"Okay. I'll get wheels in motion and be there as soon as I can. Where will you be?"

"Tony's place on Hawthorne."

He glanced at Tony, who looked ashen grey, huddled in the back seat next to Nigel.

"Do you have blood at home?" he asked. He thought he caught a weak nod.

"Yeah," Nigel confirmed.

"Enough?" Mike asked.

"O+," Tony breathed, "as recommended." He flashed Mike a weak smile.

"Ya know," Nigel commented, "I wouldn't wanna be the inspector's wife, gettin' calls at all hours o' the night, an' 'avin' 'im just up an' out the door."

Mike shook his head. "MacDonald's wife left him when I was still a kid in Sydney. I remember my mother commenting on how it took a special kind of woman to be a detective's wife."

Minutes later they pulled into Tony's drive. Mike draped a blanket about Tony, then he and Nigel carried him in. They returned to the car with the blanket.

Nigel stared at the vampire, Kamensky, who glared back at them. "'E don't look too cooperative," he commented.

Mike's right palm shot out, landing between Kamensky's eyes. Kamensky slumped, inert. "Now he's cooperative," Mike grunted.

Once inside, Mike dumped Kamensky on a couch. Nigel watched Kamensky, sword in hand, while Mike ministered to Tony.

"Where do you keep your blood?" he asked.

"Refrigerator," Tony whispered.

"Can you take it cold or does it need warming."

"Need one now—cold. Warm next one," Tony managed to sigh.

Mike nodded. He found over a dozen flat half-litre pouches in a box in the fridge. There were similar boxes stacked to the back where it was colder. Plugging the sink, he dumped the lot, ran the hot water, then took a cold pouch back to Tony. Tearing the pouch open, he put the tube end to Tony's lips. The vampire's fangs were longer than he'd ever seen, no doubt triggered by the desperate situation. He was nearing the point where he might kill to survive.

"Oi! None o' that!"

Mike glanced in the direction of Nigel and Kamensky. Nigel was perched on the sofa, atop Kamensky, holding the sword across his throat with two hands. Kamensky looked feral, eyes wide, snarling. Even with his light build and the handcuffs, he seemed too much for Nigel to handle.

"I don't need this," Mike muttered. He crossed the room in a leap and pulled Nigel away from the vampire. Kamensky tried to surge out of the sofa but a right fist slammed him back, senseless.

He went back to Tony, who had drained the bag.

"More," Tony said. The voice was a bit more than a whisper, his skin less ashen.

Mike turned the water off in the kitchen and grabbed a bag from the top of the pile, hoping it might be warmer from the constant stream of hot water hitting it. Scrounging through drawers, he found a large pair of vice grips. He returned to Tony.

"Think you can hold this with your good hand?" For an answer, Tony's right arm crept up along his chest until he was holding the bag.

As soon as he had it, Mike adjusted the vice grips and clamped them sideways onto the top of the stake in Tony's upper arm. He hooked his fingers under the head of the vice grips so that the stake was between his first and second fingers. He caught Tony's eyes. The vampire gave a slight nod. With a hand on Tony's shoulder and a knee on his elbow, he pulled the stake out. Instead of a gasp of pain, there was a sigh of relief.

The wound relaxed shut but didn't seem to be closing. *More blood,* Mike thought, and headed for the kitchen again. As Tony started on the third bag, the arm wound looked like it was healing. Mike turned to the stake in Tony's leg and yanked it out. That wound also began to close.

This time Mike came back with two bags. They were luke warm now, and Tony seemed to react to them more.

"You ready for this?"

"Go ahead, Michael." It was a tired voice now, not a whisper.

One stake had to have hit the heart. He clamped onto that one, braced against Tony's chest, power breathed, and pulled. It grated against ribs as he fought to remove it. He dropped it on the floor, prepared to staunch a welling of blood from the heart, but there was none.

"Much better," Tony said. Seizing another bag, he tore the end off with his teeth and began draining it. A moment later, Mike had the two remaining stakes out. Tony struggled into a sitting position.

"Help me into my arm chair, Michael," he said.

Mike hefted him onto his feet and eased him into the chair, then put the other bag of blood into his hands. "How many more will you need?" he asked.

Tony thought. "Just one, I think, but a moment in hot water and in a glass would be nice."

Mike grinned. "Welcome back. How soon will you heal?"

Tony pursed his lips in thought. "If I sleep all day tomorrow, and I'm sure I will, it should be scars by tomorrow night. The scars will be gone in a few days.

And, Michael, thank you very much. How is your father? And is Sean alright?"

Mike raised an eyebrow. "Dad's fine but I'd better check on Sean again. There was some mischief at the house, we're not sure what yet." Back in the kitchen, he drained the sink and ran the hot water again, then put more bags in. He called his neighbour.

"It's quiet as can be, here," Dave said. "Sean's fine. I think it just spooked him. Frankly, I'd call your alarm company in the morning and have them check it."

"Yeah, probably just a glitch in the system," he agreed. *Glitch, my ass,* he thought, but decided not to tell his neighbour what had happened. He now knew the plan was to have him on Caldwell Road at the right time. That meant getting him to SeaView and then making him head home. It was a regular, possibly known path of travel for him. Events were arranged to put him there so he could be removed—separate him from Tony, then spring a trap laid for the vampire hunter and his helper.

When he had Sean on the phone, he said, "Anything unusual before the alarm went off? Any noises outside?"

"Yeah, come to think of it, Sam went ballistic. I thought it was the wind upsetting him. You know how he can be with strange noises—starts barking and you can't shut him up. He was like that, only pathetic. He started whining and wanted to hide under my desk. And he kept demanding attention from me. He was fine when I got home from class, then he just started in. It was just minutes later that the alarm went off."

Mike nodded. "How is he now?"

"Oh, he's fine. Dave's wife gave him an oatmeal cookie and some water. He's settled now."

"That's good. Okay, Sean, go straight home. Lock the doors and set the alarm. I think you're safe now, but keep the flare gun with you. Don't go to sleep with your finger on the trigger; you might set fire to your pillow and burn the house down."

He closed his phone and looked at Nigel. "Did you sweep the place for bugs?"

Nigel nodded, then his brow furrowed in thought.

"Ye know, sweepin' fer bugs only detects localized radio transmission, like if there was a transmitter right 'ere in the room." A look of inspiration came over him. "'Ang on; gimme a bit."

He rushed upstairs and returned with something like a walkie-talkie in his hand. He donned his coat and dashed out the door. It took ten minutes.

"Yer Lordship, is your fax line a separate line or on the main line?"

"I just have the one number. I use my cell phone for most of my calls. Why?"

"Well, there you 'ave it, then, don't you?" Nigel announced. He pulled a small box with a rubberized antenna out of his pocket. "This is the transmitter. It was outside near the phone box, wired to the extra line. Ye see, every phone line is four wires, actually two lines. Most people only use two o' the wires. You could have your fax wired to the other two, wiff a second number. They ran the bug on the second line. That means, 'ere in the 'ouse, all they gotta do is tap off those lines to bug each room."

He went to the wall plug for the living room phone, unscrewed the plate, and pulled out a small microphone. "Ooh, Audio-Technica, nice. There's probably one o' these in every room. The second phone line carries the audio to the transmitter outside. Who knows? It could transmit to a receiver a block away that taps into the main phone lines and carries it to anywhere from 'ere to the Old Kent Road."

"I'll rely on you to remove the rest," Tony said. He was sipping blood from a wine glass, and looking much better. "I know the transmitter's been removed but the thought of microphones still being there is offensive. Meanwhile, Michael and I can interview Detective Kamensky."

Mike went over to Kamensky, heaved him off the sofa, and dumped him on the floor in front of Tony. He then grabbed his sword and a small, armless chair. Turning the latter about, he straddled it, chair back before him. He rapped Kamensky atop the head with the flat of his blade.

"Do I have your attention?" he asked. There was a nasty, cruel tone to his voice. It came easy after the night's experiences. "Here are the rules: Nice vampires, like Lord Anthony here, get to live and have useful, long lives. Nasty vampires who like to kill people, like yourself, get their heads lopped off. Maybe we bury you in two separate boxes, maybe we just toss you in the backyard and wait for the sun to rise. Here's a thought—instead of whacking your head off, I drive one of these stakes through your heart, then toss you out in the backyard, helpless but awake enough to watch as the sun comes up for one last time. Are you with me so far? You see, Kamensky, you've pissed me off big time. You not only tried to kill me, you implied that my son was threatened. So talk me out of killing you."

Kamensky opened his mouth several times as if to speak, then stopped. He just stared at the blood pouches discarded on the floor.

Mike prodded his throat with the tip of his sword. "Let's start with something simple. How did you set the alarm off at my house?"

Kamensky pulled what looked like a thick remote control out of his pocket. "Chernov gave me this. It interrupts the magnetic door contact. The system thinks the door's been opened."

"Who's running you? Is it Chernov?"

A look of derision filled Kamensky's face.

Tony looked puzzled. "If it's not Chernov, then who is it?"

"Chernov likes to give orders but the real orders come from–" Once more it was if he could not make the words come out.

"If that's the way you want it..."

Mike's sword moved like lightning. The blade swung an arc that ended against Kamensky's neck.

The vampire cried out in terror but the blade only touched his neck, not even drawing blood.

Mike left the blade resting against Kamensky's neck. "That was a practice swing. In fifteen seconds, you get the real one. Talk."

"I..." Kamensky did a lot of stammering but it was almost as if someone had cut his tongue out.

"Michael, let me talk to him," Tony suggested. "Perhaps, at this point, my methods might be more productive."

Mike gave Lord Dewhurst a stern stare, then relinquished his chair. "Understand this, Tony: there was a vampire at my house tonight. Sam knew it—he's my dog, a corgi. He didn't understand what was outside, but he was afraid of it. Whoever it was set the alarm off to frighten Sean and make me come home. It was part of the setup to get me, but they involved my family."

Tony nodded. He took the chair Mike had been using. "Look at me," he said to Kamensky. There was a commanding tone in his voice. "*Look at me.*" This time there was an emphasis to the works.

Mike resisted the urge to obey. He glanced back at Tony. Kamensky's eyes were locked in a gaze with the English Lord's.

"Do you know who is commanding Chernov?" Kamensky nodded.

"Do you know his name?" Kamensky nodded.

"Tell me his name." Kamensky opened his mouth as if to speak but nothing but a faint gagging sound came out.

Tony's brows furrowed. "Is this vampire European?" Again Kamensky nodded.

"Can you speak at all? Have you lost your voice?"

"I can speak," Kamensky said. His voice sounded dry and strained. His eyes passed over to Mike, fear showing in them.

"Can you speak any information about this European vampire?" Tony asked.

Kamensky's mouth opened but, as before, he seemed unable to form words.

Mike was beginning to catch on. "Could you write anything down about him? Could you write his name?"

Kamensky looked at his hands. Mike watched as he seemed to try to flex his fingers. It was as if the fledgling vampire had just acquired the most severe attack of arthritis Mike had ever seen.

"If I consider the possibility of not killing you, will you talk to me without Lord Anthony's influence," Mike asked.

Kamensky nodded. "I will try."

"You seemed willing to kill me. Did you *want* to kill me?"

There were tears in the detective's eyes. "No," he whispered. "But he won't help me—he won't feed me. I haven't fed…"

"How long since you've fed?" Tony asked.

"Never," Kamensky gasped.

Tony's brow furrowed. "You've never fed as a vampire? When were you changed? When did this mystery vampire turn you?"

"Sunday, early evening."

"More than forty-eight hours, that's not good." Tony glanced at Mike, nodding toward the kitchen.

Nigel appeared in the doorway. "Cor blime, I could open a shop wiff all the gear I found!"

"Nigel," Mike said, "bring the packs from the sink. I'm not leaving Tony alone with this guy."

Nigel nodded, "Gotcher, gov."

Tony gave Mike a weak smile and laid a hand on his arm. "Thank you for your concern but I'm probably stronger than I look."

"Not by much, I'd bet," Mike argued. He pulled up another chair and sat with the sword across his lap, plainly visible.

"Kamensky," Tony said, "We're going to let you have some blood in a moment. Why haven't you fed?"

"After—when—"

"After this mystery vampire turned you?" Tony prompted.

Kamensky nodded. "Chernov thought my hunger was funny. He wouldn't help me at all. He—he likes to watch people suffer. It amuses him."

"Why didn't you feed yourself. You've seen movies, I'm sure. Why didn't you just find some lady walking alone at night or a homeless person?"

"I tried," the cop sobbed. "I just couldn't bring myself to kill someone. Even you," he added, looking at Mike. "Tonight I was desperate, starving—even with all the resentment voiced about you by some of the other cops, it was hard—I think I might have—I was desperate enough, but part of me was rebelling at the thought."

"And who put Jenkins up to his part in tonight's events?"

"Chernov told me what he wanted to happen. I picked Jenkins because he's enough of a jerk to do it and complains about your presence more than anyone. I think your father gave him a bad report and had him before a review board before he retired."

Nigel hurried back. "This one isn't exactly warm, but it's better than cold. Can I microwave them?"

"No," Tony said. "It destroys cell structure in the blood."

Mike, meanwhile, took the pouch, tore the end off the tube, and held it for Kamensky. The vampire attacked the pouch like a ravenous beast, sucking it dry in seconds. Nigel fetched the another pouch and Kamensky gave a repeat performance.

"You'll 'ave to wait for the rest to warm up."

Kamensky seemed calmer. He nodded.

"So how did this vampire get control of you?" Tony asked.

Kamensky seemed to be struggling mentally. "He–
–I was approached after work one evening in a bar on Barrington. I often stop there on the way home. He—
my name and what I did were known. My grandfather was from Russia; he came here during the revolution. We were taught to respect the Royal Family and those related to it." He fixed Tony with a stare, then winced, as if from pain.

"Right, old man, rest a moment."

Tony seemed lost in thought, then suddenly turned to Mike. "Do you have the keys to those cuffs?"

Mike fished into his pocket and produced a key he'd lifted from Jenkins. He bent Kamensky forward and unlocked the cuffs, tossing them on the coffee table. He helped Kamensky back onto the sofa, then sheathed his sword and sat holding it in front of him.

"We are trusting you to behave, Detective Kamensky," Tony cautioned. "I hope you appreciate my friend's abilities. Should you attempt to leave that sofa he could have your head off before you could fully get to your feet."

Kamensky put his hands up in a placating gesture. "I know I'm in a hard place with no where to turn," he sighed. "You've fed me a little; that's better than I've seen in days. You've removed my handcuffs. That says you're more likely to help me than kill me."

"Don't be too sure of that," Mike cautioned.

Kamensky shrugged. "I go where the evidence takes me." He leaned his head back against the sofa and closed his eyes.

Mike helped Tony into his padded arm chair.

"Actually, Michael, I'm feeling a lot better. I'll be sore for a few days but I expect I'll be much better after a proper sleep."

Mike nodded. "So what do you make of this guy?"

"He's been hypnotized by a powerful vampire, powerful in the sense that he is old—close to my age or older. The fact that he was programmed in the early stages of his making makes the hold all the more strong. He was simply instructed never to speak of the vampire who made him. Look at the grammar he uses. He can't say 'He approached me'—that would be talking about the vampire. But he can say 'I was approached'—that's talking about himself. He also found a way to tell us that this vampire is a Russian and somehow related to the Romanovs. I think he's found himself in a bad position that goes against his natural instincts. He wants to cooperate but is under a geas of sorts. He's struggling to find a way to help us within the parameters of the force controlling him."

Mike turned to Kamensky.

"Did they—were you promised that you would be fed at some point?"

Kamensky nodded. "After you were removed. But I doubt it. After—well, I was given to Chernov as a tool, the way you'd lend someone a hammer. Chernov seems under orders himself. He's just—part of a plan. It's not his plan. I only know the part I was to play. And Chernov's into something else, something— tolerated but not liked."

"Something his boss tolerates but doesn't really approve of?"

Kamensky nodded.

At that moment there was a pounding at the door.

"Police. It's me, MacDonald," a voice bellowed through the door.

"Shit, I forgot about him," Mike hissed. He snatched up all the empty blood packs and shoved them at Nigel. "Get rid of these, well out of sight."

"Gotcher."

Mike went to the door. "Easy, Pete; no need for a battering ram."

The inspector pushed into the house, gun in hand.

"Pete, put that away and relax. We don't need saving. In fact, we've learned a lot this evening."

MacDonald looked around. Seeing Tony easing back in his chair, apparently sipping at a glass of wine, he let out a sigh and holstered his weapon.

"Cripes, Dewhurst, you look like hell! Are those stab wounds?"

"Sort of," Tony replied with a weak smile. "They're not as serious as the look. Michael would make a fine ER doctor."

Then Pete spotted Kamensky.

"Why, you..." He advanced on Kamensky, then pulled up short, hesitant.

Kamensky just sat still, head up, seemingly prepared to accept whatever might be coming.

"It's okay, Pete. We're still getting what details Kamensky can offer but, so far, he's been extremely cooperative."

"He's a vampire," MacDonald hissed in a low tone. His eyes were wide, full of fear.

Mike put an arm about MacDonald's shoulder and led him away from Kamensky. "Come on, Pete, I know you've been through this with Lord Dewhurst. Vampires have been among us for a long time. Most of them are pretty much like normal people, except they're allergic to sunlight and have a rather limited diet. Then there are those who are psychopathic or sociopathic killers. Kamensky has never fed—he can't bring himself to do it. There are people who can train him how to manage things. There are also people who can supply him with blood, pretty much like hospital blood."

MacDonald's look of fear and panic softened to amazement. "They're that organized."

"Come on, Pete. Everybody's got a club or group. It's not just alcoholics. Even the Newfoundlanders have a club in Burnside. Why not Vampires? They just can't list in the yellow pages. Lord Tony no doubt knows how to contact them. In his line of work he'd have to."

MacDonald nodded. "So you're suggesting that Kamensky can carry on, business as usual?"

"I don't know. I certainly wouldn't turn him over to Internal Affairs or whatever you call those guys here. I think he was turned against his will. They wouldn't help him feed. Once they realized that he couldn't bring himself to feed from other people, they used his hunger to control him. Chernov apparently derived some amusement from it. I think he was hoping to turn him into some kind of raving lunatic, then set him on me. Kamensky is caught between a rock and a hard place but, fundamentally, I don't think he's dangerous. Trust me, Pete, I came close to killing him myself. If you talk to him, I think it might ease this vampire paranoia you're developing.

"Now, what happened with the bomb in that building?"

MacDonald shook his head. "Nothing more than an elaborate flash-bang."

"Flash-bang? What do you mean?"

"Tactical teams use them," MacDonald explained. "They were initially made for the military—deafening bang and blinding white flash of light. Tactical units and commandoes use flash-bang grenades to deafen and blind hostage takers. It makes them easier to take down or capture without hurting the hostages. This was different, though. There was shit load of shaved magnesium. Forensics are still there but I gather they found some that hadn't ignited. There was metal sheeting under the carpet to keep it from burning through the floor. That made it even hotter in the living room. The kitchen wall was similarly protected on the other side. The kitchen's fine, the bedrooms are a bit scorched, but the living room is a charred ruin."

Mike began to nod. "Magnesium, when shaved thin, burns readily. It's easy to ignite in that form, and gives off a lot of heat. It also isn't put out easily. They use it in distress flares, and they'll burn under water. If someone was caught, trapped in a magnesium fire, they'd be burned very badly, possibly beyond recognition. There was a flare in the wall where I cut through to get Tony and Nigel out. It was wired to a small detonator cap."

"*Some people* might be burned badly enough to be completely incapacitated but not killed," Tony offered.

"Michael, Nigel is familiar with the device Kamensky showed you and can tell you about it."

MacDonald cut in. "By the way, Mike, Jenkins's next pay cheque will pay for your car repair. Just e-mail me a copy of the bill."

As Mike left them, Tony was making progress in settling MacDonald's attitude toward Kamensky.

"What have you got, Nigel," he asked.

The cockney held up one of the miniature microphones he'd removed earlier in the evening. "Bein' a musician, you know there's a magnet in 'ere."

Mike nodded.

"Well, watch this?" He set the mic on the table, held the remote device within six inches of it, and held the button down. The mic leaped through the air and hit the remote, clinging to it. "It's an electromagnet, an' a surprisingly powerful one at that. It uses two nine-volt batteries. I've made a ton o' these over the years. Ya see, your average door contact in a security system is just two magnets. Ya got your permanent magnet on the door, an' a little magnetic switch on the door trim. The magnet on the door pulls at the magnet on the door trim keepin' the circuit open. If you move that magnet away by openin' the door, a mild spring pushes the other magnet against the switch side and the alarm goes off. Or, if the alarm's not set, it activates a little *beep-beep* to tell you the door's open. I used to use these on the door side to keep the switch magnet open. Wiff the door open, the alarm thinks it's still closed, see. But tonight, all Kamensky 'ad to do was activate this on the other side of the door sensor and it would force the switch closed, making the alarm go off. That's why your neighbour could check the place out and think that no one touched anyffing. Got it?"

Mike nodded, turning the device over in his hand. "Kamensky had no intention of entering the house.

From his point of view, Sean and Sam were never in any danger."

The little black man nodded. "Precisely."

"Which still leaves us with the heart of the plot."

"Wot's that, then?" Nigel asked.

Mike had assumed Nigel was listening to Kamensky enough to have figured it out.

"Chernov is a monster. He likes what he does. He likes to see people suffer. Someone—our yet-to-be-identified Russian nobleman—knew this, knew what kind of vampire he'd be."

Mike called across the room, "Pete, any more attacks tonight? Anything like Sunday?"

MacDonald, who seemed about to leave, stopped in the doorway and looked puzzled, shook his head, then made a call on his cell phone. "Nothing," he said as he closed the phone. "The vampire killer seems to have taken two nights off in a row. Mike, I'm heading home. They've got Jenkins in lockup. The officers who picked him up were apparently disappointed in him but not surprised. I'll talk to him tomorrow and see what charges we're going to lay. He can spend the night in jail, then start tomorrow suspended, if I even let him out."

When the inspector left, Tony joined Mike and Nigel's conversation.

"My point is," Mike continued, "Chernov went out of his way to be flamboyant until it was certain that Tony was here, on the case."

"Are you sayin' that the 'ole ffing was about gettin' 'Is Lordship over 'ere—that it was all some kind o' trap?"

"That's exactly what I'm saying. Our Count doesn't like the idea of me being in the way. I'll take that as a lack of confidence on his part. He tried to have me killed and lost a flunky. This time he tried a more complicated trap. On this side of the harbour, I was supposed to be killed by the half-starved Kamensky. Elabourate means were used to put me in a precise place. All of that was put into effect after they heard Tony announce his decision to check out that address tonight. That trap was meant to cripple Tony, leaving him at this Count's mercy. Our Russian nobleman has one huge ax to grind with you, Tony."

Tony seemed perplexed. "I can't imagine who this is or what grudge he'd bear against me."

"Blime! I never thought o' that but, yeah. It all makes sense, don't it?"

Mike nodded. "What about Kamensky? What do we do with him? We can't leave him with MacDonald. Pete's almost a basket case. I hope you reenforced his hypnotism to keep him from losing it completely, Tony."

Tony nodded. "All of this seems to have shaken his rather carefully defined world more than I thought. As for detective Kamensky, he's less of a problem than you think. It requires little more than a telephone call to my blood supplier. He's part of the local network." He smiled. "They like to call it a coven. Jonathan says it appeals to their sense of humour. Jonathan knows someone on night staff at the Red Cross blood supply. Someone can take Kamensky under their wing and coach him."

"While you call, I can give ol' Barney Fife over there a decent feeding and put 'im to kip somewhere for the night, then. I'll sleep better if 'e's 'andcuffed to the bedpost, though."

Mike waited while Kamensky when through two more pints of blood, and saw him settled in a guest room. "Are you sure you wouldn't rather have me cuff him to the bed?" he whispered to Tony.

"My hearing is more acute than it used to be," Kamensky announced. "If it would set your mind at ease, Mr. Cameron, I will submit to being handcuffed, as long as you leave the key with Lord Dewhurst. Once the dawn begins to break, nothing will keep me from passing out and I'll sleep until well past sunset."

But Tony shook his head. "I don't think it'll be necessary. I'm right next door and a lighter sleeper than most vampires. Many are quite comatose during the day."

Kamensky gave a faint smile of thanks to Tony.

"Mr. Cameron, I'm truly sorry about what you've been put through. The way you handled yourself, though, tells me that you are a larger threat than ... your enemy realizes. Your enemies need to be destroyed. I don't know how much I can help but I will give whatever help I can. Also, tell the inspector that Jenkins just thought you'd be roughed up bad to make you back off, and your family threatened to keep you quiet. He's an asshole but he's not a murderer. But he has no business being a cop, either."

# 14: Aftershock

Mike got home around 1:30 am. The drive was quiet and uneventful and there was a gentle flurry of snow in the air. He'd expected to be pulled over at any moment for his smashed rear lights but had managed to escape notice.

He looked in on Sean. The boy was asleep on his side, flare gun in hand. Sam was on the mat by Sean's bed. The corgi got to his feet and hurried to Mike, wagging his butt from side to side. It made Mike smile for the first time all evening.

"Hey, bear, tough night, huh?"

The corgi grinned but Mike could sense the lingering anxiety in him.

"Come on. I'm sure you need to go potty. But first, let's disarm Sean." He eased the Very pistol out of Sean's grip and checked the chamber. It was loaded with a double meteor shell.

He accompanied Sam to the door to the deck. Sam went out cautiously, showing more suspicion than Mike was used to seeing. He was also quicker than usual to do his business and hurry back. Mike closed and locked the door, reset the alarm, then headed for his bedroom.

He set the flare gun on his desk and noticed the number six flashing on his phone. He hit the play button and listened while he unclipped his cell phone holster, pulled out his wallet, and set everything on his desk.

- *Mikey, it's Dad. I just want to know every thing's okay. Call me.*
- *Mikey, it's Dad again. Call.*
- *You're probably not expecting this—it's Carrie. Your dad was worried when I left and that got me worrying. I'll probably be awake if you call.*
- *Come on, Mikey, call me.*
- *Hi, Michael, it's me, Carrie, again. I guess I'm just worried and can't sleep. I hope you're okay.*
- *Damn it, Mikey, I'm worried here. I don't care what time you get in, just call me.*

He stripped off and collapsed on the bed. Then, getting up, he grabbed the phone, scrolled through the Caller ID to Carrie's number, and hit *select.* He started for the bath. The phone answered on the second ring.

"I'm okay," he said with a chuckle. "You can go to sleep now."

"What's that noise, water?"

"Yeah, I'm running a hot bath. I need to soak a bit. It's been a tense night."

"So, what happened?"

Mike wasn't sure how much to tell her. He had a hunch he'd eventually have to tell her everything but he wasn't ready yet. "Someone was trying to keep me away from Tony. They set a trap for him, and one to keep me busy. Sean's fine. My neighbour took Sean and Sam over there. Whoever's behind this found a cute way to trigger the alarm without actually violating the security of the house. When I caught up with Tony and Nigel, they were in a bit of bother, but I was able to help them out of it. They're fine."

"*A bit of bother, eh?* Is Lord Dewhurst rubbing off on you or is your time in Bermuda coming out in your voice?"

Mike grinned. "Probably a bit of both. Are you ready to sleep now? I still have to call Dad. You only left two messages. He left four, each one more anxious than the last."

"I'd better let you go. It's just that…"

"It's just what?

"Well, Saturday seems a long way away."

"What about lunch tomorrow? The same karaoke pub that's on your way home has decent food. Or you can come by here and I'll take you to Dave's. It's just a couple of blocks away and a bit nicer—still pub food."

"Describe how to get to your place and I'll be there around noon."

He gave detailed directions and was still smiling as he rang off and called his father's cell phone. Will answered on the first ring.

"Sleeping with the cell phone in your hand?" Mike asked.

"Sleeping? Are you kidding? But you're joking and you sound fine. I'm relieved. What's all that noise in the background?"

"Hot bath. I need one badly." He then gave his father a detailed report of the evening.

"Cripes! Pete sounds like he's coming unglued. That's not like him."

"Sure it is. Think about it, Dad. Pete's a tough by-the-book cop. He likes evidence and he likes logic, but this whole vampire thing just shatters all the glass illusions of his safe world. His world is about murderers and drug dealers, not real monsters with fangs and claws. Now all he sees is the fangs and claws. I've considered that, if he knew the truth about Tony, it might help him with his perspective. Then I fear that it would only make things worse."

"He came by here for a few minutes before going home. He was calmer than I expected. He just left about a minute ago. His opinion of you has grown.

And I'm afraid I may have given him an even more exaggerated perception."

Something in his father's tone acted like an alarm in Mike. "What did you say, Dad?" he demanded.

"I told him about China and Tibet."

Mike was perplexed. He knew exactly what he'd told his father about his visit to Tibet and he knew exactly what he hadn't told him.

"Come on, Mikey, who do you think you're trying to fool? China controls Tibet. They control who goes in and out, what they see, and who they talk to. There's a monastery tour you can take—I looked it up—and you didn't take any tour. You went straight to an obscure monastery just outside Lhasa, the capital of Tibet, very much patrolled by Chinese authorities. You sent letters from Kathmandu in Nepal, then from Thimphu in Bhutan. Your next letters were from the monastery, mailed from Lhasa. I had your cousin do a check on your passport file. You also spent more than six months at the Shaolin temple in Loyang. That's just six hundred kilometers or so from Beijing, Mikey. You can't spend six months there without a hundred pounds of red tape. My guess is the Chinese didn't know you were there, either."

"You could get Mac fired for that, you know," Mike interrupted.

"The point is, Mikey, you found a way to wander China and Tibet illegally for well over a year, then sneak out again. And you did it with a fifteen-year-old boy in tow. Now, Mike, I'm not trying to argue whether you should have done it, I'm not arguing how you did it, I just want to make the point that you did do it, however you managed it."

Mike took a slow breath, then exhaled just as slow. "Yes, Dad, I did it. Tony helped set it up so I could study with a particular Tulku. I didn't feel like going through two years of Beijing red tape to visit for three weeks. They're assholes, Dad. They stole the country and culture from those people. They terrorize the people with martial law and blame every expression of discontent on the Dalai Lama. As for the temple at Loyang, did you know that the monks the public sees are actors? The real monks and where they teach is a carefully guarded secret. The Chinese won't even allow that."

"Mike, you don't need to justify. I get it. Frankly, I think what you did was good for you. I might have wished you'd done it differently, considering you had Sean with you, but that's water under the bridge. The point is, the point I made to MacDonald, is that you have an amazing way of getting things done. Whether it was a feat of ninja skill or something worthy of James Bond, it was pretty amazing. It shows something of the unusual talents you have. That's what I was trying to convey to Pete. I think he's starting to see you as a ray of hope in this nightmare he's caught up in, some kind of lifeline."

"I suppose," Mike conceded. "Anyway, I want to work out for a few minutes, then see if I can crash. Oh, yeah, Carrie and I are having lunch tomorrow."

"That's great, Mikey. When did that happen? You tore out of here so fast…"

"She was worried and left a message for me to call her, so I did. And, Dad, I can hear it building in your voice. Don't start pushing again."

Will chuckled. "No need, Son. I think you just toppled off the fence all on your own."

Mike shut off the water and slid into the tub cautiously, easing down into the hot water, then let his head slide down 'til his face was almost underwater. He just lay there for a few minutes, then turned on the jets and slowed the speed to about half. For the next fifteen minutes he let his mind drift.

By the time he got out of the tub he felt more relaxed but still not ready for sleep. He took the sword cane and his *Muramasa* katana and headed for the theatre. Once there he turned the massive 18th century coffee table up on end, giving him room to move about.

He drew the straight blade from the cane several times until he felt like it was almost fast enough. The lack of typical katana curve made it awkward to draw.

"I'll never be a master of *iai* with this," he muttered. Iai was the Bushi art of quickdraw, drawing the sword at high speed, often striking with the same motion. He set the blade down and drew the Muramasa with lightening speed. Setting the Muramasa down, he picked up the Paul Chen again. The blade was well-crafted, though not as good as the Muramasa. He went into an elabourate kata, wheeling about, chopping, thrusting, engaging in more subtle passes that blocked and then cut with the tip. He soon had a feel for the balance but realized he'd never be as at home with it as a katana.

*Perhaps,* he thought, *there's a way to holster the katana under my coat. After all, it's really just about not attracting the general attention of the public. It's not like I don't have a permit.*

It wasn't long before he had enough and decided to head for bed. For a long time he lay there, his thoughts drifting until he began to recall his visit to the *sensei* of the Yagyu School in Japan. The ancient master must have been about eighty, yet as agile and sharp as Mike.

"You are a great warrior," Master Tekaga had said. "There is wisdom in your eyes. You are an old soul; the soul of a great samurai resides within you. He speaks to me. We call it *heregei*. You have it,

Cameron-sensei. It is the force inside you that is sensitive to the *ki* of others. It often lets you sense what they will do before they do it, and it lets you feel the presence of another master across the room."

The master stood, reached a wrinkled hand to a ceremonial rack, and took down a katana in a silk sleeve. He pulled the sleeve back, exposing the weapon. The artisanship placed it as as being four to five hundred years old.

"This was crafted by Muramasa, a legend among the great sword makers. It's last owner's story is a sad one. He rid Japan of a dishonourable warrior. He lived a life of honour but it was a short life. Part of his *kami* in believed to be in this blade. I believe the rest of his soul resides in you. An ancestor of mine was one of his teachers. Upon his death, his father, a daimyo, could not bear to have the katana in his house. He gave it into the keeping of my ancestor, to be held until a worthy owner should be found. I believe I have found that owner."

Mike relived the feelings of awe and surprise. Even his breath came in short, shallow spurts.

"This is a very large honour, Tekaga-sensei—too large an honour for me, I fear."

The old man smiled and placed the weapon in Mike's hands.

Mike had felt a thrill run through him as he touched the sheath and the ray-skin-wrapped grip. He felt both rejuvenated and a sense of déjà vu, as if he'd held this katana many times. He knew its balance and felt completely at home with it.

He sprang out of bed, rushed to his desk, and booted his computer. After typing in his password, he got the Muramasa and studied the scabbard. There were kanji characters painted on the sheath, the lacquer faded through the centuries, but still readable. Taking a

four-by-six file card from a holder, he grabbed a
Sharpie marker and copied the characters. He took a
small box out of his upper right cupboard and removed
a tool. With cautious, precise movements he pushed
out the bamboo pins and slid the tsuka, the ray-skin-
wrapped handle, off of the tang. Characters stamped
into one side gave the year, month, and day of the
sword's making, followed by Muramasa's character.
On the other side were a two kanji characters. He
copied these as well and scanned the card into his
computer, set his preferences to recognize kanji, then
Googled to find a website that could translate for him.
In the time it took him to reassemble the katana, the
program gave the results, results that sent a shiver
through him and left him staring at the screen.

The characters for the date gave the equivalent date
of April 28, 1528. On the other side was *Yama Kaze*,
the mountain wind. He knew the term, it had been used
on a WWII battleship. It referred to a cold, cleansing
wind, a wind of justice. His words under hypnosis
came back to him. *Yama Kaze will truly be a wind of
justice.* But it was the name lacquered on the *saya* that
sent the biggest chill through him—*Tomomatsu
Yakura.*

He called Tony.

"Everything all right, Michael? You sound
troubled."

"More creeped out than troubled," Mike said.
"Sorry, that's one of Sean's expressions, but it fits the
occasion. How much of tonight's hypnosis do you
remember?"

"All of it, Michael, verbatim. I've always had a
rather prodigious memory, but it seems to be part and
parcel of my condition."

Mike took a deep breath. "I disassembled my
katana—the Muramasa given to me by Sensei Yagyu.

It was made in 1528. It was named Yama Kaze or mountain wind. Lacquered on the *saya*, the sheath, is the name of its last legitimate owner, Tomomatsu Yakura. Sensei Yagyu told me he believed the soul of its owner was in me. I thought he was speaking metaphorically—you know, that I have the soul of a samurai, not that I was the actual reincarnation of the son of a 16th century daimyo."

"So, what we learned from hypnosis has been confirmed by physical evidence. You've had a very long day, Michael. Your senses, both physical and spiritual, have been rather overloaded. Get some sleep. It's after 3:00. Oh, MacDonald said not to worry about your car. He's going to have someone from the police garage come over around 9:00 or 10:00 with the parts to repair it."

"That'll let me sleep in a little, I suppose. I was going to take it to the shop for 8:00."

"He's also having a patrol check your street fairly regularly."

Mike nodded, yawning.

"I'll talk to you tomorrow, Tony."

He was about to turn out the light but one thought still nagged at his mind. He went back to this desk and rummaged through a drawer in the credenza until he found an address book, looked up a number and dialed.

"Kyoto is a twelve hour difference, so it'll be almost 4:00 pm there," he mused.

A polite female voice answered in Japanese.

"I wish to speak to Tekaga-sensei, please." He struggled with his rusty Japanese then, as if something inside him awakened, it came easier. "This is Cameron-sensei calling long distance from Canada. It is very important."

Moments later a soft, elderly voice came on the line, speaking in awkward English.

"Ah, Michael-san, it is a pleasure to hear from you. Is all well with you?"

Michael hesitated. "Strange things are happening, Yoshi-san, but I am coping with them. I have an important question. It is about Yama Kaze."

"Ah, you have found and translated the name of the blade."

"Actually," Mike explained, "I knew the name before I translated it. I believe I also know the name of the original owner, but I wish to hear it from you."

"So he finally spoke to you from within and you need me to tell you the gods have not stolen your mind, am I correct, Michael-san?"

"Yes, Yoshi-san, I need to know I'm not crazy."

"He was the best student of a descendant our our founder, an ancestor of my mother's father. Master Yagyu's pupil was Tomomatsu Yakura, son of Tomomatsu Yushita."

"And he committed sepuku after killing Toda Yoshihiro."

"Yes, Michael-san, but the event is not part of official history. The Tokugawa recorded both deaths without the details, partly to avoid disgracing Toda and partly to hide that Yakura had disobeyed shogun edict. That he did so out of honour and committed sepuku would have made him a hero among the samurai, but the elder Toda did not want this either, and persuaded the shogun."

"Thank you, Tekaga-sensei. I still treasure the memory of studying with you. It is very late here and I must retire to bed. Again, I thank you."

Mike rung off then went to bed. For a while he stared at the ceiling. It seemed impossible to believe, yet it was all true.

# 15: Interlude

**M**ike awoke at 9:45. His internal clock never let him sleep very late, even times when he was up 'til almost 5:00 am. There was a groan from Sam as Mike sat up.

*Poor Sam,* he thought, *when I'm up late you always keep me company, even if I don't notice you.*

He smelled coffee as he neared the stairs. He smiled. Sean must have made coffee before going to school. He poured some into a large mug.

"Come on, Sam" he said, sliding open the door to the deck. There was a light dusting of snow on the deck and a light flurry still falling. "Winter's a pain, isn't it, bear?"

The corgi looked at the snow then shuffled off into it, across the deck and down the steps into the yard. He took his time coming back. Mike had already made himself a bowl of instant oatmeal before there was a *huff* at the door. Sam came in grinning and gave a shake on the mat. Mike grabbed a towel from the towel bar on the island and gave him a quick wipe. Sam liked snow.

"It's going to be a slow day today, Sam. I almost wish I could sleep through it."

After breakfast he checked his e-mail, then opened his encrypted journal and typed out everything he could remember from the previous evening. He looked at his entries for the past week and shook his head. Up until Saturday, entries were a paragraph a day. After Saturday they were two and three pages per day.

*This is all since Saturday.* He tried to reconcile the reality of it all. It was too much, too fast. He thought back to the night his sailboat *Mystic Lady* had struck a shipping container and sunk in the Atlantic, partway to the Bahamas. That had been the same feeling. He remembered coming home with Susan and baby Sean just long enough to find a new boat and learn that Susan had melanoma. All that shock had been spread over four or five months, but the feeling had been the same. But he had gone on. He'd sailed back to Abaco and scattered her ashes as she'd wanted. *I guess I'm the type that just keeps going, no matter what life hands me*, he wrote.

Going to his bathroom, he looked at himself in the mirror and began shaving. *You do just keep on going, don't you? Even through the divorce—once you knew what you had to do, you just did it, got it over with and went on.* He sighed and nodded. *I guess that's just the way it is. That's how it will have to be this time. Yagyu sensei said you were in there. Well, sport, this time we'll get through it, get the job done, and not be destroyed by it—I hope.*

He studied his icy blue eyes in the reflection. *You're—we're stronger this time.* It was like a voice inside his head suddenly talking to him. *There's no we. I'm not a spirit possessing you. I am you, you are me. But you are older now. You've lived more lives and more of this life than you did in my time.*

Mike considered this, rinsed the shaving soap off his face, cleaned his grandfather's shaving brush, then nodded.

"Maybe I'll even get the girl this time," he said aloud. He smiled, thinking of Carrie.

He slipped into his southern style jing-mo—red silk sleeveless top bordered with yellow, over black silk pants—then wrapped his black silk sash about his waist. The ends of the sash were decorated with the Chinese characters for *Chi Jen Do*, the way of the man of chi, underlined by three stylized bars, his third-dan black belt ranking. He picked up the Muramasa katana and another reproduction katana with a carved imitation ivory tsuka. A serpent's body coiled about the handle, making for a good grip, and ending in a dragon's head with bared teeth.

He headed for the living room. Pushing the sofa up against the dining table gave him room to work. He unsheathed both katana and went into a series of difficult moves that became faster, more intricate. He moved in circles, eyes closed, using his inner sense to know not only where he was but where the baby grand and the sofa were, as well as the ceiling. Time ceased to exist.

The door chime and Sam's barking brought him back to the present.

At the door he found a serious-looking young man wearing a police jacket over blue coveralls. A police van was backed into the driveway up to the garage door.

The mechanic's reaction to Mike's outfit was almost comical. He took an involuntary backward step.

"Mr. Cameron? Bill Mason, Police Maintenance Division. I'm here to replace the rear bulbs and lenses on a 1999 Jeep Grand Cherokee Limited. I assume it's in the garage."

Mike nodded and pressed the garage door button. "Convey my thanks to Inspector MacDonald."

The mechanic nodded. "I gather Jenkins is suspended without pay, pending a review. Nobody in the garage has time for him. Between you and me, sir, he's an arse hole."

Mike smiled. "No argument from me."

The mechanic winked. "Rumour has it you gave it back to him in spades. Good on you."

Mike returned to the living room and his workout. Once more he let his thoughts go and became lost in the movements. It was like a purging ritual. Frustration, worries—it all fell away from him as he found that quiet center, alpha waves becoming predominant in his brain.

He came to a stand still in the center of the floor, katanas hanging at his side, then dropped to his knees, sitting on his heels. He set the swords down on each side of him, tips just a few inches apart in front of his knees, in a V-formation. He slipped easily into meditation.

Random thoughts flew through his mind. He let them pass, never allowing any to stop to be examined. Another part of his brain recognized and catalogued them, allowing patterns to form, but his conscious mind just let it all pass in a steady flow.

Eventually he arose and began to move about the floor in a slow Chi-Kung pattern of Kung Ku movements done in a Tai-Chi style, his breathing controlled and precise. Back and forth straight line techniques were mixed with spiraling circular motions. All the while his mind remained clear, his eyes unfocussed, his breathing in through the mouth and out through the nose. He paused in mid-technique, his leg raised in a high side kick.

The door bell.

"All done, Mr. Cameron," Mason announced, his eyes glued to Mike's jing-mo. "You were lucky. There were no dents in the surrounding metal and no paint damage. Oh, one more thing—I'm to give you this."

He handed Mike an envelope. Inside was a new weapons permit to replace the one Jenkins had destroyed.

"Thanks."

"Uh, sir? I hear some of the cops at work talking about you—pretty impressive stuff—and I was wondering…"

Mike smiled and told him the days and times of his adult classes. "It's ten dollars a lesson. Some students pay by the month. Whatever's convenient."

The mechanic's eyes widened. "I was expecting a lot more, especially considering your rep, sir."

Mike shrugged. "I have other sources of income and I enjoy the teaching. I'm more interested in the calibre and dedication of my students than the size of their wallets. Besides, with a sizable class it adds up."

The mechanic grinned. "I'll be there next class."

Mike closed the garage door and returned to the living room. He'd barely resumed his exercises when he sensed a car pulling into the driveway. Sam ran to the door barking.

He sighed and went back to the door.

Carrie was beaming an excited smile, both arms loaded with grocery bags. As she entered, Mike took the bags from her, then helped her out of her coat. When he turned back from the closet, he caught her looking him up and down.

"Ooh, I like this look. But don't wear it to visit your father. I'm already warning the other girls to keep their distance."

He smiled, looking into her eyes. There was a moment of hesitation in their sparkling green depths, then she launched herself up onto her toes, threw her arms about his neck, and began a long kiss. His arms came about her almost as fast. A warm, heady feeling surged through him. His workout and meditation had eased away most of his tension, but that was a slow, passive purging. This was different. It was like opening the windows to bright sunshine and warm fresh air after a month of rain.

"And hello to you, too," he said, matching her grin.

She blushed. "I don't know what came over me, but I'm glad I did that. I'm not usually that impulsive."

Mike nodded. "There's definitely something happening here. We probably should be cautious and take our time but, yeah, it's like I've known you for a very long time."

They each grabbed a bag of groceries in opposite hands and held hands as they ascended the stairs. Sam trotted along behind making an odd whiny sound. Carrie set her bag on the island in the kitchen, then squatted in front of Sam.

"I'm sorry, Sam, you're trying to meet me, aren't you?"

As she ruffled the mane of fur around his thick neck, he struggled onto his hind legs, braced a paw against her knee, and began licking her face. She laughed, continuing to ruffle his fur.

"You're precious. I've heard a lot about you, but I've never seen a corgi before." She looked up at Mike. "Is he always this friendly with strangers?"

Mike shook his head. "He's friendly enough but not with this much enthusiasm. I think he senses something about you or perhaps senses my reactions toward you. And he rarely gets up on his hind legs, even for food. He's getting a bit old for that." Going through the bags she'd brought, he added, "Lettuce, Italian tomatoes, red onions, green and red bell peppers, boneless chicken breasts—I guess this means Dave's is out. I suppose I should take a minute and change."

She caught his arm as he was about to leave. "Actually, you're fine the way you are—a bit gooey, but nothing I can't live with."

"I need a shower."

"It's 11:30. I have to leave for work in less than three hours. I don't want to spend any of that time waiting for you to shower. By the way, I passed a police van on the way up the street. What was that about?"

"It's a long and complicated story," he said. "The short version is that an ass-hole cop took out my rear lights last night. The inspector sent a police mechanic over to fix the damage."

"Why did he do that?"

"He resented the involvement of a civilian in police matters. He also had a grudge against my father."

"So he smashed your rear lights out? What did you do?"

"I lost my temper and stuffed him in his trunk. He's under suspension, pending a review board."

Carrie studied Mike's face. "Why do I get the feeling there's a lot more to this you're not telling me?"

Mike pursed his lips. "Let's just say that there's a lot going on at the moment. I'm having trouble taking it all in. Talking about it is awkward. And, since it involves a police investigation, I'm not sure how much I should talk about." He took her into his arms and held her. "I think I want to tell you about all of it sometime, just not yet."

Once more she looked into his eyes, then nodded.

"It's beautiful outside," she declared. "Have you been out? The sun is almost blinding on the snow, but they say it's supposed to rain later and ruin it all."

"That's Nova Scotia weather. Here, you start on the salad part." He handed her a large cutting board from a narrow cupboard in the island, then grabbed a skillet from the pot rack above the island. He then got a chef's knife and a santoku knife from a magnetic strip near the sink. He handed her the former while he took the latter and deftly sliced through the packaging of the chicken.

Lighting a fire under the skillet, he sliced the chicken into strips, his movements reflecting familiarity and practice with the Japanese knife. All the while he was aware of her watching him with a look of fascination. He scraped the chicken into the skillet, lessened the flame, then poured a generous dollop of olive oil into the pan. From the pantry cupboard he got a garlic bulb, broke off two cloves, pealed them, smashed them with the flat of the santoku, then diced with a rapid rocking movement of the blade. When it was all simmering, he added a splash of teriyaki sauce.

"Your father wasn't exaggerating," Carrie said. "You do cook."

Mike shrugged. "I like it."

She nodded. "And you designed this kitchen. It's a nice layout, designed by a cook, not an architect. Where were you twenty-five years ago when I was marrying Mr. Asshole?"

"In Bermuda, getting married myself."

Her face took on a more serious look. "We've both had a lot happen to us in our lives. Yours died, then there was another that you weren't meant to be with. Mine left me for something younger. Now, with both of our calendars clear, here we are."

Mike got two wine glasses, filled them with water, and handed her one. "So here's to the present," he said, clinking glasses. "We're tempered by what life puts us through. Some are broken by it, and some of us are made stronger, wiser."

Her beaming grin returned. "You're right. It's not about the past, it's about being happy for the present."

He watched her as she cut up the lettuce and the fruits into bite-sized pieces, her movements experienced, yet more cautious than his. It made him think about his natural affinity for blades, no longer surprised that his favourite chef's knife was Japanese in origin. *The more the pieces fall into place, the more mystifying it feels,* he thought. *It should be the other way around.*

Their movement about the kitchen fascinated him. While he'd made the most of the room's limited size (ten feet by ten feet), he usually found a second presence awkward. Yet, when he had to move around the island and encountered Carrie, it became a kind of dance. They laughed as they brushed around each other, often deliberately bumping into each other.

Lunch was a mix of eating and idle chatter. Their few silences were never awkward. He found himself staring at her, entranced by how readily she smiled.

"You're staring at me," she finally told him.

Instead of being at a loss for words, he found himself saying, "I could look away but the view is better in this direction."

She laughed. "I wasn't expecting you to be that direct. It's always the quiet ones that you have to watch out for."

Mike smiled and lowered his eyes, then looked at her again and shrugged. "I guess it just came out that way." He paused, choosing his words. "There's something about you I find comfortable, relaxing. It seems easier to just say the simple truth rather than try to colour it in some way."

She nodded slowly. "I can get used to that." She gestured to the piano. "You play that as well?"

"Some. I had a lousy teacher."

Carrie grinned. "Your father says you taught yourself to play every instrument you play except the bagpipes. You had lessons in those when you were young."

Mike rolled his eyes. "My family name is Cameron and I'm from Nova Scotia. It's probably in the rules somewhere."

Moments later they were at the piano and he was rolling through the opening chords of Elton John's "Tiny Dancer," followed by several more Elton ballads and love songs. As he finished "Your Song," he found himself in her embrace, his lips on hers. He held her for some time, just enjoying the feel of her against him.

"You do Elton John well," Carrie whispered.

"He's actually easier than most. You don't have to play the fancier riffs. Billy Joel is much harder. Even his gentlest ballads have such impossible runs that I couldn't force my fingers through them even if I could figure out where the fingers go."

That said, he did his best to get through "Just the Way You Are." Through the song she kept her arms about his waist.

"You managed that just fine."

"The chords in the bridge give me some trouble but fingering is easier than most of his."

She cut his comment off with another kiss. "I can't seem to stop kissing you," she said in an innocent, little girl tone.

Mike held her close, intoxicated. "I'll get through it somehow," he teased.

The shrill ring of the phone intruded.

"I hate phones," Mike growled. He went to the kitchen and answered it. "Yeah." His phone manner was more curt than usual.

"Am I interrupting something? Did Mason fix your car?" It was MacDonald.

"Yeah, Pete, it's all taken care of, and yes, you did interrupt something—something more pleasant than police business, I can assure you." He gave Carrie a wink.

"Forensics are headed to that apartment off North Street. Thought you might want a second look. MacGilvery seems to like you."

"Who's MacGilvery?"

"Mac. Forensics. You met him Sunday night at the sight of those two brutal attacks on Water Street."

"Are you expecting something in particular?" Mike asked.

"Not necessarily," MacDonald replied, "but figuring out the design of the traps that Lord Dewhurst triggered might tell us something about the person who planned this."

"Right. Okay, Pete, I'll get over there this afternoon. And thanks for sending the mechanic over. You saved me a hassle."

He hung up the phone and turned to find Carrie picking up her jacket, an anxious look on her face.

"Gotta go," she said, giving him a quick hug and kiss. "I've got twenty minutes to get to work."

He looked at his watch and glared. It was 2:25. "No way!" he blurted. "Where did the time go?"

"It flies when you're having fun, remember? Will I see you later?"

"I'll try. If not, I'll try to call."

When she left, Mike put the dishes in the dishwasher, then changed into regular clothes, pulling an Izod fleece over a cotton turtleneck. He picked up the sword cane then, looking at his Muramasa, grabbed the katana as well. He examined the inside of his drover's coat. A tailor could install a long, narrow pocket for the sheath of his katana. He draped it over the rail, donned a black suede jacket and his broad-brimmed hat, then grabbed his overcoat and weapons and was out the door.

He dropped the overcoat at the tailor's. He'd used the tailor many times; an elderly Lebanese man with a ready smile and the patient skill of a true craftsman. After explaining what he needed to the mystified tailor, Mike added, "I'm kind of in a hurry."

The man gave Mike a quizzical look. "Normally I say next week but you're good customer Mr. Mike. Okay, tomorrow, maybe noon."

Mike thanked him, then went to his car and headed for Halifax.

His conscience troubled him for much of the drive over. Part of him wanted to tell Carrie everything, part of him wanted to keep it all away from her. There was also a part of him that was alarmed by how fast things seemed to be happening with her.

*The last time the alarm bells were going off in a clangor and I wasn't listening,* he chuckled. *Carrie's not setting off any alarms, it's just my fear of making a mistake again.* He nodded to himself. *Last time I wasn't paying attention to my gut. My gut's very much in favour of Carrie. Okay, so she's in the picture, and that's fine—just keep her away from the danger. As for the rest, just bide your time with all of it, including figuring out what she's ready to know and understand.*

# 16: The Scene of the Crime

The building looked different in daytime, less ominous. Parked in front were a police unit and a forensics van. The air of tension remained, however, with tenants on lower floors peering out of doorways. Mike entered the building carrying his katana in his left hand, the weapon covered by it's navy-blue silk sleeve. Anyone knowledgeable would know at a glance what it was but he felt less conspicuous. He also felt more secure than with the sword cane.

A building tenant, obviously eastern European, grabbed at Mike's arm as he was mounting the stair. He was in his sixties with coarse grey stubble on his face.

"You are man who warn us of explosion last night," he said. "Whole building want to thank you— well, maybe not..." He jerked his head toward the second floor to indicate who might not be thankful.

"Do you know who the owner of the building is or who was using that apartment?"

The man shook is head. "Gruff, nasty man collects rent. Tall, burly, very pale. Bad breath." He crossed himself. "He have teeth almost like *strigoi*..." He seemed to be searching for a word.

"*Wampyr*?" Mike offered.

The man's eyes widened and he took a step back. "You know this creature?"

Mike smiled and lied. "From books. I know that *strigoi* is Romanian and *wampyr* is German for vampire. I read Dracula as a kid."

The man shook his head. "This is real danger," he insisted. "This *strigoi*, he like to frighten. He not hide teeth from me. He like to see fear, like he dare me to speak of him to others."

Mike nodded. "Chernov," he murmured. "Do you know what they did up there?"

The older man shook his head. "Much hammering and machine noise at first. Then boxes start coming— many small boxes." He gestured with his hands to show a size just less than a cubic foot. "Bad smells."

"What did it smell like?"

The man shrugged. "Bad smells," he repeated, "what you call—unpleasant."

"Did you tell the police any of this?"

There was fear in how fast the man shook his head.

Mike nodded. People who had escaped eastern block countries had an instinctive fear of police.

"Thank you," he said. "I will inform a policeman I trust. I will tell him what I heard but not where I heard it."

Fear faded from the man's face and he nodded. "You are good man. You not make poor Romanian feel like he not belong. I am mechanic and good welder. You need car fix, you come see Ivan. Boss give day off today because of last night but I am home on Sundays."

Mike smiled and handed the man a card. "If you see your new landlord again, call my cell phone immediately."

Ivan looked at Mike's face carefully, then at the wrapped object in his hand, and nodded. "Perhaps you cut off his head and stuff his mouth with garlic," he said, nodding at Mike's katana.

Mike smiled. "Perhaps," he agreed, then continued up the stairs.

He flashed his Interpol badge at the patrolman guarding the door and was allowed to pass under the crime scene tape and into the apartment. The cop raised an eyebrow at the covered katana but said nothing.

Inside a small team of techs were examining the charred walls and photographing evidence. Mike recognized Sam MacGilvery from the previous Sunday.

"Hello, Mac," he said. "Pete MacDonald called me."

The head forensics tech smiled. "Hi, Mike." He shook Mike's hand, his demeanor informal. "You make that extra door?" He jerked his head in the direction of where Mike had cut through the drywall to get in the night before.

Mike nodded. "I didn't have time to call a locksmith."

"That your tool of entry?" He glanced at Mike's covered katana.

Mike shook his head. "Last night I was carrying a Paul Chen straight blade in a Georgian-style long walking stick. I'm more at home with this one."

"Well, you acted fast, and it's a good thing. This room would have been a nasty place to be when those charges went off. The walls were designed to confine the effect to this room and protect the kitchen from it. The explosive was mostly magnesium, small bang, big flash in a confined space. It wouldn't have killed its victims but it would have burned them severely. Nice warning to anyone trying to break into whatever they were up to in the kitchen."

"So there's no way it would have killed anyone?"

"Not unless they had a weak heart or a lot of magnesium in their tissues. And anyone with flesh like that wouldn't last long in sunlight anyway. No, Mike, it was just a nasty warning of sorts."

Mike just nodded, keeping his thoughts of Tony to himself. "So what were they up to in the kitchen?"

"I'm waiting for special chem kit, but I have a theory."

Once in the kitchen, away from the smell of charred drywall paper and burnt carpet, Mike recognized a trace smell. "Acetone," he said to Mac.

Mac nodded slowly. "I couldn't place it at first. You work with a lot of fiberglass?"

Mike nodded. "I've owned a lot of boats, even build one once."

The stove was cluttered with pots and the counters with glass bottles, a haphazard scattering, abandoned in a hurry. Near the stove Mike picked up another smell.

"Do you have spray starch?"

"It'll be in the kit coming. You think that film of stain on the cupboards has iodine?"

"Back in a second." Mike took off out the door and down the stairs. He knocked at the Rumanian's door. Ivan's anxious frown turned to a smile when he saw Mike.

"Do you have a raw potato?" Mike asked.

Ivan looked perplexed then shrugged. "Just one?"

"Actually, just half of one, if you don't mind cutting one in half."

Ivan's brow puckered in puzzlement but he left and came back with a potato cut in half and gave half to Mike. "Is that all?"

Mike nodded. "I'm helping the police in a test. They were making drugs upstairs."

Back in the apartment Mike held out the potato to Mac but the latter just gestured at the cupboards. "You're the quick thinker, you get the honour."

Mike rubbed the sliced surface of the potato against the cupboard door and waited. In moments the surface of the potato turned dark purple, almost black.

Mac nodded. "Iodine. Here I am waiting for a hi-tech chem kit and you saved me the wait with a grade 11 chemistry experiment. Acetone and iodine gas are natural by-products of crystal methamphetamine production. Are you sure you don't want to be a CSI?"

Mike shook his head. "I'm a bit too old to go back to school now. Besides, you would have picked it up."

Mac shook his head. "I would have noticed the residue and tested it, figuring it out, yeah. But you saved a lot of wasted time. You picked up on the acetone and nailed down the meth thing immediately."

Mike shrugged. "In this part of town most cops would be assuming math lab. But what's our vampire killer doing with a meth lab on the side?"

Mac shrugged. "So our Dracula wanna-be has two nasty hobbies."

Mike flipped open his phone and called Pete.

"Pete, it's Mike. Any chance those crates stolen off the docks contained Chinese cough syrup high in ephedrine or pseudoephedrine?"

"Sorry," Pete replied. "According to the manifest, it was machine parts."

Mike thought. "Pete, check Montreal. They suddenly getting Chinese automatic weapons on the street there or used in organized crime incidents?"

"Where are you going with this, Mike?"

"Chernov is linked to Montreal, possibly the Russian mafia. Smuggled arms are often labelled as machine parts. Worried about getting your cheap Chinese arms shipment through customs? Why not arrange for an ex-KGB agent to steal them from the warehouse before they're cleared. You'd only get away with it once, maybe twice, but it might give Chernov the where-with-all to finance a building and start a meth lab."

"You found a meth lab? That would explain why the place was booby trapped. Damn, Mike, you should be on the payroll."

"I am, indirectly," Mike reminded him.

"Yeah, well tell Lord Dewhurst for me that he sure knows how to pick 'em."

"Someone went to elabourate lengths to booby trap the place," Mac said when Mike was off the phone. "The spike launchers are much more recent than the barred doors. They look like an after-thought of a couple of days ago."

Mike jumped and caught the trim of the attic hatch, then pulled himself up into the attic and examined the steel door mechanisms. They were relatively simple in design but Chernov or someone had gone to a lot of work to create the trap. He suspected that the initial plan was to trap anyone who invaded their operation. Then someone decided it was a great way to trap and eliminate Tony. Between the magnesium fire and the stakes, he'd have been helpless, probably dead. Looking at the whole picture it became obvious. Not only did someone want Tony dead but they wanted to make sure. They were afraid of him and the whole scenario seemed personal.

Near the center of the attic, right over the living room, the insulation had been disturbed. Lifting one of the thick pieces of fibre, Mike found what looked like a walkie-talkie with three rubberized antennae.

He lowered himself through the hatch and dropped to the floor.

"There is a ladder," Mac commented with a grin.

Mike pulled the device he'd found from his pocket and handed it to Mac. "Wanna bet that's a cell phone jammer?"

"No takers here," Mac said. "That's an RX9000. It'll jam cellular and 3G signals up to 30 meters."

"Almost a hundred feet," Mike mused. "No wonder my cell wouldn't work in the building. But it worked just now."

Mac shook the unit just enough to detect a faint rattle. "My guess is the shock of the blast shook something loose. The heat might also have cooked it a bit. Circuit boards don't like heat."

Mikee returned to his car slowly, pondering everything. Keeping it all clear in his head was easy—he was good at that—it was just the enormity of it all. There'd been just so much in the last four days. He thought about a book he'd read as a kid 'til he'd all but wore out the pages. In "A Princess of Mars" by Edgar Rice Burroughs, the hero, John Carter suddenly found himself on Mars. Every moment thereafter was a culture shock, but the hero was a warrior and simply coped to the best of his ability.

"Sink or swim," he said to himself in the rearview mirror. "It's like all the other crap you've been through. Just take a deep breath and keep on going."

It was just after 4:00 when he pulled into Tony's driveway. He didn't expect the vampire to be up yet, but figured Nigel would be around. He was surprised when Tony answered the door. Clouds were closing in from the west but the bright blue sky lingering to the east made Tony shield his face and step back quickly.

"I didn't think you could rise this early, especially after last night."

"I can rise just about anytime after 2:00 or 3:00, especially in winter," Tony explained. "I think my *sleep* was a restless one, no doubt related to trauma.

I'm fine, though—not at my best, but functional. How about you? You've had a lot thrown at you."

"It's better than waking up on Mars," Mike joked. Tony looked puzzled. "It's a reference to a book I read as a kid. The hero just kept on going."

Tony smiled. "Burroughs's John Carter series."

Mike was surprised. "You've read Burroughs?"

"Of course," Tony replied. "I followed his fictionalized versions of the the adventures of Lord— well, no sense in embarrassing Tarzan's grandson with revealing his true name."

"Are you kidding me?" Mike couldn't believe it. He'd lived and breathed the Tarzan novels as a boy and wished they were true.

Tony ushered him into the living room and gestured to a chair.

"Heavens, yes. It was quite the uproar in the House of Lords at the time. Of course we all knew who had gone missing, the son found years later in Africa. Everyone assumed that Mr. Burroughs had taken great liberties with his fiction but anyone who really knew the man had few doubts. He had enormous presence and a sort of jungle fierceness about him."

Mike shook his head, then laughed. "You know, after the last few days, that's not only easy to accept, but a curiously welcome piece of news. What about Sherlock Holmes? Did you know him, by chance?"

Tony smiled. "Alas, the real Sherlock Holmes was Sir Arthur himself. Holmes was fictional. Arthur applied the scientific methods of his medical professor and actually did a fair bit of sleuthing on his own. He advised Scotland Yard on several cases. Any other characters from Victorian literature you care to inquire about?"

Mike shook his head and his smile faded. "Chernov was running a meth lab in that apartment—crystal methamphetamine."

"Really? That's curious, though hardly a surprise. He was quite corrupt in the KGB, muscling in, as the Americans say, on several drug operations in Moscow. As I've said, whatever our interests were as humans, we tend to retain them as vampires."

Mike nodded. "There's a Romanian tenant on the first floor, a nice fellow named Ivan—he knows or thinks Chernov is a real vampire. He called him *strigoi*. Chernov likes to collect the rent personally."

"I'll wager he stops doing that now," Tony said. "He'd be a fool not to expect the police to have the place under surveillance, hoping to catch him or follow him."

"I agree. It's a shame. Still, I left a card with Ivan, asking him to call if he sees Chernov. We might get lucky. However, I'm now more interested in the man behind all this—the man who wants you dead so badly."

"*Me* dead?" Tony shook his head. "I rather doubt it. You seem more marked than I, old chap. What I walked into last night was just what the Yanks call a booby-trap."

"With wooden stakes and magnesium," Mike reminded him. "Wouldn't you say that combination is a bit vampire-specific? And our vampire psycho has been uncharacteristically quiet since confirming that he lured you to Halifax to find him. He just wants me out of the way to have a clearer field of fire at you. He could have rigged something to blow the top off that building. If he's stealing automatic weapons for a crime group in Montreal, he can probably get hold of Symtex or C-4. He could have scattered you and Nigel all over Halifax. Instead he chose to take you out in a nastier way. You said yourself that you could probably have survived that explosion. I was just there. Some of the carpet was melted and the walls were charred a bit, but no real structural damage. You'd have been burned horribly, especially with the magnesium content I suspect in your own tissues. It would have made a great pre-mortem torture before someone ended your existence in an up-close-and-personal fashion."

Tony mused over this, then shook his head. "Michael, I gave this a lot of thought last night. Your arguments are very persuasive, but I just can't think of anyone out there who knows what I am and what I do."

"What of the vampire community? Do they know about you and what you do?"

"Well, yes, in a vague sort of way, but it's well-approved. After all, Michael, rogue killer vampires, by their very nature, endanger the rest of us. They threaten us with exposure, and they offend most of us ethically."

"So you're telling me there are no elitists out there—no 'damn the humans, we're here to feed on them' types? You know, 'we're at the top of the food chain and humans are just cattle?' There must be a few of them."

Tiny shrugged. "Of course there are a few, but they abide by the rules."

"So far as you know. What if enough of them banded together and decided to remove the vampire Van Helsing? What if just one Russian count or prince decided he was above the rules and wanted to get rid of you. Maybe he just doesn't want some Limey cohort of George III telling a relative of Czars how to live. If he's committed enough and has the resources, there only needs to be one of him. Chernov and the others are just hired help. That notion is even supported by the fact the Chernov and company seem to have their own business operation on the side."

"You mean the crystal-methamphetamine."

Mike nodded.

"I will consider it, Michael. Your arguments are certainly persuasive enough. By the way, are you getting enough sleep? You look rather haggard. Nigel has tea on in the kitchen. Let me go check on it."

Mike smiled. "Okay, but I need to watch my time. I have to get home and make supper and I have a class tonight."

He took a seat in the living room and called out, "So what's Nigel up to?

"More complicated searching," Tony replied from the kitchen. His voice sounded as if he were still in the room. "He's following up on what Kamensky told us. If this fellow is a Russian aristocrat, he'll be rather particular about his lodgings. Back when I was alive and working with Percy, I knew a lot of those chaps from most of the major countries in Europe. Most were elitist snobs. They couldn't imagine the conditions we endured while in disguise in France. You should have seen the looks of revulsion as they held their handkerchiefs to their mouths and noses, as if shielding themselves from some foul stench we might give off. I'd expect this fellow to be in the royal suite at the Delta Barrington, ordering room service and complaining about the quality. Unfortunately, Kamensky was rather explicit. Our Russian aristo is in an old house, rather a large one, I should imagine. Nigel is searching for something sold or rented out in the last few months. He's also looking for anything to indicate that such a place might be untenanted at the moment. Perhaps our prince is borrowing a house from someone who is away. The latter would be much harder to find but, if anyone can find it, Nigel can.

He'll look for records of mail delivery suspended, etc. There's no end to the data bases he can gain access to."

"And Kamensky? What of him?"

"Sleeping soundly. I had a rush delivery of extra blood last night in the detective's blood type, as well as more of my own. Yes, Michael, you were right about your blood type theory. Jonathan thinks there should be a Vampire Nobel Prize for you.

"After giving our houseguest sufficient replenishment, I settled him in a darkened room. He was still rather comatose just before your arrival. I'm hoping to hypnotize him later. I know he can't tell us much but he may be able to reveal some clues to the location of our mystery noble's house. Perhaps he heard a train, sensed water, heavy traffic, no traffic—it all helps point to possibilities or rule out others.

"Speaking of hypnosis, Michael, how are you adjusting to what you've learned?"

Mike shrugged. "It sure explains a lot," he admitted. "It's just a lot to take in, you know?"

"I can only imagine how this must be affecting you, especially on top of all the other things you've had to accept, like the existence of vampires."

"I spoke to Master Tekaga on the phone last night," Mike explained. "He confirmed quite a few things. It seems he knows quite a bit about Yakura's— my past life. Yakura was a student of the Yagyu school, but I guess you learned that from the hypnosis."

"It's interesting and very significant that you should choose that school to visit," Tony commented. "I referred you to the Ito school with a better reference, having met one of their masters through Interpol work. It was you who chose the Yagyu school, or perhaps I should say it was Yakura.

"But, coming back your hypnosis, Michael, we need to work on your mind control. I don't know what Chernov's psychic skills are but this Russian prince of Kamensky's is a definite concern."

Mike glanced at his watch. "I can only spare fifteen minutes but at least it's a start."

Tony nodded. "No sense in wearing you out when you have to teach tonight."

There was no warning. He was there in Mike's head, forcing him to close his eyes and feel drowsy.

Mike fought back. His eyes snapped open and he shot to his feet, reaching for his katana.

Tony pressed harder. His eyes glowed red. Mike was to put the sword down and resume his seat.

Mike took in a slow, deep breath, forced it out through tightened lips. Chi-kung breathing.

Tony advanced on Mike. "Relax, Michael, and drop the weapon. Everything's fine."

Mike jerked the sleeve back, exposing the hilt of the katana, drawing the sword in the same motion. Tony's advance was stopped by the tip of the blade. Mike was struggling for control but the blade never wavered.

Tony exhaled sharply, then raised his hands.

"We're done, Michael. You can relax."

Mike took a step back but only lowered the blade an inch or two, his eyes on Tony.

Tony smiled. "I'm serious, Michael, you can relax. You did much better than I expected. You learned a lot from the Tulku. You even kept eye contact with me and resisted. It would have been easier had you avoided eye contact altogether. However, knowing that you have some resistance to that is good. People generally fail utterly once eye contact is achieved."

It wasn't until Tony's eyes returned to normal that Mike sheathed his katana and relaxed.

"That was a little scary," he said. "It was as if you suddenly became the enemy."

Mike's cell phone belted out an obnoxious dixieland version of *When the Saints Go Marching In.* He grinned. "That's Sean, probably wondering where I am and what's for supper." He flipped open the phone.

"Yeah, Sean."

"Hey, Dad. Where are you? Will you be home for supper? Should I heat up a frozen pizza?"

"That's fine but you only get half—maybe a slice more. I'll be home before it's out of the oven."

He grinned as he closed the phone. "At least some things never change."


On the way home he called MacDonald. "Pete, any change in recent drug activity in the North Street area—like evidence of a new dealer or a change in who's dealing? Any escalation in traffic?"

"Well, no one can say your timing's off," MacDonald commented.

"What do you mean?"

"Someone spotted a body in the water near Bishop's Landing, a floater. When divers went in to bag him and bring him out, they found he had company, caught against the barnacles, deeper into the water. Both had significant throat damage. However, with how long they were in the water, between the fish and the crabs, it's anyone's guess what caused the original wounds."

"Hey, Pete, when you hear hoof beats, look for horses, not zebras."

"Is that Confucius?"

"Actually, it's something my first principal in Bermuda said, but you get my point."

"Yeah, I know. How many perps do we have attacking throats in HRM. Mind you, it wouldn't be the first time one drug dealer cut another's throat."

"So they were both dealers?" Mike asked.

"Both, and their turf was around North Street, mostly the blocks around Gottingen."

"Pete, you know how quiet things have seemed, as if our Ripper vampire has taken time off from terrorizing the town? Well, I've got a funny feeling. What if he's just decided to dump the bodies somewhere else, like the harbour."

"But why?" Pete asked. "He never seemed to care before. It was as if he was taunting us."

"I think this is somehow about Tony. I told you last night: I was set up so that Tony would be on his own. What if the extravagance in the beginning was just to get Tony here? Then they adopted a lower profile while they got the rest of the pieces in place."

"What pieces are those, Mike?"

"How the hell should I know, Pete? This is just hunch, albeit a strong one."

"Hey, don't get mad at me, Mike. I'm on your side. Your judgement in this has been good so far. I was just hoping you had more hunches."

Mike sighed. "Sorry, Pete. I just think they're trying to isolate Tony, make him helpless, and dump him off with someone who holds a grudge. For what I have no idea. Who knows, maybe it's the brother or son of some perp Tony destroyed. It's all a guess."

"I hear you, Mike. You get any more hunches, let me know. And you may be right. The body count may have eased up but the number of people reported missing has risen to make up the difference."

"Check the islands and points."

"What's that?"

It had come out as one of his sudden insights. Mike thought about it. "The tide moves bodies. They might get caught under a pier for a day or so but, unless they're weighted down, the tide will try to carry them out of the harbour. The ones that don't get carried out to sea will come up against George's Island, McNabb's, maybe Point Pleasant or near Chebucto Head. I'll bet there's someone at the Bedford Institute that has a tide simulation that can pinpoint the best places for harbour patrol to look."

"Great. Now I have to convince those guys to put a boat back in the water in February."

Mike smiled. "Tomorrow's the last day of January."

"You think I can get those guys rallied by tomorrow? Yeah, maybe. I'll call their sergeant right now. Who knows? Maybe he's got a couple of guys who are keen to do this. Otherwise, I'll try the RCMP. It was their guys who pulled the two dealers out of the water tonight."

Mike pulled the bluetooth piece out of his ear and dropped it into the cup-holder near the gearshift. He suddenly wished he was headed for a bath and bed instead of supper and a class.

When Mike reached home, there was a black sedan with government plates parked in front of his house. He pulled into the garage, then walked to the car. The front seat passenger showed a CSIS ID and said, "It's warm in the car if you don't mind sparing us a moment, Mr. Cameron."

"Give me a minute." Mike went back up his walk, opened the front door, leaned on the button to close the garage, then called out to Sean.

"Yo." Sean opened his door and slid to a stop on sock feet at the head of the stair. The snow outside was melting, leaving just the banks created by the plows, but Sean was bare-chested as if it was mid-summer.

"It's not August, Sean. At least put a T-shirt on."

Sean rolled his eyes. "I'm fine, Dad."

"Humour me. Think of it as a matter of etiquette"

Sean rolled his eyes. "*Fine, Dad*," he groaned.

"I'll be back in a moment; I just have to speak to someone outside. Check on supper in the meantime, please."

"Already done," Sean replied. "I shut the oven off just before you pulled in. It's in the oven, door ajar."

Mike nodded, then went back to the car in front. As he slid into the back seat, he preempted them by saying, "If this is a pep talk about secrecy, national security, or the potential for mass panic, gentlemen, save us both the time. You're preaching to the choir."

The passenger smiled and handed Mike a leather by-fold. It looked like police ID. Mike opened it, expecting it to reveal the identity of the agent who was handing it to him. He wasn't prepared to see his driver's license photo looking back at him. It identified him as a special agent for CSIS.

For a moment he didn't know what to say. "I thought only the FBI used the term 'special agent.' Is this for real?"

"Right down to the salary and benefits while on assignment," the agent replied.

"Why? I'm already lugging around papers from the police and Interpol."

The agent nodded. "It's simple, Mr. Cameron. Your Interpol liaison position carries very little weight. It relies on the local police extending you courtesy. God forbid anything should happen to Inspector MacDonald, his successor might decide to shut you out and try to order Lord Dewhurst to mind his own business, though we can force Lord Dewhurst on the police. This gives you more official standing. It also puts us on the front line instead of waiting of Lord Dewhurst's reports. And you needn't worry, there's no conflict with Lord Dewhurst. CSIS has the highest faith in him. This isn't a pissing contest, Mr. Cameron. There was a movement to contact you soon after you came home.

"When you disappeared, your father had your cousin pull some strings to locate you. That caught our attention. We know quite a bit about Detective Inspector Cameron, now retired. He had quite a remarkable career. You, yourself, are a man of remarkable accomplishments. You spent six months in Hunan Province, China, and six months in Tibet. Yet, as far as Beijing knows, you've never been to either country. When we add this to your martial arts prowess, the results of five known IQ tests, and your achievements as a scholar and a sailor, well, Mr. Cameron, let's just say that you are a man of unique and remarkable abilities, a welcome asset to our organization.

"I've been instructed by the director to assure you that you will not be ordered about like a soldier. Your special status allows you to work assignment by assignment."

Mike considered, then asked, "What if I want to turn down an assignment?"

"I'm of the impression that you have that option, but I believe that most of your assignments will be of similar nature to what you're doing now. You may even be working with Lord Dewhurst on many of them."

"And resigning?"

"We're not the Cosa Nostra, Mr. Cameron," the agent laughed. "Of course you have to sign this, making you subject to the Official Secrets Act." He held out a clipboard.

Mike nodded and took it. He speed read through it and signed, then pocketed the ID. "Will I have a regular contact? Is there a secret phone number and password?"

Again the agent chuckled. He extended his hand. "Jean Charbonneau. I'll be your main contact. The phone number is no secret, it's the same 800 number that's in the government section of the phonebook. It's also on the back of your ID. When asked for an extension, dial the last three digits of your ID number. And, yes, we will need a password. You can chose it yourself."

Mike pronounced a word for him but the agent looked puzzled. "It's Japanese," Mike explained, then spelled it. The agent just nodded.

"Good luck, Special Agent Cameron," he said as Mike exited the car.

# 17: Clues

On the way to class, Mike called Tony. "It's about Chernov," he said after the usual pleasantries. "When he went dirty after the KGB, what was he into? Drugs and extortion?"

"Well, he was into drugs while with the KGB, so that's probable. Just a moment, Michael. Nigel has set me up with this high-tech Blackberry thing. I say, look at that! I can bring up the data file while talking on the phone. Jolly good, that! Ah, here we are. I say, Michael, that's exactly what he did—both—and the drug was crystal methamphetamine. But how did you ever...?"

"You said it yourself, Tony. Vampire's aren't that different than people. Their interests remain. Once a drug dealer, always a drug dealer."

"Rather like you, dear boy, considering your past life. Once a samurai, always a samurai. Only now you're a *bushi* for the public safety rather than a shogun. Ooh, sorry, old man, that sounds like a bad slogan, doesn't it?"

Mike grinned. "Yeah, well, I guess we can't escape what we are. My grandfather fought in France, the Camerons fought for Bonnie Prince Charlie, and, according to my grandfather, we lost family fighting alongside Wallace at Stirling and Falkirk. *Avagh na bragh*! I come from a long line of warriors... even without resorting to past life theory."

"So you've come to terms with your past life."

"Yeah," he admitted. "Speaking of warriors," he added, pulling into the parking lot, "I have to go teach a few. Look, Tony, have MacDonald dig into this. Chernov may be our unidentified Count Dracula's pit bull in whatever the dark prince is planning but he's also running his own game on the side. He's got people producing crystal meth and he's forcing his way into someone else's business, maybe taking over an established turf. If Pete can find out who he's taking over from, it might help us track him down."

Michael threw himself into the lesson, pushing his students, especially prospective black belts, to their limits. For most of the night he had them attacking him. They attacked with fists and feet. They attacked with sticks, then padded bokken, the wooden training sword of the Samurai. Then they advanced to blunted katana. Mike remained unarmed. The more he pushed, the more focused his students became.

The more he let his mind go, the faster he moved, responding naturally out of instinct with just enough conscious present to avoid hurting anyone.

"DAD!" Sean yelled.

Mike stopped, breathless and suddenly very dizzy.

Sean pulled a chair over and helped Mike sit. "Johnny, get him some water." He was still staring at Mike as the student brought a cold bottled water from the fridge."

"I'm fine," Mike assured his son. "Why did you scream like that? What's wrong? I know I didn't hit anyone too hard. Besides, I was mostly redirecting." This was what Mike called using someone else's energy to throw them around the room like a rag doll.

"Dad, you were starting to move so fast we could barely see you. You were a blur!"

Mike grimaced. "Keep it real, Sean. Maybe you need some water."

"No, *sifu*, he's right," Johnny gasped, still fighting for breath. "You're fast, but I've never seen you move that fast."

Mike puzzled over this. It seemed improbable but he decided to take them at their word. Perhaps this was some aspect of Yakura coming through. Perhaps some link between Sensei Tekaga's training and something the Tulku had taught him.

He recovered quickly—perhaps the water helped—and got to his feet.

"Alright—you four continue at me. Sean, you monitor me for control. If you see it happening again, don't stop me unless you think someone is in danger."

Once again, he followed his usual pattern. When they advanced, he moved, keeping his movements small, just enough to evade. He constantly kept another opponent between him and the most aggressive attacker. Then he'd dodge behind an attacker and take him out from behind. He took swords away from his opponents but rarely used them himself. He'd parry with a blade, then drop it as he skipped behind an attacker and brought him down.

Finally he took up a dropped katana and closed on two swordsmen. What followed was a series of feints and parries. He advanced, moving faster and faster, getting inside their guard and touching them with blows that would have been lethal.

He felt faint again when he stopped, calling for another bottle of water.

"Well?" he asked Sean.

Sean's wide-eyed look spoke volumes. "I know you won but, if I were a tough judge from a competing school, I'd say you didn't. I couldn't see much of what you did. I could tell you did something, but I couldn't tell for sure what the technique was, except when you plainly disarmed someone or took him down."

"Yeah, well we could sure feel what he did," Johnny insisted, wincing and holding his ribs.

"Ditto," Frank agreed. "You rarely leave a mark and probably didn't this time, *sifu*, but I feel like one big walking bruise."

He checked Frank for bruises and found nothing but a few red impact marks that would fade in an hour, the same with Johnny.

"Sorry if it hurts," he offered, "but you guys are really improving. So are you," he said quietly to Sean, throwing an arm about his son. "I guess I just wanted to see if I still had it. I'm getting old, you know. Fifty is just around the bend."

"*Right, Dad*," Sean snorted. "Tonight you looked more like you were getting younger. I've seen you fast but never that fast."

"Get a shower," he said, giving Sean a push in that direction.

Mike mused further on his new-found speed as he headed for the office and his own private shower. By the time he was drying himself off, he gave up and just accepted it.

*Maybe I'll speed up, then burn out, like some cancer patients*, he thought. He caught himself, realized he was getting morbid, letting his dark side slip. *I'm not only getting faster, I'm getting more cheerful. Maybe I've always been that fast*, he suggested to himself. *Maybe I'm so worried about being ready for whatever I encounter with these vampires that it's got me pushing to new limits I've never tried to reach before.*

It was almost eight o'clock when he turned out the lights and locked up. Sean was grinning all the way home.

"I wish you could have seen the looks on Johnny and Frank's faces," he said. "I think you were too wrapped up in what you were doing. They didn't know where to look. It was like they just couldn't keep track of where you were."

Mike smiled weakly but didn't find it amusing. Something about it seemed unsettling. For now, though, the best thing was to just accept it.

As he dropped Sean in front of the house, he told him, "Go straight in, lock the door, and reset the alarm. And be alert."

The words were barely out of his mouth when a white police unit pulled slowly by, turned in the turning circle, then just as slowly returned down the street. The cop at the wheel caught Mike's eye and gave him an acknowledging nod as he drove by.

"See, Dad," Sean insisted. "Even the cops are keeping extra watch. I'll be fine. Go see Tony. And, Dad, don't be freaked by that speed thing tonight. Come on, you should be psyched."

Mike shrugged and watched as Sean opened the front door and let Sam out to visit one of the cedars in front of the house.

He pulled away and coasted down the street. As he neared the stop sign at the corner he saw the police cruiser just sitting there. In Dartmouth, these units were often manned by just one officer, but this one had two. He stopped behind the unit, waiting for it to pull away. Traffic was clear. Instead of making the turn, the cop on the passenger side got out and walked back to Mike.

Mike's pulse quickened and he felt for his katana with his right hand. His left triggered the button that rolled his window all the way down.

"What's up?" he asked. He felt like every cell in his body was tensed, ready to move.

"Nothing, Mr. Cameron," the officer replied. "Just checking that everything is okay. We'll be cruising by your house about once an hour."

Mike nodded and tried to keep his sigh of relief from seeming too obvious. "Thanks," he said. "My son's almost eighteen and a talented brown belt, but he thinks he's bullet proof. He's not."

The cop grinned. "Mine's six. Thinks he's Spider-Man. Tough not to worry about them, especially with all this weird shit going on. Heard they found more bodies in the Harbour—vicious throat wounds. Could have been fish or crabs but, being specific to the throat makes us assume it's this psycho, you know.

"Look, Mr. Cameron, there are a bunch of us on the force who just want you to know we're on your side. We heard about what Jenkins pulled and we agree with what you did with him. Talk is he was setting you up. If we ever find out who he was setting you up for…"

Mike nodded. "Jenkins got suckered. He's an asshole and someone took advantage of that. When we find whoever's behind this I'm hoping to deal with him myself, on behalf of the force, as well as my new employers." He showed the officer his CSIS ID.

The cop smiled and nodded. "Well, they can't whine about a civilian doing police work now, can they? Have a safe night, Mr. Cameron. And, sir, get this guy. We'll all sleep better when he's out of the picture."

The cop got back in the car and the cruiser turned right onto Woodlawn. Mike made a left, heading for

Portland and Tony's. The conversation brought Jenkins and Kamensky back to the forefront in this thoughts. He wanted to see what what happening with Dartmouth's newest vampire.

Nigel answered the door. "'Allo, guv'nor, good to see you. Coffee or scotch?"

Mike smiled and shook Nigel's hand. "Neither, maybe some water. How's Kamensky?"

"So far so good. 'E's well-fed and a lot calmer than last night, I can tell you. 'Is Lordship's givin' 'im a crash course at the moment—you know, contacts for food, emergency help, an' such. Can you believe it? There's like this vampire help line. 911 for vampires. *Someone come an' pull this stake out of my chest, quick.*" Nigel chuckled. "I guess it's like a world-wide network. Remember those guys announced they were working on cloning blood cells? Then there was this big clamour to shut them down—you know, no cloned parts, no genetically engineered food. Well, the *network* jumped in on the sly, helped out with some funding, and 'ave been getting samples of the prototype results. So far, so good. Less pressure on getting it from the blood banks, which they also do, I guess."

"What about Kamensky?" Mike asked. "Has he been able to tell us anymore?"

"Naw, I guess 'e gave us all 'e's got. Still, I've got a program searching real estate transactions for the last few months. It's filtering sales an' leases or rentals. And, we're keeping an eye on that building. It looks like Chernov actually bought it, so I doubt if 'e'd just abandon it. And 'e can't sell it wiffout signing an agreement. By the way, speakin' o' closin' deals, Tony needs an account number and routing info. I don' know if 'e's footin' the bill or Interpol is, but you're on the payroll wiff a tidy bit o' wages due." He gave Mike a conspiratorial wink.

"Actually, there's been a recent complication in that area, but I should tell Tony first."

Nigel shrugged. "Whotever—I'm just 'Is Lordship's unofficial clark. Still, if we 'ave the info, we can use it if we need it and ignore it if we don't."

Mike leaned his katana against the wall, flipped open his phone, went to the notepad, and opened the necessary file. He handed the phone to Nigel. Nigel typed it into his Blackberry and handed Mike back his phone.

"Your dad suggested 'aving undercovers watch for drug dealers in that part of town. If Chernov killed those blokes to take over their turf, someone 'as to take their place. If we can spot 'em, maybe they can lead us to Chernov."

"That's Dad," Mike said with a grin. "In a nursing home on oxygen, he's still one step ahead. Did that get passed on to MacDonald?"

Nigel nodded. "Your dad spoke to the Inspector before telling 'Is Lordship. You want ice in your water?" Mike shook his head and picked up his sword.

There was no one in the living room so Mike took the stairs two at a time and found Tony and Kamensky in a bed room, Kamensky sitting on the bed, Tony in a chair.

"Ah, Michael, I thought I heard you come in. Did Nigel get banking information from you?" Mike nodded. "Good. Alex, here, may be of considerable help to us. His strength and speed will take time to develop but the ability to be stealthy and disappear into shadow comes quite quickly. He's offered to take on the task of assisting with night surveillance, looking for Chernov's dealers."

Michael approached Kamensky and held out his hand. "Welcome aboard, Alex."

Kamensky hesitated, then smiled and took Mike's hand. "I know what side of the law I want to be on," he said. "My new-found condition–" his hands made what Mike took as a gesture of hopeless resignation, "well, let's just say I'm glad of any kind of useful police work I can still do. I got suckered into this. I didn't want any part of Chernov, and I certainly didn't want *this*." Again he made the gesture with his hands.

"So now you help us nail Chernov and his mystery prince, Alex."

"Thanks for trusting and accepting me," Kamensky said.

Mike shrugged. "I tend to be rather pragmatic. From Lord Anthony's methods, we know your story is true. You were forced into this—suckered, as you put it, then turned against your will. Fair enough. From now on I judge you by what you do. Help us out, and I'm on your side all the way. Cross me, cross my friends, or endanger my family in any way..." he finished the warning by drawing his katana just enough to give Kamensky a view of how sharp the blade was.

Turning, he took Tony aside and said, "That banking info may be a bit redundant, double-dipping even." He showed Tony his CSIS ID and told him about Carbonneau's visit.

Tony smiled and handed it back. "Good show, Michael. It actually simplifies things quite a bit. But keep the Interpol liaison ID—never know when it'll come in handy. Who knows, this time next year I may be begging for you to help with something similar in London or Paris. Then that Interpol liaison ID will be more useful than CSIS, and you'll be back on my payroll."

Tony's cell phone rang. He listened, nodding. "Thank you," he said before putting his phone back in his vest pocket.

"That was Inspector MacDonald. Dealers have been spotted on Gottingen, Maynard, and Fuller Terrace, each within two blocks of North. He's got people watching them, waiting for us to arrive."

"Can Alex here do anything with his mind yet? Any hypnotic abilities?"

"Some," Tony said, nodding. "He can exert some influence over Nigel. Of course, I've trained Nigel to resist, so, yes, I'd say Alex can assist in this. And he will get better with time and practice."

"I'll take Gottingen," Mike said, choosing the street with the roughest reputation.

"I'll take Maynard and Alex can take Fuller. We could take one vehicle, park close to North, and walk the rest."

"We'll take mine," Mike insisted.

When he got out of his car on North, near Gottingen, Mike pulled his *sgian dubh* out of a kit bag, and stuck all three into his belt. The shortness of their blades might be laughed at by the average hoodlum but the tips were dagger-sharp and the edges honed like razors. Even the smaller two would easily sever the spinal cord if plunged into a neck.

He glanced at his katana lying on the back seat in its silk sleeve. Even covered it might be a bit conspicuous dangling from his shoulder. He decided to leave it. *These are drug dealers, not vampires,* he told himself.

Calming his thoughts, he reached out with his mind. He could feel Tony's presence, sense his movement along Maynard. Changing focus, he sensed Alex moving along Fuller. The detective was armed with his service piece. Mike knew Tony carried the sword cane, not that he'd need it against a human, considering his vampiric abilities.

Further along Gottingen he spotted two figures that didn't quite fit in with the dribble of pedestrian traffic. One appeared homeless. Dressed in rags, he rummaged in a trash can, then shuffled about, not moving too far from the can, constantly talking to himself. All the while he seemed to cast furtive glances at a shadowy figure across the street. This latter stood quietly in the recessed entrance to a darkened building.

The homeless man fell silent as a disheveled-looking young woman approached the shadow figure. Homeless mumbled then fell silent again. There seemed to be some sort of exchange between the woman Mike now categorized as a hooker/junky and the obvious drug dealer. When the woman then walked off, her stride much more purposeful, Homeless muttered some more. Mike, pegging him as the surveillance cop, assumed he was notifying someone by transmitter of the transaction and the direction of movement of the hooker.

Mike quickened his pace just slightly. He made as if to pass the dealer by, unnoticed, then wheeled about and seized the man. The dealer was wiry and strong, showing no apparent symptoms of using his own product, but he was no match for Mike. Mike slammed the dealer hard against brickwork, making sure he got enough jolting impact to be disoriented. The dealer made a mad scramble to grab a weapon hidden under his coat. Mike snatched the dealer's wrist and squeezed. Bones creaked as if about to break and the dealer cried out. Mike removed a pistol and tossed it a couple of feet.

Homeless ran across the street just in time to pick up the fallen piece and pocket it. He drew his own weapon and kept the dealer covered.

Mike power breathed, lifted the man off the ground, and slammed him against the bricks once more.

"Here's how it works:" Mike's tone was icy. "You tell me where to find your supplier and you keep breathing."

"You're a cop, cop's can't work like that," the dealer argued. Yet the fear radiating off him belied his protest.

"Wrong," Mike argued. "I'm no cop, and I work how I please to get the job done. Think of me as a garbage man. Right now my job is to take out the trash." A heavy *sgian dubh* appeared in his hand, it's needle-sharp tip puncturing about two millimeters into the skin under the dealer's chin.

The dealer cried out in pain, his eyes wide. Mike had him against the wall, feet off the ground, with his right hand, celtic knife in his left. "All I have to do is relax my right arm and you come down on the blade." He cocked his head to one side, as if estimating a distance. "Yeah," he said, "the blade's long enough to pass through your pallet into the brain. I hope my right arm doesn't get tired before you tell me what I want to hear."

"This Russian guy," the dealer stammered. "That's all I know. He comes by and gives me a backpack full of little zip-bags and takes my money. That's what I know. He sounds Russian, like in spy movies."

Mike did his best to look unsatisfied.

"On my daughter's life, I swear—wait a minute—there used to be a warehouse, at least that's what I heard—not these new guys, the old guys. No one sees them anymore. Talk was they had a warehouse somewhere on Robie, I think. That's all I know, I don't know no more, I swear! Please!"

The *sgian dubh* disappeared as fast as it had appeared. Using both hands, Mike held the dealer, forcing his mind into the other's. He found nothing but fear and truth.

*Keep up the fear,* he thought. *Maybe he can lead us to someone else.*

He made a show of turning away from the bricks before lowering the man to the ground. "Don't make me come back. I can visit you in your cell at night if I choose."

As he let the man go, the cop pulled the dealer's arms behind his back and cuffed his wrists. He gave Mike an awed look, then a slow nod.

"I can take it from here."

Mike heaved a sigh, then nodded.

He went rigid. Something intruded in his mind— surprise, fear. Kamensky. He reached out for Tony's mind. Tony was running. Mike took off, sprinting back the way he'd come. Up North, down Fuller. He could sense Tony behind him, gaining with his vampire speed, but he didn't want to look back.

Kamensky was limp in the arms of a heavier man. Mike's mind hit a barrier—something feral—a vampire! The vampire let Kamensky drop to the ground and turned on Mike. Thick fingernails had been sharpened to points. He bared his fangs and hissed at Mike like something out of a movie, then advanced with vampire speed.

Mike's hands flashed to his belt and came back with a blade in each. The vampire clamped hands onto Mike's shoulders, claws digging in. Mike's arms came up inside the grip but, instead of striking the arms away, he buried his blades to the hilt in each shoulder, puncturing the deltoids and severing motor nerves to the arms.

He pulled the blades free, dropped low and spun, lashing out with his right leg in an arc that took the vampire's feet out from under him from behind. As the creature hit the pavement, Mike was on him, atop his chest, blades crossed to cut his throat from both directions.

"Think about staying alive," Mike gasped, fighting to catch his breath. He power breathed until his respiration slowed.

"Well done, Michael." Tony had caught up and drawn his sword, adding it to the threat at the vampire's throat.

"I tried to probe his mind but hit a wall."

"It's not easy when one with vampire skills resists," Tony said. "Apply your martial training. You need to use a more rapid, forceful attack to penetrate resistance."

Mike glanced at Kamensky. "Is Alex okay?"

As Tony went to check, Mike focused on his anger. It wasn't hard, he had a well of unresolved anger—Susan's death, his ex-wife and how she'd treated Sean, bullies from his childhood. He struck out with his mind, like a fist, forcing into the vampire's thoughts.

The sound that came from the vampire was half snarl, half scream. Mike understood part of the wall. The vampire thought in Russian.

*Name,* he demanded.

*Bondarenko, Mikhail Bondarenko.*

*Okay, Mikhail, we have the same first name, something in common. Tell me more.*

Bondarenko tried to drive a knee into Mike's spine.

One *sgian dubh* left Bondarenko's throat and plunged into the vampire's pelvis. The vampire let out an agonized cry and went still. Mike tore the blade out against the serrated edge, damaging muscles and nerves further before returning it to the one that remained at Bondarenko's throat. He had to work fast. The shoulder damage might be beginning to heal.

"Pissing me off isn't smart at this point, Mikhail. Cooperation might make up for that. Now, who's in charge and where do I find him."

This time the wall felt different. It wasn't something he couldn't get through, it was like with Kamensky. There was something Bondarenko couldn't speak of.

"Is he a Russian Prince? A Romanov?"

"*Niet.*" His eyes glared. There was a mental struggle. He seemed to want to say something. "Rumanian. Last Prince of Wallachia—Transylvania."

"Name."

The mental struggle came again but no answer.

"Do you know someone with the same name?"

The Russian smiled. "I had a cousin, Stephan."

"Is there a house?"

It came in bits, like the result of intense struggle. "Big house—bigger than dacha—not his house—stolen house." This last came in a gasp of pain that lingered as a long snarl. He seemed to battle an internal conflict. "*Niet, niet,*" he growled.

Without warning, he lifted his head and thrashed it back and forth, forcing Mike's daggers to cut through his throat.

"No!" Mike cried, clamping a hand to slow blood flow.

Tony shook his head. "It'll heal with blood, but I doubt if he'll take blood. It's rather like a magical geas, the kind fantasy novels like to use. He's trying to kill himself against his will, rather than give up this Stephan, Prince of Wallachia. Odd—my Romanian history is a bit dodgy, but I can't recollect a Prince Stephan. In fact, the last princes weren't really princes. They were overlords appointed by the Ottoman Empire. The locals called them voivode. The title originally referred to a military commander but became that of the leader of a district. We British often translated it as 'prince,' 'duke,' or 'count,' but 'governor' might be a better term in this case. Our Stephan sure wants to pass himself off as royalty. Knowing that might be useful."

"Can we save him? Bondarenko?"

"Doubtful. Save him for what? A blood diet in prison? He's proved to be a killer. He was trying to turn on this Stephan, not to help us, but in hope of survival. No, Michael, if you would, I'd rather you let me step some distance away, then sever his spinal cord. Shield your mind when you do."

Tony walked away and waited. Mike hesitated. This wasn't like killing in self-defense. That didn't bother him. Being forced into the role of executioner did. *Taking out the garbage*, he told himself. Raising barriers around his mind, he rolled Bondarenko onto his stomach and drove his heavier *sgian dubh* into Bondarenko's spinal cord from behind. He levered the blade back and forth, making sure the severing was complete.

He wasn't prepared for the force that hit him. It was different than the turmoil of Petrenko's passing. An onslaught of violent images tore into him. He managed to repel most of them but what got through was disturbing in the extreme. No wonder Tony avoided it.

He staggered as he got to his feet. Tony appeared at his side, grabbing him in his arms to steady him.

"There, there, steady on, Michael. I've got you."

Mike nodded. "I'm fine. What about Kamensky?"

"Gone, I'm afraid. It may help you accept killing Bondarenko if you see what he did to Alex."

Mike walked over to the detective's body. His throat had been ravaged so severely that the windpipe was demolished and the spine torn into. Bondarenko had then ripped the head to one side, tearing the spine the rest of the way by brute strength.

Mike looked about. *Where's the cop?* he thought. *And where's the drug dealer? Surely Bondarenko wasn't the dealer.*

Recalling how Homeless had watched his man from across the street, he crossed over and found a black man, dressed in gang dress, huddled next to the dumpster for an apartment building, his throat torn almost as bad as Kamensky's. Searching the dead man's clothes, he found a police-issue handgun, a badge, and a radio with a wired hand mic.

He returned just as Tony was concluding a decapitation of Bondarenko with his sword. The English Lord cleaned the blade on Bondarenko's clothes, sheathed it in his cane.

Mike called MacDonald.

"Pete, scratch Mikhail Bondarenko off your list. We've also lost the surveillance officer assigned to the dealer on Fuller Terrace. I don't think Bondarenko is the dealer. Kamensky's dead, too. The cop died first. I think Bondarenko came upon the cop surveilling the dealer, took out the cop, then waited for Kamensky. I imagine the dealer took off as fast as his legs would carry him when he saw what was happening."

"What about the others? Did you or Lord Anthony learn anything?"

"Not much. Mine confirmed that Russians are involved, that they've somehow taken over from the previous dealers. He did say that the previous dealers worked out of an old warehouse somewhere on Robie—at least he'd heard a rumour to that effect."

He glanced at Tony. "You learn anything on Maynard Street."

Tony shook his head. "My chap was something of a weasel. Didn't know, didn't want to know. Sold his narcotics, took his money, tried not to step on any toes. Quite fearful, actually."

Mike relayed the information to the inspector.

"You okay?" Pete asked. "You were able to kill Bondarenko? You're not hurt?"

"A bit rattled," Mike admitted. "Actually, between tonight's workout at the school and being attacked by Bondarenko, I was so psyched that I just carried through on a kind of adrenalin high until it was over. Bondarenko actually tried to kill himself. I did get part of a name and a country of origin—would you believe Stephan, last Prince of Wallachia and Transylvania? I'll dig into it more when I get home."

"Be safe, Mike," MacDonald said. Mike heard worry in his tone.

"It's over for the night, I hope, Pete," he replied. "I'm sorry about your cop."

"Yeah. I guess I'd better get a wagon over there to collect bodies. We'll keep Kamensky and Bondarenko quiet and call the surveillance cop killed in the line of duty by a dealer. Damn, I don't even have a name yet."

"Wilson," Mike supplied. "Allen Wilson. I have his badge, ID, and his piece. We'll wait for the ME and turn the effects over to him."

Mike turned to Tony. "Can I use your Blackberry a moment?"

He connected to the internet and Googled "Wallachia last voivode." Clicked on a Wikipedia entry that looked the most promising. As he scrolled through the information, be became puzzled.

"What is it, Michael?" Tony leaned over his shoulder.

"All that stuff about Vlad Dracula, aka Vlad Tsepes, the Impaler, was true. His father, Vlad Dracul, was a member of the Order of the Dragon. Anyway, Dracula's success in repelling the Turks was short-lived. The Ottoman Empire eventually over-ran the region. The Habsburg Empire took over Transylvania and appointed governors. But the Draculs were voivodes of Wallachia, not Transylvania.

"Someone is really confused. Rumania as we know it today is made up of three states: Wallachia, Transylvania, and Moldavia. Wallachia, immediately south of Transylvania, became part of the Ottoman Empire, also ruled by regents, whom the people called voivode. The last voivode before Russian incursion died in office. He was actually a Greek, though born in Istanbul, one Alexandros Soutzos. He stylized it as Alexandru Sutu to sound more native to the locals. There's no Stephan, and it has nothing to do with Transylvania."

Tony smiled. "We spoke before of Abraham or "Bram" Stoker. He researched vampiric folklore for years before writing Dracula, but decided that the geography of the Carpathians and Transylvania was more intriguing than that of Wallachia, Dracula's true homeland."

Mike nodded. "Bondarenko actually called this Stephan the last Prince of Wallachia, then said Transylvania. Maybe adding Transylvania was a matter of his own confused geography."

"But we know the claim is a false one, since the last voivode's name was Alexandru, not Stephan. Perhaps our Prince Stephan felt entitled to the position.

Perhaps he's related to Alexandru. Perhaps *he* mentioned Transylvania to evoke a sense of fear or mystique about himself, drawing on the Dracula phenomenon."

A thought intruded on Mike, like the voice of another in his head.

"Like Toda Yoshihiro, back when I was Yakura," he said. It was like he was in a daze. "Another Toda, an ancestor, fought for Hideyori against Tokugawa Ieyasu. Ieyasu defeated Hideyori at the battle of Sekigahara in 1600. Toda was just one of Hideyori's generals. One of his descendants got the twisted notion that Toda might have been shogun instead of Hideyori. Yoshihiro plotted, allegedly to put his father on the throne, but it was really just a pretense. He saw himself as shogun when his father died. Yoshihiro had followers—he was a good talker and charismatic—but he was a spoiled brat. He wanted instant glory and was never willing to work for it. He had expensive, shiny armour, but was mediocre with a katana. He thought he was the best, but wasn't willing to work at being even half-decent."

"It that you or Yakura speaking?" Tony asked. His face showed concern.

Mike showed a hint of a smile and shrugged. "Is there a difference? I was Yakura, now I'm Mike. Feeling his thoughts are sort of becoming like remembering my childhood or, more correctly, something before my current childhood. I used to feel like he was a ghost trying to intrude on my life, perhaps possess me. It's not like that now. He's a set of memories. I recognize how he felt about things—we're fundamentally the same in many beliefs and ideals, but I see the world differently. It's like he's finally had a chance to grow up in me. Ideals change with new experience and new understanding. Where our values differ, there's no conflict."

Relief showed in Tony's smile. "I think your time with the Tulku did more than expand your mental abilities. I think a lot of his wisdom rubbed off on you."

Mike glanced toward North Street. "Here's the coroner's van now, along with a police unit. Good. I'm cold and would rather find a Tim Horton's than hang about here any longer."

When both vehicles pulled up, Mike handed the badge, ID, and handgun to one of the accompanying police officers and pointed across the street to where the dead officer lay.

"I told the Inspector everything over the phone," he said. "I arrived on the scene, Lord Dewhurst following, just as Bondarenko was dropping Kamensky's body. Bondarenko then attacked me. The coroner will understand the gravity of the wounds. I then found the surveillance officer dead across the street. My guess is that Bondarenko caught your man watching the dealer, killed him, heard Kamensky coming or guessed that someone was coming and waited. He then killed Kamensky. The dealer probably fled or was ordered to leave when Bondarenko killed the undercover officer."

The officer was writing it all down in a notebook. "Forensics will be here soon, maybe they'll find something to confirm things but you're theory looks probable."

———————

Mike started his car and waited for the heat to kick in. He glanced at the clock and decided to check in with Sean. Once satisfied that everything was fine there, and noticing that it was nearing eleven o'clock, Carrie's time for leaving work, he called her.

"Care to meet me for coffee on your way home?"

"Sure. There's a Tim Horton's not far from here, just up from the boardwalk at the Passage."

The enthusiasm of the responce gave him a needed lift. "Great," he said. "I'm on my way. I just have to drop Tony off at his place."

Tony was smiling at him as he put the phone away.

"What?" Mike felt a bit self-conscious.

"Your happiness is showing. It speaks volumes. I'm just pleased for you, Michael, that's all. Enjoy a precious moment with your Carrie. She is a lovely lady with a huge heart that aches to give the love it was never permitted to give because that love was not returned. It is in her eyes when she looks at you.

"I confess, Michael, I spent some time reading her that night in the pub. She is a generous, giving soul who has yearned her whole life to find a soul mate, one like her who is loving and giving. But she is strong, Michael. You cannot imagine the strength required for a woman to do the painful job she does. Can you imagine devoting your day's labour to working with people you know might die before you go home or before you come back to work? She chooses this because her immense heart has comfort to give these people, people like your father, in their last days with us. These are people, many of whom's families have ceased to visit because they can no longer bear the stress of watching a loved-one slowly die. And she gives even more care to them because they are so alone. And what toll does this take from her? Yet she does this painful duty because she can. It takes great strength, the same strength you showed when you put an end to Bondarenko, not yet realizing the monster he truly was. You think she is a bright spot in your horror-filled life? Consider what a bright spot you must be in hers. She can be a source of strength to you. Perhaps

you can tell her all. Perhaps you should. I leave it you
your judgement, even if that includes telling her of me,
old man."

"I don't know about that," Mike balked.

"Consider it, Michael. She likes me. In the short
time we met, I could tell. She's highly intuitive.
Knowing about me might put things in balance. It
helped you, didn't it? It let you adjust to the notion that
not all vampires are evil. It kept you from thinking the
night was filled with monsters. We all know there are
monsters of some sort out there. Knowing that their
numbers are limited gives us hope."

"Speaking of hope," Mike interjected, "maybe
Nigel can dig up a lead. Have him try Stephan Sutu or
Stephan Soutzos. Since Soutzos is Greek, he might
even try Stavros Soutzos. I'd look for Greeks born in
Istanbul or Constantinople. Look for entry into Canada.
I'll call Charbonneau and see if he can access
immigration files. Also, Bondarenko referred to a
house being not his, but stolen. That could be some
kind of home invasion or occupying the home of some
wealthy snow bird while they're south for the winter.
Also, there's this rumoured warehouse on Robie Street.
He could look for abandoned warehouses or ones
whose activity seems uncertain.

"There's one more possibility." He hesitated.
"Your Countess Isobelle. Are you in touch with her?
Maybe she knows of this guy."

Tony shrugged and glanced at his watch. "She
travels a lot. It's still night in France. I can try her
chateau when I get back to the house. She once knew
every noble and aspiring pretender in Europe." Tony
smiled. "You're a natural at this, Michael. I wish I had
you in MI6 during the war. You'd make a damned
good spy."

"But I am a spy," Mike joked, flashing his CSIS ID. "Cameron, Michael Cameron."

# 18: Magic

Mike's cell phone rang as he was pulling out of Tony's driveway. He picked up his bluetooth, stuck it in his ear, and activated it. "Hello–"

"Hi." Carrie's musical voice made two syllables of the simple greeting. "Where are you?"

"On my way. I just dropped Tony off."

"Oh, good, I caught you–" She hesitated. "Uh, why don't you just head home and put on the coffee or the kettle, or whatever. I'd rather have echinacea tea and I just happen to have some in my bag. I don't think I'm up for the noise of Tim Horton's, even if there is a chance of it being quiet at this time of night." Again the hesitation. "I've been thinking of you all day— mostly how nice it was before I had to go to work. Maybe we can just sit on your sofa or maybe we can watch something in your theatre?"

"Let me guess, a romantic comedy?"

"Well, I do like action and excitement but, well, the mood you make me think of at the moment is probably more Cary Grant than Nicholas Cage."

Mike grinned. "I just happen to have a few Cary Grant movies. I also have Tom Hanks and Meg Ryan, Hugh Grant, and a host of romantic movies. My tastes are rather eclectic."

"Great," she said. "I'll probably be there in ten minutes."

"You trying to race me home?"

She pulled into his drive just as he was coming out of the garage. He met her at her car. She opened her car door and got out, straight into his arms. Her lips found his in an instant, holding there for half a minute.

"I was filled with this nameless fear all night," she confided. "I don't know, I just couldn't convince myself that you weren't in some kind of danger. I feel silly, now." She hesitated, spotting the sleeved katana in his hand. "You had that with you?"

"Actually, it was in the car for most of the night," he said.

He closed her car door and walked her up the side steps to the front door. Once inside, he closed the garage, took her coat and hung it up, then removed his black suede jacket, tossing his drover's hat up onto the shelf.

"That's a good look for you—very Wyatt Earp— Kurt Russell in Tombstone?"

Mike shook his head. "You're full of surprises. I love that movie, especially Val Kilmer. I wish they'd put it out on Blu-ray."

Carrie spotted the three *sgian dubh* and froze. "You were in danger tonight—tell me the truth."

Mike assumed a gentle smile and took her hand, leading her toward the kitchen. A glance showed no light under Sean's closed door. Mike knew he'd be asleep. "Let's see this special tea of yours."

"You haven't answered me." She came close, looking into his eyes. "I knew it," she insisted, as if she could see something in his eyes. She put her arms around his waist, snuggling in close.

"I'm fine," he assured her. "Not a scratch on me."

"But you were afraid and you had to do something that upset you. And there were other things that upset you."

Mike pulled away just enough to look into her eyes. "Now who's being spooky?"

She lowered her eyes. "I feel things sometimes—from patients, mostly—never from my ex, oddly. But it's like there's a strong link with you, like we're in tune somehow."

Mike knew exactly what she meant. He just nodded. "Maybe it's time I told you some things."

While she put the kettle on, he discretely cleaned his *sgian dubh* with a damp cloth, drying them carefully. As he sheathed them he realized that she'd been watching.

"Has another of the so-called vampire killers been killed tonight?" she asked. It was as if she were afraid to ask the question. "Did he attack you?"

Mike hesitated, watching her eyes, then nodded.

"They really are vampires, aren't they?"

Once more Mike hesitated before nodding.

"Are they all evil or is it like that new TV show, Moonlight? Are they mostly kind of like good guys, with just a few bad ones?"

Mike nodded.

She put her tea back in her bag. "Maybe we should have a real drink."

"Scotch or wine?" Mike asked.

"Wine—red might be appropriate." She tried to smile at her own joke.

He opened the wine fridge and pulled out a bottle of merlot. Before he could get the opener, she was in his arms again, clinging to him. He held her until her grip on his eased, then kissed her.

"I really am fine," he assured her. "In fact, I'm amazed at how easily I managed tonight."

"Is Tony one of the good ones?"

He caught her gaze and studied her eyes. She seemed confident in her knowledge.

"Yes," he confirmed, "he's one of the good ones. What made you think he was one?"

She lowered her eyes, thinking. "He seems so old-fashioned, like he's from another time. How old is he?"

"He's the same Lord Anthony Dewhurst who helped the Scarlet Pimpernel rescue French nobles from the guillotine. He helped destroy the real Jack the Ripper, was an agent for MI6, even knew Ian Fleming, and now works informally with Interpol."

"And now he has you working for Interpol."

"Well, technically, I'm with CSIS." He showed her the ID. Her eyes widened.

"How long has this been going on?"

"I suppose I've been working with Tony since the night I was attacked down near the ferry—it made the papers."

"I saw it. And you told me Tony might be a colleague. And CSIS?"

"Since suppertime. They were waiting outside when I got home."

He opened the wine, poured two glasses, then led her to the dining table. He told her everything, starting with the night he first met Tony.

"And you think this Prince Stephan has some personal vendetta against Lord Tony."

Mike shrugged. "If the gut feeling I'm starting to get about this guy is right, it could be something so trivial that Tony doesn't even know about it. I think he has a warped psyche, like Yoshihiro—he has such an inflated image of himself and blames the world for the fact that he can't be who he thinks he should be. He's already lied twice about being some royal prince. Something about the second claim just feels close to the mark, somehow. The bottom line is, he wants very much to be impressive but just isn't—at least that's what my instincts tell me. Who knows, maybe I'm wrong."

He glanced at he clock. "It's 12:30, too late for a movie now."

"Maybe not," Carrie replied. "If I can get a hot shower to revive me, I might make it through a movie."

"How about a bath with jets?"

Her eyes sparkled. "Sounds heavenly."

Mike gave her his hooded plush bath robe and directed her toward his en suite half-bath while he ran water in the air-jet tub in the main bathroom. While she puttered, taking off makeup and earrings, using the toilet, and getting out of her uniform and into his robe, he lit candles around the tub and set a fresh glass of wine on the edge, near the buttons for the jets.

When the water was ready he called her. Tears welled up in her eyes when she saw the candle-lit tub and the awaiting glass of wine.

"Madame, your bath awaits," he announced in this best butler voice.

She kissed him and held him close, then pushed him toward the door. "If you don't get out of here fast, I'm going to drag you into the tub with me."

He flashed a devilish look with his eyes and said, "Now there's a thought," then left quickly.

The moment he heard her turn on the jets, he gathered up all her clothes, went down to the laundry, and put them in the wash. He then turned on the theatre projector and associated electronics and debated between two Cary Grant movies before choosing 'House Boat.' Soon everything was warmed up enough to put the disk in the Sony Blu-ray player and close the tray.

He returned upstairs and put his weapons away, except the katana, which he set in the corner near the bed. It had lived there ever since the night Petrenko had attacked him.

Stripping, he washed himself at the sink, then put on his Nautica pajamas, rather like a track suit made of thick T-shirt cotton.

He heard the washer alarm and the sound of water starting down the drain from the tub at the same time. Hurrying back down the stairs, he transferred her clothes to the dryer, then dashed back up just as she was coming out of his bed room.

"Um, where are my clothes?" The tone was a bit shy and held a hint of 'what are you up to?'

"Actually, they're just in the dryer now. They'll be done long before the movie ends."

"You sound like a man with a plan."

"Well," he explained in a hesitating tone, "it occurred to me that, by the time the movie's over, you may think it's awfully late to go home. But if you stayed here, you'd need a clean uniform for tomorrow. Now you have a clean uniform for tomorrow."

She snuggled into his arms. "You look so cute in your teddy-bear jammies. My mother warned me about men like you."

"Uh oh, what did she warn you?" He tried to look worried.

"Not to let a thoughtful and considerate one get away."

"Wow," she said when she saw the theatre, "you weren't kidding. This must have cost a fortune." She sat in one of five theatre seats along the back wall, experimenting with how the arm with cup-holder lifted back out of the way. She left it up, making a love-seat of the two adjacent chairs.

"Actually, the seats tie with the projector as the most expensive parts. I made the speakers myself—a hobby I've had off and on since I was about twenty. Of course it would have cost a small fortune if I hadn't been able to do the work myself."

"So this is your escape from the world."

He nodded. "This and my writing. This is where I come to really relax."

"I can relax here." She cuddled against him as he started the movie.

By the time 'House Boat' was over, they'd finished a second bottle of wine. She was looking very droopy-eyed and unsteady when they got to the top of the stairs.

"You deliberately got me drunk," she accused, smiling.

Mike shook his head. "I just poured the wine. You're the one who drank it."

She pouted. "I know. I guess it's a bit of wanting to numb the fear. I'm worried about what you've found yourself caught up in. It's also the first time in a very long time I felt like having a quiet celebration with someone. Being with you is nice."

"For ladies who've had a bit too much to drink, being with me is also very safe."

He picked her up in his arms and carried her to the bedroom. Once she was comfortably situated on one side of the bed, he drew the covers up and brushed the hair away from her face. She was already sound asleep.

He noticed his e-mail icon displaying one new e-mail but decided it could wait 'til morning He shut down his computer, turned out the lights, and slid into bed. He was just settling himself on his back—his thinking position before turning on his side to go to sleep—when Carrie reached out and found him, then snuggled against his chest. He turned so he could hold her in his arms and fell asleep in that position.

He awoke with a feeling of stiffness in his right shoulder. Neither he nor Carrie seemed to have moved all night—odd for him, he thought. He glanced across at his still-dark computer screen, his sense of time telling him it had to be almost eight o'clock. Seconds later his computer chimed to life and Sean's bedroom door opened and closed. He heard Sean descend the stairs and exit the front door. The garage door opened, then closed. There was a long pause before Sean's bike gunned to life. From the sound, Mike knew he'd walked it down the drive past Carrie's car before starting it.

*He knows I have company,* he thought. *That secret's out of the bag.*

He thought about sneaking out of bed and making coffee but he just didn't want to take his arms from around her. He held her for another hour, inhaling the scent of her hair, as if his soul were celebrating her presence.

He was about to doze off when she stirred. She smiled and snuggled harder against him. "You tucked me in and held me all night," she whispered.

"Nothing happened," he assured her.

"I know. I'd probably have lost the bathrobe if anything had. You're too much of a gentlemen to take advantage of a lady too helpless to protect her honour."

"Something like that." He smiled back.

She began to kiss his neck, one hand exploring his chest.

"What about wide awake, near-naked women in your bed, kissing your neck and feeling how muscular your chest and tummy are? Do you take advantage of them?"

"I'm only human," he said, and began some exploring of his own.

Movies loved to show couples tearing at each other's clothes like sex-starved maniacs and thrashing about in wild abandon. The reality was much slower, more cautious. There was a lot of kissing and caressing as they took joy in discovering every inch of each other. At the end, they held each other close for a long time.

"Don't say it," Carrie suddenly said. "You know what I mean. People say it in the heat of passion as if they think they have to, and it becomes meaningless."

"I know," Mike agreed. "It's better said when everything's calm, when no one expects it to be said."

"One of these days we'll disagree about something important and be too shocked by it to argue." She giggled, then, "My God, Michael, your shoulders! They're bruised—it looks like fingers with claws."

"I'm a bit stiff there, but it's not bad. I thought his claws had come through my jacket, but they didn't."

"Your black suede? That's good leather if it didn't tear."

She got up and went to the bathroom, then came back with mineral ice. "This should help a little," she said. She returned to the bathroom and he heard her helping herself to his electric toothbrush.

He went to the main bath for a quick wash up, grabbed a spare robe, then headed to the kitchen to grind coffee beans and get the brewer going. Sam huffed to go out, hurrying back in just minutes, anxious for his cookie. Mike went back to the bedroom and was at the computer, reading the e-mail of the night before, when Carrie came up behind him and put her arms about his neck.

"What is it? You're all tense. Is something wrong?"

"I told you about Tony's Countess Isobelle—she's dead."

"How? By who?"

"A hunting lodge in the woods was burned down around her. I'll bet her head was cut off first, unless the fire was set during the day when she slept. The *who* is uncertain. Tony's hoping for more information around five o'clock our time."

Mike stood and Carrie wrapped her arms about him.

"Can I say it now?" he asked.

"Nope, too soon."

Mike smiled and held her close. "Stubborn but sensible, gotta like that."

They walked to the kitchen, each with an arm about the other. Mike poured coffee, responding to his as if it was the magic elixir that kept him going.

"So what do you have on for today," she asked. He could see the worry in her face.

"Let's see: What's happening with searching for bodies in the harbour? Has Nigel dug up anything on Stephan, on a possible warehouse on Robie, on a large home in Halifax, probably the south end, where Stephan may be hiding?"

He pondered that, then reached for the kitchen phone. "Excuse me a second. I think I should call Pete—Detective Inspector MacDonald."

He speed-dialed the direct line.

"Pete, it's Mike."

"Special Agent Cameron, good to hear from you. To what do I owe this honour?"

Mike made a grimace. "You're kidding, right? Did CSIS notify you?"

"I'm just teasing, Mike. Congratulations, I think. And yes, Agent Charbonneau sent me a fax. But there's also gossip among the uniforms. You showed your ID to a cop and an ME's assistant. At least the badge has more clout around here than a vague connection to Interpol, especially with hard-ass cops who don't like civilian involvement."

"Still getting rumbles?" Mike asked.

"No, especially not after last night. The gossip is that you took out a cop-killer, almost as soon as he killed Wilson. The grumblers are now looking to buy you a drink. But that's not why you called. I'm guessing it's about searching the harbour for bodies. Three high-speed in inflatables were supposed to have hit the water at eight o'clock—that's an hour ago. It'll take time, Mike. You've spend a lot of time on the water, so you know what they're up against, especially this time of year."

"I hear you," Mike said. "Tomorrow's the first of February. We'll be back into snow again any day, and probably for the rest of the month. But there's another thing. This mystery count, Stephan–"

"You've got a name? How'd you get that?"

"I got a little from Bondarenko. Pain made him as talkative as Stephan's hypnosis would allow. Stephan's in a stolen house—Bondarenko's words, not mine. I see two possibilities. First: some aspect of home invasion. He got into an occupied house, killed the residents, and made himself at home. Second, and less likely: he took over the manor of wealthy snow birds, knowing they were in Florida or somewhere for the winter."

"Why is that less likely? I'd think it would be a lot easier."

"Easier until neighbours start wondering why there are lights and activity in a house where the people are away for the winter. Especially if said neighbours have a number to call in Florida or wherever."

"Good point," MacDonald conceded. "Would he have the nerve to introduce himself to the neighbours as a European cousin house-sitting while they're away?"

Mike considered it. "Too risky. What if a neighbour calls the owners to say they met the cousin? Even if the place is walled and somewhat isolated, there's always the chance of a neighbour getting nosy about activity where there shouldn't be any."

"Well, Mike, I could check with ADT and other security firms. They might know if owners are away with servants in the house. We can also check neighbourhoods but, short of going house to house, I doubt if we'll learn much."

Mike nodded. "Well, maybe you'll find something—nosy neighbour claiming they haven't seen the people next door in weeks—whatever."

He rang off and called Nigel, posing the same problem.

"Well, if it isn't Special Agent Cameron. 'Ow's it feel to be the Canadian James Bond, gov'nor?"

"It's not even ten o'clock and those jokes are already worn out, Nigel. Did you dig up anything?

"Oh, yeah. I do some o' me best hacking in the wee hour's. Gettin' into records in Turkey is tough, an' there is the language. But, I did find one thing: Alexandru Sutu was the eldest son. Now the Greeks were much more helpful—proud lot, that. Didn't matter that Sutu, Soutzos to them, was a citizen of the Ottoman Empire and not regarded as Greek. They'll brag 'im up and take some national credit for someone with a Greek name gettin' to be gov'nor of a European state, even if it's Wallachia. Alexandros Soutzos had one younger sister and three younger brothers. The youngest was a bloke named—you guessed it— Stavros. Greeks claim 'e an' 'is brother were close— Stavros visited a lot, but a notation in an obscure file in Rumania tells a different story. Seems someone complained to Alexandru about his annoying prick of a brother showing up all the time, gettin' in the way and gettin' on people's nerves. Seems Alexandru wanted to do something about it but little brother wouldn't take a hint and big brother couldn't bring 'imself to be rude.

"But here's the kicker: Alexandru wasn't the last ruler. There were seven after him until 1859, when Wallachia and Moldavia joined to become Rumania. Seems Stephan thought he should succeed his brother. But, depending on where you are in history, the job was either elected or appointed, interrupted off and on by Russian occupation."

Mike whistled. "So we have a compelling case for Prince Stephan being Stavros Soutzos, an Ottoman Greek wanna-be." Mike grinned. It coincided with the gut feeling Yakura kept pushing at him. "What about Robie Street?"

"Ah, now that's a bit more of a struggle. I got three prospects: two vacant, one that seems to have changed hands a couple of years ago without reopening as a business."

"What's that?"

"Well, it used to be a bus repair depot, then a motorcycle shop—repairs and customizing, mostly. The heavy bike work fell off and it changed hands again but still showed signs of being a bit of an outlaw biker hangout. Fewer bikers these days, but no one knows what's goin' on."

"And the other two?"

"A vacant car dealership and a paint-supplier's warehouse. Both are on the market, not getting much interest."

"Biker hangout would be my bet. It's the right element for the previous crystal dealers. How did you dig all that up?"

"Ah, trade secret, mate. Actually, I compared real estate deals with police complaints."

"Speaking of police complaints, maybe you can find someone in a rich neighbourhood in the south end."

"You'll 'ave to 'elp me a bit wiff the geography, gov'nor. I'm new in town."

"Sorry," Mike said. "Between a block or so south of Quinpool Road and Point Pleasant Park, and near the Northwest Arm. It'll be a large manor-style home, somewhat isolated. Maybe there'll be a complaint from a nosy neighbour of uncharacteristic night-time activity. Maybe a security-monitoring firm was told the clients would be away but servants staying in residence. It's less likely, but maybe the place is supposed to be empty but isn't. Bondarenko said it was a stolen house."

"Gotcha. Anything else, Mike?"

"How'd Tony take news of Isobelle's death?"

"Not too good. He talked about it a bit, then got all quiet. Retired early. Whot I did get is that 'er servants 'ave been in the family for generations, descendants of a couple named Claude and Marie. Her current butler, Claude, is the great-great-whatever-grandson of the original Claude and Marie. Most of the other servants are relatives of 'is. Anyway, he's in Paris dealing with business for 'er, back tonight.

"Seems she'd been off, who knows where, with some 'friend she'd known for *many* years.' You can assume that means 'e's a vampire. Anyway, someone reported a fire at this country place in the woods, posh twist on a summer cottage, I guess. Fire started middle o' the night, 'cording to reports. I'm diggin' but not gettin' much."

Mike nodded. "Okay, keep me posted," he said, and rang off.

"Is Lord Tony okay?" Carrie asked.

Mike shook his head. "I don't think he's taking this well. A vampire's perception of time would be different. For us, not seeing a friend for ten years or more would take them almost completely out of our lives. But when you live for centuries, not seeing someone for that long would be like us not seeing someone for a couple of weeks or a month.

"I can only guess the place Isobelle occupied in his world-view. She made him. I think he viewed her as part mother, part lover, certainly something like a sister or life-long friend. Nigel says he got real quiet and went to bed early. I'll be anxious to see how he is tonight."

Carrie came to him and put her arms around him. "You're a good friend. You care about people. It's one of the things I love about you."

"Careful," he teased, "you just used the illegal 'L' word."

She grinned and snuggled against him.

"I did. Is there anything you love about me.

"As near as I can tell," he replied, "I love everything about you. Now, how about pancakes for breakfast. I haven't had pancakes in ages."

"Sure. And we have four hours before I have to get ready for work. All I really need to do before 2:00 is iron my uniform."

"Well, why don't you get that out of the dryer while I make pancakes."

"Just don't rush off and get dressed," she teased. "There's no hurry to put clothes on."

"Until Sean comes home for lunch," he warned. "Wait a minute, it's Thursday. Sean said he was staying in school for lunch today."

"So we have the place all to ourselves until I have to go to work?"

"Absolutely. I'll do some writing after you leave. Nigel and Pete can do the legwork today. Until 2:00 you have my undivided attention."

# 19: The Pieces Begin to Fit

Mike held Carrie for a long time before letting her go.

"I'll be late for work," she whispered

"Tell Dad I'll call him around supper. I've got choir tonight, then I want to see if Nigel found out anything."

"Be careful."

He watched as she went down the side steps to the driveway and walked to her car. She'd already started her Neon with a remote starter, letting it warm up before she had to leave. He continued to watch as she drove down the street, then got dressed and went out.

His trench coat was ready at the tailor's, as promised. He examined the work, pleased with the result, and paid extra, the older man trying unsuccessfully to refuse the tip. Mike then pulled the coat on over his jacket and went out to the car. After assuring himself that no one was looking, he removed the silk sleeve from his katana and slid the sheath into the long, slim pocket of his coat. It fit perfectly and only felt a little awkward.

"I'll get used to that," he told himself. I just need to wear it until I do."

There was a pocket on the right side that would be a perfect fit for a flare pistol. He added that and several meteor shells when he got home, then immersed himself in writing until almost 5:00.

He was in the kitchen, prepping supper, when the thought intruded. Sean was supposed to be doing homework and working on a project, but Mike could hear him singing loudly to the accompaniment of his iPod. *Kid's got too many toys,* he thought. He glanced around the kitchen. "You just had to have the best kitchen on the block," a neighbour had teased. It triggered the epiphany.

He grabbed the phone and speed-dialed Tony's number. This time it was Tony who answered.

"Ah, Michael, how goes it?"

"I'm pretending I don't have sore shoulders where Bondarenko grabbed me. His claws didn't go through my suede jacket, but Carrie almost freaked when she saw the bruises."

"Old man, you've either said too much or too little. You've just implied that Carrie was with you and you were shirtless. Getting a bit of nursing or has the relationship deepened?"

"Oh, it's deepened," Mike replied. "Listen, about Count Stavros: tell Nigel to cross-reference his house investigations with the most expensive houses in that area. There are expensive properties out toward Ketch Harbour, but the older places are all along the Arm."

Tony was silent, as if thinking. "By Jove, you're absolutely right. I'm used to finding a place in a hurry, so I'm often less than ostentatious. Our would-be prince, however, would want to pander to his desire to feel royal. It would be a stone edifice, for sure…

"One moment, Michael, there's an incoming call. I'll get back to you as soon as I can."

Mike continued puttering about the kitchen. With choir rehearsal on Thursdays, Mike usually went for something simple—Hamburger Helper in this instance—but his basic nature still intruded. He just couldn't do such a simple dish without dicing onion and green pepper, and mincing fresh garlic cloves. He sipped a glass of merlot as the mix simmered for the required fifteen minutes. He was just calling Sean to the table when the phone rang.

"That was Claude," Tony explained. "It was a bit disconcerting, really. He looks, even sounds, so much like his ancestor that I have to remind myself that they are not one and the same."

"Did he know anything of our mystery count?"

Tony sighed. "Yes. Isobelle met a Count Stephan Sutu of Wallachia a few years after the death of his brother. His story was that Russian invaders had usurped his right to the throne. She was taken in by him, became his lover, and brought him over some time in the 1830s. He was with her rather continuously for about twenty years, then seemed to be in and out after that, showing up at odd times, sometimes in need of money.

"About two months ago, he showed up again, staying for a while. There was a heated exchange one evening. All Claude heard was Stephan screaming something to the gist of, 'I'm sick of hearing about him. Is he all you can talk about? If he's so amazing, why don't you get out and go find him.'" Claude thought that was about word for word. He insists that Stephan was talking as if he were in his own home, not Isobelle's. Apparently he had a tendency to get that way when he'd been at her chateau for too long.

"Anyway, Michael, Isobelle was so upset that, instead of sending him packing as she should have, she packed a few things and announced that she was going to her country place near Le Roi du Bois, just a rustic lodge that she was fond of. She told him that, if he came to his senses and wished to apologize for his churlish behaviour, he could find her there. Otherwise, she wished to find him gone when she returned. The fire was reported a few days later.

"But here are the critical parts. The reason Claude was away in Paris was to hear the results of an inquiry into Isobelle's will. He'd been there weeks ago to have experts prove that Isobelle's latest will was a forgery. It was filed the day after she left for Le Roi du Bois, and it left the chateau near Lille to Count Stephan Sutu of Wallachia. Also, Isobelle's journal was found in the ruins of the burned lodge, in a very old metal box—somewhat cooked, but basically intact. The diary spoke of several such arguments. Apparently Count Stephan was obsessed with one man—perhaps I should say that he felt Isobelle was obsessed with him. He became insanely jealous whenever she spoke of him."

"Let me guess. Isobelle was rather proud of and liked to speak of the many accomplishments of one Lord Anthony Dewhurst of Richmond in Yorkshire."

"I'm afraid so—I say, old chap, how did you know I was from Richmond?"

Mike smiled. "The same way I know you weren't just a friend of Percy's, you were a cousin, and the youngest of a trinity of three best friends: Sir Percy, Sir Andrew, and you. You were also an exceptional cricket player and a mediocre student. Nigel isn't the only one who can do research on the internet."

"Apparently not," Tony replied in a droll tone. "But, then, I saw that last night when you borrowed by Blackberry, did I not?"

"Did Claude succeed? Did he prove the will a forgery?"

"Handwriting analysis proved that. Also, as Stephan was leaving the chateau, Claude rescued a copy of the proper will from the fireplace in Isobelle's suite. It had a leather cover that protected the parchment from burning enough that just the edges were charred and almost all the writing was intact. The official ruling declared the new will a forgery, citing that the countess could not have filed it—she was at or en route to Le Roi du Bois at the time—the handwriting of the questionable will was clearly a forgery, and there had been an effort to destroy the authentic will, though it wasn't the only copy. Again, since Claude testified to having cleaned out that particular fireplace after the countess had left, the attempt to destroy the real will occurred after she had left. "

"Let me guess: the chateau was left to you."

"Once again, dear boy, you are right on the money—an unfortunate cliche in this instance. It was left to me with the provision that I keep the staff in their current employ and take care of their descendants, should they chose to follow the family tradition."

"Stavros Soutzos is one nasty bastard," Mike mused. "It all fits in with the trap he planned for you at the house on North Street. I think he knew his forged will wouldn't work—perhaps he has someone in Paris keeping him apprised of developments. It would make him all the more angry with you. Trust me, I know the type—or perhaps I should say that Yakura knew the type. This clown and Toda Yoshihiro would have made a good pair. He's been quiet, perhaps laying low for a few days. His plot failed the first time. Maybe he's taking his time coming up with a better plan. Either way, this is all about destroying you. We're dealing with a vampire with a psychotic fixation."

---

Sean had a smug look on his face all through supper but said nothing.

"Alright, out with it," Mike said. "You look like that cat who swallowed the friggin' canary."

"Nothing," Sean said, trying to look innocent. "You had company last night—first time since we left… well, no need to bring her up. Anyway, I'm glad. I recognized Carrie's car. Is she coming by again tonight."

"I doubt it." He grinned. "I imagine she'll draw the line at wearing the same uniform three days in a row, even if it does get washed and ironed."

"So, you guys are good? This is a good sign."

"Yes, Sean," he replied, "things are very good."

"What's happening with the vampire investigation?"

Mike froze. He'd done his best to shield Sean from it and convince him that Petrenko had been a psycho who wanted to pass himself off as a vampire.

"Dad, I'm not stupid. I hear things—you talking to Tony and Nigel on the phone. I heard some of what you told Carrie last night. I woke up and was going to go to the bathroom and heard you out here talking. You killed another one last night."

Mike nodded. "You've seen enough of *Criminal Minds* to know how some psychos can be—they get fixated on something and it becomes an obsession, totally irrational. Well, the man behind all this was weak-minded as a human. We don't know much about his background except that he's Greek, the youngest of five children, but born in the Ottoman Empire— that's…"

"A moslem empire," Sean cut in, "the capital was Constantinople, now Istanbul, the largest city in Turkey. The Ottoman Empire were the other side, the enemy, during the crusades. If this guy was the youngest of five, he either got way too much attention, being the baby of the family, or didn't get near enough."

Mike nodded. "His oldest brother achieved quite a bit—he was appointed ruler of Wallachia, near Transylvania, now part of Rumania. That was in the early 1800s, when the Moslems ruled over that region."

"He couldn't be as great as his brother, so he now wants to take what his brother had or things like what his brother had, right?" Sean guessed.

Mike nodded. "It seems he recently killed an important friend of Tony's and tried to claim her castle in France with a forged will."

"So why is Count Psycho messing with you and Tony?" Sean asked.

"It's about Tony. From the count's prospective I just happen to be in the way," Mike explained. "Tony was the real heir to the countess's castle. It seems this guy also got very jealous whenever the countess spoke of Tony and his many accomplishments over the years."

Sean nodded. "He wanted all of the countess's attention. He'd hate any hint that she was ever thinking of or proud of anyone else but him."

"You're pretty good at this," Mike said. "Maybe you should study psychology and become a profiler instead of a CSI."

"Oh, I don't know—we'll see. So what happens now?"

"Well, the Russians who have been doing the most flamboyant killings seem to have taken over the crystal meth drug trade in the lower north end of Halifax."

"Is that why the vampire killings have stopped?" Sean interrupted.

Mike shook his head. "I don't think they have. I think they just decided to hide the bodies. Being dramatic at first brought Tony in. That's what Stavros wanted. Continuing to flaunt their daring and drama would keep Tony on the job but, once he was here he'd stay on task until he located the culprit, whether horrendous killings were continuing or not. On the other hand, continuing to leave bodies everywhere increases the odds that, sooner or later, they'd leave enough bits and pieces of forensic evidence to lead us to them—they risk not being in control of the scenario. And I think it's very important to Stavros to feel in control of the scenario. What I'm waiting for is a slip-up. Chernov is a monster, and not a very calculating one. He may start being sloppy again just because he likes it. If that happens—if he decides to thumb his nose at our count—well, any internal conflict on their part might work in our favour."

"Talk about being good at something, Dad," Sean declared, "you're the one who should be a profiler or a detective."

Mike hesitated—in his enthusiasm, Sean could let things slip, especially if there was something to brag about to friends. Still, over the years he'd kept a lot of secrets. To the best of his knowledge, Sean had never spoken to anyone about Asia and what they had gone through to get in and out of China and Tibet. With a lingering hint of reluctance, he pulled out the CSIS ID.

"This is a bigger secret than most I've asked you to keep," he said.

Sean's curiosity was clearly aroused. "What is it?"

Mike showed him the ID.

Sean stared at it, then nodded silently. "Those were the dudes in the big black car out front yesterday at suppertime."

Mike nodded.

"Will you have to travel?"

"Right now the case is here," Mike assured Sean. "After this case, the next one may be elsewhere, but most likely somewhere in Canada, and probably working with Tony. Either way, I have some right of refusal of cases."

"And if it's a vampire case, working with Tony, would you ever refuse?"

Mike thought about it before answering. "Probably not."

———————

Choir practice was a relaxation for Mike, especially since they didn't have to perform the following Sunday. The church had two adult choirs that took turns, Mike's being the more formal choir, doing more classical and difficult pieces. With February on the doorstep, they were also rehearsing for their annual Good Friday evening service, more concert than service.

"Want me to drive you to class?" he asked Sean.

"No," Sean objected. "I'll just run home and get my bike." He glanced up at the sky. "See? No sign of snow yet. And if we get any, it'll be most likely after midnight, and probably no more than a dusting."

"Yeah, well, just be careful."

Sean sighed. "Yes, Dad."

During the walk home, Mike turned the ringer on his cell phone back on and noticed two missed calls— one from Inspector MacDonald and one from SeaView. He called SeaView.

"Hey, there," he said when Carrie came to the phone.

"Hello, my beautiful man."

"God, I hope this isn't a wrong number," Mike said, laughing.

She giggled. "Right number, right man. I've been floating around several inches off the floor all day— breezed through work, got everything done in record time. Of course, *everybody* noticed I had on the same uniform as yesterday, even if it was washed and ironed.

That, combined with the air of euphoria I must have been displaying, made them put two and two together. Of course, your father heard something and tried to interrogate me. I told him very little but he was grinning a lot for the rest of the day. I'm surprise he didn't call you."

"I called him soon after you left for work," Mike said. "I guess it was before the rumours started."

They engaged in typical lover's chatter until Mike reached his front door. Sean had run on ahead, opened the house, then roared off down the street on his bike.

"That was Evil Knieval, off to teach his class," he explained. Then, "By the way, I love you."

There was a pause. "I love you, too."

"Um, I've got a missed call from Pete and I'm anxious to talk to him. I think it's about the search for more bodies in the harbour. Call me again when you're heading home or after you get home."

It took a while to ring off, neither really wanting to end the call. Mike was crashed on his bed when he finally got through to MacDonald.

"What did they find, Pete?"

"Eighteen bodies, Mike."

"Jesus!" It took Mike a moment to recover. "Sorry, Pete, I don't usually blaspheme. That's more than I expected."

"And it may not even be all of them. There may be more lodged under piers or washed out to sea. If you can call it a bright side, six wore bike leathers and were hard-looking types. My guess is they were part of the previous meth connection. That leaves twelve, mostly women. With four active Russian perps until you reduced it to three last night, that's one a night each."

"Pete," Mike interjected, "We're leaving out Count Stavros."

"Stavros? You mean Stephan. Yeah, Tony had his IT-man, Nigel, e-mail me particulars about this Stephan Sutu. I gather you played a big part in that—well done."

"His birth name is Stavros Soutzos. His brother used a Rumanianized version of his name when he was ruler of Wallachia. Stavros does it to perpetuate the fantasy that he's the rightful prince. I'd rather play him down than go along with his delusions. Pete, are the boats still in the water?"

"Just a minute." There was a click, canned music, then Pete came back. "They're patrolling the waterfront. I guess they're thinking to act as a deterrent. The guys who were freezing their butts off out there all day are home; this is second shift. Why?"

"Have them check the Arm. If Soutzos is in a manor house in the south end, he's most likely along the arm. If he's feeding nightly and kills like the others, he'll dump them in the arm."

"I'll pass that on."

Next Mike called Tony.

"I'm glad you called, Michael," the Englishman said. "I took a drive along Robie Street this evening. Of the three prospective locations, two are very quiet, in fact, one seems to be having some daytime renovations done, looking like it may be an automobile dealership once more.

"Then there's the more suspect location. There are a few large motorcycles there—Harley-Davidson or similar style bikes of other manufacture. The engines were still warm on two. A few bikers loitered near the main door, talking to a large Slavic-looking chap. I didn't go close enough to ascertain whether or not the latter was a vampire, but I'd wager he is. I had the window rolled down and the breeze was most cooperative. I got a smell of iodine from the building.

My sense of smell is rather acute, Michael, a bit like that of a German Shepherd, I should imagine. No human would have detected it, but I would suggest that the smell of iodine would be detectible by a human once inside the building. I believe you said iodine is a product of crystal methamphetamine production."

"We need to talk to Pete about this," Mike said. "I don't know if it's probable cause enough to search the place but I want to go in there—tonight, if possible."

"Why don't you come over, Michael," Tony suggested. "Nigel can set up a call through the computer. It's all magic to me, but you can see the other person, and we can all talk to him."

Mike smiled. Tony clearly struggled to keep up with advances like v.o.i.p. video links. Skype had been around for years, though, Mike had to confess, he himself was old-fashioned enough to have never used it.

By the time he got there, Nigel had it all set up. They were just waiting for him.

"I never thought I'd be talking to my computer. This is like the Jetsons, for Christ's sake." MacDonald looked uncomfortable staring out at the three of them from the screen.

"And he can see all three of us on his monitor?" Tony asked.

"In the pink, Yer Lordship," Nigel replied, "just as long as we're not crowding too close to the vid-cam there, mounted to the top of the screen."

"And you say Michael's computer has this vid-cam, as you call it, built into the screen?"

"That's right."

"This is a bit creepy," Pete insisted. "Can we just get on with it?"

Tony laid out what he'd discovered and its implications. On the screen, Pete was shaking his head.

"I need more to go on than that. Any *normal* thugs involved in this will be back on the street tomorrow and I'll be arm-pit-deep in shit with the chief. There just isn't anything to get me a warrant and no probable cause for a search without one."

"I've got your probable cause." Mike pushed his head in front of the camera so that he took up the whole screen. "A reliable source here-by informs you that there's going to be a break-in at that location one hour before sunrise. Can you act on that?"

"Call it in to the tip line and I can."

"Fine. I'll call it in to the tip line that it's going to happen and, when we're on site, Nigel can report that it's in progress. We'll wait for your units to get there."

Pete puffed his cheeks and blew out a long breath. "Good luck. I hope you guys know what you're doing. Please don't be leading my uniforms into a nest of— things I don't want to explain."

# 20: Drug Lab

It was cold in the pre-dawn air. Nigel had his hands wrapped around an extra-large cup of Tim Horton's coffee. He was chatting with Pete and one of several cops, two doors away from the building. The building, a run-down structure with painted-over windows, was tucked back into trees. Mike stood apart from the rest, burying any sense of anticipation or anxiety by concentrating on deep breathing, Chi-Kung power breathing. He could hear Nigel's nervous banter.

"Is 'e always like that? 'E looks so aloof, like we're not even 'ere."

"I imagine he has a lot on his mind at the moment," Pete commented.

"Yeah, I bet 'e does. 'E looks like Van 'Elsing, you know, Hugh Jackman—great movie. Anyway, 'e looks like 'im, 'cept for that mustache. Wi' that, he looks like Asterix the Gaul, you know, the comic, well, 'cept for the dark 'air. But the 'at an' the coat, that's Van 'Elsing."

Mike smiled. Nigel had become unused to field work, except for the odd bit of skullduggery when he knew he'd be the only one in a building. This was definitely out of Nigel's league.

Mike settled his drover's hat more snugly on his head. It was keeping his head warm and gathering a slow accumulation of light, powdery snow. Sean was right. The flurry had held off for most of the night, starting around 6:00 am. He glanced at his watch—

6:25. Sunrise was predicted for 7:34. At the moment
there was very little activity in the building. There
were four biker types loitering near the door and no
sign of the Russian Tony had seen. Mike hoped he was
inside. Part of him hoped all three were inside, though
he knew hoping to take on three vampires was crazy.
Still, he'd be glad of any more that he could cross off
his list. His mind brought up the list Nigel had given
him, clear as a photo in his memory. Petrenko: gone.
Bondarenko: gone. That left Chernov, Chekinovich,
and Vollinkoff. And, of course, there was Stavros
Soutzos, the want-to-be prince.

"Close enough," he announced. He removed his
hat, tossed it on the front seat of his car, and caught
Nigel's eye. "Give me a couple of minutes."

He walked up the street and circled around the
property outside the trees, taking advantage of the
shadows. He came across two pieces of steel pipe, a
couple of feet long, and picked them up. He paused,
still in shadow, as close as he could get to the biker-
types without breaking cover. He hefted one of the
pipes, then launched it at the back of the head of the
nearest biker. It flew like a spear and impacted with a
thud. The target dropped without a sound.

"What the..." One of the bikers turned quickly,
looking for the source of the interruption. The other
two reacted more slowly.

Mike caught biker number two dead center of the
forehead, dropping him next to number one.

Out of pipes, Mike moved in.

The other two looked confused, not ready for a
fight.

*Are they stoned?* Mike wondered.

He drove rapid one-two thrust punches into the gut
of one, then slammed a palm up under his chin. As

number three dropped, number four seemed to wake up and produce a knife.

Mike leaped into a dragon kick. Launching off his right leg, his left foot swung an arc to the left, the outside of his foot knocking the knife out of the biker's hand. The right foot swung a higher arc to the left, the inside edge smashing into the side of biker four's face. He went down, struggling to rise. Mike came down, dropped onto the biker's chest, and brought his fist down like a hammer on the biker's forehead. Lights out.

He dragged two of them back to where the police waited, "Anybody got handcuffs?" then disappeared, returning moments later with the other two.

"Your turn at bat, my hobbit thief," he said to Nigel. "Just pick the lock, then run to Tim Horton's and call the police." He grinned at Pete. "I hope your chief doesn't figure out you were here before the call came in."

"Routine check," Pete replied. "I sent a couple of cars to have a look, based on the earlier call. I'm off the clock. No one knows I'm here, no one need know when I got here." MacDonald made sure every officer had his kevlar vest securely in place. They also wore the extra kevlar collar.

Mike moved silently toward the building, taking advantage of every bit of cover offered, waiting for Nigel to catch up at each stop. He listened at the door. There was movement inside, but not enough to account for more than maybe three or four people.

He nodded to Nigel, who produced a set of picks and went to work. Moments later he turned the knob and eased the door in less than a quarter of an inch.

Glancing up at Mike, he whispered, "Give 'em 'ell, gov'nor," and flashed him a thumbs-up.

"Go make that phone call," Mike replied. "Do you think you can do it without sounding like the Artful Dodger?"

"How's this, Mike? Do I sound Canadian?"

"No, you sound like a Texan in a bad movie, but it'll do."

Mike eased the door open until he could slip through, then eased it back, making sure it didn't latch. The room was a maze of tables, covered with large pots on portable electric hot plates. Above was a half upper floor that appeared to contain a collection of offices that overlooked the floor area. On the floor were four men wearing vapour masks, going from pot to pot. They were scrawny, ill-kept, scraggly-haired types, all showing the unkempt and unhealthy look one associated with serious drug use.

*Chernov must pick people he can pay off in product*, Mike thought. *No sign of vampires.* He felt both disappointed and relieved. He'd yet to go up against one voluntarily.

He waited in the shadows, a shadow himself, taking in the details of the tables, watching the four monitor the boiling of product on the stoves. Over against a wall were crates of cough medicine.

He studied the gallery. Two offices showed hints of light but no obvious activity.

*No vampires tonight,* he thought. *Okay, let's do this.*

"POLICE," he yelled. "EVERYONE ON THE FLOOR!"

Pandemonium broke loose. Two came at him, while the other two began turning off the burners, possibly hoping to destroy evidence. After all, Mike was only one man. He hoped Pete had men covering any other doors that might exist.

The first to reach him slashed at him with a knife. Mike caught the arm, swung the thug off-balance, and threw him into the second attacker. He moved in, jerked the knife wrist, and drove his palm into the shoulder. He heard both the wrist and the shoulder pop.

He grabbed the other before he could react. Heaving the man's shoulder, he forced him to bend, then brought a knee up into the man's face, then jerked him back upright, and drove a fist into the sternum. He felt the breast bone separate from the cartilage and punched again, displacing the centerline of the ribs. As both men collapsed, he took off after the remaining two.

There was a commotion in the offices above.

Two burly slavs appeared from separate offices.

Mike's mind felt the same wall he'd encountered with Bondarenko. They thought in Russian and their psychic abilities exceeded those of humans.

*Shit! Be careful what you wish for!*

Both vampires ran to the rail of the gallery and vaulted over it.

Mike's left hand dove inside his coat and came back with the flare pistol. *Shit! No!* He thought. He cast it aside, pulled a *sgian dubh*, and launched it in the same motion. It caught one vampire in the chest. The moment the creature crashed to the floor, Mike rushed in, katana drawn, and hacked it's head off

Mike wheeled about, his stance low, katana in an overhead guard position. The second vampire landed a few yards away. He glared at Mike, wild-eyed, fangs extended. Mike retrieved and pocketed his Very pistol, then gave the katana a twirl and went back into his prepared stance. Something about Muramasa's blade sent a surge of confidence through him. Then the vampire was on him.

Like a springing panther, it leaped at him, eight feet in the air before it began to descend upon him.

Mike lowered his stance and raised his sword, impaling the creature on the blade. In the same motion, he turned and heaved with every ounce of his strength, flinging the vampire through an arc. But the vampire clutched at the katana with both hands, tearing it loose from Mike's grasp, then crashed to the floor on its side.

It got to its feet and, laughing at Mike, drew the katana out of its chest and tossed it to one side. Reaching into a pocket, it pulled out a small pouch of blood. Mike expected the vampire to tear open the pouch and drink it. Instead it tore open its shirt and thrust the pouch against its chest. The pouch burst and the vampire held it in place. The blood was closing the wound!

Mike jumped up onto a table, then leaped to the other side. He made a dive for his katana but the vampire was too fast for him. It, too, vaulted the table and landed barely two feet away, flailing at him with stiff-armed blows, like some Russian version of Tae Kwon Do.

Mike blocked and attacked nerve points that would have made the arms useless in a human, but the vampire came on, its arm motions only slowed and stiffened a little.

Mike kept blocking everything, then drove a foot into the creature's groin. Mike snapped his foot back and drove a second kick into the vampire's abdomen, then leaped and thrust a side-kick into it's chest, slamming the creature back over a table.

There was a loud crash as the table collapsed. Mike's heart raced, fearing a stray spark might cause an explosion. The air was getting to him. He seized a hot plate and hurled it through a window.

He turned, made a dive for his katana, and came up with it in his hand just as the second vampire was getting off the table.

It went into a classic beginner's karate stance, then came at him again, flailing arms and legs in the windmill technique of Tae Kwon Do.

"Are you kidding me?" Mike almost laughed.

Two slashes of the katana severed a hand and a foot. Mike skipped to one side as the creature crashed to the floor. Then, stepping in, Mike took its head off with a downward slice.

"MIKE, ANY MORE?"

MacDonald was bellowing at him from the doorway.

Mike shook his head. "Break a few windows and get some air in here," he said. He sheathed his katana, found a large fire extinguisher, and threw it through another window.

"Leave them," Mike called as Pete was about to break more windows. He heaved the body of the first vampire onto a table, then dragged the other one over, heaving it up next to the first, then tossed the heads and severed hand and foot there as well.

"Clear the area," he warned. "I'm going to make sure this crap can't ever hit the streets." As he spoke, he drew his Very pistol.

"Come on, Mike, that's tampering with evidence." Pete grabbed his arm but Mike just shook him off.

"Report me to Charbonneau," he said.

Outside, Mike yelled, "EVERYBODY AWAY FROM THE BUILDING, NOW!"

"Okay, Mike, it's clear," Pete said. "Jesus, this is crazy."

Mike shot a flare through the open window.

Since the room had been partially ventilated, the explosion was minimal, blowing out the rest of the windows. But the fire would rage inside for hours.

Nigel ran up and handed him his hat.

"You need a bath," he said. "I 'ope none o' that blood is yours."

Mike shook his head. "My guess is Chekinovich and Vollinkoff. I wish one was Chernov, but I doubt it. I think this would be his natural hangout, but my gut tells me Soutzos will be keeping him close at hand as a watchdog. He probably comes by to check on things regularly, though."

"Well, he'll have nothing to check on now." Pete shot Mike an angry look, then pulled out his cell phone. "911, this is Inspector MacDonald of the police. We've got a fire and explosion at a meth lab on Robie Street. We'll need chemical extinguishers." He gave the precise location, then closed his phone.

"I guess I can explain this away as an accident or the actions of one of those drug freaks in there," Pete said to Mike. "And maybe those two bodies will burn enough that no one notices they were decapitated."

Mike shrugged. "Any descent ME will find tool marks on the adjacent edges of the cervical vertebrae, and similar marks where I hacked off the second guy's hand and foot."

"Lord Dewhurst will look after that," MacDonald assured him. "I don't know what the deal is, but there's one coroner who seems good at overlooking awkward details, like the fact that Petrenko's head was removed after you severed his spinal cord with your knife thrust."

"Let me guess," Nigel piped up, "Does 'e work the night shift?"

———————

"You're a sight," Tony said when he opened the door. "Here, give me your coat. I have some protein cleaner that should remove the blood stains, especially since they shouldn't have had time to set in too much. Nigel, be good enough to pour Michael a scotch. Feel free to have a bath if you like, Michael."

Mike thought about it when he got to the bath room, but settled for running hot water in the sink and lathering up soap in a face cloth. Before long he felt and looked a lot better, though the navy fleece jersey he'd worn under his coat was also splattered with blood. He pulled it off and checked his black turtleneck. That seemed blood-free. He scrubbed at the fleece pullover for a minute or two, then decided to let Tony's blood remover have a go.

"'Ere you go, gov'nor," Nigel chirped, handing him a double Glenlivet on the rocks.

"Thanks." He took the drink and handed his fleece to Nigel. "Let Tony have a go at that, too," he said, and followed the cockney down the stairs.

He collapsed in an armchair and put his feet up on a foot stool. His katana and Very pistol lay on the coffee table, along with six meteors for the pistol. He pulled his three *sgian dubh* from his belt and tossed them onto the table as well. Leaning back in the chair, he sipped at the scotch. He breathed deep, letting the vapours clear his sinuses and his thoughts.

Nigel was in the corner, fingers clicking away at his laptop.

"You've got a dangerous job, sport," he said, looking up from the keyboard. "I guess I kind o' took it for granted at first. I 'eard the coppers talkin' about you when it was all over—an' you done it all, didn't you? You set their mouths to yappin,' you did. Took out two thugs with your bare hands, then two o' them fanged buggers. Now I've 'ad an 'and in 'elping 'Is

Lordship with a few—loppin' off 'eads just before sunset or just after sunrise 'cause 'Is Lordship can get up earlier an' stay up later than most o' these buggers. But I ain't never 'eard tell of anyone going toe to toe with 'em on their own turf, with them wide awake an' all. You got more guts than I'll ever 'ave."

Mike just shook his head. "Years ago, before we knew my first wife had cancer," Mike said, "we moved aboard our sailboat and took off for the Bahamas. Her mother had a fit. She actually rewrote her will. Other people thought what we were doing was wonderful. I realized then that for my wife to go against her mother's approval like that took amazing courage. It gave me a new outlook. It's easy to run into a burning building when the crowd on the street are cheering you on, ready to sing your praises for saving the child caught in the fire. Doing something you want to do, that you know is right for you, when all of society thinks you're wrong or stupid or escaping responsibility or whatever—that's courage.

"Nigel, I was scared half numb when I went in that building. I'd killed two vampires already, but each one had taken me by surprise. I was coming home from a martial arts exhibition when Petrenko attacked me from out of nowhere. I was going to Kamensky's aid when I realized that Bondarenko was a vampire. Tonight, for the first time, I entered a place where I knew there might even be three vampires. It took a lot of determination. When they leaped at me from that gallery, I went into automatic mode. It got me through."

It made him think of the vampire with the blood pouch.

"Tony," he called.

"Yes, Michael." Tony appeared in the doorway carrying Mike's coat. "I think you'll find this acceptable," he said, setting it on the table on top of Mike's things. "The fleece jersey was another matter. I've treated it and have it on a gentle wash cycle. I've become something of an expert at getting blood out over the years. Of course, it's much easier today." Tony had the air of someone struggling to stay busy.

Mike got up and dragged Tony back into the kitchen. He looked into his eyes.

"You okay?" He asked.

Tony looked perplexed.

Mike put a hand on Tony's face then, on sudden impulse, gave him a hug. "I know all too well what it means to loose someone important." As he continued to hold the vampire, a wave of emotion flowed through him—a strange mix of affection and need, even hunger for this simple act of compassion. It took him a moment to realize that the feelings weren't his own but Tony's. He became aware of wetness where Tony's face touched him.

He let Tony straighten and saw the tear running down one side of his face.

"You Brits sometimes take this stiff-upper-lip business way too far," he suggested.

Tony smiled. "You're right." He pretended to hoist a glass. "The Monarch and the Empire." He gave a brief chuckle. "Go back and sit before you fall down. I'll be right in. Just let me get my drink."

Tony sat in a chair, crossed his legs, wine glass in hand, and began to sip what Mike knew was blood. "I'm anxious for details, but I can tell there's something in particular on your mind aside from concern for my reaction to Belle's demise."

"It was either Chekinovich or Vollinkoff—I don't know which was which, and I'm assuming that neither was Chernov—one of them had a pouch of blood. He flew at me through the air. I caught him in the chest with my katana and hurled him away from me. He came up with my sword, pulled it out and tossed it aside, then produced this pouch of blood. Instead of drinking it, he broke it against his chest. The wound started to close."

Tony was nodding. "It's no mystery, Michael; I'm just surprise that Stephan, or Stavros, as you prefer to call him, would be so accommodating. But then, knowing how effective you've been against his lackeys, he would want to give them an edge."

"Are you saying that it was Soutzos's blood in that pouch?"

Tony nodded. "Had you checked the other, you would probably have found a similar pouch. Vampires learned a long time ago that the blood of an older vampire can help a younger vampire's wounds heal. Indeed, there's a centuries-old practice. If we take what we call the small drink—drawing just a sustainable amount of blood without killing the victim—we can close the wound so that it is undetectable the next day by placing a drop of our own blood on the wound.

"Now, Michael, if you don't mind telling me from the beginning what occurred tonight..."

He listened, nodding, as Mike gave him a detailed play by play. When Mike was finished, he asked, "What did you feel when the vampires were passing— when you beheaded Vollinkoff as he hit the floor, and again when you decapitated Chekinovich after your prolonged combat?"

"How do you know who was who?" Mike demanded.

"In good time, dear boy. This is important."

Mike thought about it. "There was nothing with the first one, but I was focused on locating the second. I was afraid he might go into my mind and was blocking him out. But the second—Chekinovich?—for a moment it was like all hell broke loose in my mind, like a whirlwind. There was a chaos of violence and bloodlust, like looking inside the mind of Jack the Ripper or Mister Hyde. Then I blocked it out. Pete was yelling at me, wanting to know if there were more."

"That force in your mind, Michael, that's the reason I cannot do what you do. It's much harder for a vampire to block it out. A part of us hungers for it as much as we can hunger for blood. It's what drives a monster like Chernov to kill the way he does."

"What about Stavros? Does he kill or just take what you call the small drink?"

"Both; it depends on his mood," Tony explained. "Claude scanned everything he could find about him in her diaries—scanned it to text and e-mailed me the text files. Our Prince Stephan, as he likes to call himself, took the small drink when it was too dangerous to do otherwise but, if he thought he could get away with it, he would kill and dispose of the body. He doesn't seem to like others dictating rules to him. His pride and stubbornness seem to exceed his intelligence."

"So, how did you know which was Chekinovich and which was Vollinkoff?" Mike asked.

"Elementary, my dear Michael," Tony joked. "Chekinovich and Chernov both trained for Spetsnaz, Russia's special forces. Chekinovich washed out early but still had considerably combat training. Chernov almost made it but his superiors thought him too much of a loose cannon. It was that penchant for ruthlessness that made the KGB recruit him. Also, Chekinovich was of stockier build than Vollinkoff, though not as big as Chernov."

"So I still have something to look forward to," Mike muttered.

He set his glass down, then gathered up his things. Once the celtic knives were tucked into his belt, he donned the coat and slid his katana into its special pocket. He pulled the spent meteor out of his flare gun and reloaded it before placing the gun in its pocket, then pocketed the remaining flares.

"I'm heading home to a hot bath, then to bed for a few hours," he said, placing his hat on his head.

Tony walked him to the door. "Your fleece will be here for you tomorrow."

Mike nodded. He had other things on his mind beside one blood-stained fleece pullover.

"This is all going much better than I expected, Michael," Tony continued. "With a bit of luck, we might be able to isolate Chernov and Soutzos, take them out separately, and be done with this business in a few more days—all thanks to your skills."

"We'll see," Mike said.

# 21: Making Sense

Mike closed his eyes and let his body revel in the heat of the bath. Sean was rattling about in the kitchen prior to heading off to school. He'd tried to pester his father for details of his pre-dawn adventure, but Mike would only tell him it went fine and was over. At intervals he added more hot water, easing the aches and pains that pervaded his upper body and arms.

*I don't remember it hurting this much twenty years ago,* he mused.

It bothered him how easy things had gone, then he reflected on his battle with Chekinovich. *Perhaps that wasn't so easy,* he thought. *Perhaps I was simply better than he was, or luckier.* His new-found speed still troubled him. But, he was tired, too tired to belabour every little detail. "Take the successes and improve on the failures," he reminded himself, swallowing the last of his scotch.

He exited the tub, dried himself, took two Excedrin, and buried himself under the covers, hiding from what light leaked through the blinds. He was asleep in moments.

At first he wasn't sure what had awakened him. He got up and listened. Nothing. He checked the window. Carrie's car was in the driveway. She was just getting out. He quickly pulled on pajama bottoms and met her at the door.

She came through the door and into his arms.

"I've only got two hours before I have to be at work," she explained, "but I thought we could have lunch." She looked him up and down. "Perhaps breakfast in your case." She spotted the bruises and touched them with her fingertips. "My, God, Michael, what are you doing to yourself."

"Late night," he explained. "Actually, a very early morning. If it's any consolation, the one who did this is toast—literally. He and a colleague are no doubt lying on morgue tables, looking like to over-roasted chickens. And I blew up a meth lab. Pete's not too happy about that, but I don't give a crap. None of that stuff can ever hit the streets now."

"Please tell me you got another vampire and this is all that happened to you!"

Mike smiled. "I got two other vampires and this is all that happened to me. I seem to bruise more as I get closer to fifty," he joked. "The good news is that bruises fade fast, and the stiffness and achiness rarely last through the day. "

"Have you always been a fast healer?"

Mike nodded. "As far back as I can remember."

"Well, if you'd like to freshen up and get dressed, I have the makings of a fruit salad and can probably have it all ready by the time you reach the kitchen."

She picked up the cloth shopping bag and over-sized carry bag she'd let fall when she came in, and headed up the stairs.

"Hello, Sam." She patted the corgi's head. He'd just come waddling out from the bedroom and looked like he was still waking up. "Getting old doesn't mean getting lazy, Sam," she chided. "Take a lesson from your daddy there. He seems to be getting more active as he ages."

Something in the remark hit a nerve with Mike. He dwelled on that while washing up. Mike hated showers, preferring a bath, but with Carrie in the kitchen he wasn't about to waste time on that.

When he reached the kitchen, she hugged him again.

"I'm glad you put a shirt on," she teased. "I don't dare arrive at work today looking all happily disheveled. I'd never hear the end of it."

"I'll try to get out there later today, maybe this evening," he commented. "I've a few things to talk to Dad about and, while he claims talking on the phone is as good as a visit, that's crap and he just doesn't want to admit it."

"I think your father always put work first," she suggested.

"You hit that nail on the head. I think he carries a lot of guilt about Mom's death. He wasn't there. He was in the office late at night, his detectives working 'round the clock to crack a tough case."

"And did he?"

Mike shrugged. "The detectives cracked it while he was on leave to prepare Mom's funeral."

"I never realized. It explains a few things, like why he's so protective of you. You're all that's left, really, since your brother's not here."

Mike shrugged. "This looks good," he said, picking up a plate.

He told her everything about the raid on the drug lab, including his fears and worries.

"I can understand your being afraid of going one-on-one against a vampire—with all the stuff in movies, who wouldn't?" she agreed. "But, from what you've said, you seem to be really fast. And you can see them move when other's can't. Maybe you just can't bring yourself to accept that you're almost as fast as a vampire. But, with all the training you've had, you're more than a match for any vampire in skill."

Mike shook his head. "It just can't be that simple. Something about it feels so unnatural and I don't know why."

Carrie smiled. "At heart you're an introvert, Michael. All through school you were the smartest, sometimes the second smartest, in your class. Yet you never took it for granted or recognized it as a part of who you are. You have an IQ of 145, yet you think you're ordinary. Your father told me a lot about you. It's the same with your music—you have an incredible voice but think you're just a decent singer. It's the same with your skill as a martial artist. You're incredibly good but you act like you're just average, maybe a little better than average. How you can still be lacking in confidence after all you've accomplished is amazing, yet there you are."

Mike sighed. "I wish it were that simple. Part of me accepts all the things you've said but just wants to cling to an air of modesty—maybe it's the Shaolin passion for humility. But another part of me just knows there's something weird and not normal about this, and that part just won't let go."

She gestured with her fork at his plate. "Let go long enough to finish your lunch."

Though the remainder of lunch they talked about what Tony, Nigel, and he had accomplished and what still lay before them.

"There's been nothing on the radio about the bodies in the harbour," she commented.

Mike thought about that. "It may be too soon. Pete may be keeping a lid on it to avoid further panic. Then again, he may just be keeping a lid on it until all the bodies have been identified. Perhaps he'll let the names out one at a time to give the impression that there wasn't a mass body count in one day. Our local news media are a bit more cooperative with the police than in the States."

"That reminds me," Carrie interrupted, "you made Frank magazine. I guess not all the media are so cooperative." She handed him the small gossip paper. There, taking up most of the front page, was a black and white photo taken, presumably, from a window overlooking the sidewalk. He was wearing his black suede jacket and drover's hat, grappling with Bondarenko, twin *sgian dubh* imbedded in Bondarenko's shoulders. The headline asked the blatant question, ***Halifax's Own Van Helsing?*** The text inside told of an unidentified vigilante avenging the killing of a local police officer moments after he was murdered by one of the alleged vampire killers.

Mike took his time reading the article.

"Great, that's all I need," he said. "It's obvious that someone in an apartment was watching out the window, took some pictures, and saw most of what happened. Shit!"

He flipped open his cell phone and called MacDonald.

"Pete, have you seen Frank magazine?"

"Yeah, I saw it," the inspector said. "They called me last night looking for confirmation. I sent a man over to Fuller right after I got back to the station. The camera angle narrowed the search considerably, so it didn't take much door-to-door before we located an elderly lady with a digital camera. She was more high-tech than my mother, I can tell you. She sold the magazine the story of what she saw along with a photo CD. We have a copy. Here's the good news: you never looked up, and her camera battery died before anyone official arrived on the scene. While you were talking to police and the ME's people, she was getting dressed and coming down the stairs to join a small crowd rubber-necking in the doorway. No one can corroborate a connection to the police. They can't claim that we know who you are."

"Well, that's some consolation," Mike agreed. "What about checking the Northwest Arm for bodies?"

"It's in the works," Pete said. "The boats headed there about nine o'clock this morning. They've got a couple of those glass bottom things for looking into the water, and a diver in each boat. I told them to check along the private docks on the city side."

"I know they're going to find something, Pete. I can feel it."

"How are you doing today?" MacDonald asked. "You went above and beyond this morning. Shit, man, you cleared the path for Nigel, took out two of the lab rats, then nailed two more on our list of Russians. Blowing up the place wasn't exactly protocol, but I understand your motives. My guys were really impressed. Any cop who grumbles about you after today will get hauled off and taught some painful manners by any of the crew on scene."

"You getting any heat from the chief or the mayor about the explosion?"

"Let's just say I was a bit vague in my report about the cause of the explosion," Pete replied. "Meth labs are volatile, Mike. You have to be extra careful not to have an explosion. And my cops are behind you like one of their own. I cautioned them about mentioning you and your flare gun. One cop, MacKenzie, grinned and said, 'What flare gun?' The rest just laughed and nodded. So, Mike, I may have given you hell about it this morning, but we're square on it, okay?"

Mike raised an eyebrow. "That's nice to hear."

"So, Mike, you haven't answered how you are," Pete said. "Are you okay? You got pretty banged up in there."

"I'm fine, Pete—having lunch with a lady friend at the moment. I've got a few aches and pains from Chekinovich, but the mineral ice is helping. Thanks for asking."

"So, who's the lady friend?" MacDonald inquired. "Is it the nurse who looks after your father? He told me about you and her—Carrie, is it? He's a huge fan of hers."

"Yes, Pete." He gave Carrie a wink. "I'm a fan, too. And that's enough questions about that."

MacDonald laughed. "Good luck. Maybe you can have tonight off."

After Carrie left for work, Mike kept turning things over and over in his mind. He felt like a dog with a bone. Finally, he looked up a number in the phonebook and dialed.

"Good, Sandy, you're in the office," he said when he got through. "Will you be there for a bit? I'd like to come over and talk."

"Well, I was going to do an afternoon of visiting at the hospital, but you're just around the corner—come on over. I'll get to the hospital after we're through."

Mike buzzed at the church house door and told the secretary who he was. There was a buzzer sound of the lock holding open long enough for him to get in. He sighed. When he was a teenager you could knock and walk in. Times had changed.

He trotted up the stairs of what used to be the old manse and found Sandy waiting at his office door.

He took a long look at Mike and gave him a warm hug.

"Come on in, Mike. You look like the world's weighing heavy on your shoulders."

Mike tried to be as concise as possible as he unloaded everything.

"That's a powerful pile of revelations for anyone," the reverend commented. "The church is no stranger to past life phenomenon, you know."

That caught Mike off guard.

"Come on, Michael, you know what the United Church is like. Most of us don't buy the whole 'Jews killed Christ' bit. You only need to study a little history to know that Romans used crucifixion as torture for rebels. And no occupying force ever made a habit of doing favours for the people they occupied. But then, when the Roman Church was first preaching in Rome, they weren't about to tell their Roman congregation that it was the Romans who killed their new god. The Council of Nicaea in 325 AD decided what could be told and what couldn't. The Gnostic Gospels were suppressed."

Mike nodded. "I know about that. I even have a copy of them, or what survives of them. I haven't had time to read it yet. But what's your point?"

"Well, Mike, when you find time to read them, you'll learn that, according to some of those texts, Jesus spoke of reincarnation. I've done some extensive reading on past life memory. There are a lot of conflicting theories. One that sticks to the wall more than others, so to speak, is that past lives intrude most on present lives when there's something terribly relevant—when something in this life relates directly to a past life. It may be an effort to keep us from making a mistake over again. It may be that skills from a past life are needed in this life. There are even those who believe that, sometimes, we are destined to reencounter people from our past lives. Maybe we rediscover a lost love, maybe we are meant to foil an old nemesis. There can be powerful links between souls."

"So how does all this sit with your role as leader of the flock?" Mike asked. "Don't these beliefs create a contradiction?"

Sandy smiled. "Did you read or see The Da Vinci Code, Michael?"

He nodded.

"Did you find any of it credible and, if so, does it create contradictions?"

Mike thought about it. "Yes, I found it credible and, no, I don't find contradictions.?

"What? No contradictions in the Son of God having children like a mortal man?"

Mike shook his head. "I figure God came here as Jesus to make sense out of who we are—to understand what it means to be human. If he was to experience all our pain, all our joy, parenthood is a natural part of that. And if he wanted to spread a message of peace, what better person to do it than the heir to the throne of David married to the heir of the line of Benjamin—an uncrowned king espousing peace, not war. But, Sandy, I don't have to preach on Sunday and keep it in line with what the congregation and the Halifax Presbytery expect to hear."

"Some of our congregation see Him as God in another form, and some insist He's the Son," Sandy argued. "We've always had to work around these things. To help our parishioners effectively, we must have an understanding of their experiences and beliefs, whether we concur with them or not."

"Fine, I'll give you that. So what about all these strange things about me, Sandy," Mike persisted. "Why am I so fast? Why do I heal faster than most people."

"You know the answer as well as I, Michael; you used to teach anatomy and physiology. You heal fast because you have a hyperactive immune system. You process protein efficiently. It's why you have arthritis. How is that, by the way?"

Mike shrugged. "Exercise, hot baths, and pain killers."

Sandy nodded. "Now, about your speed. Maybe you're just wired differently. You've always been fast, even as a kid. And sharp as a tack. Your brain is fast, Michael. I think your nerve synapses, both motor nerves and the connections in the brain, just transmit faster than most people's."

Mike finally nodded. "I suppose." He couldn't keep the reluctance out of his voice.

"Okay, Mike, you need a higher, more spiritual explanation? I'll give you one. God needs you right now, doing what you're doing. He needs you to be fast, and he needs you to heal fast and be back on your feet without delays. Does that help?"

Mike broke into a smile and suddenly felt a bit foolish. "I suppose," he conceded.

When he left the church office, he went to SeaView to see his father. Running into Carrie in the hallway brought a chorus of oohs and ahs from her coworkers. After a quick kiss she scurried off on her rounds.

He found his father sitting in his chair, like always, reading a paperback. The oxygen tubes were at his nose, held in place by a band about his head. "Hey, Mikey. Okay," he said, gesturing to the tubes, "You caught me. I was just reading."

Mike glanced at the cover of the book.

"Jeese, Dad, **Bloodlist**? I didn't know you were an Elrod fan. Finished my book already?"

"Hey, what have I got to do but read? Pull up a pew." He put a book mark in place and closed the book. "With all that's going on, one of the girls here told me about the books and loaned me this one."

"Want it in hard cover?" Mike asked. "I have the whole set."

"Well, I'll finish this one first—Maggie was so excited that I was willing to borrow a book from her. So how are you doing? I gather you and Carrie decided not to wait for tomorrow night's big date."

Mike grinned and shrugged. "It just sort of happened. But it's good—it feels right, and she gives me something I've been missing ever since Susan died—that feeling that I'm where I'm supposed to be, with who I'm supposed to be with."

William put a hand on top of his son's. "I'm glad for you, son."

"Dad..." Mike hesitated

"What is it?"

"That night when I was a kid and had that accident on my bike? I remember falling off my bike and hitting that pipe, I remember the pain of it tearing my throat, but I don't remember you being there, and I definitely don't remember Tony. I thought I was in an ambulance."

Will shook his head. "What exactly do you remember?"

Mike thought about it. "I remember voices—someone telling me it would be okay. I remember someone holding me—I remember a hand against my throat."

Will nodded. "You knew from the voices that there was more that one person and assumed it was an ambulance. I was driving and it was Tony's hand against your throat. If I remember right, I think he even had a finger in the wound, trying to stop bleeding from a major blood vessel.

"I think you touched his heart in some way. I guess it was the sight of one so young so close to death. I got letters from him in the years between that visit and the one about seven years later. In every single one he asked about you—if the injury had healed, were your throat and voice okay—showing true concern."

"In the Orient they believe that, if you save a life, you become responsible for that life," Mike offered.

Will nodded. "I think Tony had a sense of this. When I told him about your singing and the solo festivals between grades five and seven, he was most enthusiastic. I guess he was relieved by conclusive proof that your throat was fine."

Mike stared at the floor, deep in thought. He was picturing Tony's reaction to his offer of comfort that morning. It reminded him of what the Englishman had said when Mike became so suspicious after learning Tony was a vampire—how becoming attached to a human, as if he were a son or a nephew, made it easier for a vampire to deal with the passage of time and retain a sense of his own humanity. And how it eased the incredible loneliness that vampires risk by being reclusive. It cast Tony in such an innocent light that it made Mike feel guilty for ever doubting his motives.

He had quite a long visit with his father. Sean surprised them by showing up unannounced.

"Shouldn't you be in…" Mike was about to say 'school' but a glance at his watch showed him it almost four o'clock. "How are the roads?"

Sean tossed his helmet on a chair and peeled off his blue and red leather jacket. "Fine," he said. "Maybe two centimeters of snow. I came the back way—you know, Caldwell Road? No cars but they haven't plowed. It's not packed down by traffic, so my treads kind of just go through it. Relax, Dad, I kept it easy on the turns, allowed for the snow. I'm careful, you know."

He gave his father that disparaging look teenagers can give when they think grownups are treating them like children.

"Cut him some slack, Dad," Will said.

Mike shot a direct look at his father. "Did you cut me any?"

Will turned his head away, looking sheepish. "Oops," he said, giving Sean a wink. Then, looking at Mike, added, "So learn from my mistakes."

"Some help you are" Mike chided.

"This isn't a domestic scrap, is it?" Carrie stood in the doorway.

"No, Carrie, it's just Mikey being a bit over-protective."

"Yeah," Sean chimed in. "Tell Dad to gimme a break. He might listen to you."

"Is that so?" Her smile sparkled. "Perhaps I should listen to him before I take sides."

"My son seems to think his motorcycle is a snowmobile just because they make snow tires for it."

Carrie nodded. "And your father has so little to worry about that you should pitch in and contribute to his worries," she said to Sean.

Sean sighed. "Point taken. Hey, you guys have a big date tomorrow night," he added.

Mike grinned. Sean liked to change the subject when he felt he was losing an argument. Maybe her comment would stay with Sean long enough to make him more careful.

"As a matter of fact, I do have a date with a very handsome man—an author, no less. And, since I have the weekend off, I will have all day to get ready."

"I have to get home and make supper, then I have a class to teach at six," Mike announced. "Would the lovely lady care to walk me out?"

She took his arm. "My pleasure, sir."

He glanced back at Sean. "Don't be too long, and be careful coming home. There'll be more traffic then."

Sean nodded. "I will, Dad."

"So," he whispered to Carrie, "any hope of you coming by tonight. You don't need a clean uniform until Monday."

Carrie grinned. "You can be very bad, you know."

"I'm not bad," Mike defended himself, "I just want to see you as much as possible."

She checked to make sure no one was watching and gave him a quick kiss. "By strange coincidence," she whispered, "there seems to be a small suitcase in the back of my car—just big enough for a change of clothes and some cosmetics."

"And something nice to wear tomorrow night," he prompted.

"As a matter of fact," she replied, "I was planning to go shopping for something new tomorrow afternoon. I also have an appointment to have my hair done, not far from your place. So you have the afternoon to yourself. But when date time rolls around, watch out."

Mike took her in his arms at the elevator and held her close until another care giver called out, "Get a room."

"Tonight," Mike whispered, then got into the elevator.

# 22: Plans

The rest of Friday night was as uneventful as Mike could have wished. The class went on for an extra hour, all of his students, especially the more senior ones, seemed to be very focused and at their best. He even went so far as to tell Sean, Frank, and Johnny that they should prepare for possible black belt testing in a month.

He and Carrie watched "The Scarlet Pimpernel" in his theatre and kept joking how the actor playing Lord Dewhurst looked nothing like Tony.

They slept late into the morning, then, after breakfast together, Carrie kissed him goodbye and said, "Just wait 'til you see me tonight. And I'd like it if you can wear your black suit with that silk knit T-shirt." She widened her eyes in dramatic fashion, kissed him once more, then headed for her car.

Mike was looking forward to a relaxed afternoon of writing and actually got half a chapter written before the phone rang. It was Inspector MacDonald.

"Yeah, Pete, what's up."

"Six bodies, weighted down, ten feet out from private docks in the Northwest Arm," he said. "They weren't savaged in the fashion we've come to associate with Chernov, but they aren't pretty."

"Can you tell which dock they were thrown from?"

Pete sighed. "Not really. They were far enough out that they could have moved with the tidal current. Still, it localizes us to the areas off the southern part of Beaufort Avenue or off Francklyn Street."

"Nigel is looking into properties in that area," Mike pointed out. "He can get into security company reports and stuff that you'd need a court order to access. You should acquaint him with all of this."

"Why don't you meet me at Lord Dewhurst's. Can you be there in thirty minutes?"

Mike looked at the clock. Two-twenty. "Okay," he agreed with a sigh, "but I'm not going snooping in Halifax tonight. I have a very important date, Pete. She's out buying a new dress and getting her hair done as we speak. I plan to be back here to get cleaned up by five."

"Mike," Pete begged, "give me an hour, two at the most. I promise you'll be home before five."

"Okay." Mike felt reluctance as he said it. He took his black suit out of the closet and laid it on the bed, set his silk knit T-shirt on top, even laid out clean socks and underwear and his Tony Lama boots.

He grabbed his keys, then hesitated at the door. Instinct made him grab his trench coat and drover's hat. "Van Helsing on the case," he joked to himself.

———

"I like this place here," Nigel said. "It's in the right area for your bodies, it's got the biggest dock, a motor yacht worth several million quid, it's got a tennis court, an' enough square footage for a small 'otel. I'm telling you, this is the place. An' the trees around it keep the neighbours from seeing anything."

"Yes, but the bodies were so spread out it could be any of those properties," Pete argued. He circled an area in the Arm. "Who knows how the tide moved them? The incoming tide could have pushed them up, then the outgoing tide dragged them down."

Pete was about to continue to argue the point when Nigel got exasperated.

"If I could just get a word in 'ere, Inspector, I could settle this. A week ago the alarms go off. Security calls the 'ouse before calling the coppers. Somebody tells them it's a false alarm. Thing is, there's a delay in giving them the identification password. Now, mind you, they record all this. You wanna 'ear it played back? I got it right 'ere."

He played the recording. The voice claiming to be the homeowner had a relatively bland accent but there was a hint of something.

"Play it again," Mike said. Nigel complied. "There's something—I just can't place it."

"I can," Tony said. "It's in the vowels but more noticeable in certain consonants."

"Yes," Mike agreed. "I was about to suggest he was New Brunswick French, speaking English so long he has no real accent, but it's different."

Tony nodded. "He's Dutch, but he's had years of speaking English and French, particularly English. His accent is quite washed out, but the subtle Dutch inflection is there."

"It's Soutzos," Mike insisted. "The delay was him getting the password from one of the homeowners. Chernov probably had them in another room. I can just see him with his teeth against the wife's throat, waiting for her husband to cave in."

"So what do we do?" Pete asked. "There's no probable cause and, in this case, manufacturing it like last time isn't much help. What can my cops do against Chernov? And we know next to nothing of Soutzos's capabilities."

"Well, we got nothin' on the count's physical appearance," Nigel pointed out. "I can't find a bleedin' thing, 'cept that 'e's blonde. No references to height, weight, or build. No references to any sport or fighting skills. Even bloomin' Von Richthoven was known as a skilled fencer."

"Let's poke around tomorrow, say around noon," Mike suggested. "It's supposed to be sunny. Even if he can be up and around indoors, noon places the sun at its highest, and Chernov and Soutzos at their weakest."

He looked to Tony for confirmation. Tony nodded. "By noon I'm catatonic, no matter how hard I try."

"But what about the homeowners?" MacDonald argued. "He's had them for days."

"They're probably among the bodies recovered yesterday," Mike pointed out. "Once he had the alarm system figured out, they'd be just food to him. I doubt if he'd keep them around in case relatives showed up."

Pete sighed. "I can't imagine the scandal I'll have to deal with if a total victim count ever gets out about this case. Even if we get all the culprits, it won't help the image of the police. No offense, Mike, but after that photo of you in Frank Magazine, this Van Helsing figure they're trying to sensationalize will get all the credit."

Mike rolled his eyes. "And letting the body count continue to rise is going to help things? Let's deal with stopping this guy first, then we can worry about police reputation. For God's sake, Pete, just plant a story that the man in the photo was an undercover cop acting in self-defense. You want probable cause? Then identify any of the bodies from the Arm as one or both of the homeowners, and there's your grounds for a warrant. However, I do agree with you—I don't think your cops will be able to handle Chernov—unless you want to arm them with flare guns."

"Or shotguns with shells filled with wooden pellets," Tony suggested. "They wouldn't be lethal, but they'd keep the wounds from healing. But Michael's right. With Chernov's speed and strength, he might kill several of your officers before anyone could seriously incapacitate him."

"I'll go in around noon," Mike said. "Your cops can deal with any human guards he might have, while I look for resting vampires." He turned back to Nigel. "Can you get me more information on the property?"

"Well, I wish I could access blueprints, but the fact is, gov'nor, I can't. Near as I can tell, there noffin' on file. Maybe in a cabinet in some architect's office, but there noffin' online. 'Owever, I can give you an aerial overview of the grounds. That's easy."

He booted Google Earth, then zeroed in on the neighbourhood. The property stood out easily for it's size and the contrast against the buffer of trees around the property. Nigel zoomed until the entire screen was filled with the property. He then pressed print, made preference selections, then said, "Be back in a jiff, mate. I got a whopper of a printer in my room— wireless router."

He returned moments later with rolled up a 33" x 42" color print.

""What the hell have you got up there?" Mike asked.

"Well, it's an architectural printer, i'n't it. Does a nice job with playmate o' the month, too."

Mike studied the aerial view. It was just beyond the resolution of the image, making it a bit fuzzy, but he could easily tell details of the yard, where balconies and other possible points of entry might be.

He went off to one side and studied the layout. The very trees that granted privacy to the property offered concealment to an approach. There'd have to be security measures. It took him a while to spot it—hints of a tall iron fence about the property. It might be electrified, there might be motion sensors or surveillance cameras. Even in daylight, he couldn't just walk in. He remembered places like this in Florida. The mailman left mail in a box outside the gate that servants could access from inside.

"Cripes," he exclaimed, "this guy could be a Columbian drug lord from the layout of the place. Can you hack into ADT and see what electronic security there is?"

"I'm on it, gov'nor," Nigel said, then started typing at his laptop.

Mike continued to study. The docks looked like the easiest point of access. He assumed there'd be some security there as well, but it was still the easiest physical access. Approaching boats would be heard and, no doubt, picked up by surveillance cameras. A swimmer? The water would be below zero Celsius. He'd dived wrecks in sub-freezing water as a young man. He could remember seeing the water clouded with ice crystals. Salt water froze at colder temperatures that fresh, but it did freeze. Often it was just wave movement and tidal flow that kept certain small bays and inlets from freezing. He knew the upper reaches of the Arm could freeze in very cold winters. The very coldness of the water would be a security system and his only wetsuit was custom eighth-inch suit he'd had made in Florida, good for a half hour in Nova Scotia water in August.

"Pete, can you get me a dry suit?"

"Probably," the inspector replied. "Anything else—tank, mask, fins?"

Mike shook his head. "Just the suit and weights."

Pete made a call, spoke for a few moments, then closed his phone. Five minutes later Pete's phone rang. He nodded and smiled, spoke briefly, then closed the phone and put it away. "One of our divers lives about a mile from here and he's about your size. He'll be here shortly to drop his suit off."

"Electrified gate, seven outside cameras, an' sensors on all downstairs windows," Nigel reported. "An' you better check your time, mate."

Mike glanced at his watch. "Shit! It's quarter to six! Gotta go." He rolled up the photo and gestured with it. "I'll be back here by noon."

MacDonald stopped him at the door. "Look, Mike, I…"

Mike cut him off. "You're getting rattled, Pete. This whole thing is weighing on you—I get it. So we shut it down. That's our job."

"And this doesn't scare you?" Pete demanded.

"Jesus, Pete, it scares me shitless!" Mike shot back. "What do you think? But somebody's got to take these to monsters out. I don't see any other volunteers coming forward, do you?"

Mike wasn't too happy with the plan. As he drove home, he realized that, while he had tried not to plan to far ahead, he'd been looking forward to having a lazy Sunday with Carrie. "Now I know why James Bond was never successfully married," he muttered. Then, imitating Sean Connery, "Sorry, Dear, I'll be late for dinner again. It's Blofeld. Shouldn't take more than a few hours, but don't wait up. No, Dear, I'm not seeing Moneypenny on the side."

As he neared his street, a knot formed in his gut. The closer he got, the worse the feeling got. Dave, his neighbour, was milling about at his front door. Something made him pull up in front instead of using the driveway. Exiting the car, he grabbed his katana and bolted for the front door.

Horror filled him. He fought the urge to retch.

The glass of his front door was shattered. Sam's limp body was impaled on a shard of glass rising like a fang from the bottom of the pane. Feeling drained from him as he approached. The corgi's throat was also torn out. His nausea quickly subsided as cold rage took its place.

Carrie's car was in the drive, driver's door open. A large wardrobe bag, probably her new dress, lay in the snow.

Dave opened his mouth to speak. Mike raised a hand to cut him off, pulled out his phone, and voice dialed Sean. No answer.

He looked at Dave and nodded for him to speak.

"The police are on the way. There was a strange van parked in the turning circle for about a half hour. The engine was running and I just figured it was someone Andy knew." He gestured toward the house two doors past Mike's. "I got curious enough to watch it at intervals. Mike, it all happened so fast. There was a crash. I saw a car pull into your driveway—it's been there a few times, so I figured it was someone you knew.

"It looked like a terrorist raid! I heard a horrible yelp from Sam, the van moved and blocked that car in just as a blonde lady was getting out. They grabbed her and hauled her into the van. When the van pulled away, there was poor Sam hanging in the broken window. That's when Sean came roaring up the street on his bike."

"Sean? What about Sean? Did they grab him?"

Dave shook his head. "I don't know that they even noticed him. They just sped away. Sean noticed them, though. Maybe he spotted your lady friend in the van. Anyway, he spun his bike around and took off after them."

Mike stifled a curse.

"I decided to wait for the police here," Dave went on. "I've got heavy plastic and duct tape to cover the window when they're through—wait, Mike, don't touch anything–"

Mike ignored him, lifted Sam, and laid him on the ground. Drawing his katana, he entered the house. It took only a few moments to prove the place empty. He'd given Carrie a key and left the alarm off. At least he didn't have to deal with that noise.

His cell phone rang.

"Michael, it's Tony." The crisp British accent was an unexpected source of calm in a sea of chaos.

"They've got Carrie, Tony," he blurted, fighting tears. "And Sean's gone after them."

"I know about Carrie, Michael, but I didn't know about Sean. Perhaps they don't either. A note was delivered by special messenger just moments ago—parchment tied with purple ribbon.

"It says, 'I'm entertaining a charming friend of a friend of yours. She may not last long, so perhaps you should hurry over. Bring your friend and bring *Yama Kaze*. It's more than fitting for *Yama Kaze* to be here for this very different ending of our long rivalry.'

"It's signed 'Prince Stephan Sutu of Wallachia and Transylvania,' accompanied by what may be his brother's former seal in purple wax. The address we already know, but this confirms it."

"It also gives Pete his probable cause, not that I care a crap about that. They killed little Sam, Tony. I know it was Chernov—he tore his throat out and hung his body in the broken window of my front door. They smashed that to get in. No one was home. Then Carrie got back from her shopping and they grabbed her. I think they were hoping for Sean. Now he's on his bike, riding right into their hands."

"You need to calm yourself, Michael. Emotions won't help you right now. Sean is well trained. He's a teenager but he's not without discipline. You said yourself, he's ready to test for his black belt. You can't get there without discipline. You'll hear from him. He probably isn't answering his phone because he's too busy driving his motorcycle."

"Yeah," Mike sighed. Then, "Did that dry suit arrive?"

"Shortly before the note," Tony said.

"What about Pete?"

"I'm still trying to get through to him, Michael."

"I'll be there as quick as I can."

Closing his phone, he thought a moment, then grabbed his wetsuit out of the closet. Stripping down, he pulled it on, right there in the entry hall.

"What in God's name are you doing?" Dave asked, but Mike ignored him.

He snatched the heavy plastic Dave was holding. He spread the plastic on the floor, dropped his three *sgian dubh*, and the Very pistol and flares onto it. He ran to his bedroom and came back with two pairs of *tabi* socks, a pair of ninja boots, and his climbing claws. Like the *tabi*, the big toe of the boots was separate from the rest of the foot. He added them to the bundle, then grabbed a black stocking cap and *Thinsulate* leather gloves from the entry closet and toss them in as well. He then rolled the whole thing into the tightest mass possible, rolled the ends, and taped it all with Dave's duct tape.

Dave glanced at the drover's hat Mike had tossed on the cedar chest at the base of the stairs and started to nod. "You're him. You're the one they're comparing to the Van Helsing movie."

Mike grimaced, then flashed his CSIS ID. "I don't suppose you could keep that a secret."

Dave whistled, then nodded.

Mike put the package and his katana in the back of his Cherokee, then went back to the house. It took but a moment to locate his scuba tank and dive gear in the basement.

Dave forestalled him in the doorway. "Be careful. I'll wait here for the police, then get more plastic for the window. If they don't take Sam, I'll wrap him for burial."

Mike put a hand on Dave's shoulder. "Thanks." He loaded his gear in the car and took off.

He stopped at Tony's just long enough to grab the drysuit and weights.

As he tried to leave, Tony grabbed his arm. "We should plan something—some strategy, Michael."

Mike tore free, shaking his head. "They've got Carrie, Tony." It came out as a snarl. He breathed deep, then nodded. "You're right, Tony. Any rage I feel helps them more than me. No room for feelings tonight. I'll hit the property from the water as planned. I'll use the shadows and take out any guards one at a time as I find them."

"Michael, I don't think you want to waste time trying to tie up guards. I know they're human but you may have to just put that out of your mind in this case."

Mike gave Tony an icy look. "Anyone guarding that property is an accomplice to ruthless murderers and involved in making and selling poison. They're up to their necks in this. Don't worry about me, Tony. Tonight is business. I'll deal with my conscience tomorrow." He handed Tony the Muramasa katana. "You're my diversion."

"I'll give you a few minutes head start, then set out," Tony said.

Mike raced across the bridge and through downtown Halifax, ignoring lights and the speed limit. Twice police cars had pulled out, sirens and lights activated, only to give up chase. He could only assume that Pete had alerted dispatch with his plate number. He was on Tower Road, headed toward Point Pleasant Park, when his cell phone rang, singing out with Sean's ringtone.

"Sean, stay where you are and wait for me. Don't do anything without me."

"Dad, they've got Carrie! I saw them grab her. And, Dad, they killed Sam." Sean sounded like he was fighting to not be hysterical. "I had to just leave him there, Dad. If I'd stopped to look after Sam, they'd have gotten away, and we wouldn't have known where they went." He rattled off the address.

"I know, Sean, I have an aerial photo of the place. Sean, I don't want you anywhere near there."

"Dad, I'm calling from inside the grounds. Okay, I won't enter the house 'til you get here. I can even help you get over the fence the way I did. I climbed a tree and used the branches to get into another tree on the other side. The fence is electrified, so be careful."

"What about surveillance cameras and motion sensors?"

"I didn't see any, Dad."

"Did you look for them?"

"Well, no, not exactly…"

The sound of a thump ended the call.

"Shit!" The knot on Mike's stomach returned.

# 23: "Some Big Date!"

Mike reached Francklyn Street and pulled into a posh driveway two doors away from the target property. When a man answered the door, Mike let him have a good look at his CSIS ID.

"We have an incident in progress and I need to use your property to get to the water," he explained.

The man nodded, wide eyed, then told Mike, "I'll open the gate and you can drive right down to the dock."

"Thank you. It's important that you act as if nothing's wrong. Close the gate behind me, wait about twenty minutes, then activate any security systems you might have. Stay off the phone, and keep your doors and windows locked."

Once at the dock, Mike arranged his plastic package, scuba tank, weights, mask and fins at the edge of the dock. He pulled the borrowed drysuit over his wetsuit, then grabbed his Sherwood Magnum regulator and installed it on the tank, turned it on, and checked the gauges. The tank was full—he hadn't used it since he'd come home, but he'd had it tested and filled the previous summer. The harness straps wouldn't adjust large for the bulk of the dry suit but he didn't care. He only had to go about two hundred yards.

He donned the weight belt, which did fit the suit, got his fins on and adjusted, and slid into the water. He had to let air out of the suit to avoid feeling like an ungainly cork. It took a moment to spit in his mask, rub it around, put the mask on, and then grab the tank. He hoisted a strap over one shoulder and held it, got the regulator in his mouth, then grabbed his package.

The icy water was painful against his face, feeling ironically hot. He ignored it and finned his way up the shoreline. He fought to keep his breathing relaxed, falling into a Chi Kung meditation to calm his anxiety about Carrie and Sean, willing this thoughts to become those of a predator.

Locating the second dock up the Arm was easy. The dock was empty. He'd half expected to find the giant motor yacht, almost forgetting that pictures on Google Earth could be as much as five years old. He swam closer to shore, keeping his leg movements smooth and silent. A rocky patch, miraculously free of ice, made it easy to climb out.

He lowered the tank, turned off the valve, and gently breathed the regulator dry. The last thing he wanted was for the regulator to purge itself, announcing his presence to anyone patrolling the grounds. Moments later, he'd opened his plastic package, was out of the drysuit and pulling his ninja boots on over two pairs of *Tabi* socks. Everything had stayed dry, but he'd been careful not to submerge the package. His custom wetsuit, more than warm enough in the winter air, was covered with pockets of various shapes that soon held his *sgian dubh*, the flare gun, and his flares. He pulled on his gloves and adjusted his climbing claws so that they were on the backs of his hands.

———————

Sean felt a groan escape him, then forced his eyes open. He felt like he'd been struck by a bus in the back of the head. He tried to reach back there to feel for a bump but his arms wouldn't move. It took a moment for his vision to clear so that he could see the cords tying his arms to the arms of a heavy wooden chair.

*Come on, look around,* he thought, *there must be something that can help me get loose.*

"Carrie!"

"Shhh!" she urged, keeping her voice to a whisper. "I yelled out a while ago. All it got me was that monster coming in—my God, he's horrid! He slapped me and warned me to stay quiet or he'd come back for a drink." She shuddered. "He's got teeth—they're not like in most vampire movies, they're more like a cat's—needle-sharp at the tips and just thick enough to be strong." She turned her head to show the red mark on her face where he'd struck her.

"If I could break the chair, I could get free," Sean declared, "but I think it's too strong for me to break."

Carrie nodded. "Don't try," she whispered. "I've got one arm almost wriggled free. The guy who tied me up didn't tie the rope too tight—probably took pity on me as a women, or else figured a woman couldn't get free. Besides, I clenched my fists hard to make my arms as big as I could. I read about Houdini doing that."

Sean watched, enthralled. Little by little, keeping her arms as limp as she could, she slowly wormed one arm up and finally out of the cords. Sean heaved a sigh at the same time as Carrie. She rested a moment, then tried to reach behind her back at chest level. There were still cords about her upper arm, just below the shoulder, keeping her from getting enough arm movement. "There's a knot back there but I can't reach it."

She began working her right arm, just as she'd done with the left. It took longer, but patience paid off. Once both arms were free, she did a slow shoulder shimmy, forcing the ropes around her chest to gather slack from the arms.

"Good thing they tied my arms first," she whispered.

She wormed both hands up behind her back, fingers working at a knot Sean couldn't see. He marveled at her flexibility. *Bra straps,* he thought, recalling movie scenes of women reaching behind their backs to do up or undo bra straps, a movement no man could duplicate.

Moments later the ropes fell away from her chest and she doubled over to work on the knots tying her legs to the chair legs. As soon as she was free, she rushed to him and began to untie the knot behind his back. Unlike her, they'd made a point of tying Sean tight. Soon she had him loose as well.

Sean got to his feet, rubbing his arms and trying to shake better circulation into his legs. He grabbed Carrie and gave her a kiss on the cheek.

"I can see why Dad fancies you," he whispered.

"Fancies? There's a term no one uses anymore."

"Then you clearly haven't watched the Harry Potter movies."

Footsteps were approaching in the hall. Sean crept to the door and flattened himself against the wall by the doorframe. Carrie looked about for something to use as a weapon but there was nothing. Sean pointed for her to get back in the chair, then put a finger to his lips.

The man who entered wore a leather vest over a T-shirt, tattoos showing on his arms and neck. He took one step into the room, his eyes seemed to spot Sean's empty chair. Sean drove a fist into his kidney, then yanked him about by the shoulder and drove a fist into his gut. As the air was expelling from the biker's lungs, Sean launched a palm strike into his jaw, then leaped and clobbered him with a jumping roundhouse kick to the side of the head. He caught the biker so that he didn't make a noise hitting the floor.

Carrie helped him drag the man to a chair, then Sean tied him up. "No granny knots for me," he whispered, and secured the biker's right arm to the chair arm with multiple clove-hitches. He found a switchblade in the biker's pocket, cut the rope, then duplicated his technique on the other arm. He clove-hitched the remaining rope to the chair frame, then wound it tight about the biker's chest, securing it to the chair frame at the end with another clove-hitch.

He cut a long strip from the prisoner's leather vest, then grabbed the front of his T-shirt in a wad and cut it away. He forced the cotton wad into the biker's mouth, securing the gag in place with the strip of leather, making sure to tie it extra tight.

"He won't choke on that, will he?" she asked.

Sean gave her a blank stare, then said, "Like I give a crap? He's lucky I don't cut his throat with his own knife. Maybe he's the one who belted me in the head." He felt for a bump and found one. "Come on."

He was about to lead her toward the door when she grabbed his arm. "I'd rather try going out a window," she said. "That monster's out there, and he's not the only one. There's a smaller one who thinks he's Count Dracula. And, Sean, please believe me, you don't want to fight with the big one, Chernov. I think he's the one who did the most horrifying killings. He's about six-and-a-half feet tall and built like Arnold Schwartzenegger."

"So let's try the windows," Sean agreed. "But it's going to be cold out there, and they took our jackets."

Carrie shook her head. "When they took mine off of me they threw it in a corner over there." She went to the corner and, grinning, held up Sean's jacket in one hand and hers in the other.

"Luck of the Irish," Sean commented, pulling on his sport-biker jacket.

The room seemed to be some sort of attic storeroom with dormer windows. He opened a window, checked outside, then climbed out. Finding there was enough roof in front of the window for the two of them, he beckoned to her, helped her out and closed the window.

"If they find us gone," he said, "they may assume we're still in the house. Now, you stay here, I'll be back. I want to find an easy way down." He climbed away from the dormer and disappeared.

---

Carrie waited what seemed like a long time. She was getting cold and there was no sign of Sean. She was afraid someone would check the room, find them gone, then find her on the roof.

She couldn't decide whether to follow where Sean went or go the other way. Glancing at the steepness of the roof, she decided on the other way. She'd barely gone a few yards when she reached another dormer, but this one was bigger, with no roof in front of it. She could go up over the roof, but that frightened her. In a panic, she looked about. The gutter ended in a drainpipe. Instead of modern sheet metal, it was thick metal pipe. She decided to risk it.

Hanging by her hands, she got herself onto the pipe and, keeping her feet against the wall, began the terrifying downward climb. Her hands were freezing, losing their feeling on the metal pipe. She was maybe twelve feet from the bottom when her hands slipped and she fell the rest of the way.

She came up short, into a pair of strong arms.

"Gotcha," a deep voice declared.

Mike crept from shadow to shadow, getting ever closer to the house. He spotted three sentries patrolling that part of the grounds, darkly dressed, giving him the impression of bikers.

*These clowns give bikers a bad name,* he thought. One of his best friends had a heavy road cruiser, as did his wife. They took a vacation every year, touring somewhere scenic on their bikes. *But these clowns think dealing in crystal meth and hanging with a psychotic vampire is cool.* He pictured the body of his corgi hanging from the remains of his front door window. He had no compassion for Chernov's human accomplices.

He made a break for a trio of birch trees, ducked back into shadow, and waited. The nearest sentry was coming toward him. He waited 'til he'd just passed his location, then came up from behind. Grabbing the back of the biker's jacket, he drove a fist into his lumbar spine. There was a crack, then the man's legs buckled. As he fell, Mike brought his fist down on the back of the biker's neck. Another crack.

He wedged the biker in the birches so that he looked as if he were watching the docks.

Footsteps approached—another sentry. He looked like he might have heard something and was coming to investigate. Mike crept to one side, staying low, using the shadow of the birches. As he approached, the new sentry drew what looked like an old Colt automatic from inside his jacket.

Once more Mike came up from behind and drove a fist into the man's spine. The sentry, another biker, fell. Mike wrenched the biker's head to one side, snapping his neck, then dragged the body behind the next clump of trees.

He found the third sentry smoking a cigarette near the corner of the house. He was lit by an outside light, back to the house, with no way to sneak up on him. Mike debated the odds, pulled one of the pair of thin *sgian dubh*, and felt its balance. He straightened and launched the blade in one motion. It caught the sentry in the throat. Whatever cry the man may have wanted to utter died in a gurgle. Mike rushed in and yanked the blade to one side as he pulled it out. The biker's eyes went lifeless. Mike eased him down and dragged him to a nearby hedge and hid him behind it.

There was a chuckle behind him.

"This night has no end to entertainment."

It was a heavy slavic accent coming from a burly Russian, well over six feet tall. He wore what looked like a military-issue sweater—drab light brown with leather shoulder and elbow patches—and no jacket. His face looked almost flat in the front, his features showing the mongol traits of eastern Russia. The most alarming features, however, were his fangs. They showed traces of blood, and there was a smear of blood about his mouth.

He must have caught the direction of Mike's stare. Dragging a sleeve across his mouth, he grinned. "Somebody piss me off. Not good for them," he bragged. "Tasty, though. You have been nuisance to me. You kill my friends and burn down my product-making facility. We have your woman inside. She looks tasty. Let's see how you taste."

He came at Mike in a blur of speed. Mike blocked Chernov's attempts to grab him with crane strikes and drove a fist into the vampire's chest.

Chernov staggered back, rubbing his chest.

"You are strong and quick," he declared. "That is good. I like good fight. You are martial art instructor, no?"

He squared off against Mike in a classic karate stance, left fist stiff-arm forward, right fist cocked at the hip. Mike eased into a zen stance, a relaxed, almost flat-footed modification of a cat stance, made popular by Bruce Lee. He swayed a little on the balls of his feet, prepared to go in any direction.

Chernov came in fast. He faked a thrust punch to the gut, then tried to rake his claws across Mike's face.

Mike had hardened his abs as a teenager to the point that he used to welcome punches there. He'd joke that, while his opponent was hitting him in the gut, he'd be hitting him in the head.

He ignored the gut shot that never materialized and parried the claws with a right crane-wing block. The back of his left wrist came up to trap Chernov's wrist while he drove a right fist into the Russian's ribs. The cracking sound didn't seem to faze Chernov in the least.

The vampire jerked his hand free and launched a one-two punch combination at Mike's face.

Mike reacted fast. Left and right hands did mirrored preying-mantis blocks, pinning of Chernov's forearms atop each other in a Wing-Chun sticking hands maneuver. He drove a right palm into Chernov's jaw. It should have felled him instantly but failed.

Chernov butted Mike in the forehead, wrenched his hands free and brought them down on each of Mike's shoulders.

Mike dropped to his knees, dazed, but only for a second.

Chernov was still laughing when Mike drove his fist full force into the front of the vampire's pelvic girdle. The cartilage joining the two arches of bone coming from the hips detached, breaking the connection. Mike roared, turning it into a massive, chi-releasing power exhalation, and drove both palms into each of Chernov's hips, completely displacing both pelvic arches.

It is the pelvic girdle that holds a man up. The legs carry the weight, but it's the pelvic girdle that transfers that support to the spine and the rest of the body. It was like blowing up the foundation of a building. Chernov collapsed to the ground, unable to rise.

Mike pulled out the flare gun and aimed it at Chernov's chest. "Do you believe in Hell, Vladimir? Here's a preview of what you can look forward to."

He fired a double meteor into the vampire's chest. The flares tore into the vampire with the energy of a shotgun blast, making a hole filled with fire. Chernov went wide eyed in agony, then his skin responded and burst into flame.

Mike's body ached from Chernov's blows but he ignored the pain. He loaded another double flare into the barrel, and crept to the corner of the house. He paused, trying to work the pain out of this shoulder muscles. Rounding the corner, he found another biker, gun in hand, staring at the house. He drove a fist into the base of the biker's skull. When the man dropped, Mike grabbed his head, then stopped himself. *You'll be out for a while,* he thought. *Still*—he stomped his foot down on the side of the man's knee, bringing a snapping sound—*can't have you sneaking up on me.*

He looked where the man had been watching. Something or someone was coming down a drainpipe. As the shadowy form neared a patch of light, he recognized Carrie's pink ski jacket and ran forward. He arrived beneath her just as she fell, managing to catch her before she hit the ground.

"Gotcha," he said, then fell to his knees with her in his arms.

She went rigid, eyes wide, then recognized him. She gave a soft cry and threw her arms about his neck.

Mike struggled to his feet and steered her away from the house to the rows of trees lining the inside of the fence. He cast a glance at the gate. It was open. Then he spotted Nigel, leaning against the opening.

"Evenin,' gov'nor. Care to bring the missus over 'ere? I got a nice warm car she can sit in while you carry on wiff your business."

"How did you…?" he started to ask.

Nigel gestured to a steel spike driven into the ground at his feet. A set of jumper cables ran from the spike to the fence, shorting it out.

"Once the juice was gone, I just cut the power to the electromagnet that 'olds the gate locked. After that it was just a matter of cutting the power to the motor that opens and closes the gate and wheelin' 'er back."

Mike shook his head, amazed.

"Well, it's whot I do, i'n't it!" Nigel said, grinning.

Mike helped Carrie to Tony's car.

"Some big date!" she joked, and gave him a quick kiss.

"Where's Sean?" he asked once she was in the back seat.

She shook her head. "We got out onto the roof. He went over the roof to look for a way down. He never came back. I was afraid they'd find me and found another way down."

Mike remembered the blood on Chernov and felt that familiar knot in his stomach.

"I've got to find Sean."

"Whot you've got to do, my warrior friend, is get inside. 'Is Lordship 'as been in there for about ten minutes an' I'm not feelin' good about it at all. You take care o' Count Dracula, an' I'll look for your son."

Mike nodded. "The sentry over by the drainpipe has a gun. He's the only one alive on this side.

Everyone in the back is dead. I don't know about the
other two sides."

Once he saw that Nigel was armed, he turned his
claws around and prepared to climb up the wall.

A muffled blast like a gunshot came from inside
the house.

# 24: Nemesis

Mike climbed up to the roof as fast as he dared, the sound of the gunshot still echoing in his mind. From Carrie's description, he had no trouble finding the window to the attic storeroom. The biker Sean had tied in the chair was squirming, watching Mike with hatred in his eyes. Mike struck him between the eyes with a palm thrust, then tiptoed along the corridor and crept cautiously down the stairs.

The house was a nineteenth century stone mansion, complete with inner stone walls and marble stairs. *It cost a fortune to build and it costs a fortune to heat,* he thought. He paused at the second floor. All his senses were alert for company but the only sound was a muffled voice from the main floor. He looked in all directions and listened intently before continuing down the wide stone stair.

From the corner of his eye he caught a movement and ducked into shadow. Another biker, gun in a shoulder holster, was coming out of what must have been a kitchen, a huge sandwich in his hand. Mike waited until he was in the middle of a big bite. He stepped from cover and drove a fist into the man's gut, then wrenched his head, breaking his neck.

"You disappoint me, *Lord Anthony*." The voice said the name as if voicing it made him ill. "I expected so much more from you. However, you did bring me the Muramasa katana as I asked. I shall enjoy killing you with it."

The voice came from a large room at the back of the house. A cautious peek through the door revealed a library or office. One wall was lined with bookcases that reached to the ceiling and he caught just a glimpse of a large mahogany desk in front of a window.

"You're such a pale replica of my Tomomatsu Yakura. Yes, I see you know the name. It's been coming back to me so slowly. I hired a hypnotist who specialized in past-life regression. He told me much about my former life before I drank him dry. Well, after all, he knew such personal things about me—even my current condition. Hypnosis reveals so much." It was the voice from the security company recording.

"Why did you kill Isobelle?"

That was Tony's voice, but there was something wrong. It came in feeble gasps.

"Have you ever had to live with a constant stream of prattle about someone else? No, well, perhaps that's why you left her and were never around."

"I was around," Tony gasped, "but I had other duties, obligations. At least she spoke kindly of me. She never mentioned you that I can recall."

There was a clang of metal on metal, then a grunt.

"Come, now, *Lord Anthony*, you must keep your blade up. Where's that stirling form I'm so tired of hearing of. *Lord Anthony* helped Sir Percy Blakeney rescue so many aristocrats from the guillotine. *Lord Anthony* found and killed the *real* Jack the Ripper. *Lord Anthony* spied for the British in the two Great Wars. *Lord Anthony* helped start the British Secret Service. He even knew the famous Ian Fleming, the former MI6 agent who created James Bond. *Lord Anthony* **was** James Bond. *Lord Anthony* works for

Interpol. Well, enough! Lord Anthony bleeds like a gutted pig!"

Mike had enough. He burst into the room, kicked one biker guard in the gut, then turned, spotting another aiming a gun at him. He spun a circle, lashing with his back foot. The reverse roundhouse kick sent the gun flying and double snap sidekicks caught the man in the solar plexus and jaw, dropping him in a heap.

Lord Tony was backed against the desk. He had a huge wound in his chest that wept blood continuously. His shirt showed signs of several sword wounds, but those seemed to be closing, leaving little blood. It was the circular pattern of wounds that wasn't closing.

The 'count' was about the same height as Mike, but smaller, less muscular through the chest and shoulders. He had a thin, wiry physique.

"So you're this annoying piss-ant, Stavros Soutzos," Mike jeered, hoping to distract the vampire's attention away from Tony.

Tony relaxed and tried to smile. As his friend edged away from the desk, Mike spotted a modified shotgun. The barrel and butt had been sawed off, making it almost a pistol. He guessed that the wounds in Tony's chest were from wooden pellets fired from the gun.

"Stacking the deck in your favour?"

"I intend to win," Soutzos declared. "I deserve to win."

"And yet you always lose," Mike taunted. "You're no Prince of Wallachia—and just when did you decide to throw Transylvania into that claim? You're the piss-ant youngest brother of Alexandros Soutzos. You're not even Wallachian or Rumanian or whatever you're claiming to be these days. You're Greek. And you can't even pick the right man.

"Did it start as dreams? Did you awaken from a nightmare of being hacked to pieces by a better swordsman? When the countess kept speaking so proudly of Tony, you decided he had to be the great nemesis from your nightmares. Wrong again, Soutzos.

"I am Tomomatsu Yakura," he said in Japanese. "And you are the coward, traitor, and murderer of women, Toda Yoshihiro. I killed you once, and tonight I plan to kill you again."

The colour left the vampire's face. "Good," Mike said. "So you understand enough Japanese to know who I am."

Soutzos snarled in rage. Wheeling about, he snatched up the shotgun pistol and aimed it at Mike. He squeezed the trigger but it was just a futile click.

Tony coughed a weak chuckle and tossed a shotgun shell past Mike, into the hall. He'd apparently removed the second shell while the vampire was distracted by Mike.

With a roar of rage, the vampire hurled the gun across the room but Mike was far enough away to dodge easily.

Mike pulled out his flare gun and tossed it to Tony. "I want to take him in a fair fight, Tony, but you can keep that on him, just to keep him honest."

"Here," Tony said, and tossed him the katana he'd been trying to use.

Mike caught it, examining the blade. Stamped into the sides near the *tsuba* were *440 stainless* and *China.* He snorted a chuckle at the inferior weapon and tossed it toward Soutzos, where it clattered to the floor.

"No thanks; I'd rather have my own sword."

Soutzos sneered at him. "It's mine now. If you want it so bad, come and get it. Maybe you can take it from me." He went into a classic prepared stance, katana held almost like a baseball bat.

Mike smiled. "That's more or less what I had in mind, *Soutzos.*"

Still smiling, he mimicked a classic Bruce Lee gesture, going into a stance, right hand extended, making a beckoning gesture with his fingers.

Soutzos grinned with confidence and came on the attack. Mike skipped and dodged, the blade just missing him with each slash. All the while he got a sense of how Soutzos moved, his timing and style. There was a bit more polish this time, but the old Yoshihiro was still evident in his movements.

He ducked a lateral slice at his head and lashed out with a side kick, propelling the vampire back so that he fell on his ass on the stone floor.

"Come on, Soutzos, hurry up. I want my katana back."

Soutzos scrambled to his feet and. With a snarl, charged Mike with a downward strike. Mike stepped inside the vampire's guard the moment he raised the blade. His right hand struck Soutzos's hand just behind the *tsuba* or guard. As he drove his left palm into the vampire's ribs, his right struck the *tsuba*, tearing the katana out of Soutzos's hands.

Mike stepped back and held up the Muramasa blade. "Have a good look. Here is Mountain Wind and it's here for your blood."

He kicked the *made in China* imitation toward Soutzos and stood in guard position while the vampire picked it up. Then Soutzos attacked with a fury.

Blades rang like the clangour of steel bells as the two combatants moved about the room. Mike had strength and superior swordsmanship, but Stavros's vampire speed and strength were alarming. But the vampire feared losing. Having sparred with swords against Tony, Mike was sure Tony would have won a fair fight. Stephan must have shot him just as the duel was starting.

Stavros cast his eyes about the room.

"What's the matter?" Mike asked. "Fight going longer than anticipated? Looking for a way to cheat or looking for a way to escape?"

The vampire came at Mike in a burst of speed.

Mike blocked every stroke, then his blade flashed in, cutting a long slice in Stavros's upper chest. What would have been a nasty wound on a mortal began to close after a few seconds.

Back and forth they fought.

Stavros, in a blur of speed, sidestepped a thrust and shoved a hand into his pocket, nonchalant, parrying the thrust with one hand.

"Showing off?" Mike asked.

Stavros surged forward again. A handful of coins flashed from his hand directly at Mike's eyes. At the same time, the vampire slashed at his throat.

Mike threw himself backward, his back slamming against the hard stone of the outer wall. In a blur, the vampire was suddenly in front of him. Eyes glowing with anticipation, cat-like fangs exposed in a malicious grin, he thrust with his katana. Mike ground his teeth and grunted. He barely dodged the heart-thrust. The blade felt white-hot as it entered his shoulder, just below the right clavicle.

Mike ignored the pain. His right leg launched a front kick, catching Stavros in the chest. The vampire flew back, coming up hard against the desk. Mike stepped away from the wall and pulled Soutzos's katana out of his shoulder.

"Just watch him for a moment, will you Tony?" he asked.

Tony seemed to enjoy holding Soutzos at bay with the flare gun.

Mike set Soutzos's katana aside, drew a *sgian dubh,* and cut a piece from his wetsuit. He clenched his teeth and forced the nylon-covered neoprene into the wound. Disadvantaged now, Mike didn't dare prolong the fight. But he still had one advantage—the reason the Tokugawa shoguns had so hated Muramasa blades.

He walked slowly toward the vampire. Soutzos, wary, backed away toward the door. Having no honour himself, he didn't seem to trust the honour in others.

There was a disturbance in the doorway—another biker. He had Sean before him, an arm about the boy's throat, a gun to his head.

"Sorry, Dad," Sean said.

"I found this one sneaking in a bedroom window while I was trying to sleep. I thought he was tied up upstairs. Shall I blow his brains out or cut his throat?"

"Just kill him and be done," the vampire growled.

Before anyone could move, there was a loud gunshot. The biker fell to the floor.

"'Ave I got good timing or whot?" Nigel asked.

Sean reached down to pick up the biker's gun, but Soutzos moved in a blur, snatched the gun, and snatched Sean. Gun in one hand, he jerked Sean about and held his own sharpened nails against the boy's throat.

"Drop the gun and kick it into that corner," he told Nigel. "Like my servant suggested, I can either put a bullet in his head or cut his throat."

Nigel tossed the gun, raised his hands, and moved over by Tony.

The vampire shoved the gun into the back of his pants. Keeping his claws at Sean's throat, he held out his hand toward Mike.

"My sword."

Mike tossed Soutzos the katana.

Sean thought he saw his chance. He drove his right elbow into the vampire's gut.

Stavros let out a grunt and flashed his nails across Sean's throat.

"*NO!*" Mike screamed, moving toward his son.

"Uh-uh," Stavros warned, extending his katana toward Mike.

Nigel and Tony both ran to Sean, Tony clamping a hand on the wound.

Stavros unleashed a burst of speed, as if to finish Mike in a few seconds. Back and forth he slashed, eyes ablaze.

Instead of blocking in his usual, minimal manner, Mike swung as if trying to hit a baseball.

The Muramasa blade smashed through the inferior blade, shattering it near the hilt.

Mike's blade reversed in a return slash that took the vampire's head off in one clean slice.

Before the body hit the floor, Mike was at Sean's side.

"Why aren't the police here?" Tony moaned.

"I'll call 911," Nigel said, heading for a phone.

"There's no time for that," Mike insisted. Looking straight into Tony's eyes, he said, "You know what you have to do. You've done it before."

"The carotid is torn, Michael."

"So was mine. Do it, Tony."

The vampire nodded. Biting the tip of his finger, he pressed it into the wound until a couple of drops of his blood touched the carotid artery.

Mike let go a sigh of relief as the artery closed and the worst of the bleeding stopped.

"How did you know?" Tony asked. He looked pale. "Your father didn't even know."

"He said doctors told him they could see the carotid, that the pipe barely missed it. A miracle. What are the odds that a wound made by a jagged pipe would expose the carotid and not cut it. And I'd lost so much blood I needed a transfusion. How did I lose so much blood unless the carotid was torn? It's why I'm so fast and heal so well—I have vampire blood in me—not much, but enough to be slowly changing me. How long will it take?"

"Maybe the rest of your life, hopefully never," Tony said.

"And if I'd died tonight?"

Tony shook his head. "I've never heard of one such as you rising. But then, I've never heard of one getting the healing drops at such a young age."

"Does this mean I'll get fast, like your speed, Dad?" Sean asked in a hoarse whisper.

Mike smiled and nodded. "You're eighteen, I was six—maybe by the time you're sixty."

Turning back to Tony, Mike said, "We have to get you to a hospital and get those pellets out."

"The morgue would be better," he coughed.

"You're not dead, Tony, we can get them out."

Tony smiled. "You forget my friend Jonathan, the ME who works nights," he said. "He can remove them and he knows my blood type. Your car should get us both there faster than waiting for paramedics."

There was a noise in the hall and Inspector MacDonald stepped in, pistol drawn.

"Great timing, Pete," Mike chided. "Get some cops in here to help carry Sean and Tony to the back of my car—Shit! It's two doors away. The keys are in it. Send a car two doors south with someone to get my car and bring it here. And I need four men to help carry Sean and Tony out."

Pete pulled out a two-way radio and gave orders.

"So, Pete, where have you been?" Mike asked.

"Waiting outside for the last fifteen minutes, afraid it might not be safe to send my boys in, unless you can hypnotize them into not seeing vampires. Christ, Mike, it looks like Custer's last stand out there."

Mike shrugged and gestured to the wound in his shoulder, then to Tony and Sean. "There were casualties on both sides, but I got the job done. We were lucky—only one death on our side tonight." Tears formed in Mike's eyes.

# 25: Recuperation

"And I'm holding him to the promise of that date," Carrie assured Tony.

Lord Anthony Dewhurst was sitting up in bed, in his own bedroom, heavy curtains drawn over a thick pull-down blind. He seemed barely conscious.

"Shouldn't you still be in hospital?" Tony murmured. "Your shoulder…"

"Jonathan took care of it, remember?" Mike gave Tony a warning glare. "Besides, my shoulder was checked by a doctor an hour ago." His left arm was in a sling. "The stitches are fine, no inflammation. I checked myself out." Seeing Tony's questioning look, he added. "It's easy—you get up, get dressed, go to the desk, and sign yourself out."

"A doctor tried to make him stay," Carrie interjected. "Michael asked him if he was the one who was going to physically stop him from leaving." She shook her head. "We have residents like him at SeaView, one in particular."

Tony tapped the folded newspaper lying next to him.

"You made the paper," he murmured.

Mike unfolded the Halifax Herald an tensed as he read the headline.

*Samurai Vampire-Killer*
*The last of the so-called vampire serial killers may have been destroyed last night. The unidentified*

*vigilante previously compared to VanHelsing (from the graphic novels and the movie, not the Character in Bram Stoker's Dracula novel), is now being referred to as a samurai. According to on-scene witnesses, the ring leader of the gothic cult, composed mostly of members of an outlaw biker gang, was beheaded by a samurai sword. A local resident claims a man used his property to gain access to the suspect property after showing CSIS ID but the Canadian Security and Intelligence Agency so far refuses comment on this. One thing is certain, citizens of Halifax may be sleeping more soundly tonight thanks to the actions of one intrepid individual.*

"Well, at least there are no photographs this time," Mike said, tossing the paper back on the bed.

Tony breathed a soft chuckle, his eyelids drooping.

"Is this a normal reaction to the time of day or are you having trouble healing? Do you need anything?" Carrie asked.

Tony smiled. "I'm fine. Show her, Michael."

Mike opened Tony's pajama top. There were no bandages, just round red marks on his skin the size of the shotgun pellets.

"His body wants to be asleep," Mike explained. "It's nearing noon, weakest time for his kind. His friend at the morgue took all the pellets out, gave him lots of blood, and the healing started right away. The skin heals first, the inner wounds more slowly. He'll be up and around tonight—probably not dancing, but up and around."

"Michael pulled quite a few wooden stakes out of me a week ago," Tony breathed. "He's seen first-hand my recuperative powers."

Carrie kissed Tony on the forehead, then took a possessive grip on Michael's arm.

"I promised Sean we'd bring him lunch," Mike said. "Gotta feed the boy!"

Tony didn't answer. It was as if he'd slipped into a coma.

"He'll be like that for a couple of hours," Mike assure her, "then like sleep, then wake up around four. He might sleep late today, though."

---

They were watching Sean work though his second bowl of Tim Horton's chili when Mike's cell phone rang. Mike looked at the caller ID, then open his phone.

"Come on, Pete, can't I have a day off or did I forget something?"

"Hey, be nice. Who do you think had your scuba gear picked up, not to mention a borrowed drysuit and weight belt?"

"Point taken," Mike agreed. "So what's up? Not another 'unique serial killer,' please." It was their code for 'vampire' when there was a chance of being overheard.

"Two more months to retirement," MacDonald said, "Then I only have to read about that stuff in the papers. No, Mike, I think I might have a job for another of your talents. Can you meet me at the SPCA Shelter?" He gave Mike an address in Burnside.

"Why?" Mike didn't feel like seeing animals just yet.

"Maybe you can keep a beautiful animal from being killed."

That hit close to home. "We're with Sean at the hospital. How about in an hour?"

Pete agreed.

"What is it, Dad?" Sean's voice sounded much better than it had the night before.

Mike shook his head. "Pete thinks I that might be able keep an animal from being put to death at the SPCA." He shrugged and picked up his jacket. He got his right arm into the sleeve, then Carrie brought the jacket up over his left shoulder.

"I'm okay, Dad, really."

"You weren't okay last night, young man," the doctor announced from the doorway. "I'm told you awakened and made quite a stir until the duty nurse put a sedative in your IV."

"Nightmare?" Mike asked.

Sean shrugged and looked evasive.

"Give us just a second, doctor, then we'll be out of your way."

Mike stared into Sean's eyes, then his mind took a grip. "Look at me, Sean. No more nightmares. There's nothing to have nightmares about. Right?" His voice was stern but low.

"Right." Sean's voice sounded like he was in a daze.

"The people we had to deal with last night were just two psychos and some creeps from an outlaw biker gang. Right?"

"Right."

"Now, you'd better get some rest or they won't let you home tomorrow. Go to sleep, Sean."

He took the bowl from his son and set it on the bed table.

"Now, young man," the doctor said, "let's have a look at those stitches. What the…?"

As the doctor removed Sean's bandages, the boy let out a soft snore.

Mike shrugged. "He snores a lot but, other than that, he's a good kid."

––––––––

Pete met them at the shelter entrance.

"After you guys left, my men searched the house. An officer heard this guy yowling from a room in the basement. The room was cold. This fellow was in there, half starved. There was a large patch of dried blood on the floor, but no trace of blood on him. Usually blood will attract them and, if they're hungry, they have been known to drink it. Not this one. But when my officer tried to touch him, he went vicious. Animal control had to use one of those nooses on a pole to get him into a cage. I remembered your Dad's story about you and the skunks."

"Skunks?" Carrie asked.

Mike smiled, remembering the incident from this childhood. "We were spending the summer at a friend's cottage. Dad drove back and forth to work each day. I was almost twelve. There was a mother skunk and her babies under the cottage. I used to crawl under and visit them."

"You never got sprayed?" Carrie asked.

"We were friends," he said with shrug. "I heard my parents talking about how they might have to get an exterminator to get them out. I crawled under the next day, explained to the mother what I had to do, gathered up the babies, and took them down a path toward where it was more wooded. The mother followed. I found what must have been an abandoned fox den and put the babies inside. The mother went in after them. It never occurred to me that they might spray me. I think I just figured they were like some kind of cat or something."

At that point, a shelter worker who'd been standing by took up the tale. "We sedated him for the night and put food and water in the cage, but nobody can go near him. He snarls and hisses and flies at the bars like an angry leopard. He's had nothing to eat for over a week, unless he caught bugs or mice in there. I gather you're something of a whisperer, Mr. Cameron. You know, gifted at dealing with upset animals. He's so beautiful, but too vicious. If you can't deal with him, no one else will take him, and he'll have to he euthanized."

Mike followed the employee into the room. As they neared a particular cage, the occupant went into a fit of hissing, attacking the bars, and growling like a small leopard. It was a young Siamese cat. Mike guessed its weight at maybe seven pounds.

"He's a blue-point. How old—six or seven months?"

The attendant nodded. "He's been neutered, maybe a month ago."

Mike nodded. "If I can do this at all, I'll need to be alone. If you step back by the door it should do. I want him to start by thinking it's just me."

Mike fixed his eyes on the kitten. Fear raged in the animal. Mike understood that easily enough—a monster that looked like a human had killed his family, then locked him in a cold room to starve. Soon he had the kitten's attention, sapphire-blue eyes locked onto his blue-grey eyes.

"Shhh," he said repeatedly, "shhh—calm—yes—be still." He kept his voice low, gentle, soothing. "Shhh—it's alright, little one, everything's going to be fine."

He placed the backs of his fingers against the bars. The kitten sniffed at his fingers, then made a strange meow. When the kitten rubbed its head against his fingers, he opened the door and placed his hand in the opening. Once again, the kitten rubbed against his hand, then made the same forlorn meow. Mike picked up the kitten and settled it on his left arm, against his chest, inside his shoulder sling.

"My God," Carrie said, "I can hear the poor thing purring from here!"

The attendant shook his head. "The inspector said you were good, but I never expected anything like this."

"Do you know any of his story?" Mike asked.

"Just that his people were murdered and he was found in a cold room. Starved as he was, he apparently never touched the blood. That gave me hope. Siamese cats are smarter than dogs—their mannerisms are a lot like dogs, actually. Still, cats go feral more easily than dogs."

Mike nodded. "I've had a few Siamese cats." He glanced at Carrie. "Susan and I had one on the boat with us when were were cruising." She smiled and nodded. "I think I'll call him Kato."

"So, you're taking him?" the attendant asked.

Mike nodded. "I'm taking him."

"Can I pet him?" Carrie reached forth a hand, then withdrew it immediately when a low moaning growl came out of the kitten. "I guess not," she declared.

"It'll take time, maybe a few days, but he'll come around," Mike said. "This little guy's been through a lot."

"That little guy has a growl ten times his size," she countered.

He handed Carrie his keys. "It looks like you're driving."

———

Mike was enjoying a rare moment of tranquility when the interruption came. He was lying on the bed, reading a book—well, trying to. Kato, now eight months old, was settled half on the pillow, half on Mike's shoulder, purring, and constantly getting his furry head in Mike's line of sight.

"You don't make it easy to read, you know," Mike chided. That's when the doorbell rang.

Mike set the book down and headed for the door, the Siamese cat at his heels.

"Stay there," Mike said when he reached the door, and the cat dutifully sat on the bottom step.

Mike opened the door to find Charbonneau there, one shoulder hunched in an effort to block the March winds from his face.

"What's up?" Mike asked. "You got my e-mailed report; did you get the hardcopy? I mailed it weeks ago."

Charbonneau nodded. "My supervisor wants to speak with you—in the car."

Charbonneau looked uncomfortable, almost guilty, but said no more. He just stepped away from the door as if waiting for Mike to follow him.

Mike stuck his feet into hiking boots, laced them quickly, then grabbed his black suede jacket from the closet. He ignored the icy wind as if it didn't exist and followed Charbonneau to the car. Charbonneau opened the rear door to the black limo and closed it once Mike had slid into the back seat.

The sole occupant of the spacious compartment was an impeccably dressed man in his early sixties with a dour expression on his face. In his hands he held a file folder with the word *CLASSIFIED* stamped in red capitals on the cover. Mike saw the word "Samurai" on the tab.

"And you are...?" Mike asked, looking the man in the eye.

"My name doesn't matter, Mr. Cameron; what matters is our concern for the manner in which you handled this case."

"Six vampires were killing at will in this town. Chernov and his cohorts were setting themselves up as drug merchants, peddling crystal methamphetamine. They subordinated a local outlaw biker gang to be their pushers and watchdogs. The vampire problem has been eradicated. No one can prove they really were vampires, but the public knows they're gone, and are relieved. So just exactly what part of this are you unhappy with?" Mike was beginning to categorize the man as a detail-oriented bureaucrat, obsessed with procedure and discipline more than results, and instinctively didn't like the man.

"Mr. Cameron, what I have here is little more than a massive body count," the man retorted, colour rising in his face. "You killed almost every human on the property as well as the... the creatures you were commissioned to destroy."

"So let me get this straight:" Mike rebutted, "you're fine with me killing vampires. It's just the drug-peddling hoods who kidnaped by girlfriend and captured my son, men who happily pulled guns on me with the intention of shooting me—these are the men who have inspired your compassion and sympathy. Done any fieldwork, sir? You have to make on the spot decisions, like the fact that the man you leave unconscious on the ground might come-to and shoot you in the back."

"The bottom line, Mr. Cameron, is that I will not tolerate such behaviour. This is not a James Bond movie and you're credentials do not give you a license to kill. CSIS has been subjected to enough scandal already, simply because we passed on information to other agencies and the press wants to hold us accountable for other countries' actions. The government has been sued!" His eyes widened and his colour deepened as he reached the end of this tirade.

Mike had enough. Shaking his head, opened the car door and got out. Luckily, his CSIS ID was in his inside jacket pocket. He pulled it out and tossed it on the seat.

"Now you can deny my involvement," he said. "And don't worry, mister paper-pusher, I'll keep your vampires a secret, but don't ever get in my face again."

"Oh, on the contrary, Mr. Cameron, we'll be keeping a close eye on you."

"Oh, I doubt if you'll be that close, sir. You're not the type to risk getting any blood splashed on him."

———

Mike's jaws were clenched tight as he gently placed the urn into the ground next to that of his mother. He straightened and stepped back. Carrie took a tight grip on his right arm and Sean moved closer on his left.

Pete MacDonald, in full dress blues, donned his uniform hat and nodded to a sergeant. A file of seven police officers fired three blank shots into the air, giving the late Inspector William Cameron a rare twenty-one gun salute.

Mike fought to hold back the tears but they came regardless. He took a deep breath, blew up the bag on his pipes, struck them in, and blew *Amazing Grace* followed by *Going Home*.

———

A steady westerly breeze filled Windward's sails. She was heeled a stately twelve degrees, about as far as the Hunter would lean. The only sound was the lapping of the waves against her hull and the occasional sound from the sails.

Carrie snuggled against Mike. He had his left hand on the helm, his right arm about her.

"This is like magic!" she said.

There was a childlike sparkle in her face when she smiled. For Mike it was her most attractive and compelling feature. It spoke of imagination and the child within that hadn't been stifled by the experiences of adulthood.

"It is a kind of magic," he agreed. "We're riding the wind like a bird."

"And you couldn't have picked a better day. If the rest of May stays like this, June might be fabulous."

Mike nodded. The trees on the shore were opening new leaves, the sky was a clear blue, dotted with cumulous clouds, the temperature a pleasant seventeen degrees Celsius.

"Maybe we can use your vacation time to sail down to Mahone Bay—a week or two on the boat, quiet coves, picturesque towns with nice restaurants, the moon on the water."

She kissed his cheek. "Aye-aye, my captain."

They passed under the MacKay bridge and into The Narrows. Mike eased over to the Dartmouth side for a better shot at the wind. The hills on the Halifax side tended to kill the breeze in The Narrows.

Kato, who had been lying on the seat next to Mike, crept into his lap, purring. He reached out a paw, playfully batting at Carrie's fingers. She scratched at the side of his neck, making him purr louder.

"His colours are filling in beautifully," she said.

Mike nodded, keeping his eyes on the rocky Dartmouth shore. "He's handsome. He'll be even more handsome when he's fully grown—that's about two years for a Siamese."

"Will you get more beautiful as you get older?" she asked him.

"No," he joked, "I'll probably stay homely, maybe even get uglier.

"I'm serious, Michael," she persisted. "You've got vampire blood in you from when Tony saved you as a child. Will that change you? Will you slowly become a vampire?"

Mike's jaw clenched. He'd never told her about that night in the morgue and Jonathan. At first he didn't want to worry her. Then, as more time passed, he just didn't know how to bring it up. How do you tell your girlfriend that there's a strong risk that you'll become a vampire?

"I hope not," he said, shaking his head. "Tony insists it's never happened. But then he's never heard of it being done to a six-year-old. It will change me somewhat—it's been changing me all my life. I heal fast, I seem to be able to move faster than I remember..."

"And I swear you don't have even half the grey in your hair that you used to have," Carrie asserted.

Mike grinned. "Yeah, but you can fix that with a box from the drugstore."

"And have you coloured your hair since we got together?"

Mike made the face of a kid who just got caught doing mischief. "Ah, no, I haven't."

"So what happens when we're seventy. What if I look seventy and you only look fifty?"

Mike smiled. "Everyone will wonder how such a boring looking fifty-year-old landed such a gorgeous, sexy-looking seventy-year-old."

Carrie pressed the issue. "I'm serious, Michael."

"If that happens I'll bite you and give you some of my blood. And if that doesn't work, I'll send for Tony."

"That monster who thought he was a prince—was he really the same person you killed in your past life? It all seems so—I don't know what to call it."

"Farfetched?" Mike suggested. "That's how it seems to me. I wrote a lot of stuff down, just to prove to myself that it was real. I even have copies of the police photos—Charbonneau made sure of that on the sly. It seems he doesn't approve of his supervisor attitude. That clown's name is Monahan. I'll continue to help Tony when he needs me. It's a chance for me to do something that perhaps only I can do. Toda Yoshihiro and Stavros Soutzos just didn't have a clue about what it means to be bushi. It's about protecting and serving. The very word, 'samurai,' coined as an insult, means 'to serve a lord.' He thought the world was here to serve him."

Carrie nodded. "I fear for you being in danger, but I can understand how you feel. That guy in the car, he was an ass, but he may not always be in his position. Maybe someone like Charbonneau will replace him. So what if CSIS calls on you again?"

Mike shrugged. "Once a samurai, always a samurai."

Coming Soon:
...ALWAYS A SAMURAI

For more information visit http://DCRhind.ca